DEATH WAS ONLY SECONDS AWAY!

This is it, Brent said to himself. Then he prayed as his pilot fought the controls like a madman. Brent tracked his gun as the Arab ME banked for another run. The front of the fighter blazed. There were thuds, pings, and bangs from hits, and then the explosion of a twenty-millimeter shell knocked Brent to the left side of the cockpit where he hung helplessly, filled with disbelief. Something hot and sticky was running down his chest.

Biting his lip, Brent pushed himself back to his gun, grabbed the pistol grips, and swung the Nambu back to the right. The enemy was off their right elevator, throttled back and moving in for the kill.

"Bank, Takii! Give me a shot!" Brent yelled. But Takii seemed not to hear. Was he frozen by panic. Wounded, too?

The ME moved in and death began to wink . . .

ATTACK OF THE SEVENTH CARRIER

PETER ALBANO

ZEBRA BOOKS
KENSINGTON PUBLISHING CORP.

ZEBRA BOOKS

are published by

Kensington Publishing Corp.
475 Park Avenue South
New York, NY 10016

First printing: December, 1989

Printed in the United States of America

ACKNOWLEDGMENTS

The author makes the following grateful acknowledgments to:

William D. Wilkerson and Dennis D. Silver for advising on the many problems facing the pilots of antique aircraft;

Master Mariner Donald Brandmeyer who gave freely of his time to counsel on the proper handling of a ship in port and at sea;

Mary Annis, my wife, for her careful reading of the manuscript and thoughtful suggestions;

Robert K. Rosencrance for generously lending his technical and editorial skills in the preparation of the manuscript.

For charming, delightful Teresa

Chapter I

The early morning air at nine thousand feet struck as if it had been blown off of the polar ice cap. Hunching down in the gunner's cockpit with the cold wind sucking the air from his lungs and ripping the breath from his lips in white banners, Lieutenant Brent Ross wished he could close the canopy of the ancient Nakajima B5N—the *Tora II*. But with Oberstleutnant Kenneth Rosenscrance and his Arab assassins reported combing the skies of the western Pacific, a man's momentary carelessness could be his last moment of existence. Reacting to the bitter cold like all men who are convinced they are freezing to death, the young six-foot-four-inch blond giant tried to contract and shrink himself within his brown, fur-lined flying suit, turtleneck US Navy sweater, and grossly oversized foul-weather jacket. But the vicious cold caught at his clothes with icy fingers and seeped insidiously down his collar, intruding in the tiny areas left unguarded between gloves and sleeves and froze his cheeks and nose. Frigid air even probed beneath his tightly strapped helmet like slivers of icicles and his eyes felt dry as sand, the gale whipping the moisture away, causing him to blink constantly. He ached to lower his goggles, but, they interfered with his peripheral vision, so they remained high on his forehead.

Brent cursed and crossed his arms across his chest, gripping his biceps with massive hands and rocked as he pushed gently on his footrests. Yielding to the gentle pressure, his swiveling and tilting seat revolved smoothly on its circular steel track, its dozen ball bearings rolling so smoothly they felt liquid. The young lieutenant's scan was that of the trained aerial observer; short, jerky movements of the head, never allowing the eyes to be trapped by the glaring morning sun, a spectacular display of cloud formations or sea birds drifting on rigid pinions. Over the years, he had developed the knack of depending on his peripheral vision to detect distant objects as tiny as fly specks that would often be imperceptible to a direct, intense stare. Strange how this technique worked; but it did, and all experienced pilots and observers used it.

Swinging from beam to beam and glancing ahead, Brent Ross scanned the length and breadth of the aircraft and wondered how such an anachronism could still club its way through the skies over forty years after the end of World War II and half a century after it had been assembled at the Nakajima Aircraft Factory. "Truly, a wonder of its time," the *Tora II*'s tiny old pilot, Lieutenant Yoshiro Takii, had said proudly one afternoon on the hangar deck. And then gesturing as he led Brent around the big aircraft. "Ahead of its time — nine-hundred-eighty-five horsepower Sakae 11 engine, variable pitch three-bladed Sumitomo propeller, retractable carrier-stressed landing gear, integral tankage, Fowler flaps, stressed skin construction, and folding wings. Much superior to the Douglas TBD and the British stone-age death-trap Fairey Swordfish." Stiffly, he had reached up and proudly patted *Tora II* lettered on the huge cowling. "Wrecked Pearl Harbor twice and sank *Lexington, Wasp, Hornet, Yorktown,*

8

Repulse, Prince of Wales, Hermes, and dozens of others. And then contritely, "Sorry Brent-san, did not mean to offend." Brent had assured the crestfallen little man he had not, despite a roiling, empty feeling deep in the pit of his stomach.

First flying with the old man in the Mediterranean on a mission to Tel Aviv, Brent had learned to respect the ancient pilot who was perhaps still the best single-engined bomber pilot in the world. One of the original members of carrier *Yonaga's* crew, Yoshiro Takii had withstood the ship's unbelievable forty-two-year entrapment at Sano Wan on Siberia's Chukchi Peninsula. After the great carrier's breakout, he had flown in the vortex of the ship's rampage down from the Bering Sea and led a squadron in the attack on Pearl Harbor. Then the terrible fighting against Colonel Moammar Kadafi and his murdering hoodlums in the Mediterranean and western Pacific that had decimated *Yonaga's* air groups — battles that dispatched the spirits of many brave samurai to the Yasakuni Shrine, including Yoshiro's navigator and best friend of more than a half century, Ensign Morisada Mochitsura. Brent had been on that mission and been only three feet from the navigator when he bled to death after being hit by a half-dozen 7.7 slugs.

Slowly Brent revolved his seat and raised his scan high over the tail plane. They were about a hundred miles north of Saipan and were on a southerly heading — a course that would bring them over Saipan and its neighbor, Tinian, in about forty minutes — if the navigator who was seated in the middle cockpit was correct. A young ensign transfer from the smashed Self Defense Force, Ensign Takashiro Hayusa — a big, strong lad from a farm on southern Kyushu — had been brought up on the highly computerized navigational devices of the micro-chip age. Equipped with superannuated equipment from the thirties, the B5N forced its navigator to resort to sextant, stopwatch, an air almanac and pencil, and paper computations to figure latitude and longitude. Perhaps still more important, his dead reckoning was suspect, Brent convinced Hayusa did not have a feel for the set and drift to which an aircraft could be subjected by the capricious winds of the western Pacific. Brent sighed. If they were to return safely to carrier *Yonaga,* they would need luck and favorable smiles from God, Amaterasu, Allah, and whatever other deities dwelled in the infinite skies.

With a flash of theatrical brilliance, the sun suddenly broke from behind scattered blobs of morning clouds and bathed every horizon with long, probing fingers that brought to mind Japan's sobriquet, "land of the rising sun." Despite the cold, the bloody fighting, the lack of sleep and fatigue, Brent Ross loved flying and the many breathtaking delights nature reserved for the few men who dared to enter this most private sanctum. This morning was no exception. Overhead, the clear sky was like an inverted cup painted heron's-egg blue while far to the south and west, gray clouds massed and rolled, sweeping in monstrous, terrifying mushrooms and anvil heads across the sky, flashing with internal lightning angrily as if to battle one another. Here, an aircraft could lose its wings. Below, as far as he could see, the flat plain of the sea stretched in radiant blueness to the great circle of the horizon, the sun catching the feathery tips of the chop and reflecting like a tray of blue diamond chips.

He glanced at the wing tips less than thirty feet away, and the miracle of flight overwhelmed him. Over two miles high, freezing to death under layers of wool and fur, he was a gnat suspended in an infinite void. There was nothing between him and extinction except a pair of thin-skinned wings, frail formers, spars, stringers and wires, and a fifty-year-old engine. He could see the wings bend up and then snap down as the bomber charged through invisible barriers of turbulence, could feel the whole structure vibrate with the strain, the seat tremble. He was witness to more than a triumph of human skill, it was a miracle. Abruptly, the young lieutenant was seized by a mournful thought: *How insignificant was man in these limitless dimensions where he hung motionless and time and distance had no meaning. An intruder. A speck of dust, transient and gone in a blink.*

Takii's tinny, rasping voice in his earphones shocked him from his reveries. "Gunner, we are approaching our patrol area. Load and lock."

"Load and lock," Brent Ross repeated into his microphone. With quick, practiced motions, the young lieutenant unsnapped the upper strap of his harness, stood, released the Nambu's well lock and pulled the Type 96, 7.7 millimeter machine gun from its well, releasing the locking lever. Bracing his feet against the footrest and gripping the double pistol grips, he swung the perfectly balanced twenty-four-pound weapon from beam to beam and from the vertical to the horizontal. He nodded with approval. It was like moving a feather. A line from one of Emperor Meiji's most famous rescripts came to mind, *Death is as light as a feather.* He chuckled to himself as he thumbed a spring-loaded latch, raised the top cover, exposing the feed mechanism. As usual, the belt had been pulled through the receiver, but the armorers had not seated a round in the firing chamber. The belt was perfectly aligned and showed a mix of projectiles, color-coded alternately red and blue for antipersonnel and armor piercing with every fifth round-tipped yellow for tracer. He snapped the cover shut and grabbed the cocking handle on the right side of the weapon, pulled back hard, and released. Ringing metallically, the spring pulled the handle back and the bolt snapped back into place. Brent knew a round was seated in the firing chamber.

However, the usual gnawing worry of the aerial gunner nagged him and he partially opened the breech, tilted his head close to the side of the Nambu, and assured himself there was a cartridge in the chamber. Still, nothing reassured like the feel of the gun bucking in his hands. He made the inevitable request: "Gunner requests permission to clear weapon."

Takii made his usual response: "Granted. But do not shoot off my tail."

Smiling, Brent swung the weapon to the side and squeezed off a short four-round burst. The airframe bucked and a single tracer arced high and then rainbowed downward toward the sea. "Tail still intact, sir," Brent reported solemnly.

"Very well. Thank Amaterasu." Brent felt the aircraft vibrate again as Takii cleared his own single fixed 7.7.

A glint high in the sky caught the American's eye. A bird? An airfoil? Nothing but a tiny cloud catching the sun. The Chinese orbiting deuterium-floride particle-beam system came to mind. A mistake that had set the world's war-making potential back forty years. Or was it a mistake — a malfunction as the Chinese had claimed? Indisputably, their inexhaustible manpower now became one of the world's most potent forces. Three command stations in geo-synchronous orbit at 22,300 miles and twenty low-orbiting weapons platforms at 930-mile altitudes, equipped with laser systems that homed in on both heat, infrared, or combinations of the two emissions. All communications satellites had been destroyed instantly and not a jet, not a rocket, could operate. Ignition of either meant instant annihilation from the heavens like a thunderbolt hurled by an angry god. With jets, rockets, and cruise missiles grounded junk, the waging of war did not stop, but paused while the nations searched frantically for old WW II aircraft with their laser-immune reciprocating engines and big-gunned ships from the same war and even earlier. In fact, the old Japanese museum-piece battleship, *Mikasa* — a veteran of the Japanese-Russian war of 1905 — had been pressed into service as a monitor, her four twelve-inch guns still finding service in the Israeli war with the Arabs.

With the hegemony of the two super powers broken, Kadafi's madness had spread worldwide like a new black death. He organized an Arab holy war — *jihad* — against the hated Israelis, and with the exception of Indonesia, brought OPEC to heel and imposed a crippling oil embargo on the West. Hard put to meet its own demands, the US could only send Japan enough oil to barely maintain its industrial plant and provide fuel for *Yonaga* and her air groups. An Arab battle group had been defeated in the South China Sea when Kadafi had tried to destroy the Indonesian oil fields and sink *Yonaga*. Now a modest stream of oil was flowing to Japan from the Indonesian fields, but, again, an Arab battle group of at least two carriers, cruisers, and destroyers was stalking the western Pacific. A powerful force, it had all but obliterated the Self Defense Force in strikes on Tokyo Bay and the Inland Sea, delivered while *Yonaga* was at sea attacking Arab bases in North Korea. Now the great carrier and her valiant samurai was the only force standing between international terrorism and the enslavement of Japan, and, perhaps, the entire free world. Certainly, the dominoes were set in a neat line and a leer-

13

ing Kadafi had his hand poised over the first one marked *Japan*.

Now *Yonaga* was hunting the Arab force; a dozen Nakajima B5N's and Aichi D3A dive bombers protected by high-flying echelons of Mitsubishi A6M2's — the lithe, acrobatic Zero — searching all four quadrants for the Arab battle group or newly established bases. Launching its search from a position eight hundred miles southwest of Honshu — according to the point option data on Brent's clipboard, latitude twenty degrees, thirty minutes north, longitude a hundred sixty-one east — *Yonaga*'s search planes were ideally positioned to reconnoiter the Marianas and the old airstrips at Guam, Saipan, and Tinian; the Bonins to the west, Iwo Jima and Kita Jima; the Carolines to the south including Truk and Ponape; the Gilberts and Marshalls including Tarawa, Makin, Kwajalein, Enewetak, Bikini, and a half-dozen other atolls suitable for strips and anchorages. Even Wake and Midway were slated for reconnaissance by narrow, curious eyes. Ominously, Radio Saipan and Radio Tinian had both mysteriously gone off the air almost simultaneously that morning just before takeoff. An atmospheric phenomenon? A raiding party? The entire ship's company of *Yonaga* had been uneasy, long memories recalling that the *Enola Gay* had taken off from Tinian. If something was amiss in the Marianas, the *Tora II* was to sniff it out.

Brent shifted his weight as he continued his restless sweep of the sky and the horizon. The cockpit was built with much smaller men in mind and the muscles of the small of his back and shoulders were beginning to ache their objections to the cramped quarters and his rigid posture. As usual the young officer rubbed the small of his back, his shoulders, and thighs to stimulate circulation grown sluggish because of the

14

cold and lack of movement. A new thought brought a chuckle to his lips. What set of insane circumstances had brought a twenty-five-year-old NIS (Naval Intelligence Service) officer and Annapolis graduate to the gunner's cockpit of a WW II relic vibrating its way over the Pacific? His mind ran down a mental checklist: *Yonaga*'s breakout from her secret Arctic entrapment; the mysterious disappearance of ships and aircraft as the undetected carrier moved south toward Pearl Harbor; fruitless investigations by NIS; Pearl Harbor devastated; the mission to Tokyo Bay with Commander Craig Bell and Admiral Mark Allen to meet *Yonaga* and investigate her incredible story. Then the Chinese orbited their star wars system and his assignment to *Yonaga* with Admiral Mark Allen.

Brent smiled as he thought of *Yonaga*'s captain, Admiral Fujita. Not quite five feet tall, the old man was said to be over a hundred years old. Yet he was alert, strong, quick to make decisions and, above all, a charismatic leader. His samurai would gladly die for him and often did. Brent tightened his jaw and tucked his lips under with the realization he had casually put his life on the line several times for the old man, too. The old admiral was a Svengali.

Not only had Admiral Fujita appeared to defy time, so had all of the crew of *Yonaga*. True, many of the senior officers had died, but all of the crewmen Brent met seemed youthful despite their years. Admiral Allen tried to explain the phenomenon: "Holdouts age very slowly, keep their youth and vigor. No liquor, no women, and no tobacco. I know, Brent. I debriefed Sochi Yokoi after twenty-seven years on Guam and Hiroo Onoda after thirty years on Lubang. Physically and mentally they remain young men." Brent had shaken his head in wonder and disbelief.

A flash of white high and to the southeast caught his

eye and broke his maundering thoughts. He unstrapped his binoculars and pulled them from their canvas case mounted on the forward bulkhead above his clipboard and between his flare gun and oxygen bottle. Raising the glasses, he thumbed the focusing knob and brought three gleaming white Zeros into precise focus. The leader of the *V* had the red cowling and green hood of Commander Yoshi Matsuhara, Brent's best friend and fighter group commander. Each had a single blue band around the aft part of the fuselage, as did *Tora II*—the identifying stripe of the Koku Kantai (First Air Fleet), *Yonaga's* air group. The young gunner felt a new surge of confidence, a reassurance all men need when they hang alone in uncertain skies like an insect dangling from a collector's ceiling. "Yoshi," Brent said to himself. "Hang around, old friend. We're not flying the friendly skies of United."

But the agile white fighters turned abruptly and climbed toward a gathering cloud cover. Brent switched on his microphone, "Three Zero-sens at two-six-zero, high. Climbing high and into the cloud cover."

"Very well. I see them," Takii said back. "Stay alert, both of you. Saipan must be just over the horizon. And Brent-san. Keep your mind on our business, not some Madam Butterfly back in Tokyo."

Brent chuckled. At the moment he had no Madam Butterfly. "Aye, aye, sir," he answered. And then with mock gravity, "If my sword is broken, I will strike with my hands. If my hands are cut off, I will smash the enemy down . . ."

"Very well, Very well," Takii snapped in exasperation in Brent's ears. "I have read the *Hagakure,* too. Secure the moralizing back there."

"Aye, aye, sir," the gunner said, laughing to himself at Takii's quick recognition of the old samurai adage

16

and reference to *The Hagakure (Under the Leaves)*, the handbook of the samurai where Brent had found it. Ensign Hayusa's laughter was clear in the intercom. However, bringing up his glasses, Brent's mood of sparkle vanished with the fighters. Hayusa's laughter faded. The Zeros had disappeared. A great empty loneliness crept in. *Where are you, Yoshi Matsuhara? Where are you?* Brent asked himself, staring into a sky empty of everything except clouds and the red-white ball of the sun.

Commander Yoshi Matsuhara palmed the throttle of the Zero ahead two notches and enriched his mixture by pushing ahead the control lever on the quadrant attached to the left side of the cockpit. Pulling back on the control column and countering the increased torque with a feathery touch of left rudder, he watched his tachometer needle zoom past three thousand, his manifold pressure toy with the red line at eighty centimeters of mercury and his airspeed indicator reach three hundred forty knots as the new two-thousand-horsepower Nakajima Sakae IV engine roared and rocketed the light airframe upward like a berserk express elevator. Designed for one half the horsepower of the new engine, the Mitsubishi's airframe and main wingspar had been strengthened to take the new stresses and loads. Yet, the Zero-sen was still the lightest fighter in the skies, almost a half ton lighter than its principal opponent, the ME 109 which also boasted a new power plant; the Daimler Benz Valkyrie II with 2,200 horsepower.

Yoshi had just sighted the B5N, *Tora II,* low and far to the north and west, and he was chuckling with thoughts of his big friend Brent Ross freezing in his cramped cockpit when the corner of his left eye had detected a movement where there should have been none. Then moving the control column to the left and balancing with the rudder, he had dropped his port wing, and just over the tip he saw a lone four-engined aircraft lumbering in a westerly direction and perhaps five hundred meters below his section. He knew the Americans still kept a small presence on Guam, their last base in the western Pacific, despite fuel shortages and nearly continuous warfare between Colonel Moammar Kadafi's forces and the Japanese. He guessed the big plane was probably a commercial airliner enroute from Enewetak to Guam. But a good fighter pilot — one with longevity — assumed nothing. He had seen years of Arab trickery, deceit, and treachery, and a close reconnaissance was mandatory.

Sinking back into the bucket seat and pressed down into his parachute pack by g forces, the commander's eyes widened as he watched the white needle of his altimeter wind clockwise with a speed it had never shown before. He was gaining altitude — the fighter pilot's most precious commodity — at a rate that would have put the A6M2's designer, Jiro Horikoshi, in a state of shock.

Glancing quickly to the right and then the left he grunted with frustration, finding his two new wingmen, NAP (Naval Air Pilot) First Class Masatake Matsumara trailing far off his right elevator while Ensign Subaru Kizamatsu was nearly astern. Both of the young pilots were slow, had lagged despite his wing-waggling and hand signals. He yearned for his old comrades from China, Shio Yoshida and Yozan Sakanishi, who had died in the great battles over the Straits of Malacca. Even their replacements, Akiko Yosana and Junichiro Tanizaki, had been better than Matsumara and Kizamatsu. But, Yosana and Tanizaki, too, had joined their ancestors over Tokyo Bay;

Yosano shot to pieces by Johannes Friessner, Tanizaki murdered in his parachute by the American renegade Kenneth Rosencrance. At night when sleep was slow, he could still see Tanizaki's tumbling body trailed by his shredded chute and whipping shrouds, plummeting into the Uraga Peninsula. Someday, Yoshi Matsuhara would gorge himself on revenge, kill the butcher Rosencrance. He hoped to do it slowly, face-to-face; burn the American, cut him, inflict exquisite pain, and savor the screams.

Commander Yoshi Matsuhara had spent so many years in the cockpit of a Zero-sen, the aircraft seemed to be an extension of his spiritual self. He never consciously moved a control. Instead, his concentration, the power of his mind seemed to attune itself to the *kami* (spirit) he was convinced inhabited the fighter. He thought of turning and the Zero turned; he thought of firing his two twenty-millimeter Orlikons and two 7.7-millimeter machine guns and they blazed to life. The control column, the rudder peddles, were extensions of his own limbs, fusing with his being and propelling him through space in pursuit of the emperor's enemies. And he had killed many — so many. It began in China when he was a young ensign just out of flight school.

Born and raised in Los Angeles, Commander Yoshi Matsuhara was a *nisei* with dual citizenship. Fiercely loyal to the emperor, each evening his father, Oto-san, sat with the young Yoshi on *zabutons* in the main room under an equestrian of Emperor Hirohito and studied Bushido (the code of the samurai) and the wisdom to be found in the *Hagakure*. In 1938, the young Yoshi returned to Japan and enlisted in the Naval Air Arm. A month after enlistment, he met the beauteous Sumiko Makihara and they were married after a short courtship — unusual for Japanese, but the

19

war in China had caused the abandonment of many customs. After training at Tsuchuira, he was sent to China with the first squadron equipped with the *Rei Sentoki* Zero-sen. The dogfights took on the character of massacres, the slow Chinese Illusian 16's and Curtis P40's no match for the Mitsubishi. It was a happy time when Yoshi's squadron shot down ninety-nine enemy aircraft while losing only two to antiaircraft fire.

After a year's service, he returned to Tokyo where Sumiko presented him with a magnificent son, Masahei. Yoshi's joy was unbounded, and he and Sumiko began to make glorious plans for their beautiful boy. Within two months, Sumiko was pregnant again. A month after his second son, Hisaya, was born, the young ensign was sent to Hitokappu Bay—a remote anchorage in the Kurile Islands about sixteen hundred kilometers northeast of Tokyo Bay. Although Yoshi had heard rumors of super-battleships and carriers for years, he was not prepared for *Yonaga*. As the whaleboat approached the behemoth—which loomed gray in the cold mists—Yoshi felt he was nearing a gray mountain. And indeed it was an island; a gigantic steel structure of eighty-two thousand tons, over three hundred meters in length and thirty-four meters at the beam. An incredible, breathtaking giant that could operate one hundred fifty aircraft and steam at thirty-two knots. "A steel *Fujisan*," he had said under his breath as he climbed the accommodation ladder.

Here at Hitokappu Bay, Yoshi first learned of Kido Butai—the Pearl Harbor strike force. Seven carriers, *Kaga, Akagi, Soryu, Hiryu, Shokaku, Zuikaku,* and *Yonaga* were assigned to the force. But *Yonaga* was too large. With the usual paranoid thinking of the naval general staff, it was feared the great carrier would be too easy to discover and the seventh carrier was detached from *Kido Butai* and sent on a great circle north to the Bering Sea and the hidden anchorage at Sano Wan on the Chukchi Peninsula. From here she was to sortie on December 1 and join in the attack on Pearl Harbor. Tragically, the overhanging glacier slipped, covering the entrance, trapping *Yonaga* hopelessly.

For forty-two years the loyal samurai remained entrapped. Notwithstanding, morale remained high and the men maintained their equipment, their minds, and their bodies, waiting for the day of freedom — the moment they, too, could honor Bushido and carry out their orders. The moment came one summer's day in 1983 when the glacier slipped away. Then came the attacks on ships and planes as the great carrier steamed on a southerly heading toward its objective. Finally, the devastating attack on Pearl Harbor where the Americans were found sleepily wallowing in their usual ineptitude.

On returning to Tokyo Bay, the horrified Japanese learned it had all been for nothing. The unthinkable had become reality. Japan had surrendered. Yoshi was nearly destroyed when he learned his wife and two sons had been burned to death in the great Tokyo fire raid of March 9, 1945. He withdrew into a venomous shell of bitterness.

Brent Ross came aboard that first day in the bay, and Yoshi hated the American instantly — all things American. Then the Chinese orbited their laser system and the world changed dramatically. The nuclear terror of the Ivans and the Yankees was broken and Kadafi's madness went worldwide. Then came the alliance with the Israelis and the bloody fighting in the Mediterranean and southwest Pacific. Now dozens of his friends lay at the bottom of the sea or were nothing but ashes poured into white boxes. But all the fine warriors had filled the most rigid demands of Bushido and Shinto. *It is a cleansing act to give one's life for the Mikado. All the gods of heaven will respect the spirit of the samurai who dies in a righteous cause,* he had been taught. And an inviolable truth the adage was, indeed.

Over the years, fighting side by side with Brent Ross, Yoshi's hatred eroded, gradually turning to respect and then genuine affection. The young American was brave and, in many ways, more Japanese than most of the officers on *Yonaga.* Then Kimio Urshazawa entered his life and Yoshi found love did still exist in this hate-filled world. But love died in a blast from a terrorist's AK 47 in an ambush in Tokyo's Ueno Park. Since Kimio's death, Yoshi had hurled himself into combat with new recklessness: *shinigurai,* the Japanese called it—"Crazy to die." He saw his friend Brent Ross become distraught with worry. But death was a reward, a purification. No one could argue with that.

Leveling off, he shook the cobwebs from his brain and studied the mysterious aircraft which was now a thousand meters below him and lumbering along at about two hundred forty knots. A Lockheed Constellation C-121. Unmistakable with its triple tail fins, long, slender nose, four huge 3,250 Wright turbo-compound radial engines. With a range of 3,400 kilometers, it was ideal for the long hops between island bases. It wore Pan American markings. There was no indication anyone in the stranger had seen the Zeros.

Yoshi's five senses were fine-tuned to danger—so sensitive he seemed to possess a sixth sense that searched for threats when none seemed likely. A slight bank, change in pitch of a propeller, sudden acceleration, a shadow flickering in a cloud could all bring his head up. Something was wrong with the stranger and the alarms rang. He studied the fuselage where Plexiglas glinted from a dorsal bubble, and then he saw the outline of a door in the Lockheed's side which spoke of an unusual modification he had seen on several Arab aircraft: a quick opening door that concealed a deadly Gatling gun. As the flight commander led his section in a wide sweep around the giant, it nonchalantly changed its heading to west and north—a heading which would take it to Japan. But Pan American had given up its Japanese service because of the fighting and the loss of a transport with all of its passengers and crew off Hokkaido. Could it be headed for Iwo Jima? Pan American had no service to that island, either. He would investigate.

Glancing at a chart attached to a clipboard strapped to his knee, he pulled his microphone to his lips and barked *Yonaga's* code name. "Iceman. Iceman. This is Edo leader. Over."

Immediately, a scratchy voice acknowledged in his earphones. Matsuhara continued, "Sighted a Lockheed Constellation with Pan American markings. Latitude eighteen, longitude one-five-one, speed two-four zero, altitude three thousand, on a heading of three-zero-zero. Am investigating."

"Roger" came back.

The flight leader glanced from side to side and grunted with satisfaction—Matsumara and Kizamatsu were close on his elevators, precisely where they should be for the first time on the patrol. The commander disliked the radio because it told the whole world what he was thinking. Both his wingmen had heard his transmission and both acknowledged his signal of a single finger stabbed downward and a clenched fist punched upward twice, which meant a sweep around the mysterious plane by the leader while his wingmen remained on patrol high above. This could be a trap. He had seen the worm dangled before eager hunters before as far back as China. Turn your

23

back, get lost in a reckless approach, and the skies very often rained enemy fighters.

After a quick glance upsun to assure himself no squared-off wing tips of ME 109's lurked there, Matsuhara thumbed the ring of the gun button from Safe to Fire, opened the throttle another notch, kicked left rudder, and horsed the stick back and to the left. Responding like the thoroughbred it was, the Zero lifted its red cowling and began to roll to the left into a split-ess. Yoshi felt his stomach sink with the pull of gravity and the horizon dropped out of sight. Then he arced through the top of the roll and plunged into a dive, the horizon reappearing above his cowling and then his vision was filled with the blue expanse of the sea. He centered his controls and pointed the fighter at the Constellation which was five or six kilometers to the north and a thousand meters beneath him.

As he streaked toward the transport, he became uneasy. Then alarmed. The Plexiglas dorsal bubble had sprouted two black snouts and doors had been opened on her sides. Another Arab conversion? Perhaps even a bomber trying to sneak in over Tokyo Bay or seek out *Yonaga* and destroy her with a single stick of bombs. The Arabs and their German and Russian technicians were clever—had even converted old Douglas DC-3's to bombers. Now, there were no doubts; the multiple barrels of a Gatling were visible in the port door.

Yoshi's stomach suddenly felt empty and his mouth was sour and dry—the way it felt the morning after too much sake. Death was there. Did he not seek it? Crave it to cleanse away the guilt of Kimio's death? Strange that that insidious interloper *fear* should suddenly find a home in his stomach. Gritting his teeth angrily, he punched the Sakae to full military power and it roared like a predator smelling the kill, accelerating the tiny fighter to over four hundred knots in a blink. A diving Zero at full military power was a terrible gun platform. But a speeding fighter was also a difficult target. He would need every advantage the Zero could give him. He faced awesome firepower and he would be in range within a heartbeat.

The dorsal turret glowed cherry-red and tracers whipped toward him but dropped off. "Too far for thirteen millimeter, you amateurs," Yoshi snorted disdainfully. Then tracers stormed from the port door, which blazed a fearsome orange like an open blast furnace as the pilot cleverly banked the huge plane, giving the crew of the Gatling a shot. A three-barrel twenty-millimeter, these tracers did not drop off, streaming and smoking past the Zero like a hail of glowing meteorites.

The fighter was bouncing and vibrating, its control surfaces buffeted by pressures that nearly froze the rudder pedals and made the control column as rigid as a tree trunk. It took all of the commander's strength to bank away from the Gatling's fire and bring the glowing reticle of the electric gunsight to the center of the fuselage of the huge plane. Suddenly it filled all three rings of his range finder. He had his killing angle. He thumbed the red button.

Jarred by the recoil of two twenty-millimeter cannons and a pair of 7.7 millimeter machine guns, the little fighter slowed twenty knots and, already tortured by its dive, seemed to be shaking itself to death like a man with epilepsy. Empty shell casings bounced against the guards and spilled down their chutes and into the slipstream gaily like a hail of glistening yellow confetti. Holding the button down and clenching his teeth, Yoshi felt an atavistic glow of pleasure spread deep within him — a hot, visceral feeling he had not known since Kimio's death.

It was only a four-second burst at one-quarter deflection. But the Japanese pilot never wasted a round. His laugh was wild and high as he saw his shells grind through the great fuselage like a buzz saw, chopping off pieces of skin plating and hurling them into the slipstream like paper in a gale. A breath on the stick and the sledgehammer blows tore through the turret, smashing it in a blaze of glittering Plexiglas and red-gray shower of gore as a shell exploded the gunner's head.

A little right rudder and he flashed past, too fast for the starboard Gatling to make an accurate full deflection shot at a target moving at over four hundred knots. Nevertheless, the door glowed with huge orange flashes and a cloud of smoking firebrands dropped off toward the sea. Yoshi laughed as he pulled back on the stick with all of his strength. The enemy's rounds were all behind him.

The commander's laughter turned to groans as at least six g's pounded him down into his seat, the little fighter bouncing and groaning, her main wingspar bending upward with the enormous load. His head was suddenly a lead slug and he felt the skin of his cheeks sag downward, stomach and abdomen bulging against his flight suit. Then as he pulled back on the stick with all of his strength, his vision blurred and rockets flashed across his retinas. He felt as if a giant were pounding him into his seat with an enormous sledgehammer. Screaming to relieve the pressure and shaking his head to clear the fog, he continued to pull back on the stick until the vast blue mat of the Pacific dropped from view and the cowling climbed above the horizon.

The Constellation should have been directly above him, but it was not. Instead, he caught sight of it fleeing far to the west. Easing the control column and working the rudder peddles, the commander brought the fighter onto a course of interception. Slowly, the underside of the big plane grew in his range finder. "Prepare to join Allah, Arab pigs," he said under his breath. The belly of the Lockheed filled the first ring. It was almost in range.

Then the expected bank and the Constellation began to circle to its right as the pilot tried desperately to bring his starboard Gatling to bear on his tormentor. At the moment Yoshi punched the button, the Gatling boiled to life like a volcano spewing lava. His shells blasted into the fearful Gatling, four twenty-millimeter shells blowing it from its mount. He watched it fall from the aircraft and tumble toward the Pacific like junk. His laugh was maniacal, out of control. He felt the heat in his groin grow.

Punching the stick to the right and balancing with rudder, the Japanese barrel-rolled to the right while the enemy, slowed by hits to his fuselage that had blasted off big chunks of aluminum exposing "U"-stringers and frames from the door all the way back to the shattered turret, banked carefully to his left with his speed cut by at least fifty knots. Yoshi felt a familiar crystal-clear clarity, a charge of energy that caused his hands to tremble and his breath to be short. He wanted to kill his enemy with a knife, his hands, his teeth. He was almost disappointed with the knowledge he would be forced to destroy him with gunfire.

Streaking at at least a hundred fifty knots more than his enemy, Yoshi bored in below and to the right of the Constellation, avoiding the deadly Gatling on the port side. With the stick pulled back into his stomach, the fighter rocketed up and under the starboard wing of the lumbering giant and slightly ahead of it.

Hanging on his prop with the Sakae screaming with the strain, Yoshi risked a stall and moved the glowing reticle to the two starboard engines, boring in so close

27

he could see the copilot's wide-eyed white face staring at him out of the cockpit's side window, a dead gunner with no legs hanging out the starboard door and flopping in the wind, held by his safety harness like a red-and-brown pennant, his severed arteries spilling a red haze into the slipstream. Matsuhara was so close, the engine nacelles streaked black from exhaust not only filled the gunsight but the antiglare gunsight screen as well. It was zero deflection and point-blank. Seesawing his rudder pedals gently, he moved the nose of the fighter back and forth like a hunter tracking a game bird and sprayed the right wing. The burst blew the cowling and hood from the number-three engine exposing the two rows of cylinder heads of the huge radial engine, turbo-charger, the bulging Power Recovery Turbine, and fuel and hydraulic lines. Severed lines streamed red fluid like the gunner's blood, and a hole in the recovery turbine spouted hot exhaust gases like an old locomotive puffing up a hill. More shells punched into the wing tank, blew the cover off the right main wheel well, shot off the flap hinges causing the flap to rip free and dangle from its control linkage, ripped off big chunks of skin exposing the main spar, formers, ribs, and color-coded control lines. The big transport staggered and dipped erratically but thundered on.

Despite Yoshi's pleas to Amaterasu, the Zero would take no more. Standing on its tail with its airspeed nearly zero, the Sakae screamed in agony like an animal caught in a steel trap, the airframe yawed and shook as if it were trying to shake itself to pieces like a wet dog, and the fighter began to fall off on its right side, pulled by the Sakae's weight and torque. Stick-horsed forward and sharp right rudder followed by a correcting kick of left rudder turned the embryonic spin into a spiraling dive. Picking up airspeed, Yoshi looked into his rearview mirrors and then over his shoulder. He exulted joyfully and saliva ran down to his chin as he saw flame streak from the Constellation's number-three engine and wing fuel tank. Shouting with joy, Yoshi pulled back on the stick and leveled off, banking toward the doomed Lockheed. He had used thirty-six rounds of twenty millimeter, fifty-eight rounds of 7.7 and had not even been scratched.

Circling and climbing back up to his wingmen, he watched the great plane fall off into a tight spin. Weakened by shell hits, the right wing bent up at its root like a piece of wet cardboard and then broke off completely, flopping grotesquely behind the stricken transport. Leaving a thick black column of greasy smoke and pulled to the left by its port wing, the big plane tumbled and gyrated wildly, no longer a graceful thing of the air but now a shattered, crumpled insect of monstrous proportions that had been swatted from the air and set aflame. With a huge splash and cloud of spray, it finally plunged into the Pacific while the wing twisted into the sea at least two kilometers to the south. Quickly the cold water covered the grave and only a long, thin shroud of black smoke remained as a marker. Then the wind ripped at the smoke and within seconds there was nothing left to mark the tomb.

High above, three Zeros sped off to the west.

From six thousand feet the island of Saipan looked like a wolf's head, mouth spread wide in a mortal scream of agony. Approaching from the north astride the 145th meridian, Marpi Point first became visible to the crew of *Tora II*. Grim, high cliffs dropping off to seaswept rocks like dragon's teeth gave the bluffs a murderous aspect. And, indeed, thousands of civilians and soldiers had shattered themselves on the rocks and drowned in the wild surf during the final days of the great battle for Saipan in 1944. Takii's scratchy voice filled Brent's earphones and the little pilot gestured over the combing. "A cemetery. I lost a brother there." He seemed to be talking to himself. No one answered.

Banking to the west toward the wolf's mouth, Magicienne Bay, details of the entire fourteen by five mile island became visible; Mount Tapotchau rising from the island's center like a green sentinel, to the north and east the rolling hills and high plateaus ending abruptly in narrow coastal flats. But to the south and west Tapotchau flattened into a long coastal plain, fringed by inviting white beaches, protected by a great coral reef. It was here that Brent saw the towns of Garapan and Charan Kanoa. Strangely, there was no movement.

Takii's voice again: "There, on the southwest beaches, that's where the landings were made." Brent looked at the lovely beaches and the protective reef and shuddered. There were three openings in the coral. They must have been zeroed in. *Very expensive real estate,* he thought.

Takii seemed to be reading his mind. "Thirty thousand Japanese troops and sailors died here, and most of the civilian population — over twenty thousand more — General Saito, Admiral Nagumo . . ."

Brent could not remain silent. "But thousands of Americans died, too." He stabbed a finger at the island and his voice was hard. "My father was here and so was Admiral Allen. That place didn't come cheap."

The pilot's voice was conciliatory. "I know, Brent-san. I did not mean to offend. It was a terrible tragedy — all for nothing. All those fine boys."

Commander Yoshi Matsuhara's voice calling "Iceman" interrupted the conversation. All three members of the bomber's crew sat bolt upright as the report of

30

the destruction of the Libyan Constellation poured through their earphones. There was no cheering. Instead, three pairs of eyes searched the skies even more anxiously. Takii said, "The Commonwealth of the northern Marianas maintains an airdrome on the southern end of Saipan and another on Tinian."

The nearby island of Tinian was now clearly visible. In fact, even tiny Aguijan jutting from the sea off the southern toe of Tinian like the dot of Tinian's exclamation mark could be seen. The storm was much closer, thunderheads looming high and hostile, tossing their monstrous, billowing heads to the sky and filling the entire southern horizon—a great black-and-gray promontory charged with lightning and crashing thunder. Its precursors, scudding gobs of cumulus like a rolling line of skirmishers, already flanked Aguigan. The air itself also seemed to have changed. It was charged with static that made Brent's skin prickle and filled him with new unease and deep forebodings. He tightened his jaw and patted the breech of the Nambu.

As Takii banked the Nakajima to the west over the channel between Saipan and Tinian and away from the storm, Brent adjusted his glasses. Airstrips like Xs were visible on the southern end of Saipan and in the middle of Tinian, which was almost flat. Now Brent understood why Tinian had been a favorite of B-29 crews.

Takii's voice: "Ensign Hayusa, are you monitoring your bands?"

"Yes, sir. No transmissions on channel eighteen or FM ten."

"Not even citizens' band?"

"Nothing, Lieutenant."

"Continue your search." Then to Brent, "You have the eyes of a hawk, Lieutenant Ross. See any parked fighters?"

Brent leaned over the combing with his glasses on Saipan. The place not only showed no movement at all, it looked dead, almost as if the thousands who had died with such great violence over four decades ago refused to let go, their troubled spirits overwhelming life with an aura of death. The young lieutenant shuddered, feeling a new cold, but this time not from the wind. He spoke into his microphone. "I don't even see an airplane, Lieutenant Takii."

Takii punched his instrument panel so hard the tachometer needle jumped a hundred revolutions. "Sacred Amaterasu, we need your help," he muttered to himself. And then to Brent, "Something is wrong down there."

"I agree. Nothing's moving. Not even a car—no fishing boats."

Brent saw a mound near the strip on Saipan. He leaned over the combing, stared with new concentration. Sandbags. Brush. He keyed his microphone. "Lieutenant Takii, I've spotted something—could be a camouflaged revetment."

"Fighters! High and to the east—one-eight-zero!" Ensign Hayusa screamed, stabbing a finger at the sky.

Bringing up his glasses, Brent saw a frightening spectacle: a wedge of three Messerschmitt 109's rocketing at them from far to the east. Two tar-black fighters led by a blood-red machine that looked like the point of a lance just pulled from the guts of a dead foe. The red machine belonged to Oberstleutnant (Squadron Commander) Kenneth Rosencrance, leader of the Vierter Jagerstaffel (Fourth Fighter Squadron) mercenary, killer, and Kadafi's leading ace. Brent knew the renegade well—had been amazed at the man's arrogance and courage when Rosencrance became *Yonaga*'s prisoner after Yoshi Matsuhara shot him down over Tokyo. Virulently anti-Semitic, the man had the soul of a cobra and the instincts of a shark. It was rumored the Arabs paid him one million a year American plus fifty thousand dollars for each kill. Rosenscrance had snickered to Brent, "If I bust enough Kike and Jap ass, I'll be a millionaire before this is over, ol' buddy. I'll buy San Simeon, Hearst's old pad, get me some young pussy, and fuck and booze myself to death."

It was instant hatred. Brent wanted to kill the big American with his bare hands. Had almost done as much in *Yonaga*'s sick bay after Roesncrance had nearly beaten the wounded Taku Ishikawa to death. But Commander Tashiro Okuma had stopped the insensate Brent Ross before he could deliver the coup de grace with a pair of surgical scissors. Then the kidnapping of Prince Akihito, the exchange that led to the release of Rosencrance. Rosencrance's last words were a vow to kill Brent, a pay back for the beating. "I was wounded, you chicken-shit son-of-a-bitch," the burly American shouted as he left. "Someday I'll square it."

"Be my guest," Brent had snorted. But now Kenneth Rosencrance had his chance and all of the marbles. As Brent brought the machine gun to bear he heard Ensign Takashiro Hayusa calling frantically, "Iceman, Iceman, this is *Shonendan* (Scout) Two a thousand meters over the island of Saipan. Three enemy fighters closing high and to the east."

"I read you, *Shonendan* Two." Then to Bren'ts joy *Yonaga*'s call to Yoshi Matsuhara: "Edo Leader, Edo Leader, this is Iceman."

Brent heard Yoshi's strong voice acknowledge. Then *Yonaga*'s fighter-control officer continued, "Enemy fighters have intercepted *Shonendan* Two over the island of Saipan. Engage! Engage! Your vector two-three-zero."

"Roger and out."

33

The cold, dispassionate tones of the control officer and Yoshi Matsuhara, like men ordering lunch, maddened Brent. "Jesus Christ, Yoshi. Hurry! Hurry! I'm going to get my ass shot off."

Brent felt himself thrown violently to the side of the cockpit as Takii banked sharply to the south and headed toward the storm, stick forward, the big plane in a dive, engine at full military power. The old pilot was doing all he could: bring *Tora* low to the water and let the ocean protect her belly and take his chances with the storm — if the enemy did not kill him first.

With the precision of a trained group of acrobats, the three ME's banked gracefully into a wide, sweeping turn and swooped down on the Nakajima's tail. Then they split into three petals like the bloom of a poisonous flower; Rosencrance almost into a vertical climb and the two black machines veering to the right and left. Brent felt the hair on his forearms and neck come erect, each follicle freezing and tingling, and his bowels seemed to drop out of his body. Unable to swallow because of a rock lodged in his throat, he steadied his hands and brought the right-hand ME into the first ring of his large ringsight. He cursed. They had made him choose. And, no doubt, the Arabs would attack simultaneously from both sides and with far greater firepower.

Rosencrance was high above, staring down like an amused spectator. Then Brent was anguished as a new thought grated through his mind: *They're using us for practice. A target. Sharpening up some new men.* He bent his long legs until they ached, squatting low, set his jaw, and was suddenly filled with a new calm. He had shot down a DC-3 over the Mediterranean and a fighter over Korea with the same gun and the same pilot. He was considered a gifted gunner with an instinctive sense for the maddening multi-dimensional

34

gunnery problems of aerial combat. Anticipation, an inherent grasp of deflection and steadiness were all qualities Brent Ross possessed. He waited as the ME grew in his sights.

Now he could see the aircraft was not all black; the spinner gleaming white with the fearsome muzzle of the engine-mounted twenty-millimeter gun protruding. The sun glared from the flat gunsight screen and, as the Messerschmitt closed at a speed that exceeded the bomber's by at least a hundred knots, even small details became clear: the exhaust manifold fairing strip, oil cooler intake under the fuselage like a double chin, the nonretracting tail wheel, the D/F loop just back of the cockpit, the Libyan markings on each squared-off wing and fuselage, the muzzles of the two cowling mounted Borsig thirteen-millimeter machine guns. Now he could see the pilot, a goggled black lump, rigid and fixed behind his range finder as much a part of the aircraft as the Daimler Benz engine, the aerial mast, the guns. Not a man at all, but a machine whose only function was to kill him.

Now he realized the two black machines were not in precise sync—the right ME at least a quarter mile ahead of the left. Either they were new, careless, or so supremely confident they intended to take target practice individually. But it was a mistake. They had given their enemy a slight advantage. He would grab it.

He felt the bomber flatten, bounce skyward, and then down again as they skimmed the sea parallel to the east coast of Tinian. A quick glance downward and he saw the sun- and shadow-dappled water blurring past only a few feet beneath him—so close their propeller threw up a fine plume of spray; so close their backwash left a flattened, rippling wake behind them. The chop was clear, white froth on a deep reddish-black sea like a turgid mass of dark blood, showing

35

great depth even this close to shore. He glanced at a chart fastened to the bulkhead. He found *ME 109 — First ring eight hundred yards, Second ring five hundred yards, Third ring two hundred yards*. He would force himself to wait until the enemy filled the three rings. The young gunner set his jaw and tightened his trigger finger.

While his companion lagged farther behind and gradually climbed to get a better view of the sport, the attacking Messerschmitt banked gracefully to its right and closed the range slowly. *He's throttled back,* Brent thought. *The son-of-a-bitch is really confident — thinks we're easy meat. He'll try for a zero-deflection shot*. The propeller boss and then the ME's cowling began to wink red at him. A swarm of fire beads smoked toward him, at first coming quite slowly but accelerating miraculously as they closed. Violently he was thrown to his left as Takii banked sharply to the right and headed the big plane for the cliffs of Tinian's southeast coast. Fooled by the maneuver, the Arab's tracers dropped off harmlessly.

The enemy pilot corrected quickly, gunned his engine, and slashed in above the Nakajima's port elevator, all of his armament blazing. He filled two rings.

Brent's aiming point was the orange-red flashes of the engine-mounted twenty-millimeter gun. He held fire until the wing tips of the ME stretched far enough to form a diameter of the outer circle of his range finder. Two hundred yards. It seemed time slowed for Brent and his vision suddenly intensified to brilliant clarity. Holding his breath and with his lips pulled back in a rictus of determination, he forced himself to caress the trigger gently, taking up the slack until he felt the resistance of the trigger spring. Then the hard, even pull through the spring and the Nambu came alive, kicking, chattering, sending a stream of smoking tracers into the bull's eyes of the enemy's propeller. Bright yellow strikes erupted on the Libyan's cowling and spinner, ricochets flung from the propeller like sparks from a pinwheel.

Shocked and panicked by Brent's accuracy, the Arab rocketed the ME to the right, crossing the Nakajima's tail. And then back directly behind the bomber, firing now in short bursts, trying to confuse Brent's aim with the B5N's rudder. He was clever and brave—too courageous to be an Arab. Probably a German or Russian. Holes appeared miraculously in the Nakajima's right wing. With his own tail assembly in his sights, Brent released the trigger and shouted into his microphone as more tracers burned past, "The rudder—he's directly astern. Give me a shot, Takii!"

The plea was unnecessary. Takii, watching carefully in his rearview mirrors and anticipating the Arab's tactics, had already begun to bank to the left, giving Brent a shot free of the rudder. Brent squeezed off two short bursts, saw paint and bits of metal kicked loose by small fire motes of bright yellow strikes as his slugs ripped into the ME's cowling. The ME banked away and then began curving back again.

At the instant the bomber bounced up and over the cliffs of Tinian's coastline riding upward on the cap of a thermal Sinian's radiating from the hot, rock-hard surface, the 109 began another run high above their right rudder and this time his aim was better, the Nakajima rising in his sights. *Bang! Bang! Bang!* The bomber vibrated as thirteen-millimeter bullets shot off the geared rudder tab and tail wheel leg cuff, exploded the rear navigation light and plucked at the fuselage just behind Brent's cockpit, leaving haloes of bright bare metal around the rents in the aluminum.

Brent heard his pilot cursing as he fought the change in the bomber's trim and managed to bring the cowling down again. Takii's voice: "He will pass over us. You will have his belly." Brent wondered how the pilot could know so much, prophesy the enemy's moves. Then he was thrown forward as Takii cracked the flaps full down, cut throttle, and jammed his pitch-control lever to full forward, turning the Sumitomo propeller into a brake.

The Messerschmitt loomed so close Brent was seized by a panic when it appeared the three blades of the big VDM constant-speed propeller would chew into their tail. Frantically, the enemy pilot pulled back on his stick and banked to his right. Brent had his belly. Lips skinned into a hungry leer, the big American filled his sights with the ME's underbelly. Judging his deflection perfectly, he pulled the trigger, sending a long burst that caught the ME just behind its spinner backplate and forward of the big scooplike oil cooler intake. As the fighter passed and banked away, Brent held the trigger down and let his enemy fly through the murderous stream, swinging the gun with his target so that his tracer stream stitched through his enemy from hub to tail wheel.

Sharpening his bank, the Libyan streamed glycol from his ripped oil cooler in a white mist. And then a fierce burst of flame licked back from the huge engine followed by a spoor of dense black smoke. Screaming with joy, Brent stood in the cockpit and waved a clenched fist as the stricken fighter made a full roll upward, spilling its own epitaph like shiny black silk behind it, pointing its nose for the heavens in a last desperate effort to escape the clutch of gravity and the inevitable.

Fascinated, Brent watched as the black fighter's canopy flew open and a brown bundle tumbled out, caroming off the wing and slamming into his own stabilizer, his right arm neatly severed by the stabilizer's leading edge. Legs and arm spread-eagled, the Arab pilot sailed over Brent's head, the brown flying clothes mottled red while the pilotless ME rolled again and pointed its nose down into its final dive. Streaking at full throttle, it exploded on the island's flat surface with a violence seen by only those few who fight and die in the sky. Rotating slowly like a bloody Frisbee, the pilot's body crashed into a rocky promontory just above the beach.

Brent felt the Nakajima jerk as Takii kicked rudder and pointed the aircraft south again. They roared over a few farmhouses and then Tinian town shook to the vibrations of the big Sakae. Brent glimpsed rows of small shacklike houses, narrow roads, animals, and frightened white faces staring up. Anxiously, he searched the heavens and found the second black ME now high and to the west while Rosencrance's blood-red machine was curving downward in a shallow dive. "We're going to catch it now," Brent said to himself.

Abruptly, the sea was beneath them again and the green tablelike island of Aguijan loomed only a few miles ahead. And the storm was there, licking at the trees that crowned the sharp peak at the island's center like a single candle at a formal setting. But they would never make the storm. This time the attack would be coordinated, swift, deadly, and from two quarters simultaneously. No more casual target practice.

Brent brought up the Nambu, tightened his finger. He had no trouble making his choice — Rosencrance. He would die emptying his belt into the red ME. Remembering an old samurai adage Admiral Fujita had quoted years ago during the fighting in the Mediterranean, he squared his shoulders, smiled grimly, and repeated it to himself: "If you are to die, Brent-san, die facing the enemy."

A flash of white to the east on the very periphery of

his awareness turned his head. Three high-flying Zero-sens. One with a red cowling and green hood. *Yoshi! Yoshi Matsuhara!* Joyfully, Brent shouted into his microphone, "Zeros. It's *Edo One,* high, bearing one-zero-zero."

"Very well. I have them."

Then Ensign Hayusa's cold, trembling voice. "More enemy fighters at zero-four-zero, elevation forty."

Brent found them, a pair of black crosses roaring in from the southwest, arrowing toward Matsuhara's Zeros. "For God's sake, Yoshi. ME's! ME's!" Brent screamed into the slipstream. "Can't you see them?" Abruptly, Matsuhara's wingmen broke, banked sharply and streaked toward the pair of new enemy fighters. Yoshi rolled into a vertical dive, nose pointed toward the Nakajima, Rosencrance and his wing man. A murderous daisy chain had been formed; the B5N, two ME's and Yoshi Matsuhara. Soon, cannon shells and bullets would break the chain.

Brent glanced ahead at the Aguijan. They were so low the cliffs of the forbidding island loomed above them, the swells slowed by the shoaling bottom and angered by the storm rising into successive mountain ranges like waves of attacking infantry, hurling themselves furiously against the unyielding rock cliffs where they creamed and leaped high in explosions of purest lacy white mist catching the slanting rays of the sun and flashing the colors of the rainbow. In any other circumstances, the spectacle would have been beautiful. But not today.

Brent was seized with a chilling thought. Was Takii's samurai's mind determined to hurl them all to their deaths against the cliffs in a spectacular gesture of seppuku? Cheat the enemy of the glory and pleasure of the kill? It was consistent with Bushido, had happened thousands of times in the past. Brent tore his eyes from the cruel cliffs and hunched down behind his weapon.

The black ME was close, jockeying for his killing angle. Brent watched the aircraft grow in his sights. The enemy was alone, Rosencrance looping into an Immelmann in an interception of Matsuhara while high above Matsuhara's wingmen were engaging the pair of high-flying ME's. Then, suddenly, the sun was gone, hidden by the first outriders of the storm and Brent was hurled to the side, the restraint of his harness saving him from injury against the side of the cockpit. Takii was banking hard, skimming the cliffs so close, the left wing tip clipped off the top of a clump of scraggly brush like a chain saw through celery.

But the fighter was moving in for a point-blank shot and the pilot was smart, pulling up sharply, not allowing Takii to lure him into crashing into the side of the cliff but losing his firing position at the same time. Again Brent was hurled to the side, the big plane turning, canopy close to the curving side of the island as Yoshiro Takii called on every horsepower and taxed every spar, former, stringer, and wire in a desperate attempt to throw off the Arab's aim. The Arab veered away and Brent knew he was setting up for a belly shot. He jammed the breech of his Nambu high bringing the muzzle down, but the ME was off their right rudder and the tail plane was in Brent's line of fire. "For Christ's sake, Takii! Give me a shot!"

The pilot seemed not to hear him. Instead, Takii continued to hug the curving sides of the island with his wings nearly vertical like a yo-yo spun around a child's head. But the sharp inclination of the wings lost lift and Brent could feet a gut-wrenching drop. Then the quarter-roll to the right, a flattening as airfoils found cushions of air, and another quarter roll to the right, a sharp lunge upward, and then down like the wildest roller-coaster ride, forces reversing, Brent abruptly lifted from his seat by centrifugal force and straining against his shoulder restraints as the big plane crested its climb and hurtled downward, banking again close to the island.

Blood surged to the young lieutenant's head, his eyes bulged, nose ran, and a million needles tried to push their way through the flesh of his cheeks and forehead. Despite the wild gyrations, he fought the Nambu bringing it to bear on his enemy. For an instant he had a clear field of fire and the ME skidded into his sights. They fired simultaneously. Tracers snapped past and Brent felt the big plane vibrate from bullet hits. With the winking twenty-millimeter in the center of his sights, Brent held down the trigger and sprayed the front of his enemy like a man using a garden hose squirting firebrands. But again his burst was cut short by his pilot's maneuvers.

Takii threw the stick to the right and kicked rudder, throwing the big plane into a wrenching turn. He spoiled the enemy's aim, but could only hold the turn for a moment. With the bomber's airfoils nearly vertical and the aircraft threatening to side-slip into the sea, he horsed the stick to the left, dropping down to the wavetops and banking only a breath away from the sheer sides of the island. Suddenly a downdraft and the plane plummeted while Takii pulled the stick back into his guts, slapping the sea with his elevators like a sperm whale in a mating frenzy. Out of control, the big bomber staggered drunkenly, lurching from side to side and threatening to stall and smash into the breakers.

This is it, Brent said to himself, convinced death was only seconds away. Then he prayed as his pilot fought the controls like a madman. Finally, by a miracle of piloting, Takii regained control and trimmed the aircraft level.

Muttering thanks to God, Brent tracked his gun as the fighter zoomed far out and then banked in smartly for another run. The front of the ME blazed, the Arab trying for a difficult full-deflection shot. He was an excellent marksman. There were thuds, pings, and bangs from hits as Brent opened fire. Struck by a 7.7 millimeter slug, there was a "pop" as his oxygen bottle exploded and his binoculars and flare gun were blown from the bulkhead by a half-dozen more slugs. Then an explosion of a twenty-millimeter shell that knocked him from the gun and over the left side of the cockpit where he hung helplessly for a moment, filled with disbelief, a black door slamming in his head. Then reality began to return with the smell of cordite, burned cloth, and screams in his earphones that turned his blood to ice water. Something hot and sticky running down his chest. He shook his head, trying to clear the dregs of night from his brain.

The middle cockpit had been hit and Ensign Takashiro Hayusa was screaming, spraying blood, chest blow open, his pulsating and ripped right lung exposed to the wind. His shrieks were high and shrill, the eerie cries like sharp fingernails raked across Brent's soul. Blood sprayed Brent's face, stuck to his helmet and jacket where it coagulated immediately in the cold wind.

The American had no time for the wounded navigator or the pain in his chest and the blood he could feel running to his waist and pooling against his belt. Biting his lip, he closed his mind to the screams, the pain, grabbed the pistol grips and swung the Nambu back to the right. The enemy was there, off their right elevator, throttled back and casually moving in for the kill.

The young gunner glanced skyward. Yoshi and Rosencrance were locked in a personal duel, while high

43

above a Zero burst into flame and began its curving descent into the sea. A black Messerschmitt had rolled out of the fight trailing smoke. No help there.

Groggily, Brent brought the Nambu to bear and squeezed the trigger. But the ME dropped behind and slightly above the horizontal tailplane. He was directly behind the rudder. Seething with frustration, Brent released the trigger. "For Christ's sake, give me a shot, Takii," he screamed over Hayusa's fading groans.

Takii seemed not to hear. Instead, he seemed to be trying to keep the Messerschmitt precisely where the Arab chose to be; behind and slightly above the horizontal tail plane. A new pain brought the gunner's hand to his chest. His flight clothes were ripped and slimy gore stuck to his glove like red paste. Chunks of shattered bone imbedded in coagulating blood. Dully Brent stared at the offal on his hand, his ripped jacket, and the huge hole in the forward bulkhead. Pieces of the navigator had been blown through the bulkhead and mixed with his own wounds. Two or three slugs had ripped his clothes and opened wounds on his chest. Now the rents in his flesh burned — flamed with the intensity of branding irons. For the first time in his life, Brent Ross felt hopeless — defeated — and deep down, the floor of his stomach boiled as an atavistic clutch of horror uncoiled like a great loathsome maggot.

Slugs cracking in his ears like whips jarred the gunner. Brent pleaded feverishly, "Bank, Takii. Give me a shot!" But again, Takii seemed not to hear. Was Takii frozen by panic? Wounded, too? The ME moved in and death began to wink.

When he heard the call from *Shonendan* Two, Commander Yoshi Matsuhara was fifty kilometers to the east and north of Saipan. From four thousand meters he could already see the hump of Saipan and the tabletop of Tinian in the distance, with the enormous black hulking storm looming just to the south and obscuring the southern end of Aguijan. Brent was in trouble. With his throttle jammed to the fire wall and his wingmen straining to keep station, Yoshi had raced toward the Marianas, his compass heading 230. A fearsome flash of orange low and to the west caused him to groan and feel fear deep down in the very essence of his being. Was he too late? Brent, Takii, and young Hayusa dead already? Then he exulted. A black Messerschmitt. Crashing into Tinian. Brent Ross's uncanny gunner's eye had scored again.

At that instant, Yoshi's trained, experienced eyes had picked up the B5N racing toward Aguijan with another black fighter in pursuit. Then Rosencrance's red 109 curving upward toward him and two more ME's, which were nothing more than black mites to the south caught his peripheral vision at the same time. With the speed of a computer, Matsuhara's mind weighed and analyzed each problem and the best possible decisions were made in a millisecond. A waggle of wings followed by a flurry of hand signals and NAP Masatake Matsumara and Ensign Subaru Kizamatsu had gunned into split-esses, diving toward the pair of Messerschmitts closing from the south and four hundred meters below.

Now Matsuhara had just completed a half-roll and was screaming down hard on the fighter closing for the kill on the B5N which was hugging the cliffs and racing toward a tall steel derrick. Anchored on the sea floor just off the south coast of the island with a long cable attached to a tower on top of the cliffs, the rig was the only way to off-load cargo to the inhabitants of the island. But Rosencrance was intercepting him, cutting him off, growing in his windshield.

The red fighter was at a disadvantage, climbing on his interception. Yoshi hunched forward, jaw set, eyes squinting, his left hand first rubbing his *hachimachi* headband and then trailing across his waist where he could feel his belt of a thousand stitches. Softly, he called on the gods and Buddha.

Yoshi cursed. The renegade Rosencrance was a talented flyer and fearless in a fight. The red ME was closing on him head-on. There was no chance he could help the B5N without fighting the red Messerschmitt first. And he was low on ammunition — had fired for eight seconds in shooting down the Constellation. He had nine seconds of firepower left. He would make every round count.

With the engine in full overboost and in a steep dive, the white airspeed needle chased around the indicator — 300, 350, 400 — the white needle overtaking the slower red danger line. The stick vibrated in his hands like a live thing, and all the strength in his powerful arms and hands could not hold it still. The airframe was bouncing and vibrating as enormous pressures built up against wing and tail surfaces. He had called on a punishing dive in attacking the Constellation and Yoshi knew his wingspars and airframe had been strained to the limit and were in jeopardy again. But he had no choice.

At a combined closing speed of almost one thousand knots, the fighters came into range in a blink. Fighting the controls, Yoshi brought the red machine into the bouncing, glowing reticle and the red bead onto his enemy's engine. Rosencrance began firing but Yoshi held his thumb above the red button. Then at a hundred and fifty meters, with shells and tracers snapping around his canopy, he jammed the trigger. A two second burst and the red machine flashed past like a bolt of lightning.

The commander knew Rosencrance would roll and dive on his tail, looking for his killing angle. With a groan, he glimpsed the Nakajima far below, flying directly for the derrick and the steel cable. If the black ME did not kill them, the derrick would. A quick glance over his shoulder and he saw a burning Zero high and to the north. Matsumara was hit. And a ME was smoking, falling off into a wide chandelle. A white parachute blossomed. Kizamatsu needed him and so did the crew of *Tora II*. But Rosencrance had him — dictated his actions. Cursing his luck, the commander pulled back on his stick.

The black ME was directly behind the Nakajima as Takii screamed down on the steel derrick and slender steel cable which was almost invisible in the shadows of the overhanging thunderheads and the mist which was rapidly turning into slashing rain. Clinging to the B5N as if it were attached by a cable of its own, the fighter was close astern and firing in short bursts as the big bomber bounced up and down in the turbulence of the storm. Eyes stung by the rain, Brent pulled down his goggles and screamed curses, choking back the pain and feeling trails of blood oozing down his thigh. Triggering off a dozen rounds at a time, he took chances with his tail assembly and saw holes appear in his tail fin.

Suddenly the bomber staggered as a twenty-millimeter shell hit the right wing like a sledgehammer, blowing away a huge chunk of aluminum, exposing the main wing spar, stringers, and ribs. Praying frantically, Brent sent a burst into his enemy's cowling, shooting off a cowling fastener and riddling a wing root fillet. With the left side of his cowling ripped

47

loose and threatening to crash back onto his tail, the Arab pulled up abruptly just as the B5N slashed under the cable. The enemy pilot never saw it.

Caught just inboard of the left mainwheel well, the cable sliced through the ME's wing structure like a hot razor through butter. Staggered by the impact, the fighter was hurled by its own momentum upward into a twisting, agonizing turn, severed wing flopping and tumbling far below with the left main wheel and part of a wing tank breaking free, cowling ripped loose and shedding aluminum sheeting like a molting reptile.

Screaming with joy and whipped by huge raindrops, Brent forgot his wounds and half stood, cheering as the big fighter continued climbing and writhing and disintegrating in its death agony like an eviscerated jackal, finally stalling and dropping off into a dive, twisting around its one remaining wing. The canopy flew back and a figure maddened with fear scrambled over the combing and was hurled into space by the savage motion of the fighter. Too late. The plane crashed into the tumbling surf and smashed itself to pieces on the rocks while the pilot pulling on his D-ring with the white parachute leader trailing was smashed to bloody gelatin at the base of the cliff.

Brent's cheers turned to gasps as rain, pearly strings and snakes of it, stormed into the cockpit, coating his goggles with streaming curtains. He was blind — absolutely blind in a world made of gray jelly. And his wounds pained him and he was suddenly weak. But he was alive.

Cheered by Takii's clever maneuver and the violent end of the ME, Yoshi braced his feet and pulled back on the column with all his strength, screaming *"Banzai! Banzai!"* to the heavens. The B5N was out of it, either protected by the storm or destroyed by it. In any event, he was free now to kill Rosencrance—if the renegade did not kill him first. He was in his second full-power dive in thirty minutes. Could the souped-up Mitsubishi take it? Hold together? He knew Rosencrance was turning. He had no choice. Either die in a collapsing aircraft or in the cone of his enemy's fire.

As the Zero began to flatten its dive, it bounced even more severely than before, its wings bending to the stress and turbulence of the storm. There was a familiar dull pain in his stomach again and his skin was chain mail, sagging with its new weight, forcing him deep into his seat, blood draining from his brain, vision darkening and clouding into patches of blackness. He shook his head to clear the darkness and only with the samurai's tremendous strength of will resumed control of himself and his aircraft. New jolts and pounding and his wings were actually flapping as they fought the tremendous inertia of the oversized engine.

But he had reached the bottom of his dive and the Mitsubishi had held together. Aguijan was below his cowling and the horizon dropped, crowned by the great storm, all black gargantuan fingers, battlements, and flying buttresses. Suddenly there was blue above him and a red machine streaked into his vision. Yoshi laughed. The Messerschmitt was slightly beneath him and had not completed its turn. No doubt Rosencrance was waiting for the Mitsubishi's wings to rip off. A moment's preoccupation. Foolish. Matsuhara laughed out loud. "Never try to turn with a Zerosen, you fool," he muttered under his breath.

A great flash of light high and to the north caught his eye. Kizamatsu had collided with the black ME and had exited this earth with the glory of a newly formed nova. Fascinated, the commander watched as smoking chunks of debris rained like white and brown tentacles and the wind began to rip the great cloud of smoke to pieces. *"Banzai!* Great *Yamato damashii* (Japanese spirit)," he screamed.

Now it was just Rosencrance and himself. Just what he wanted. Zero against Messerschmitt. But he was low on ammunition. Perhaps only six seconds left in his ammunition tanks. It made no difference. He would kill the fatuous renegade if he had to ram him. Find his niche in the Yasakuni Shrine the same way Kizamatsu found his. And, perhaps, if he had lived an exemplary enough life, had honed his karma well enough on the whetstone of *bushido,* he might even find Kimio in nirvana. Yes. Eternity with his one true love. What could paradise be beyond Kimio?

Pushing the stick to the left and trimming gently with the rudder, he half rolled the Zero and swept into a shallow dive, bringing the red ME which was just completing its turn into his reticle. He poised his thumb. Not yet. Still a thousand yards. Under his breath he thanked the supreme sun goddess, Amaterasu-O—Mi-Kami (Heaven Shines Great August Deity) for smiling on him and giving him this superb fighter plane. He ran a finger over the hilt of the great Matsuhara sword which was locked into its brackets at the side of the cockpit. It had served the family well, had belonged to his father and his father before him. "You are my sword now, oh, Zero-sen." He rubbed the *hachi-machi* headband which showed his determination to die for the emperor. "Perhaps, we will die together for the emperor."

Realizing he could not turn with the Zero and that Matsuhara would be on him before he could bring his armament to bear, Rosencrance resorted to his one advantage—the Messerschmitt's great diving power. Brutally, he flipped over on his back and streaked into a dive, nose pointed for the storm. Cursing and pounding his instrument panel, Matsuhara charged after his diving enemy, guns blazing. But the heavier 109 pulled away, vanishing into a low layer of clouds.

Yoshi pulled back on his stick and kicked rudder, avoiding the clouds and pulling up into a maximum climb, hungrily buying back altitude—the fighter pilot's most valuable commodity. He knew the renegade American was doing the same thing, somewhere in the clouds. Because all dogfights degenerate into speed-killing turns and near stalls, smart pilots always sought altitude-height which could be traded for speed. Yoshi had learned the lesson over and over again. But so had Rosencrance.

Leveling off at four thousand meters and turning north toward Saipan, the commander found he owned the sky. A glance at his fuel gauges told him it was time to turn for home. He was reaching for his throttle and propeller pitch control to reduce power, thin his mixture, and reduce fuel consumption when the red ME burst from the clouds above him. "Impossible!" the Japanese screamed. But the American was there, closing in behind him.

Instinctively, the commander pulled the stick back and kicked rudder, looping and rolling off the top to meet his enemy in another head-on pass. But by the time he brought his four guns to bear, Rosencrance was already firing. There were thuds and ripping sounds as slugs struck home in his fuselage and tail assembly. But he had the red machine in his reticle. *Careful, ammunition is low,* he said to himself. He squeezed the button and the guns' vicious recoil kicked the airframe.

He shouted with joy as his stream caught the ME at the wing root. Trying for a petrol tank, Yoshi touched rudder without banking, sliding the stream along the

51

leading edge of the left wing. First the wing went glossy white as his bullets and shells burned silver chunks out of the red paintwork, then the entire top of the wing began to bulge up as the wounds scooped up air like a great vacuum cleaner and tremendous pressures built up inside the structure, threatening to peel off the entire top all the way back to the flap. The American had no choice. As Yoshi flashed past, he reduced power and veered away, desperately turning back toward the storm. But the killer would not escape this time. Matsuhara had him. Turning toward his enemy, he licked his lips, savoring the coming moment.

No one could ever challenge Rosencrance's courage. He fought his controls, regaining balance instead of bailing out. Perhaps he knew Matsuhara would shoot him in his chute, anyway. Maybe he chose death in his cockpit instead of slaughter in his harness. Yoshi shrugged as he curved in behind the crippled aircraft and set up a perfect killing angle. It made no difference. He would kill the butcher with his bare hands if given the opportunity. The old familiar deep heat returned as he squinted through the reflector of his gunsight, bringing the bead to Rosencrance's head and shoulders. He caressed the button lovingly. In fact, he squeezed the trigger so gently, he allowed the gun-camera pressure to slow his thumb before pushing through to the firing position, distinctly feeling the click as the switch closed the firing circuit. There was a hiss of compressed air.

"No! No!" Matsuhara anguished into the slipstream. He was out of ammunition. Helplessly, he watched as the Messerschmitt vanished into a cloud. At the last instant, he saw the pilot turn in his seat and laugh at him — big, white pearly teeth like the mouth of a shark mocking him. Pounding his instrument panel, the commander felt tears stream down his cheeks. Two wingmen dead; Brent, Takii and Hayusa probably dead and Rosencrance had escaped. *All for nothing — it had all been a waste,* tortured his mind.

Outriders of the storm flitted past all around the aircraft like demented spirits, coating his windscreen and threatening to blind him. Checking his artificial horizon, he pushed the stick hard right, kicked rudder, and turned back north toward Tinian. Breaking from the clouds, he looked at his fuel gauges. The needles were flickering dangerously low. An overboosted Sakae devoured petrol like bathwater down an open drain. A glance at his clipboard told Yoshi he was still over two hundred kilometers southwest of *Yonaga's* point option. Quick instinctive fingers flattened the prop to a fine pitch, leaned out the mixture, and then throttled back until his tachometer read twelve hundred, the manifold-pressure gauge indicating the maximum eighty centimeters of mercury. The aircraft mushed along just hanging on the edge of a stall, a few misses and an occasional backfire telling the pilot the Zero would take no more.

With battle-lust fading, a deep sense of loss and sadness seeped through him like cold oil. Many had died this day and the empty sky seemed to mock him — a tiny lonely speck in the vast rotunda of the afternoon sky. Matsumara and Kizamatsu gone. Yoshiro Takii, Takashiro Hayusa, Brent Ross and their bullet-shredded Nakajima vanished into the jaws of Susano (the storm god and "Impetuous Male") and the killer drafts of the squall line. He had lost Kimio and now Brent Ross — the two most important people in his life. Side by side he and Brent Ross had fought with guns and fists, saved each other's lives time and again and had grown close together with a bond of camaraderie known only to men who go to war and place their lives on the table while other men roll the dice. They had survived torpedoes, aerial bombs, truck bombs, shells, fists, knives, and even AK 47's in the hands of ambushers. The young American had shown he measured up to the most rigid standards of Bushido; personifying the finest traits of *giri* — devotion to duty, boundless bravery, and a deep sense of honor.

Some of his happiest hours had been spent drinking sake and reading his *haiku* aloud while Brent Ross listened thoughtfully and sipped his own drink. They had talked endlessly of the drives that set men on the paths of war and made them become cogs in the machine, obeying orders without hesitation, without supplying rationale, killing, destroying, and finding honor and glory in slaughter. They agreed there was no counterpart in civil life, nothing to lure a man away from the road to destruction, his fascination with terror and horror. War tested a man as nothing else ever could, honed the edge of a samurai's blade and determined if a man could take his place amongst men. Only with Brent Ross had he been able to voice the thoughts, indeed the doubts that assail all men who follow the god of war, Hachiman-san.

Two movements widely separated caught and divided his attention almost at the same time. First, a red machine burst from a cloud directly beneath him, approaching the strip on Tinian cautiously. It was Rosencrance, and he was making an approach for a landing. Should he ram him? End it all here and now? Kimio and Brent were both dead. Why not? As he reached for the throttle a second image caught his attention; a flash of wings in his rearview mirror. Joyously, he realized a miracle had happened. It was *Tora II* emerging from the front. Old Yoshiro Takii had grappled with Susano and bested him. True, the ungainly old bomber was out of trim and dragging one wing, but still the ancient magician was keeping her in the air.

And he could see Brent's huge figure in the rear cockpit, waving.

Banking into a wide, sweeping turn, Yoshi looked down. The red ME had landed and he could see frantic antlike figures pushing it off of the strip and into what appeared to be a camouflaged revetment. Was Tinian an Arab base? Saipan, too? He had assumed the enemy fighters had been carrier-launched. After all, an Arab battle group was known to be operating in the western Pacific. But he had seen trained crews many times, and the group of men who had trundled the Messerschmitt off of the apron had appeared to be too efficient to be ordinary airport personnel. Then, perhaps, the Constellation, too, had taken off from Tinian or Saipan and had been on a routine sweep to the east and, in that case, most certainly looking for *Yonaga*.

He stared below. Where was the rest of the Rosencrance's Jagerstaffel? They always operated in twelves. Uneasily he scanned the sky, the storm. Nothing. And, with the exception of the red 109, no wheel marks below in the dirt surrounding the airfield. He breathed easier. If the enemy fighters had been transported to the Marianas by a carrier, perhaps the captain of the ship had been loath to strip himself of his CAP (combat air patrol); especially with *Yonaga* searching for him. That was probably it. He could spare less than half a fighter squadron—the five they had fought. Otherwise, the sky would be swarming with enemy fighters. Nevertheless, an Arab presence was in the Marianas and doubtless more were coming. He banked over Tanapag Harbor, a small cover on the west side of Saipan protected by coral reefs. A medium cargo ship, a dozen fishing boats, and a mysterious lack of activity. He must report to *Yonaga*.

Leveling off behind and above the laboring Nakajima, he pulled the microphone from its bracket: "Iceman, Iceman, this is Edo Leader." Yoshi knew that with possible enemy RDF's (radio direction finders) in the vicinity, *Yonaga* not only might remain silent, but could change course and speed without informing her aircraft, leaving their crews to die slowly in the cold Pacific. But the response was immediate.

Yoshi recognized the voice of the new, young American radio and radar technician, Martin Reed: "Edo Leader, this is Iceman. I read you loud and clear. Over."

The commander opened his throttle slightly and began to creep up on *Tora II*. As the two aircraft passed over Saipan, he mulled over his brief message and then spoke: "Possible enemy air bases on Tinian. One medium-size cargo vessel in Tanapag Harbor." He glanced down, saw suspicious piles of brush but no wheel marks. "Camouflaged revetments on both islands at the existing airfields but only one damaged fighter. No antiaircraft fire. Engaged five enemy Bf one-oh-nines. Destroyed four, damaged one. NAP Matsumara and Ensign Kizamatsu both casualties. *Tora II* severely damaged. Am escorting her to point option. Any change?" The commander did not mention his lack of ammunition. If attacked, he would ram.

"Your point-option data still operable. Out."

As the two aircraft left Saipan behind and headed northeast into the vast wasteland of the Pacific, Yoshi moved in close to the bomber. His eyes widened. Her right wing had been badly hit and she had taken a shell amidships which had blown a huge hole in the fuselage opposite the navigator's cockpit. He could see Ensign Hayusa's head lolling to and fro on the padded combing with the motions of the aircraft. Part of his jaw and his right ear had been blown away and the comb-

56

ing and parts of the fuselage were streaked with blood. The upper part of his torso was visible through the hole, a mangled mix of churned flesh, torn cloth, and broken bones. The young ensign was most certainly dead.

Brent Ross was seated upright, goggles back and their outline smeared red on his face. He could see the big American's shoulders and the brown foul-weather jacket was mottled red, too. But Brent waved and turned a thumb up. Yoshi clenched his jaw and swallowed hard, returning the gesture. Brent pointed aft to the damaged tail and the aerial whipping in the slipstream. The Nakajima's radio was out. Yoshi nodded understanding.

The commander banked in closer and examined the pilot's cockpit. Apparently unhurt, the marvelous old pilot stared back, managing a grin despite laboring at the controls. The old man nodded at his right wing and then stabbed a finger at the Zero. Pulling the stick back and dropping his wing Matsuhara moved in just above the bomber's right side and stared at the huge hole in the wing. Not only could he see the main wing-spar, stringers, and ribs, but control wires and the fuel tank were visible. Yoshi leaned over his combing. No leaks. The new self-sealing tanks were priceless. Just a few years earlier, the Nakajima would have been doomed. He stabbed a fist upward. Takii answered with his own fist and nodded.

Yoshi held up a hand and spread the first two fingers downward like legs. Takii nodded understanding. The commander dropped beneath the bomber and stared up. In a moment the B5N's landing gear rigged out from the wells and locked down. There was a huge hole in the right tire. Carefully, Yoshi ran his eyes over the bottom of the aircraft; the cowling, torpedo crutches, slotted flaps, ailerons, tapering fuselage, nonretractable tail wheel and tail assembly. All appeared undamaged except for the shell hits on the navigator's cockpit and right wing and a score of bullet holes in the tail assembly and a few back of the gunner's cockpit. Slowly, Matsuhara banked away and then curved up above the bomber.

Takii and Brent Ross stared at him expectantly. Yoshi held up a hand, dropped two fingers, pointed to the right one, and crossed his throat with the universal symbol of damage. Takii appeared confused. Yoshi knew Takii's green locked-down light must have glowed when his gear came down. Besides, any pilot could feel the vibrations of the gear descending and the locking mechanism thudding into place. Yoshi held up a hand, made a circle with his thumb and forefinger, and then flattened the circle. Takii smiled, nodded, repeated the gesture, and stabbed a finger at his right wheel. Yoshi held up a fist and signaled agreement.

Slowly the commander gained altitude and dropped back of the Nakajima, protecting its tail. From this position he could see Brent Ross staring back up at him. He could also see Brent's chest. His flying clothes were ripped and covered with bloody stains. Yoshi shuddered. The young man was obviously wounded and needed medical attention. But they were still over an hour from *Yonaga* and Takii had to land on a damaged wheel. Then Brent waved, a warm confident gesture. Yoshi laughed bitterly to himself. *Would he feel secure if he knew I was out of ammunition?* taunted the fighter pilot's mind. But Brent steadied his Nambu with one big hand and held the other up again, fist clenched. Yoshi answered with his own salute and grinned his most confident smile.

Despite the pain and weakness, Brent stared up at Yoshi's Zero and waved. After the horror of the fighter attacks the hit on Hayusa, and the unbelievable violence of the storm, the lithe white fighter appeared as a savior, a divine shepherd to guard, protect, and deliver them from mortal dangers. He was sure Hayusa was dead. Even from the rear Brent could see the savaged shoulder, ripped jaw, and missing ear, blood splattered everywhere. And the young ensign moved only with the aircraft like a sack of rice.

Brent examined his flight clothes. The front of his jacket was torn and a tracer had burned a track with its white-hot magnesium, leaving a black sear in the gore and tough sailcloth. Hesitantly, he ran a hand under his flight clothes, found tears, and startled himself with slashing pain when he touched a long rip across his chest. A slug had cut him like a knife. Perhaps a tracer. He remembered the terrible burning sensation when first hit and the smell. But it appeared the bleeding had stopped. He had lost blood — a lot of blood. He could feel its slippery presence around his buttocks, crotch, and down his legs. Then he noticed the white cloth on the floorboards. His parachute had been hit and tatters of white nylon torn from his seat pack. He grinned laconically. Perhaps the dead Arab would kill him yet. A new fear. Could he fight?

He clutched the pistol grips, tried to swing the gun, and was stopped by a thousand hot needles stabbing at his chest and stomach. The cold was exacerbating the wounds, stiffening, cramping. *More than one slug,* he said to himself in frustration. Grimacing, he forced himself to swing through the pain, but he knew he was almost useless and the thought enraged him. Defeat was impossible, unthinkable, and totally unacceptable. If the Arabs came again, he would force himself to fight, not be killed slumped down in his cockpit like

59

dead meat. Watching the magnificent Zero-sen hovering protectively, he sighed. Yoshi was there. Commander Yoshi Matsuhara the greatest fighter pilot in the world. Reassurance flowed back into his veins and he managed to straighten his back.

The storm had been a Dantean madhouse. Brent was still wet and shaken by it. When they had plunged into the first thunderhead it was like being trapped in the bowels of a ravening beast. Instantly, they were caught by the wall of a powerful updraft that hurled the big plane upward like a butterfly caught in a typhoon and he seemed to leave his guts behind. He had actually felt the aircraft flip over and over, and for a few unbelievable moments it seemed to windmill end over end. All was swirling gray and black making orientation impossible, the very pull of gravity that should have defined a simple up or down confused by vertigo like a mad carousel. And the rain was so thick it poured into his cockpit not in drops, but in a solid torrent, and he felt like a man caught beneath a dam that had suddenly collapsed.

His senses had been overwhelmed. There were blinding flashes of lightning and thunder rolled and crashed painfully, assaulting his eardrums like heavy artillery. He was convinced he was a dead man and had already entered the gates of hell. Not even the greatest pilot on earth could manage the insane turbulence; updrafts, downdrafts, hail like frozen stones. But a caprice of the storm saved them. Hurled upward, downward, rolled and tumbled and then shot upward again by another freakish draft even more powerful than the first, the bomber exploded out of a cloud bank into brilliant clear sky. Brent was shocked to find the horizon vertical instead of horizontal and the wings still on the aircraft. Then as Takii regained control, the horizon rotated back down into its proper position. It was then that Brent realized he was completely disoriented and had even lost his feel for gravity.

Thanking a variety of gods, they turned north and fled toward Tinian. Then they found Yoshi Matsuhara.

Takii's voice scratched tinnily, breaking into his consciousness. "You are wounded, Brent-san?"

Brent turned his seat. Tried to maintain his watch, staring up and into the distance despite the pain that had even stiffened his neck. The pain was frustrating but even more disturbing was his inability to focus his eyes. He concentrated on a great cumulo-nimbus thunderhead hulking on the southern horizon, first wide-eyed and then through slitted lids, but found everything out of focus like looking through a gauzed lens used to film aging Hollywood glamour queens. He spoke into the intercom honestly. "I've been grazed across the chest — lost some blood." He clenched his jaw, disliking the admission to follow: "I'm weak — may not be at top battle efficiency."

"Ammunition?"

Brent had done a lot of firing and had been concerned. He looked down at the floorboards where the belt disappeared into the ammunition tank. "Maybe a hundred rounds."

Takii's voice was heavy. "Ensign Hayusa has moved on."

"Yes. But I'm sure his karma was strong."

Takii looked skyward. "Life and death are part of the same whole. On the fortieth day he will be reborn on a higher plane." The little man's head came down and his eyes moved over the damaged wing. "Perhaps we will be close on Ensign Hayusa's heels if that wing gives way."

"It's taken a lot. We should've lost it in that storm."

Brent could hear the old pilot sigh. "Amaterasu had us in her grasp."

"Nakajima engineering helped, too," Brent answered, staring at the hole. He could see the spars and braces, could see the aileron control wires moving as Takii worked the controls. A remarkable aircraft. He looked down at the sea. The Marianas had vanished and the storm was nothing but the tip of a dark toadstool protruding over the horizon. From a thousand feet, the five thousand fathoms of the Marianas Trench gave the sea a purple hue and the surface appeared crenulated by the chop, a swell spreading across it like ripples across a pond, from the disturbance in the south. Another thought disturbed Brent. "You can navigate us back to *Yonaga*, Ensign Takii?"

The old man chuckled. "Of course, Lieutenant. My compass works, I have my charts and you know I have a small amount of experience."

"But if *Yonaga* changes course — speed . . ."

"Then hope the commander still has his radio." Takii jerked a thumb over his shoulder at the Zero which droned steadily above their tail.

For over an hour, the two aircraft threshed through the empty sky. Brent examined his wounds as much as the tender flesh would permit. Apparently, the bullets that had ripped his flight clothes had also served to help staunch the bleeding, the cold air causing the flowing blood to coagulate quickly. But his muscles not only ached, but now he felt severe cramps in his shoulders, back, and neck. Nevertheless, he shook the gathering malaise from his head, forced his seat to rotate, and even raised his glasses in attempts to maintain his watch. But his glasses were heavy, his head doddering as if made of concrete and his eyes still refused to focus.

Takii's voice: "We are at twenty-three degrees of latitude, one hundred fifty eight degrees of longitude. We just crossed the Tropic of Cancer and should sight the carrier dead ahead soon."

"Good."

"And bad, Brent-san."

"What do you mean?"

"The northeasterlies are taking us by the head and we are low on fuel."

"You made my day," the young American snickered to himself in a sudden giddiness that brought a wild burst of laughter and sent saliva streaking from his chin. He shook his head, rubbed the top of his head, and hunched over the breech. He knew he was close to slipping from consciousness, clenched his teeth until his jaw hurt and the cords of his neck bulged and the encroaching darkness pooled away to the outer bounds of his awareness. But he knew he could not keep the blackness away much longer—not by sheer willpower. He had lost too much blood. Now he could feel lumps of it like liver against his thighs, his buttocks, squishing under his legs when he moved.

Takii shouting, "Ships! Ships! Three-four-zero" shocked Brent upright out of his lethargy. Forgetting his wounds, the weakness, he stared forward over the left wing. On the far horizon where the sea and sky met in a curving blue-gray line, he saw two white slashes in the sea. Eagerly he leaned into his glasses and brought first a graceful Fletcher class destroyer into focus and then another. Captain John "Clubber" Fite in the lead and far behind, another Fletcher protecting the still-invisible *Yonaga*'s side. Must be. Had to be it. He prayed. Felt joy when he finally recognized the Japanese battle ensign flying from both. Where was the CAP? If the carrier was nearby certainly her patrols would be sniffing them out. Then, looking around with the pain forgotten, he found them: three specks high in the pale, ethereal cobalt of the sky, swooping downward on him from the rear with the grace and precision of the Bolshoi. He stood, cheered, waved, and collapsed.

Takii's voice again. "*Yonaga* bearing three-three-zero."

It took a hard look to finally discern the great ship which was still "hulled down" by the curvature of the earth, only her soaring foretop, flag, and flight control bridge protruding above the horizon. But she was unmistakable. The director, foretop cluttered with antennas, elegantly curved upper works, single huge stack. Brent felt joy swell like a young wayward boy finally coming home after a long absence. "Home. Home," he said to himself with disbelief, making levers of his elbows against the combing and forcing himself erect. In the battle and storm he had become convinced he would never see the great carrier again. But there she was with her gigantic thousand-foot flight deck now completely visible. Sighing, he sagged back.

Takii's voice: "Fire a single red flare, Brent-san."

Brent looked down at the floorboards. The flare gun had no handle and its barrel had been bent by an armor-piercing round. "Sorry, Yoshiro-san," Brent answered. "My flare gun is junk."

Takii cursed artistically, unleashing his wrath on Daikoku and Ebisu, two minor gods whose lack of stature limited their powers of retaliation. Brent turned to Yoshi's Zero, held up one hand over his head simulating a pistol, and snapped his thumb down as if firing it. Matsuhara looked puzzled. Leaning forward painfully, Brent picked up the pieces of the flare gun, held them up, and threw them over the side. He repeated the pistol signal with his hand. This time Yoshi nodded understanding, reached down, and then held a flare gun high over his head. He fired a single red flare which arced high into the heavens leaving a smoking phosphorous trail behind.

Takii spoke: "We are badly damaged—trim is hard to maintain, and our right tire has been shot out. I will fly over an escort and you can bail out. I will land alone."

"Sorry, Yoshiro-san, my chute is full of holes. We'll ride her down together."

Takii said, "I could try a water landing, but the swell is large and you are wounded."

"I know."

"We will be forced to try for a deck landing and I have very poor control. We could crash into the stern or overshoot and . . ."

"I know that, too, Yoshiro-san. I'm ready. I am flying with the finest pilot on earth and, anyway, we have no choice."

Takii muttered an oath and then spoke softly and Brent recognized a famous passage from the *Hagakure:* "It is a cleansing act to give one's life for the Mikado. For a man to end his life in the cause of righteousness, there is no need to call on the rewards of death. All the gods of heaven will smile on him and his tributes will come in abundance." He paused, resumed with a strong, hoarse voice Brent had never heard before. "You are a fine samurai, Brent-san. It has been my gain to know you. I cannot find a better man to die with. Ensign Hayusa is waiting at the gates to Yasakuni for us and, perhaps, if the gods will it, we will all join hands and enter together."

Brent spoke softly. "I could not improve on the company, Yoshiro-san."

"Banzai! Banzai!" Takii shouted. Without hesitation, the American answered the salute with his own *Banzai!* The old man hunched over the controls with new determination.

Staring over the damaged wing, Brent could see the carrier clearly, only a few miles to the northeast. Responding to the distress signal, she was curving into the wind and there was frantic activity on her flight deck; yellow-, red-, green-, and brown-clad handlers and deckhands rushing in every direction like a colorful upturned ants' nest. Beginning the first leg of his approach, Takii slowly flew the start of a great ellipse, paralleling the starboard side of the leviathan and passing her. Looking down with a new energy, Brent could see aircrews releasing a half-dozen ready Zeros secured amidships from their tie-downs and manhandling them toward the forward elevator while a pair of new fire trucks equipped with the smothering American foam raced from their compartments just abaft the superstructure. Crews swarmed amidships, cranking up the fearsome steel-mesh barrier designed to halt any errant aircraft that failed to hook one of the five cables with its arresting gear. A high-speed collision with the barrier could crush an aircraft like a swatted fly, and several aircrewmen had been killed when they overflew the cables. Brent felt a tremor watching white-clad hospital orderlies with stretchers and kits over their shoulders run to their positions just abaft the island and next to a cluster of twenty-five-millimeter gun tubs.

Despite his wounds, despite his weakness that fogged his mind and cramped his muscles until they ached, and despite the mortal danger about to be challenged, Brent still felt a stir of the old pride, the awe always inspired by the sight of the noble gray juggernaut powering her way through the swells. Displacing eighty-two thousand tons, Yonaga slashed through the sea, leaving a widening white wake to the horizon. Her six escorts, all Fletchers, had assumed standard steaming stations; one directly ahead, two off each side covering her quarters and one astern on lifeguard station. The small narrow escorts gave the carrier a regal aspect — a *daimyo* with an entourage of fawning courtiers.

Circling across her bows and beginning their run down her port side, Brent could see the entire vessel: the great rectangular flight deck longer than three football fields; 186 twenty-five-millimeter AA machine guns in triple mounts and 32 dual-purpose five-inch guns pointed skyward from her galleries and superstructure like stands of saplings and young trees; the island reaching into the sky like a steel Everest with its tiered flag bridge, navigation bridge, flight control bridge all topped by the gun director and radar antennas like perforated dishes and bent colanders; the huge stack bedecked with rows of life rafts and a pair of searchlight platforms; the aft director, crane, and more antennas and the stern with the flight deck overhang almost concealing the four twenty-five-millimeter mounts in a pair of tubs. The entire sweep of the graceful hull revealed her battleship genesis, the 406 millimeter armor belt protruding just above the waterline like a ridge on the side of a gray cliff. "A *Yamato,* bigger and faster than her sisters, *Yamato, Musashi,* and *Shinana,*" her old officers had told him pridefully, over and over again.

"She has two-blocked 'Pennant Two,' " Yoshiro Takii said. "They are ready to receive us." Brent glanced at the signal bridge, found the bright blue pennant with the white dot whipping from a halyard. "Are you strong enough to secure your Nambu and check your canopy lock, Brent-san?"

"Affirmative," Brent said, not sure he was telling the truth. Slowly he brought himself into a crouch, lowered the machine gun, and locked it into its well. The pain was excruciating, spinning his head. Then, while

Takii banked into the final leg of his approach, the young American turned and faced forward. The canopy had been shattered by gunfire and the lock appeared damaged. Wracked by pain he tried to stand, sank back, and tried again. Finally, with *Yonaga*'s deck looming close, he leaned forward and grasped the lock. Either it was jammed or he was too weak to turn it. Despairing, he sank back and almost whispered in his microphone, "Nambu secured, canopy lock is jammed."

"Very well. Brace yourself. Here we go, Brent-san," Takii shouted into his microphone.

The deck was very close and jutted toward them like a steel shelf while beneath their belly the chop skimmed by like sharks' teeth. Brent felt jolts as the landing gear locked down and the tail hook was extended. Surprisingly, the beat of the engine did not drop, Takii, forced by the damage and lack of trim, to maintain more throttle than usual. They were high enough, but the speed of the B5N was far too fast. Takii would be landing out of trim, with one wheel damaged and at a high speed.

"Pray to your Judaic-Christian God—I will call on Buddha and my Shinto kami," Takii grunted breathlessly. Brent glanced skyward but knew not even a platoon of gods could land the wreck he was riding.

Suddenly, the bomber dropped. They were below the flight deck and headed for the twenty-five-millimeter mounts. Panicked gunners scrambled. More power. The nose came up and the deck was obscured by the wings. Abruptly, the nose dropped and the flight deck was beneath them. Glass glinted on the bridge, men were staring down while other fearful faces stared up from the galleries, catwalks, and deck. The landing operations officer was waving them off, his fans gyrating frantically like a pair of yellow windmills.

Brent heard Takii scream, "Out of the way, fools!"

At a hundred-ten knots, thirty knots above designed landing speed, *Tora II* made her final lunge, tilting to the left as Takii cut the switch and crossed his controls, bringing the right wheel high, trying to land on his left wheel. A jarring thud as the left wheel struck the deck, a report like a gunshot as the tire burst followed by sudden deceleration and Brent was flung forward against his harness as the hook caught. But the speed was too high and the cable snapped, whipping steel strands to port and starboard, the end of one catching a handler at the waist and severing his torso neatly. His legs were sent flying into a gun tub while his head and chest were lashed over the side, trailing viscera and blood.

There was no time to react, to think. Brent, weak and numbed by fear, clung to his hand grips, jerked from side to side by the forces ripping *Tora II*. Free of the cable, the bomber accelerated, nose pointed at the sky but hurled down the deck almost horizontally at the barrier like a wounded gull looking for a perch, tail dragging across the deck, hook broken and useless.

The Nakajima caught the top of the steel mesh with its left wheel faring at least a hundred knots. The wheels, oleo legs, retraction mechanisms, and brake lines spewing red hydraulic fluid were ripped free as if gripped by the hand of a giant and the aircraft flipped up and over the barrier, smashing down on her propeller and skidded along the starboard side of the deck like an injured dog rubbing its nose in the grass.

The horizon revolved and there was the scream of tortured aluminum, crashing, banging, ripping as the bomber flipped completely over, shedding both wings and spilling high-test gasoline behind. Screaming, Brent pulled down his head like a frightened turtle, trying to make an accordion of his neck and make himself smaller, sheltering himself against his headrest and the fuselage decking which screeched like an animal in a steel trap as it scraped across the deck only inches from the top of his head, leaving a trail of ripped teakwood, sparks, and splinters.

The plane bounced off the island, pounding Brent's head against the coaming. Black drapes swung across his consciousness, gongs and drums crashed, thundered, and reverberated in his head. Meteors and comets flashed and suddenly it all ended. There was a sweet silence and he sagged, upside-down, held by his harness above the deck. So this was death—complete relaxation—peace. He let his arms hang over his head. Then he smelled the gasoline.

There was a whoosh like a balloon deflating and he smelled smoke. Fire! Cold, paralyzing fear coursed through him as if icicles had replaced his blood. He was alive, but the greatest fear was there—death by burning. He tried to release his harness, but his arms were lead and his nose and mouth were filled with blood. He felt heat and flames raced beneath him. He would be broiled alive. He screamed again and again. There were shouts. Then the bomber rocked and he heard a hissing. White foam sloshed through the gasoline and then there was the sound of ripping metal as the jaws of a huge cutter slashed through the aluminum of his cockpit. Suddenly, strong hands gripped his shoulders while others released his harness lock and he felt himself slide down and slip into the foam. As he was pulled across the deck, a tranquil darkness closed about him.

Chapter II

Brent rose slowly from the depths of sleep, conscious of a growing sense of disquiet and unease. He was a deep-sea swimmer, flat on his back, arms and legs extended, rising without effort on a whim of the sea toward the surface which was only a faint glow high overhead. On the edge of consciousness a misty dream image swirled overhead. Slowly a great cavern formed and descended to meet him — a maw lined with serrated teeth like rows of daggers. It was a mouth — the jaws of a great, predatory creature about to envelop and shred him. Hot breath fouled his face. He gagged. Tried to scream. There was a rumble. More heat and flames erupted from the beast's bowels, reaching for him with yellow incandescent fingers. Terror froze the deep primal recesses of his being. He cried out, tried to throw up his hands, but they were trapped. He rolled from side to side in desperation. He heard screams. But it was not his voice. He was sure of it.

He broke through the surface. The jaws vanished and the light was brilliant — so bright it ached against his retinas. His head felt as though someone had knotted a piece of barbed wire around it and twisted it up tight. The time-ravaged face of Chief Hospital Orderly

Eiichi Horikoshi, like parchment preserved in spirits, loomed above him, and he was directing a tiny beam into Brent's eyes, his ears. The young American rolled his head from side to side. "He is almost back," he heard Horikoshi mutter.

Mercifully, the light vanished and he could see Commander Yoshi Matsuhara, Admiral Mark Allen, and Admiral Hiroshi Fujita staring down at him silently. Brent tried to focus his eyes on Admiral Fujita's face, but the old admiral's features appeared fogged by mist — like the ghost of King Hamlet.

Admiral Fujita, The Ghost of the Seventh Carrier, an Arab newsman had dubbed him. And, indeed, not five feet tall, the tiny admiral appeared as a wraith about to be swallowed by the tunic of his blue uniform. With only a few wispy white strands on a nearly bald head, his skin was like that of a prehistoric reptile, browned to the color of tobacco juice and splotched with dark stains of age and benign sun cancer from too many decades on the bridge of a warship. The nose was flat and indifferent, his lips almost vanished in a web of deeply chiseled lines. But his chin was well formed and strong, and his eyes were remarkable. Charged and vital, they were shrunken into their dark cavities like a skull, glittering with intelligence and probing deep as if they could penetrate not only a man's mind but his soul as well. There was steely command and latent power there.

No one knew Admiral Fujita's exact age, but everyone agreed he was over a hundred years old. Descended from a famous samurai family, he was a graduate of Japan's Annapolis, Eta Jima. He had fought the Russians at Tsushima and acted as a liaison officer in London and Washington during the First World War. Like most Japanese officers of that period, he studied abroad, and after the Armistice he took his Master's in English at the University of Southern California. He attended the Washington naval conference where the despised 5-5-3 rule for capital ships—a ratio that reduced Japan to a position inferior to the United States and Britain—was adopted over his objections.

An advocate of naval aviation, he learned to fly in the early twenties, serving on carriers *Kaga* and *Akagi*. For over fifteen years he helped develop dive-bombing and torpedo tactics and oversaw the building of the incomparable Tsuchiura Air Training School. He was a captain when the Second World War broke out. On November 11, 1940, naval warfare was changed forever when the English carrier *Illustrious* launched twenty-one antique Swordfish torpedo planes which sank three Italian battleships and damaged two more in a daring night raid on the Italian Fleet in the harbor at Taranto.

Within a week, Fujita, Kameto Kuroshima, and Minoru Genda were ordered by the Commander-in-Chief of the Combined Fleet, Admiral Isoroku Yamamoto, to develop contingency plans for a carrier attack on the American fleet at Pearl Harbor. With typical samurai logic, Fujita decided to go for all or nothing, risking the seven fleet carriers of *Kido Butai* in a single massive stroke on the American bastion. Plans completed, Fujita, now an admiral, was given command of *Kido Butai* and he moved his flag from *Kaga* to the new giant, *Yonaga,* leaving the remaining six carriers in command of the incompetent Admiral Chuichi Nagumo. Then came the oil embargo by the Americans, British, and Dutch. Without oil, Japan was forced to attack. The order was given and *Kido Butai* began to gather in the Kuriles.

Yamamoto grew uneasy with the massing of the force at Hitokappu Bay, especially with the movements of the colossus, *Yonaga,* and he ordered the great carrier to the secret anchorage at Sano Wan where she was to await the radio signal to attack Pearl Harbor, "Climb Mount Niitaka." Then she was trapped by the sliding glacier and assumed lost. After the war, surviving senior officers in Japan, honor bound by samurai tradition and the power of Bushido, kept the existence of the carrier, which everyone assumed lost, secret. Gradually, the old sailors died off and *Yonaga* was forgotten.

But Admiral Hiroshi Fujita and his crew of samurai had not forgotten. Trapped in a prison of ice, supplied with power from an inexhaustible steam vent releasing power from the Pacific Ring of Fire and tunneling to the Bering Sea to harvest food from one of the world's great fisheries, the crew waited for over four decades. Many of the older officers died, but the men goaded by Fujita, trained daily, kept themselves in superb physical condition, maintained their equipment, waiting for the day—the miracle when they would be free to carry out their orders and attack Pearl Harbor. Similar to holdouts who had held out after decades on Pacific islands, the men of *Yonaga* aged slowly, kept their youth long after most men had collapsed into geriatrics.

The miracle happened in 1983 when the world's warming from the greenhouse effect caused the glacier to slide away like a curtain opening on a great drama. And indeed it was a great drama, *Yonaga* finally escaping and her maddened crew bent on carrying out her orders to the letter. She destroyed ships, planes, captured Brent's father, Ted "Trigger" Ross, wrecked Pearl Harbor, sinking *New Jersey* and *Peleliu.* Then the return to Tokyo Bay to find the impossible had happened; Japan had surrendered. Within a day, Hiroshi Fujita discovered his wife and two sons had been vaporized at Hiroshima in 1945. He was crushed by the news, but the war against Kadafi and his Arab *jihad,* and the personal orders from Emperor Hirohito to attack brought new vitality to the old sailor — gave him a new purpose in life. And then Ted "Trigger" Ross's suicide and Ensign Brent Ross's assignment to *Yonaga* by his NIS (Naval Intelligence Service).

Staring upward and concentrating with all of the strength of his will, Brent Ross began to focus his eyes, and Admiral Fujita's inscrutable stone face actually showed concern, the crosshatch of a century of wrinkles crinkling in incipient lines of anxiety at the corners of his narrow eyes. Brent tried to speak, but his lips refused to form words. He felt terribly frustrated and helpless.

Brent heard the admiral's familiar soft, rasping voice: "He will recover, Chief Horikoshi?"

"He has a mild concussion, and his chest and head and the side of his face have been lacerated by bullets and shrapnel and he has first and second degree burns to his right side which are not life-threatening. There is danger of shock and he is in much pain and we have kept him heavily sedated. He has lost enough blood to kill the average man. Fortunately, he is not an average man and we are giving him whole blood intravenously. His response has been miraculous."

"You said lacerations."

"Yes, Admiral. I spent the evening sewing. His chest is a *tatami* mat stitched by a madman. It took over a hundred twenty sutures to put him back together."

Christ. I'm a Humpty Dumpty, Brent thought. He tried to laugh but only gurgled deep in his throat. He heard Yoshi Matsuhara's basso profundo, "He groaned, Chief."

"Perhaps. He's probably trying to talk," the chief orderly suggested.

"I am, you stupid shit," Brent finally managed.

"See. He's back," Chief Orderly Horikoshi said. There were chuckles of relief.

A soft cultured voice spoke. "You'll be all right, Brent. You're as tough as your father." The speaker, Admiral Mark Allen, loomed over the bed, his pallid face appearing as white as linen, surrounded by the tanned leather skin of the Japanese around him. A tall man in his mid-sixties with gray-green eyes and a strikingly thick shock of white hair that hung over his forehead like a valance, Mark Allen had been COMNISPAC (Commander Naval Intelligence Service Pacific) when he and Brent Ross had been assigned to *Yonaga*. Allen had spent his formative years in Japan where his father, a naval officer, had been moved about from legation to legation as an attaché. An expert in languages, he spoke Japanese fluently and became an expert in Japanese history and Oriental cultures.

After graduating from Annapolis, he served on S-Boats and was captain of one of the first Gato class fleet submarines. But his first love was aircraft and after receiving his wings at Pensacola, he was assigned to the *USS Lexington* as the pilot of a Douglas SBD dive bomber. It was on *Lexington* that he met Brent's father, Theodore Ross, who was assigned as his gunner. Mark Allen gave Ted Ross the sobriquet "Trigger" after Ross's temper exploded following a particularly frustrating mission.

Mark Allen flew twenty-three combat missions and was sunk at Coral Sea when *Lexington* went down. Then duty as assistant air operations officer on carriers *Yorktown* and *Wasp*. He was on board both when they were sunk. He began to be known as "Deep Six Mark," and men were reluctant to serve with him, calling the ill-starred flyer, "A sure ticket to Davey Jones's

76

locker."

But his luck changed and he served with distinction on a succession of new Essex class carriers as an air operations officer. In fact, he commanded the air groups that sank battleship *Yamato* when she made her insane run on Okinawa on April 7, 1945. In all, he participated in twelve carrier battles earning the Navy Cross and the Distinguished Service Medal. He was nominated for the Medal of Honor after sinking the *Yamato*. He was not awarded the medal, but he was mentioned in reports and received a personal commendation from President Truman.

After the war, he and Ted "Trigger" Ross were reunited and served on the staff of Samuel B. Morison, aiding in the writing of the monumental, *United States Naval Operations in World War II*. The two men grew very close and served as best men at each other's weddings; Ted marrying Kathleen Egan in 1953 and Mark marrying the exquisite Keiko Morimoto a year later. When Brent was born, Mark Allen was the only choice for godfather.

Brent looked up into the concern in Admiral Mark Allen's eyes. The young man tried to smile. "I'm all right, sir."

"Yes. Of course," Mark Allen agreed. And then thickly, "You're the toughest SOB I've ever known." The two Americans chuckled. The Japanese missed the humor.

Yoshi stepped forward. "You did well, Brent-san. Shot down one ME and damaged another." He reached down to his waist, unsnapped a scabbard. "I brought you this. Your sword. All officers of *Yonaga* have the privilege of bringing their swords here." He gestured at the bulkhead. "I will put it there on those brackets above the bed." Reverently, the air group leader placed a sword in a magnificently jeweled scabbard above the head of the bed.

Eagerly, Brent watched as the pilot locked the sword in place. The storied Konoye blade; a superb piece of tempered steel sheathed in an elaborately crafted scabbard encrusted with precious stones which were fashioned into ideograms explaining heroic feats performed by members of the famous samurai clan. Brent had been given the sword by the last Konoye to own it, Lieutenant Nobutake Konoye, when Brent served as his *kaishaku* (second) for Nobutake's seppuku. Although Konoye despised Brent and had once tried to kill him, the American was chosen because of his courage and great strength. Lieutenant Konoye was not disappointed. Goaded on by Admiral Fujita and a hundred other officers, the big American beheaded him cleanly with one stroke. Afterward, Brent vomited and continued to vomit for two days.

Brent's wandering thoughts were interrupted by Chief Hospital Orderly Eiichi Horikoshi. "You have done very well, Mr. Ross. You can start taking liquids instead of taking all of your nutrition through that tube." He gesticulated at the IV dripping down a long plastic tube to a needle in his arm. Then, turning, he spoke to a white-smocked third-class orderly standing at the foot of the bed with a clipboard in his hand. "Continue the dextrose five-percent solution, one-half normal saline concentration, at one-thousand-fifty cc's an hour, Orderly Takeda."

"Yes, sir," the young man said in a nervous, high falsetto, scribbling furiously.

Horikoshi continued as if reading a manual, "For pain, give him one hundred milligrams of Demerol every four hours—and no more."

"Yes, sir."

Brent interrupted. "Takii. Lieutenant Yoshiro Takii, my pilot. How is he?"

Before Horikoshi could answer, a loud groan from the next bed turned all heads. Rolling carefully to his side, Brent saw a form under a cradle used for burn patients. The head was completely wrapped like linen rolled around the skull of a mummy. There were tubes in every orifice, even the nose, which was the only part of the man's face exposed. But there was no nose, only two round black holes where oxygen-carrying tubes disappeared. "Takii! That's my pilot," Brent gasped in horror.

"He was trapped — soaked in petrol," Admiral Fujita said hoarsely. "It took time . . ."

"Third degree burns," Chief Orderly Horikoshi said. "Entire head and neck, both arms, posterior surfaces of upper and lower trunk. By the *Rule of Nines,* forty-five percent of his body."

"Please! I don't want to know about your *Rules.* He has no nose! What about his eyes, ears?"

Horikoshi looked above Brent at the Konoye sword. His voice was almost inaudible. "Gone. Gone . . ."

"He has no eyes, no nose, no ears and forty-five percent of his flesh has been destroyed! Then why keep him alive?" Brent asked angrily.

The chief orderly's black eyes flashed like chips of polished ebony. "Because that is why I am here. I try to restore what you destroy out there." He waved a hand over his head angrily. "This is a place of war just like the skies where you do these things." He stabbed a finger at the burned man and then gestured at the pilot's sword which was bracketed above his head next to Brent's. "But I war against death while you war against life." He glared at the circle of officers, showing no fear of the high ranks. "Expect no miracles from me for what you do."

Admiral Fujita drew himself up, eyes blazing a warning. But before he could speak, Takii screamed, a high, endless, piercing sound like a flutist testing his instrument to the limit. The screech stabbed like a swordpoint scraping glass, chilling a man's blood, and sending tremors racing along his spine. Horikoshi shouted at the orderly, "Takeda! Demerol! One hundred milligrams!"

"But, sir. I just gave him . . ." Takii screamed, groaned, tried to move his head.

"I do not care what you gave him." Horikoshi stabbed a finger at the patient. "Now!"

"Yes, sir." Jaw working, Orderly Third Class Shingen Takeda took a syringe from a table loaded with medications and injected it into one of two IV bottles feeding liquid into Takii. The groans began to fade.

Composure returning, Eiichi Horikoshi turned to Admiral Fujita. "With your permission, Admiral, we must tend to our patients." He waved at the large ward and the patients occupying twelve of the thirty beds.

"Very well," Fujita said. "It is time we return to our duties." With Fujita leading, the officers turned toward the door.

Gripped by a sudden terrifying thought, Brent spoke with all the strength he could muster. "The Arab battle group?"

Yoshi shouted back over his shoulder, "We put two *gyos* into one of the carriers. They are retiring."

"Good. Good," Brent whispered, sinking back into his pillow. As sleep gathered, he felt contentment.

Brent recovered his strength with amazing speed. Although his stitches pulled and his burns itched, by the next morning he was ravenous and his headache was almost gone. Old Chief Horikoshi, Petty Officer Takeda and a half-dozen other orderlies ministered to him. A small cradle had been erected over his right leg where he had been seared by burning gasoline.

"Excellent capillary refill," Chief Eiichi Horikoshi said on the morning of the second day, pulling back the sheet and examining the burned leg. Takeda stood close behind Horikoshi, clipboard in hand.

"According to *The Rules of Nines?*" Brent quipped.

A smile rearranged the wrinkles on the old man's face into unaccustomed patterns. "You learn fast, Mr. Ross. One leg—nine percent." He hunched close, probed the burn with a stainless steel instrument. Brent winced but said nothing. Horikoshi spoke to his assistant without turning his head. "Blistering and some eschars are forming—a partial-thickness injury to the dermis, only."

"What do you mean?" Brent asked.

The old chief looked up. "Scabs are forming and you have some second-degree burns, Lieutenant. But not deep. If they were deeper, they would be third degree." He returned to the leg, said to Takeda: "Continue with the saline soaks at room temperature."

"What do you know of Rosencrance? The Arab battle group?" Brent asked suddenly.

"Nothing. We leave the killing to them." Horikoshi waved airily in the direction of flag country.

"Liquids?" Takeda asked as if he were totally unaware of the exchange.

Horikoshi's voice returned to clipped professionalism: "Continue with the Parkland point five solution and the five-percent dextrose solution. Force all the water down his throat that he can hold without drowning him and monitor his urine output. If his vascular system holds colloids well enough, we can draw off edemous fluids with diuretics and take him off the IV tomorrow morning."

"I don't get it," Brent said in frustration. "You know nothing about the Arab battle group?"

Horikoshi straightened. "No! Nothing!" He nodded at a bedpan. "Just fill that, Lieutenant, with quarts of urine and we will pull that out of your arm." He pointed at the IV hanging over Brent's head. "As you Americans would say, piss your guts out."

From the first moment Brent met Chief Orderly Eiichi Horikoshi over a year earlier, he had been amazed and confused by the old man. A "plank owner" (an original member of the crew), he had reported aboard *Yonaga* in 1938 as a hospital orderly "striker." During the forty-two-year entrapment at Sano Wan, the ship's five doctors began to die off. Admiral Fujita recognized a rare talent for medicine in Eiichi who quickly learned even the most complex surgical techniques by assisting *Yonaga's* outstanding physicians. Gradually, Horikoshi took charge of the sick bay. Finally, one morning in 1967, the last doctor died and Horikoshi was given command and he began intensive training of a cadre of the most promising orderlies. Having a deep distrust for the medical profession which he considered peopled with "charlatans and fakes," Fujita was confident of Horikoshi's competence. He knew surgery was taught on the time-honored journeyman-apprentice relationship and not through textbooks. He did not hesitate to give Horikoshi a free hand.

Horikoshi considered the sick bay his domain, not showing the subservience of enlisted men to officers that typified the Imperial Navy. In fact, even when Admiral Fujita appeared in the sick bay, obeisance was missing from Eiichi's demeanor. Respect and loyalty were there, true; obsequiousness, however, never. Indeed, there was a confidence that approached arrogance in the old orderly like a *daimyo* ruling his realm. He had been offered a commission but refused it, telling Fujita he was just a simple uneducated farmer's son and not a professional.

When *Yonaga* returned to Tokyo Bay, professionally trained doctors were offered immediately by the Self Defense Force. To Horikoshi's delight, Fujita refused. Instead, new young strikers were brought aboard and Horikoshi and four of his most competent assistants began their training. Eiichi studied the latest medical literature and ordered the most modern equipment and medications. His intelligent staff learned quickly and *Yonaga's* sick bay became one of the most efficient medical facilities on earth. And with heavy fighting against the terrorism riding roughshod over the world, there were many casualties and terrible wounds of every description. Many crewmen died in the ward – some new and very young. Chief Orderly Eiichi Horikoshi added a strand of bitterness to his cloak of arrogance.

The old man's next words shocked Brent: "See to it he eats at least thirty eggs a day."

"Thirty!" Brent said in astonishment. "Christ, I'll start clucking."

"You need protein. Eat the eggs if you want to return to duty." A sly grin twisted Eiichi's face. "That should please you, Lieutenant."

"What do you mean," Brent asked, not trusting the expression and feeling like a straight man in a low comedy routine.

The old man continued, "A good rooster can take care of a barnyard full of hens. I understand you have kept many hens happy."

A groan turned their heads. It was Takii. The smiles vanished and a grim silence filled the room like a cold viscous fluid, seeping into every corner and coating everyone with its chill. Quickly, Horikoshi and Takeda moved to the next bed and pulled the sheet from the cradle which covered the patient.

"More sedatives, Chief?" Takeda asked. "We have not changed the dose and he may be building up a resistance."

The old man shook his head. "Continue with the same dosage of Demerol, but after my examination."

To Brent's knowledge, Lieutenant Yoshiro Takii had never been conscious. He had lain like a burned vegetable, breathing shallowly, every need provided by tubes, bottles, and attendants who changed bottles and emptied pans. "What are his chances?" Brent asked in a soft voice.

"Considering the extent and severity of his burns and his age—about ten percent."

"Jesus Christ," Brent murmured. "And no eyes, ears, nose . . ." He was stopped by a sudden flash of pain across his chest. Horikoshi gestured at the medication chart. Quickly, Takeda removed a syringe, and in a moment Brent winced as a needle pricked his arm. "I didn't need that," the American said. "You just wanted to shut me up."

"That is my decision," the old chief said, turning back to Takii. His voice droned on with a timbre of cold professionalism: "Continue with the endotracheal intubation and watch his urine output."

"A tracheostomy, Chief?" Takeda asked.

"Not yet. Only if severe edema develops with fluid retention."

"I understand, Chief."

"Continue with the saline soaks, Takeda. And I want an arterial line to monitor mean arterial pressure—the femoral artery."

Takeda muttered understanding. "Continue with the ten-percent Sulfamylon, Chief?"

Horikoshi pondered for a moment. "It penetrates the eschars well, but we are getting some metabolic acidosis. Reduce sulfamylon to five percent for two days, three times daily."

Confused by the medical terminology and with his eyelids turning to lead, Brent listened with a deep, sinking feeling as Eiichi droned on, prescribing new medications and canceling others. Anger began to grow in the young American. Why keep Takii alive? It made no sense. The old pilot had been cremated before death. An invalid who could only live in pain, without eyes, ears, nose, and almost half of his flesh burned away. A horror that would challenge Hollywood's most talented special effects men. The droning continued, became a bass viol in a vast auditorium. Brent drifted off into the dream world of Demerol.

That night Brent heard the strange sounds for the first time — rustling and popping sounds like a stiff wind bending trees, soughing through the leaves and rubbing small branches against each other so that they broke and tumbled to the ground. The wind formed letters — a word. His name. "Brent-san — Brent-san," it said, before fading away.

The lieutenant turned to Takii's bed. The pilot was as still as death. *Could he speak?* Brent asked himself. Impossible. He had seen Takii's face when the bandages were changed. Not only had his mouth been burned away, but his right jaw was gone nearly to his ear, exposing his blackened teeth like two rows of badly tarnished silver. Brent remained awake for nearly an hour. Finally, an attendant brought a familiar needle to his bedside and sleep returned.

The next day pain was reduced to persistent itching of the leg and chest, and Brent managed to refuse painkillers and his headache was completely gone. To his relief the IV was removed, and for the first time since being wounded, he was wide awake when Commander Yoshi Matsuhara entered the sick bay. "Where ya' been, man?" Brent asked in a boisterous mood.

"Working. We can't all take catered vacations in luxurious surroundings like these." The pilot seated himself next to the bed.

"I haven't seen you for two days."

"It's been six, Brent, and I've been here every day. You have been asleep."

"Six days," Brent repeated with wonder. And then quickly, "How long have we been in port?" With a lack of motion and the whine of auxiliary engines replacing the thump of the main engines, like any experienced sailor, Brent knew the ship was in a sheltered body of water.

"We moored at dock B-Two, Yokosuka, yesterday."

Brent felt sudden distress as an aching worry returned. "The Arab carriers—you said we put two fish into one." And then in sudden confusion, "You did say that yesterday, didn't you, or did I dream it? They've shot me so full of morphine I can't tell fact from fiction."

Yoshi smiled, a deep, contented look. "No, you did not dream it and I told you that at least six days ago, too. The morning after you were wounded we found them two hundred kilometers east of Yap. We put two *gyos* into a Majestic class carrier. They are making for the Makassar Straits, probably put in at Surabaya."

Brent waved at the glass-enclosed office at the end of the ward. "Horikoshi wouldn't tell me anything. I don't get it."

"He is a strange one. He hates war, Brent."

"But he serves in *Yonaga*. He could transfer."

Matsuhara shook his head. "No. His family is dead and this is all he knows. And Admiral Fujita would never release him. He is the best in his field."

"And the craziest."

The air group commander grinned. "Aren't we all, Brent. Look at our profession—the way we make a living."

Brent grunted at the logic and then was struck with a new thought. "According to international law, the Arabs only have seventy-two hours in a neutral port."

Yoshi grinned sardonically. "There is no law and who is neutral? Only strength and 'King Oil' count."

"Then you think they'll be repaired in the Indonesian yards?"

"Indonesia is OPEC, Indonesia is pro-Kadafi, Indonesia wants to survive. Yes, indeed, the *Majestic* will be repaired."

"It'll take months. We'll nail her there—in the harbor."

Yoshi shook his head. "No. The Arabs have bases on Borneo, Halamahara. You know Admiral Fujita would never knowingly take *Yonaga* within range of land-based aircraft unless he had no choice. He will wait until she comes out—attack in the open sea where he has maneuvering room."

Brent's mind returned to its former speed and questions crowded to be answered. "The Marianas, Rosencrance, Arab LRA's . . ."

Yoshi waved him to silence. "When I flew over the west coast of Saipan I spotted a transport in Tanapag Harbor."

Brent raised an eyebrow. "We flew down the east coast—over Magicienne Bay. We didn't see it."

Yoshi continued, "Apparently, they landed a special force."

"The Fifth Special Combat Battalion or a parachute brigade?"

"Very good, Brent. It is the Seventh Parachute Brigade and both units were landed. They are in regimental strength."

"I remember Bernstein's briefing. Israeli Intelligence spotted those special troops, a couple of transports, and ten new subs months ago. Israeli agents staked out the whorehouses in Tripoli and Benghazi—picked up all the dope from their own whores."

"Best way to handle Arabs." They both chuckled. Yoshi said, "Those subs were Zulus and now they have eight."

"Eight? I don't get it. Bernstein was sure of ten."

The pilot laughed softly. "We sank two Zulus and the transport just east of Rota. We took prisoners. That is how we got our intelligence."

"Interrogation?"

"Yes, Brent. Admiral Fujita can be very persuasive." He snickered.

Brent knew how "persuasive" a samurai could be. He had seen prisoners beaten, tortured, shot, and beheaded. Yes, indeed, Fujita was a master at persuasion. At first the American had been shocked and sickened. But now he had learned to expect it, especially since the Arabs had butchered all of the passengers and crew—over a thousand prisoners—of the cruise ship *Mayeda Maru* in the harbor at Tripoli two years earlier. Most had been killed slowly by garroting.

Yoshi moved on: "They have occupied both Saipan and Tinian."

"Air bases, Yoshi."

"Of course. Bases for strikes against us with their long-range aircraft."

"Have they landed any LRA's?"

"Not yet. But they have three squadrons of converted Constellations, Douglas DC-4 Skymasters, and DC-6 Liftmasters training in Libya."

"Did they take Aguijan?"

"No. We have agents there now. The place is like a table—hard to assault. Our men can watch both islands for aerial activity."

"The Arabs will pick up their radio signals."

"We know. As you would say, 'that comes with the territory,' Brent-san." He studied his big hands spread across his knees. "We know nothing about Rosencrance. I know he landed on Tinian."

"You know?"

"Of course. I damaged him badly with twenty-millimeter." He punched an open palm with a clenched fist. "But the gods turned away. I ran out of ammunition."

"Someday we'll kill that swine, Yoshi-san."

"I want the privilege, Brent-san."

"Take a number." They both chuckled.

Abruptly, Yoshi's jaw hardened and the black eyes gleamed with new intensity. He moved his eyes to the Konoye sword and spoke slowly as if each word was coated with acid and had to be forced from his lips. "The emperor is very ill. It may only be a matter of time. There are rumors of cancer—internal bleeding. I feel he will join his fellow gods in a few weeks."

"I'm sorry, Yoshi-san. I know how important he is."

"Important!" the Japanese raised his eyebrows. "You know of *Kokutai?*" It was more of a statement than a question. Yoshi knew better than anyone how well Brent had been indoctrinated into Japanese culture and traditions. He himself had spent long hours discussing the *Hagakure,* Shintoism, Buddhism, poetry, painting, literature, and Japanese history with the young American.

"Of course. The emperor is Japan."

"Good, Brent-san. But he is much more—our heart and soul, the national essence itself."

"Crown Prince Akihito is a good man."

"Yes. Japan is fortunate to have him." The pilot rose slowly, broke the somber mood. "You look well, Brent-san."

89

"I hope to return to duty in a few days," Brent said, welcoming the change in subject.

A slow smile spread across Matsuhara's face. "Do not hurry it, Brent-san."

"No doubt the Arabs will invade Tokyo and wreck the Ginza worse than Godzilla if I don't get out of this sack."

Matsuhara was chuckling as he walked out of the door.

That night Brent was awakened again by the wind moaning through the branches, the rustling of leaves. "Brent-san. Brent-san," the wind said. Slowly Brent swung his feet to the deck and stood in the dim light coming from a single shielded bulb at the far end of the ward and the brightly lighted office at the opposite end where the duty orderly sat at his desk. Again "Brent-san." It came from Takii. But that was impossible. The man was petrified wood.

Carefully, Brent leaned over the wrapped, immolated form and lowered his ear over the head. Then he heard it, distorted and hissed through mucus that caused a continuous popping sound like tiny bubbles bursting, but distinct and unmistakable. "Kill me, Brent-san. Kill me." The young American recoiled as if he had just heard a ghost speak.

A high, anxious voice interrupted. "Mr. Ross. What is it? You should not be out of your bed." It was the young duty orderly, Third Class Petty Officer Haruo Kayatani, who was hurrying down the isle, rubber soles squeaking with each step on the highly polished vinyl floor.

For some reason unknown to himself, Brent concealed the truth. "I thought he said something."

"Impossible, Mr. Ross." The young man pulled a

syringe from the service cart. "He probably groaned." He emptied the syringe into an IV bottle. "Here. That should quiet him."

Brent sank back onto his bed. "Yes. That was it, I'm sure. Groans, Orderly Kayatani." Brent lay on his side and eyed Yoshiro Takii until finally, early in the morning, he drifted off.

The next day, Yoshiro was as silent as a corpse. Brent began to doubt himself—question his own memories of the sounds. But he was off painkillers, strong again, in charge of his faculties and alert and would be discharged the next day. He stared hard at the wrapped head, the tubes, watched as the orderlies changed dressings. Looking at the pilot's head, Brent remembered the burned logs reduced to black charcoal that filled his father's fireplace on winter nights when he was a little boy. Takii's head was a charred log, the skin so completely destroyed it would not even blister. Purple and black, it was ridged, crusted, and devastated, like the side of a volcano scoured by a lava flow.

Then, that afternoon, he heard the popping again. Uneasily, Brent stared at the pilot. It was unmistakable, air was hissing through Takii's trachea, making tiny volleys of pops as it forced its way through collected mucus. Suddenly, Takii coughed, a deep, liquid sound that sent yellow mucus flying. Immediately, Kayatani and Takeda were at Takii's side. "Suction," he heard Shingen Takeda order. With quick movements Kayatani forced a tube down the pilot's throat and there was a faint sound like a vacuum. Lieutenant Takii was silent for the rest of the afternoon.

That night it began again. First the popping and then the rustling sounds. This time Brent was on his feet and hunched over the pilot's bed in seconds. The words were run together, nearly formless and garbled, but Takii was speaking and Brent understood. "Brent-san. Brent-san. Can you hear me?"

Brent leaned close and spoke to the place where his pilot's ear had been. "Yes, Yoshiro-san. I can hear you."

"Kill me, Brent-san." Stunned, the American stared down mutely. "Please kill me, my friend."

"I can't."

"You must." The wrappings fell silent and Brent thought Takii had lapsed into unconsciousness. But the voice returned. "You love me, Brent-san?"

"You are my friend, Yoshiro-san. Of course."

"Then kill me. Let me die like a samurai — not like this. The way you honored Konoye. My sword. A single stroke."

"I can't."

"Please." The figure shook. Takii was sobbing. "In the name of Sacred Buddha, it hurts. Help me, please. The sword. The sword . . ." The voice trailed off.

Brent Ross came erect slowly, like a man hypnotized. Tears streaked his cheeks and his heavy shoulders trembled as he gasped for breath like the victim of a killer's garrote. His eyes moved the length of the dark ward to the office where the duty orderly hunched over his desk, lost in a novel. Everyone had been sedated for the night and not a patient stirred. It was then Brent realized Takii must have built up immunity to the painkillers — had deliberately suffered pain in periods of wakefulness, saving himself for a few short periods of consciousness and time to persuade Brent to dispatch him in glory.

Stiffly, like a wide-eyed automaton, Brent turned toward the Takii sword. He reached up, grasped the scabbard and the leather-wrapped *tang* (grip). The sword came free from the bracket with a loud click.

The attendant stopped reading.

"The north — my head," Takii hissed. Brent nodded

92

understanding. Buddha had died with his head to the north. A devoted Buddhist, the pilot knew dying with his head in the same direction would improve his karma and enhance his chances for reaching nirvana. Slowly, the American pushed the foot of the bed around until he estimated Takii's head pointed to the north. One of the rubber tired wheels squeaked.

The attendant looked up curiously.

With one quick motion Brent tugged on the handle and the fine steel blade leaped eagerly from the scabbard with a high, ringing sound like a temple bell struck by a priest.

The attendant came to his feet.

Gripping the sword with both hands and raising it over his right shoulder, Brent chanted a litany of Buddhist supplications, "Death is as ephemeral as a wave of the sea and rebirth awaits you, dear friend. May you walk the Noble Eightfold Path with the Blessed One at your side, find the middle way and the Four Noble Truths to the peace that passeth understanding, Yoshiro-san." But it was not enough. He spoke to the samurai with lyrics from the *Kamigayo* (anthem) and verses he remembered from the *Hagakure:* "Corpses on the mountains, corpses in the sea, I will die for the emperor and the gods shall smile . . ."

The attendant threw a switch turning on the ward's bright overhead lights. He stared the length of the room. "No!" he shouted, bolting for the door.

Tightening his hold on the silver fittings of the *tang* and raising the sword higher and higher in the classic posture of the coiled and charged samurai, Brent looked down at his friend with a measure of his own peace. A samurai was born to Shinto rites; died as a Buddhist. He had done his best. He stared at the tiny neck. It would not be much — very easy, like chopping through a sliver of balsa. He heard heavy footsteps racing near, the shouts of "No! No!"

Brent smiled. "Good-bye, dear friend," he said. With all of his strength he whipped the blade over and down in a vicious semicircle. A fabled blade drawn in the seventeenth century by the master Yoshitake, the Takii sword was fashioned like the incomparable Damascus blade, layered and tempered metal, folded and drawn nine times, as finely wrought as jewelry and sharp and spare as a haiku verse. Born to the task, the sword hissed through the air with a high, lilting note — a gay, hungry sound that ended in a crunch and whacking thud as flesh and vertebrae were sliced and severed. Striking with every ounce of the American's two hundred twenty pounds behind it, the blade not only severed Takii's head, but the mattress was slashed all the way to the springs as well.

Brent pulled the sword free and dropped it to the deck with a loud clatter. He stood stiffly, staring down at his friend, the head that had rolled down to one side and lodged against the body's right shoulder. Blood was hosing from jugulars and the body was twitching in its final spasms. "Find peace, dear friend," Brent said.

"He is a murderer, Admiral!" Chief Hospital Orderly Eiichi Horikoshi screeched, standing before Admiral Fujita's desk in the admiral's cabin. The chief orderly's face was livid, lips a thin white line, bushy white eyebrows almost meeting above the snapping black eyes.

Brent, dressed in green number-two combat fatigues, which was the uniform of the day, stood rigidly at the opposite end of the desk. The cabin was well furnished with two leather chairs flanking the large oak desk, and four more straight-back chairs were clustered around a small table bolted to the deck in the center of the room. In the corner, a petty officer sat at communications center equipped with two phones and a pad. Two armed, burly seaman guards stood at the room's lone entrance. A large equestrian of Emperor Hirohito hung from the bulkhead behind the admiral while charts of the Pacific and the Japanese home islands were attached to the sides. There were no computers or monitors in the cabin.

"It was cold-blooded, premeditated murder. Savage, unconscionable . . ."

Admiral Fujita removed his small steel-rimmed glasses and stared up at Brent Ross. Silently, the old man studied Ross as if he were trying to penetrate the expressionless mask and read the wildly churning thoughts racing through the young man's mind. Despite the turmoil, Brent was at peace with what he had done and had not explained, tried to justify. Somehow, the lieutenant felt he would demean Takii's memory.

"You won't speak, Mr. Ross," the admiral said.

"I won't degrade Lieutenant Yoshiro Takii's memory with excuses, sir."

"Of course. No one expects that." Fujita drummed the desk with fingers gnarled like dead roots. As usual, the old man's insights were almost metaphysical. "He requested it — death by his sword. Is that not true?"

Brent sighed, spoke softly. "That is true, Admiral."

"Nonsense," Eiichi shouted. "He could not talk." He glared at Brent. "You were tired of the burned body — the groans — the smells."

The admiral's eyes moved back and forth from one antagonist to the other with that strange, calculating stare Brent had seen so many time when conflicts had erupted before him. Sometimes Brent felt the old man enjoyed the bitter exchanges and even physical combat that had exploded in his presence. Or was it a catharsis, a washing clean of antagonism by exposure that he had learned to tolerate, even encourage, during the forty-three-year confinement at Sano Wan? No. Brent had seen pleasure on the old sailor's face.

Brent felt heat grow in his chest, a formless anger that uncoiled like a hot snake and beat against his ribs for release until he thought he would burst. Unflinchingly, he stared down into Horikoshi's eyes. "That's not true. He deserved better than what you would give him. He couldn't go on as a burned vegetable. And I don't give a damn if you or anyone else don't like it — he got the death he had earned."

Horikoshi's voice was acid with derision, "Oh, are you not the warrior? So you gave Takii a samurai's demise. I find your gallantry overwhelming." He thrust his jaw toward the American and his voice hardened. "We had him stabilized. He was growing stronger — could have lived for years."

Brent said, "Yes, indeed, kept him alive. And for what? No eyes, no nose, almost half of his flesh destroyed, perpetual pain. Is that the goal of medicine? To torture — inflict pain?"

Horikoshi shook a finger at the young lieutenant. "You inflict the pain! You are the killer! I repair what you destroy. Preserve life. All you know is death!"

Brent brushed the finger away with a big hand like he was chasing a fly. "Don't you ever stick a finger in my face."

Horikoshi's sarcasm was palpable. "What will you do, Mr. Ross, kill me?"

Refusing the bait, Brent's tone was casual. "No. But I might break your hand."

Admiral Fujita took charge: "Enough!" Silence filled the room, only the sounds of blowers and the high whine of auxiliary engines intruding. The four enlisted men stole looks at the admiral as he spoke. "I can understand your feelings, Chief Horikoshi. You are devoted to the saving of life and I commend you." He moved his eyes to Brent. "Sometimes, Mr. Ross, your thinking is more Japanese than any one of us." He gripped a single long white hair hanging from his chin with a thumb and forefinger, tugged it meditatively. "I understand your decision — and even if Yoshiro Takii could not speak, he deserved what you gave him." Horikoshi winced. Brent sighed and felt the tension drain away. "It is the way of the samurai — the way of Bushido." He shifted his eyes to Eiichi Horikoshi's face. "I find no crime here." He gestured at the American. "His actions were appropriate — even commendable."

Horikoshi was out of control. "This is insane! Murder commendable?" he stabbed a finger at Brent. "He should be courtmartialed! Hanged!"

Fujita came to his feet slowly. "Return to your duties immediately or I will have you thrown off the ship." He punched the desk with a tiny fist. "You do not challenge my judgment. Ever!" He pointed at the door. "You are dismissed!"

Glaring, Horikoshi turned and left. Brent knew it was not over.

Brent's cabin was in "Flag Country," the former quarters of a long-dead staff officer. Still, it was small and Spartan, not more than eight feet long and six feet wide with a narrow bunk, small table, two chairs, a sink, and a mirror. However, it did have the luxury of a shower-equipped head tucked away in a tiny alcove.

Brent had no more than sagged down on his bunk with a double Chivas Regal in his hand when Yoshi Matsuhara knocked and entered. As the pilot seated himself, Brent rose, pulled a bottle from a cabinet beneath his sink, filled a small porcelain *sakazuki* with sake and handed it to the air-group leader. "You served Yoshiro Takii well, Brent-san," Yoshi said after taking a long drink. "The perfect *kaishaku.*"

"Horikoshi does not agree," Brent said.

"I know, Brent-san. I heard."

Brent was not surprised at the pilot's knowledge of the conversation that had taken place only minutes before. Four enlisted men had heard the violent exchange and Brent knew the news had spread on the ship's mysterious "unofficial telegraph" like wildfire.

Yoshi continued, "It makes no difference, Brent-san. Eiichi is a farmer, despises Bushido, fights us but saves our lives."

"A living, walking contradiction."

"Yes. And more Japanese than any of us for it."

Brent nodded understanding but was still confused by the irrational concept that a man's strength lay in the number of contradictions he could entertain without conflict; the greater the number, the stronger the character. "There is no doubt he is a man of great strength of character, Yoshi-san."

The pilot nodded solemnly and emptied his cup. Brent refilled it. "You did a great service for your pilot. He was cremated this morning and soon his ashes will rest honorably on a sepulchral pillar in the Temple of the Calm Light at Kyoto. His family was from Kyoto."

"But his spirit lives at the Yasakuni Shrine, Yoshi-san."

A smile widened the strong jaw. "Good, Brent-san. With the heroes — with his navigators, Morisada Mochitsura and Takashiro Hayusa." He made a temple of his fingers. "This is important. Takii was a follower of Nichiren. You must understand this."

Confusion beetled the young American's brow with

tiny crow's-feet. "It is a Buddhist sect which is the most Japanese of them all," Yoshi explained. "It was founded by the old monk, Nichiren, seven hundred years ago. Takii was a follower, believed Buddhism had been corrupted with metaphysical nonsense. Like all good Nichirens, he felt he must return to Buddha's original teachings. In the West, he would have been a Protestant rebelling against Catholicism."

Brent nodded. Drank. Felt the warmth spread while his mind was occupied with thoughts of the strange teachings of Gautama Buddha that challenged the foundations of his western mind and governed his best friend's consciousness: the belief that all men are essentially meat and bones with minds was mere illusion, and only the belief that this was actually the case created each other. The fact that Yoshi Matsuhara was big, strong, brave, and the finest fighter pilot in the world was essentially an illusion, a fabrication of Brent's consciousness, which was an illusion, too. There could be no objective and external universe, no reality existing eternally, absolutely and independently of mind and observations.

Yoshi continued, "Takii lived his faith with more fervor, with fewer dogmatic trappings, simple ceremonies — pristine and clean."

"That's how he checked out." Brent swallowed the last of his Chivas Regal. Poured another drink. For the first time, he felt relaxation spread in warm waves.

The Japanese stared at the bulkhead behind Brent. Narrowing his eyes, he spoke softly. "If he could have prayed, it would have been simple — *Namu Amida Butsu. Namu myo-ho-renge-kyo.*" He smiled at the questioning look on Brent's face and continued, "Literally, 'Let us worship the Buddha Amida — the future — and the doctrine of the good law'."

"You should say those words over his ashes."

"I already have, Brent-san. In the *Shrine of Infinite Salvation*."

"You're a good man, Yoshi-san."

Grinning, the pilot tapped the table with a forefinger. "There are other words, Brent-san — we owe Captain Kenneth Rosencrance a debt. Not only Takii, but my wingmen, Masatake Matsumara and Subaru Kizamatsu cry for vengeance."

"The vengeance of 'the Forty-seven Ronin'?"

"Yes. And more."

"More?"

Yoshi took a long drink. "You've heard the story of Ono Doken?" Brent shook his head. "He was a famous samurai who lived in the seventeenth century. He was unjustly accused of cowardice and condemned to death by fire. When his enemy came to check his remains, Ono grabbed the man's sword and stabbed him to death. Then he dissolved into ashes." He drank again. "You will find this tale in the *Ohanashikikigaki* by Naoshige."

Brent was not surprised by the story. It was fanciful, and in a way ludicrous, but very samurai and he knew Yoshi believed it just as firmly as Christians believed biblical parables. "I haven't read Naoshige, but I intend to soon," he said. "But Rosencrance did escape — the only one who got away?"

"Yes."

"Do you think his staffel is operating out of the Marianas, Yoshi-san?"

The fighter pilot shrugged, turned his palms up. "Our observers on Aguijan have not reported fighter activity. But we know Saipan and Tinian are occupied."

Brent pondered for a moment. "If you shot down his wingmen and damaged him, maybe they just haven't been able to reinforce. After all, their transport was sunk and we put a couple of fish into their *Majestic*."

"Logical, Brent-san. But they'll reinforce, even if they must bring them in by submarine. And they do have the subs."

"A sweep. We must make a sweep with our air groups."

The pilot shook his head. "I do not think Admiral Fujita would risk it. Remember, when we were attacking their bases in North Korea, they sank most of the Self Defense Force. Even the amphibious squadron."

Brent spoke, thumping the table with a big fist for emphasis. "We've got to kill Rosencrance. He's beneath humanity. An animal." He looked up. "Why—why are there always these creatures roaming the earth. Why are good men always called on to stop them? Why must so many good men die?"

Yoshi scratched the afternoon stubble on his chin thoughtfully. His question took the American by surprise. "Have you ever read *Julius Caesar?*"

Brent knew Yoshi was an inveterate reader with eclectic tastes; first Naoshige and now Shakespeare. Nevertheless, the question seemed strange even for Matsuhara. "Why, yes. I enjoy Shakespeare."

The fingers tugged at the chin. "Do you remember, I think it is in Act One before Caesar's assassination, when Casca is troubled by the plots of evil men?" Brent stared expectantly. Yoshi moved on. "Caesar said to Casca, 'Against the Capitol I met a lion, who glared at me, and went surly by.' "

"Rosencrance is the lion," Brent observed.

"And Kadafi, Arafat, Khomeini. There are always lions."

"But there are lion hunters."

Matsuhara laughed. "Yes, Brent-san. We must pick up our pistols, chairs, and whips."

There was a loud knock. Brent opened the door and

Admiral Mark Allen walked in. He saw Yoshi Matsu-hara and hostility flared in both of the men's eyes. The old admiral seated himself as far from the Japanese as the small room would permit and faced Brent Ross. Brent knew the admiral liked his Scotch straight, too. Pouring a stiff measure, he handed it to the older man, who accepted it without comment. He was troubled and Brent knew what the trouble was. The old man came to the point immediately, "You killed a man, Brent."

Brent answered without giving ground, "I know, sir."

The admiral reached for Brent's early Catholic training. "A mortal sin you can't erase. No penance . . ."

Yoshi Matsuhara interrupted. "He served a friend. Honored his duty in the finest tradition of Bushido."

"He killed in cold blood—has done it twice."

Brent squeezed in, "Please, Admiral. I know. I know. It was not an easy decision."

Mark Allen showed his perceptiveness. "Admiral Fujita understands, doesn't he?"

Brent sighed. "Yes."

"No court-martial?"

Brent nodded. Took a stiff drink. "Horikoshi would have me executed."

Mark Allen looked at the young lieutenant over his drink thoughtfully as he sipped the fiery liquid. "You should leave this ship, Brent."

Matsuhara sputtered angrily, "That is nonsense. He belongs here."

"Don't you tell me what's nonsense, Commander."

"I will when you make no sense, Admiral."

"You don't speak that way to an admiral, Com-mander."

"I am a line officer—a member of ship's company.

102

You are from the outside—from another navy. Another world. If this be insubordination, take it to Admiral Fujita's desk. And I will fight you there."

"Very well. Then that's where it will go."

"Yoshi-san!" Brent shouted, visibly upset. "Please leave."

Silently, the pilot glared at the admiral. Slowly, he rose and stalked out of the room.

Brent turned to Admiral Allen. "Please, Admiral, understand him. He lost both of his wingmen—been under terrible stress."

Allen emptied his glass. "I know. I know." Brent poured the admiral another drink. "Haven't we all."

"Don't put him on report, sir."

"I can't drop it."

"If he apologizes?"

"I don't know, Brent." He shook his head as if clearing cobwebs. "There are more important things."

"You want me to leave *Yonaga?*"

"Yes. Return to NIS Washington—widen your experience. Think of your career."

"The action is here, Admiral. With *Yonaga*. She is the only force capable of stopping the Arabs and you know it."

"I appreciate your altruism, Brent, but you must think of yourself, too."

"I am. I belong here."

The old man took a large swallow. Brent drained his drink, enjoying the spreading warmth. The iron began to drain from his veins and the room moved slightly. He recharged both their glasses. Mark Allen continued, "Matsuhara—the rest of them have too much influence on you. You've changed, Brent. How could you, a clean, rational American, an All-American fullback, a boy raised in the American tradition behead a man—two men?" Grimly, Mark set his jaw, stared

103

deep into Brent's eyes. He waved a hand in an encompassing gesture. "It's those men—the samurai, Fujita, Matsuhara, Okuma, Arai—the lot. They've made you one of them. This is dangerous, Brent." He waved a hand at the overhead. "You'll never fit in back home and you don't really fit here. Think of it. This can destroy you."

"My decision, sir?"

The older man's jaw hardened and deep lines fissured the wide forehead. "I can't force it. I would if I could, but Admiral Fujita has too much influence in the Pentagon—in the Cabinet, and, I hear, in the Oval Office." He slammed a fist down hard on the table. "It must be your decision, Brent, but for God's sake use that big brain of yours."

Brent tossed off his drink with one motion. "I've made it, sir. I'll remain, Admiral."

"Have it your way." Angrily, Mark Allen stood, emptied his glass, and left.

Chapter III

"Flag plot" was the largest room in flag country. Located between the flag bridge and the admiral's quarters, it was furnished with a long oak table, a dozen chairs, bulkhead-mounted charts, two blowers, a speaker, phones mounted on a table manned by a rating, and the usual picture of young Emperor Hirohito astride a white horse. The room was brilliantly lighted by a dozen light bulbs shining from wire-shielded fixtures nested in the inevitable maze of conduits and cables cluttering the overhead.

The staff meeting had been called for the middle of the morning. Although Brent's burns had healed quickly, a few itching scabs remained and the flesh was scarred and discolored like a burgundy-colored birthmark from his ankle to his groin. Seating himself at his place near the far end of the table, Brent Ross almost groaned. His headache had returned, a dull, merciless pulsing behind both eyes that told him he had not completely recovered from his concussion. But he would not report to Eiichi Horikoshi, did not mention it to anyone—not even Yoshi Matsuhara.

Yoshi was already there, seated next to him, thumbing through a sheaf of reports. Across the table, Admiral Mark Allen sat, apparently lost in his own documents. At the far end of the table, Admiral Fujita was busily engaged in a conversation with his executive officer, Commander Mitake Arai.

Tall and ramrod straight, Arai was in his mid-sixties and a survivor of destroyer service in World War II. He had been the captain of destroyer *Rikokaze*. By a freak of the fortune like a macabre joke, he had fought against two of the officers seated at the table: Admiral Mark Allen and escort commander Captain John Fite, the big, burly bear of a man who had commanded destroyer *Bradfield* in the fighting in the Solomons. Fite had engaged Arai's ship, *Rikokaze,* the night Arai destroyed cruiser *Northhampton* with two of the Imperial Navy's magnificent Type 93 torpedoes, the *Long Lance*. Arai had fought against Mark Allen when Yamato sortied to meet her death and Allen's air groups sent *Rikokaze* to the bottom with the battleship. Most of Arai's crew had died.

At first the fires of hostility had flickered amongst the old warriors. But now, with a common enemy and the sharing of mortal dangers, old animosities had been put aside and replaced by the close-knit harmony found in the fraternity of war. But Brent knew it was not completely gone—suspected the old warriors could never forget. It was there in the quick looks, the inflection, and in the extreme politeness that bordered on the frigid. It could explode again. Brent was sure of it.

On the other side of the admiral sat the ancient scribe, Commander Hakuseki Katsube. An antique of a man, the tiny scribe was withered and wrinkled as though too many decades of sun, salt spray, and wind had evaporated every trace of moisture from his flesh, leaving his skin tanned to the consistency of old leather dipped in tannic acid. His back was permanently bent as if he wore a heavy weight around his neck and he had a disconcerting habit of giggling to himself and sometimes drooling into his work. Both he and Admiral Fujita rejected modern recording devices and the old man hunched over a pad and brush.

Next to Admiral Mark Allen sat the new dive-bomber commander, Commander Kazuoshi Muira. Muira was the replacement for Lieutenant Daizo Saiki who, when accused of cowardice, had blown his brains out in that very room only six months before. Sixty-years old but looking much older, Kazuoshi Muira had a flaccid build and flat, expressionless face that looked as though his countenance had been run over by a heavy roller. However, his stomach had escaped the roller and hung over his belt in layers. An Eta Jima graduate and thorough professional, he had seen action in WW II as the pilot of a Aichi D3A in the Solomons and had put a bomb into carrier *Hornet* at Santa Cruz. In 1944, he was wounded in the Battle of the Philippine Sea when he was one of the turkeys shot down in the Marianas Turkey Shoot. He volunteered for kamikaze duty, but his injuries kept him out of action until the end of the war. A close friend of Minoru Genda, who headed the Self Defense Force, he was given a commission in the Self Defense Force where he spent twenty-two years before retiring. He was a highly skilled and respected pilot. Brent was wary of the baleful looks Muira directed at him and Admiral Mark Allen, as if the old fire still smoldered. Uneasily, Brent realized the old pilot still remembered the turkey shoot.

Next to Muira sat the new torpedo-bomber commander, Commander Shusaku Endo who, similar to Muira, was attending his first full-staff briefing. Descended from the famous samurai Endo family, Shusaku proudly traced his lineage back to the Heian period and the establishment of the Tokugawa shogunate in Kyoto by Iyeyasu Tokugawa in 1600. A fearless warrior for Iyeyasu Tokugawa, Tonishio Endo was honored with the title of *fudai daimyo* (hereditary lord) and was bequeathed vast estates with thousands of vassals. It was in 1610 in one of the many wars against the Maeda at Kanazawa (the *daimyo* in the island of Shikoku) that Tonishio distinguished himself by committing seppuku after a bitter defeat. His disembowelment was done before Shogun Iyeyasu Tokugawa on the day of the *o-bon* (Festival of the Dead) on the steps of the palace in the new capital at Edo. There were thousands of witnesses. The magnificent gesture was still spoken of amongst the highborn.

In 1873, with the Meiji restoration, the Endos fell on hard times with all of the other disenfranchised samurai families. But they managed to hold on to some of their property near Kyoto and curry favor at court. In 1903, the family's fortune and future was assured when Emperor Meiji conferred the title of "Marquis" on Shusaku's great-grandfather and sent him as his personal representative to the coronation of Rahma VI of Siam. Brent Ross was convinced that Tonishio Endo's seppuku of so long ago had influenced Admiral Fujita into accepting Shusaku Endo as his bomber commander. There were rumors that Emperor Hirohito had interceded in Endo's favor.

Looking at the bomber commander, Brent was impressed by Shusaku's size. He was large for a Japanese at an even six feet and, perhaps, two-hundred pounds. With glistening black hair, alert eyes, and clear skin, his age was deceptive, as was true with most Japanese. He appeared to be about thirty-five, but lines like deep commas trailing cruelly downward from the corners of his eyes and mouth spoke of at least four decades. His shoulders were broad, chest thick, and he carried himself like a trained athlete. There was latent malevolence in his eyes, and whenever he looked at Brent, the American saw a challenge flash. He did not trust this man. He expected trouble.

The CIA man, Jason King, had been relieved and his chair was empty. The new CIA man, Dale McIntyre, had not yet arrived. According to Admiral Allen, McIntyre had been scheduled to arrive at Tokyo International Airport just two hours earlier. In addition to the hand-carried encryption box destined for Brent, the CIA man would deliver the latest reports of Arab naval and air activities and expected terrorist strikes. Everyone was anxious to see McIntyre enter the conference. Staring at the empty chair next to him, Brent fretted restlessly and palmed his head with spread fingers. His head still ached and he suppressed a groan.

Dressed in desert combat fatigues, Colonel Irving Bernstein of Israeli Intelligence sat across from the empty chair. Elderly, with white hair, a neatly trained mustache, and pointed beard, Bernstein was the only man in the room with hair on his face. His slight build showed wiry strength and his most notable feature was six blue tattooed numbers on his right forearm. "Auschwitz, class of forty-five," he would say blankly to anyone foolish enough to inquire. Bernstein had been on board on liaison since *Yonaga's* voyage to the Mediterranean and her attack on Arab forces in North Africa over two years earlier.

Fujita stared down the table at McIntyre's empty chair with irritation. Restlessly, he tapped the table and the conversation came to an abrupt halt. The old sailor nodded at Matsuhara. Yoshi stood, glanced at his reports. He said, "All air groups are up to full strength. All Zero-sens are equipped with the new Sakae two-thousand-horsepower engine. We can put fifty-four fighters in the air." He looked up, set his jaw in a hard line. "But thirty-four of my pilots are new —

need training."

"But you have been training continuously at Tokyo International and Tsuchiura," Fujita noted.

"True, Admiral," Matsuhara answered. "But most of my new men were raised on jets — have not fully found a *feel* for a propeller-driven fighter — the huge torque of the new engines can kill."

Commander Shusaku Endo said to Yoshi Matsuhara, "Perhaps, if you did not lose so many of your wingmen, we would not need so many replacements, Commander." The insult brought a deadly silence into the room. All eyes turned to Yoshi. Brent was sure he saw a look of delight on Admiral Fujita's face.

His eyes locking with his tormentor's like those of two great bull buffaloes, Yoshi spoke slowly, a slight tremor betraying the depth of his anger. "No one grieves my losses more than I. You foul the memories of good men with your pedestrian remark."

"If my memory serves me, six good men," Endo countered, the broad face as expressionless as sheet metal.

Brent knew that Endo, like many of the new pilots, felt Yoshi Matsuhara was too old for the responsibility of Air Group Commander. He had probably been influenced by the man he replaced, Commander Tashiro Okuma, who had returned to the Self Defense Force. Okuma hated and envied Yoshi Matsuhara, and the two men had almost come to blows on several occasions. Brent was sure that only the Korean operation that forced cooperation had prevented bloodshed, perhaps, a fight to the death in the ship's combined Shinto shrine and Buddhist temple — the Shrine of Infinite Salvation — where Fujita insisted blood feuds be settled.

"If you have any criticisms of my conduct in the air or in my ready room, I will be happy to entertain you privately in the Shrine of . . ."

"Enough!" Fujita shouted. "This can be settled after we entertain Colonel Kadafi's murderers in the western Pacific."

Yoshi spoke with unusual candor. "You cannot deny a samurai . . ."

The admiral unwound slowly, drawing himself up to his full four-feet eleven-inch height. He spoke and his voice was suddenly deep and resonant as if he were speaking in a great cavern. To Brent, the little man was suddenly seven feet tall. "Commander," he said. "You do not tell me what I can and cannot deny — what I can do and cannot do."

Yoshi bristled. "That is not my intent." He waved at Endo. "He insulted me — my men."

"Not your men!" Endo shouted.

"Quiet! Both of you. Save your anger for the Arabs," Fujita commanded. "I will decide how, when, and where to resolve this." He glared at both of the pilots and then spoke to Yoshi. "The CAP?"

Yoshi sighed, collected his thoughts, and said, "As before, Admiral — six Zero-sens out of Tokyo International and six more ready fighters on the apron." He knuckled the table, "No one is permitted to violate *Yonaga's* airspace."

"Good," the admiral said. He turned to Shusaku Endo and asked for the torpedo-bomber leader's report.

Endo reported fifty-four aircraft combat ready while twelve more were in the process of overhaul. Three had been so badly damaged over Korea they were good for nothing more than being pirated for spare parts. Eyeing Yoshi Matsuhara, he closed. "We are terribly underpowered with our old nine-hundred-fifty-horsepower Sakaes. These engines are fifty years old. We need the new Sakae two-thousand horsepower engines, but the fighter squadrons have all of them."

"My decision, Commander," Fujita said. "You will be issued the new engines as soon as they come on board." He dismissed Endo with a wave and nodded at Commander Kazuoshi Muira.

The fat dive bomber commander rose and spoke in a reedy, petulant voice that squeaked like the falsetto of an effeminate rock singer. He reported forty-nine Aichi D3A's operational, eight in repair and four damaged beyond repair. He closed with a plea for new engines.

Then, in quick succession, the chief engineer—the clever, redoubtable Lieutenant Tatsuya Yoshida—gave his report, followed by the gunnery officer, Commander Nobomitsu Atsumi. Yoshida assured the admiral the four main engines were in perfect working order and all sixteen Kampon boilers, except three and six which were down for descaling, were on line. However, Auxiliary Engine Two had burned out a generator armature and a new one had to be hand wound. The engine would be down for at least four more days. The fuel tanks were topped off and eight boilers maintained a constant pressure of three hundred pounds. The ship could put to sea in a moment's notice.

The gunnery officer took the floor. Slender and of average height, Gunnery Officer Commander Atsumi was a wiry man whose lean frame promised great reserves of strength and endurance. Although he was over sixty years old, he was another "plank owner" who showed an amazing contempt for the ravages of time with a shock of lacquered black hair, unlined skin, and sharp black eyes under beetling brows. In strong, professional intonations he reported all batteries ready for action with new barrels installed in all 25-millimeter machine guns. A half-dozen 127-millimeter guns of the main battery needed barrel replacements,

112

but they would not be available for two months. Nakajima was rolling them in its plant in Kyoto. All magazines were fully loaded. He paused in his report and stared at Admiral Mark Allen before asking, "When will we get our new computerized fire control for our main battery? You promised to requisition one."

Fujita nodded at Mark Allen. Allen, Bernstein, and the still-absent Dale McIntyre represented the ship's intelligence effort and their reports were the most eagerly awaited. Mark Allen stood. "I ordered the new SPY-One-A three dimensional fire-control system."

Atsumi surprised Brent with his knowledge. "Phased-array radar. It can send out multiple pulses capable of simultaneous tracking of hundreds of targets. The heart of the Aegis system."

"We need it," Endo and Muira chorused.

"Well, we can't have it," Allen retorted. He waved a document. "I received this rejection just before the meeting."

"Why?" There was anguish in Atsumi's voice.

Allen swallowed hard. *"Glasnost."*

"Glasnost!" Fujita and Atsumi chorused. And then Fujita spoke. "Another word for détente. And it did not work, either."

"True. But you must understand, the two major powers are working hard at rapprochement — hold continuous meetings at Geneva."

"Still trading off," Fujita said derisively.

"Yes, Admiral Fujita," Allen acknowledged.

"We are denied the new guided Mark Forty Eight acoustic torpedo and the Russians refuse to deliver the Five-Three-Three guided torpedo to the Arabs," Fujita said.

Atsumi spoke to Mark Allen. "My one-hundred-twenty-seven-millimeter guns are wearing out and I am denied the new fully automatic Mark Forty-Five, five-

113

inch, fifty-caliber gun because we are assured the Arabs will not be given the new Russian automatic seventy-six-millimeter gun. Right, Admiral Allen?"

"The Russians are as dishonest as Arabs," Fujita said before Allen could answer. "Lying and cheating are endemic with them. I know . . . I started fighting them over eighty years ago."

Allen tightened his jaw, but remained silent.

"And we do not have radar fire control for our escorts." Fujita waved at Captain Fite who nodded back.

"You must understand the position of the United States," Mark Allen finally said. Then with irritation rising in his voice. "I have told you before, the US and Russia have agreed to not supply *any* nation with the most modern weapons. Both nations are trying to cool the fires of war."

"Cool the fires of war?" The Japanese rocked in their chairs with laughter.

"Yes! Yes!" Mark Allen shouted over the din. Fujita waved his hands in a suppressive gesture and the noise ended as if it had been cut with a sword. Red-faced, Mark Allen continued, "The US and Russia cannot afford to give their latest weapons — their secrets away. We must continue to use our original armament." His eyes flashed at Fujita. "Those torpedoes that hit us south of Pearl Harbor were not wire-guided — were not *homers.*"

Fujita acknowledged the truth of the statement with a grudging nod.

Mark Allen turned to Escort Commander John Fite and pursued his point. "You have never encountered enemy fire-control radar, John."

The burly captain nodded his shaggy head. His voice rumbled like a heavy train on a bridge. "True, Admiral. If we had, my entire squadron would have been sunk twice over on our torpedo runs." He shrugged, tapped the oak with a huge fist. "What is a smoke screen to radar?" The rhetorical question died unanswered in the silence.

"The best fire control is still the eye of a samurai to a gunsight," Fujita said emphatically, with a gesture of finality. Accepting the nods of approval from the Japanese, he changed direction in his usual mercurial fashion, directing his words at Colonel Irving Bernstein. "The Chinese satellite system. Is it deteriorating? What does Israeli Intelligence say of it?" Brent knew this question would ordinarily be directed at the CIA. However, with McIntyre's chair empty, Fujita had no choice.

Coming to his feet, the Israeli leaned forward on clenched fists and stared down at the table at his notes. Moving his eyes to Muira and Endo, he spoke in a voice that rang as clear as fine-leaded crystal. "As you know, the Chinese laser system consists of twenty weapons platforms orbiting at nine hundred thirty miles, controlled by three command modules in geosynchronous orbit at twenty-two thousand three hundred miles." He looked around the room. "Two of the weapons platforms are in trouble—their orbits are decaying."

There was a rumble and the Japanese exchanged worried looks. *Yonaga's* position as the world's dominant force at sea depended on the laser system's instantaneous destruction of all jets and rockets. Now it was deteriorating. The fact that the lasers had unleashed world terrorism and menaced the world's freedom was of little concern to the samurai. *Yonaga* was their world, and her supremacy and survival their paramount concern. Fujita waved a hand and Bernstein continued, "Tel Aviv computes the two platforms will reenter the atmosphere in about two years."

"This will leave a hole in their effectiveness?" Atsumi asked.

The Israeli smiled. Not really, Commander Atsumi. The Chinese were clever—built layers of redundancy into their system."

"Inscrutable Orientals," Fujita said slyly, in a rare moment of humor.

Taking their cue, the Japanese officers rocked with laughter, Katsube spraying spittle and nearly falling from his chair, his pad and brush sliding to the deck.

The laughter faded as the Israeli pushed on. "The satellites' footprints—ah, areas covered by individual stations, overlap and we suspect the entire system is programmed to adjust and compensate for losses. In other words, anticipated casualties to enemy attacks had been programmed into the command computers systems. We feel they can lose half their weapons stations and still command every square inch of the surface of the earth."

There were sighs, expansive looks exchanged, and a palpable aura of relief filled the room. "The other machines—their orbits?" Fujita asked.

"Firm, sir."

Fujita leaned forward, withered hands flat on the table. "The situation in the Middle East?"

Bernstein spoke without reference to his notes, his brown eyes narrowing and moving over the seated officers. "The Masada Line is holding."

"Masade Line?" Endo asked.

"Yes," Bernstein said. "The new name for our system of blockhouses and fortifications stretching from El 'Arish in the south in the Sinai Desert to a line running through Be'er Sheva and Jerusalem in the east and anchored in the north at Haifa, twenty-five miles south of the Lebanese border."

Commander Muira addressed the Israeli. "Kadafi's

116

jihad—ah, holy war. I hear the Arab coalition is falling apart."

"There are always those rumors. But their oil embargo against the West and Japan shows no sign of cracking," Bernstein said, tapping the table with a single finger. "As you know, an Arab is as predictable as a typhoon at latitude zero. True, they have their problems. The Iraqis and Iranians have gone back to killing each other, which is their favorite pastime and Iranians aren't Arabs, anyway, they're Persians. But Lebanon, Syria, Jordan, Libya, the PLO, and volunteers from Egypt and Saudi Arabia have provided Kadafi with a fighting force that encircles Israel."

"But they can't break through, Colonel," Mark Allen offered.

"True." The Jew's eyes narrowed and moistened, the crystal-clear voice suddenly low and diffused with emotion. "No one—absolutely no one can fight like a Jew with his back to the wall—the wall of the gas chamber, the wall of the crematorium. There was one holocaust, and there will never be another—not unless the executioners are prepared to die with their victims." He punched the table with a clenched fist, cried out in an anguished voice, "No more 'final solutions,' no more 'special actions.' Never again!"

Silence, broken by only the sounds of the blower overhead and the whine of auxiliary engines, dropped like a cold curtain. Finally, Fujita broke it with uncharacteristic concern in his voice. "There are a hundred million Arabs—only four million Israelis, Colonel," he said. "You still feel you can still hold out?"

"Yes! It makes no difference, Admiral," Bernstein said huskily, wiping his face with a palm as if the tragedy of so long ago was a mask that he could tear from his face and discard. The gesture seemed to restore his control, his balance, and his voice was firm again as he continued, "Israel is nothing but a small enclave in the Middle East, true, but we've already inflicted a half-million casualties on Kadafi's armies." His eyes moved over every face. There was pride in his voice. "It's a stalemate — we've fought them to a stalemate. The Israeli Air Force has been unbeatable and when we need her, *Mikasa* moves along the coast like a monitor. Nothing the Arabs have can stand up to her twelve-inch guns."

The gunnery officer, Commander Nobomitsu Atsumi, suddenly came to life. "Those old three-hundred-five-millimeter guns only have a range of twenty kilometers."

Bernstein smiled pridefully. "We've equipped her with new twelve-inch guns that can fire a new *sabot* charge."

"Sabot?"

"Yes. *Sabot*. 'Shoe.' We fit a *sabot* charge into the breech that reduces the bore to six inches but doubles the range to over twenty miles and twenty miles will range most of the Arab positions."

Mark Allen joined in. "The *New Jersey* uses *sabots* to reduce her sixteen-inch bores to eight-inchers — can fire an eight-inch shell fifty miles." There was a babble and the Japanese looked at each other in wonder.

"So Kadafi attacks us," Muira said with sudden bitterness. "Cuts off our oil."

Bernstein nodded. "He hates you almost as much as he hates us. His speeches are filled with it."

"Kadafi's courage is all in his mouth," Fujita said. He tapped the leather-bound copy of the *Hagakure,* which was in its customary place on the table in front of him and his words dropped like stones in a pool, the ripples spreading and bringing every man upright, "The man who sins in soul and speech shall be reborn a dog in the next life."

118

Shouts of "Banzai!" filled the room. Brent found himself waving a fist and crying out with the others. Mark Allen looked at him quizzically out of the corner of his eye and smiled sardonically.

Fujita raised his eyes to a small man almost as tiny as himself, dressed in the uniform of a lieutenant of the Self Defense Force, seated not at the table but in a far corner next to one of the communications men. He was a stranger Brent had never seen before, and the young American realized the stranger must have entered quietly during the meeting and sneaked unnoticed to his place. The man rose to the admiral's gesture as if he were a puppet attached to a string tied to Fujita's hand. Fujita introduced the officer, gesturing. "This is Lieutenant Tadayoshi Koga of the Self Defense Force."

Koga kept his black ferretlike eyes fixed on his notes as he spoke in soft, halting tones. "As you know, most of our vessels were caught and sunk or damaged at their moorings while *Yonaga's* air groups attacked the enemy fields in North Korea."

There were angry grumbles. "You should have joined us," Katsube squeaked, looking up from his pad.

Koga glared at the scribe. "First you must convince the Diet to declare war."

Brent could not contain himself. "My God, what does it take, Lieutenant?"

"An act—a legal act of the Diet," Koga retorted hotly, showing the first glimmer of emotion besides fear. He continued, "Most of you," he gestured at the elderly Japanese, "have been away from Japan for over four decades. You were lucky."

"Lucky?"

The voice thickened. "Yes. You did not see the fire raids, the obliteration of Hiroshima and Nagasaki,

119

people starving in the streets. We had two million dead." His eyes moved over the silent faces. "Of course there is a strong pacifist movement — a movement that disavows violence for any reason."

"But you were attacked," Nobomitsu Atsumi insisted. "And they have embargoed oil even from Indonesia."

The little man sighed. "According to Article Nine of our 1947 constitution — " He hooded his lids and spoke as if he were reading, "Aspiring sincerely to an international peace based on justice and order, the . . ."

He was interrupted by Mark Allen's booming voice as the admiral continued the article, "Japanese people forever renounce war as a sovereign right of the nation and the threat and use of force as a means of settling international disputes." Stunned, Koga stared at the American admiral. "I wrote it," Allen explained, smiling.

The little man pulled himself together, said with surprising timbre and resonance, "It makes no difference. The document exists. And you must remember that when the Arabs attacked, none of our missiles could be fired. Our frigates were not equipped with Phalanx or any other quick-firing antiaircraft guns for in-close defense. Some of our ships were equipped with a single five-inch gun. That was all. They were target practice."

"Some survived," Mark Allen said suddenly.

"Of course. Two frigates and three destroyers. But, as I have said, their armament will not function."

Atsumi said to Koga, "I still cannot understand why the Diet still refuses to act against these international terrorists."

"You have seen the press," Koga lashed back. "There have been peace riots." He waved at the dockyard. "There are pickets out there right now! Why, I

120

understand two of you were ambushed in Ueno Park by Red Army terrorists."

Brent winced with the memory of the ambush and the killing of Yoshi Matsuhara's fiancée, Kimio Urshazawa. Brent glanced at Yoshi. He was staring at a pad on the desk, punished by cruel memories.

Mark Allen came half out of his chair. "Your subs. You have some fine submarines—especially the Yuushio class."

Koga drew his breath audibly. "All seven Yuushios were sunk." There was a groan.

"All seven!" Mark Allen cried with disbelief.

"They were nested next to their tender, which was also sunk. Her magazines exploded. That is what did most of the damage."

"But the others?" Mark Allen said. "A half-dozen others—good boats, the Uzushio class."

Koga looked at the table. His voice was very soft, almost a whisper, "Gone."

"Gone?"

"Scuttled and abandoned after the air raids by their cowardly crews."

Fujita came to his feet angrily, face red and swollen with rage. "Sacred Buddha, I never thought I could live long enough to see this—Japanese rebelling, deserting."

"It was the Rengo Sekigun (Japanese Red Army)," Koga said. "They infiltrated the crews—spread their poison."

Fujita was unconvinced. "This could never happen to samurai. What has happened to *Yamato damashii?* Respect for Nippon—for the emperor?" The men looked up. Fujita brightened. "At least the emperor still has steel in his backbone."

Everyone knew Emperor Hirohito was gravely ill and everyone knew the mortality of a god was a subject that agonized the Japanese. Brent stirred uneasily in an absence of sound disturbed only by ship noises. Finally, Fujita broke the mood by standing and stepping to a chart of the Pacific mounted on the bulkhead behind his chair. He spoke grimly to Koga. "Since Commander Matsuhara damaged a Libyan DC-3 that violated *Yonaga*'s airspace, that madman Kadafi has vowed to destroy us. But he has failed and it has cost him dearly." He was interrupted by cheers and shouts of "Banzai!" He picked up a pointer and the shouts faded. He stabbed the chart, "The Arabs are repairing their *Majestic* here in Surabaya, three thousand kilometers." He glanced at the Americans, "ah, nineteen hundred miles. Far out of our aerial surveillance range." He moved the pointer to the Marianas. "And, here, in the Marianas, they are setting up bases possibly for LRA operations." He fingered the single long white hair dangling from his chin. "An amphibious operation. That is what it will take." He stabbed the pointer at Koga as if it were a weapon. "Amphibious craft. Can you provide us with assault craft?"

"We have four LST's, Admiral," Kaga said. "But we would have to find a way to transfer them to the Department of National Parks with *Yonaga*."

Brent almost chuckled thinking of *Yonga*'s status as a national park. The subterfuge was the only device the Diet would recognize as a screen for her maintenance. But resistance had been fierce, debates at times violent, and only the emperor's personal intervention had turned the tide in favor of Fujita and his carrier.

Fujita's voice filled the room. "Find a way, Lieutenant. Do you understand me? I will not have LRA's bombing *Yonaga* in her anchorage."

Koga stared down with blank eyes. "I will try, Admiral Fujita."

"No! Results, Lieutenant, or this matter will go to

the Imperial Palace and you can bid your career farewell."

Tadayoshi Koga bit his lip. "Yes, sir. I understand, sir."

Fujita turned to Bernstein. "Any new information about long-range aircraft, Colonel?"

"Yes, Admiral. Three squadrons of Constellations are training at Tripoli and an assorted bunch of converted DC-6's and DC-4's are being assembled at the same field."

The old admiral glared at Koga and then thumped the table and turned to Mark Allen. "There is a Dallas nuclear submarine — ah, you call her a SSBN — off Vladivostok?"

"Yes, a boomer, Admiral. It's on permanent station."

"Indonesia?"

"None, Admiral Fujita. There is no strategic threat to the United States from Indonesia. The US Navy is hard put with shortages of every kind to just maintain stations off Archangel, the Barents Sea, Murmansk, the Baltic, Black Sea, the Med."

Fujita struck the chart angrily. "We need reconnaissance. We cannot put to sea again just for reconnaissance. We do not have the fuel and we could be ambushed by aircraft — submarines. That is not the way to use *Yonaga*. We must save her for decisive actions against the enemy battle fleet. Not risk her casually. We need submarines. Just one sub — "

He was interrupted by a knock, and an armed seaman guard stepped into the room. His face was constricted with a strange amalgam of wonder and concern and he appeared to be strangely stimulated and agitated as he announced, "Lieutenant Dale McIntyre is here, Admiral."

"Show him in — show him in," Admiral Fujita said

brusquely. Brent was sure he heard the young guard giggle as he turned to the door and ushered Dale McIntyre in. There were gasps from the officers and a grunted "Sacred Buddha" from Fujita. Dale McIntyre was a woman.

Carrying a valise and a small box, Dale McIntyre walked into the room with long, confident strides. Tall and slender, she appeared to be in her late thirties. She was wearing a tailored blue suit of fine wool that accented the narrow waist and sculpted hips of a graceful, almost coltish body, with long fine limbs and muscles toned by hard exercise. Her breasts appeared large and rounded even under the suit, skin clear and tanned from the effects of long hours in the sun, and her thick mane of magnificent golden hair further testified to a life devoted to the outdoors. Streaked with silver, platinum, and copper-gold, it was swept up elegantly into a chignon that was wrapped behind her head like a rope as thick as a man's thumb. Although not beautiful in the classic sense, with a nose a little sharper than it should have been and lips thin where they should have been full, she was a striking woman who exuded sexuality with every hip-swinging stride. Struck to breathless silence, the old officers, so long deprived, stared hungrily.

It was then Brent realized that most of the old men had probably never seen the full breasts and sculpted hips of a western woman. Dale McIntyre must have appeared as a shapely Amazon to them.

"You are Dale McIntyre?" Fujita said incredulously.

"I am," she said, timbre of her voice low and resonant with strength. She was obviously not cowed by the roomful of Japanese officers who, both old and young, were known for their medieval attitude toward women that challenged the chauvinism of the Arabs they hated. "I have a report," she added. Fujita gestured to the chair. Dale seated herself next to Brent Ross, placed the box on the deck between her chair and Brent's and spread documents before her. Glancing down at the box, Brent caught sight of a shapely nylon-covered calf that shone like polished ivory. His headache faded.

Fujita fired an opening broadside. "Women are not allowed on *Yonaga,* madam."

The woman's large green eyes seized Fujita with glacial coolness. "The CIA is not in the seventeenth century, Admiral."

The admiral slapped the desk with a palm. "Proceed with your report, madam."

"I am *Ms.* McIntyre."

"Proceed, madam."

Dale McIntyre came to her feet, stuffing documents back into her valise. "I refuse, *Mister* Fujita," she said, voice cracking ice. The slight brought a gasp from the officers.

"Very well," Fujita said. The woman paused and all eyes moved to Fujita. Every man in the room knew the report could be critical, could possibly even hold *Yonaga's* survival in the balance. He spit the words as if each was a bite of rotten fruit. "Give your report, Ms. McIntyre," he conceded. And then to save face, "And then leave this ship."

"My pleasure on both counts," she said, standing erect and holding several documents before her. "The United States cannot send Japan any more oil," she began.

"We are having trouble maintaining our training schedules, now, with our ration of petrol," the executive officer, Commander Mitake Arai, said. "What about the Persian Gulf states, Kuwait, Bahrain, Oman, and the United Arab Emirates. They have not joined Kadafi's *jihad* and they have enormous oil re-

125

serves."

"True," McIntyre agreed. "But they don't dare challenge Kadafi and, with Iran and Iraq back to open warfare, it's too risky to try to send loaded tankers through the Straits of Hormuz anyway." She tabled a document and looked up. "Don't forget, the US is on strict rationing and we are hard put to maintain our allies in western Europe. Japan gets most of the Alaskan production now."

Fujita waved a hand and spoke to his executive officer. "We will manage, Commander Arai. Let the civilians drive their Hondas less." There were tension-relieving chuckles.

McIntyre continued while a dozen pairs of eyes fixed on her like shipwrecked sailors dreaming of a feast. "Our information indicates the *Majestic* being repaired in Surabaya will take at least four more months to repair." She looked around, "She's a seven-hundred-foot ship, can operate forty-four aircraft, speed thirty knots, numerous rapid-fire AA guns and dual purpose seventy-six-millimeter cannons."

"Where is the rest of the force?" Arai asked.

"Tomonuto Atoll."

"Why, it's radioactive still from our hydrogen-bomb tests over thirty years ago," Mark Allen said.

"Yes," McIntyre agreed. "And uninhabited."

"This is confirmed?" Fujita asked.

"Negative, Admiral," Dale said. All eyes followed her hand as she placed it on her hip. Then, self-consciously, she dropped it to her side. She continued, "With our satellite system destroyed and with a shortage of LRA's and—don't forget—the US has been forced to pull back to Hawaii—it is impossible to reconnoiter every backwater on earth." She rubbed her temple thoughtfully. "But we have heard rumors about great ships from the natives."

"Natives?" Mark Allen exclaimed. "But you just said Tomonuto Atoll is uninhabited."

McIntyre nodded. "Yes. Of course. That makes intelligence gathering more difficult. We picked up rumors at Truk."

"A base is more than just an anchorage," Mark Allen offered.

The CIA agent smiled, a brilliant display of perfect white teeth. "I know," she said, glancing down at a dossier. "We have information they have two depot ships and a forty-thousand-ton oiler anchored there." A rumble of alarm filled the room.

Fujita said to the woman, "According to our information, the other carrier is the new Spanish ship *Principe de Asturias*—seven hundred feet, fifty aircraft, speed thirty-two, heavily armed with AA and the latest radar."

McIntyre nodded agreement. "And they have two cruisers," she continued. "The Arabs bought the old Babur—ex-British *London*—from Pakistan. Seven thousand four hundred tons, length five hundred seventy feet, main battery six, five-point-two-five-inch Armstrong-Vickers, Mark twenty-six rapid fire guns and 'numerous' twenty-millimeter Orlikons and forty-millimeter Bofors in dual and quadruple mounts." She continued reading while the officers stared. She described the Arab cruiser *Umar Farooz*, ex-British HMS *Llandaff* bought from the Bangladesh Navy. The ship was only three hundred sixty feet long, but was very fast with a top speed of thirty-four knots and she was loaded with armament: four, four-point-five-inch cannons in her main battery and a reported twenty-four twenty-millimeter Orlikons and twenty forty-millimeter Bofors in her secondary."

The officers eyed each other grimly. Brent's headache seemed to grow again. He gripped his forehead as Fujita spoke. "We know about their cruisers. Our information indicates their escort consists of seven Gearing class destroyers."

"Yes, Admiral," she said. "But our information indicates at least twelve Fletchers and Gearings with their standard five and six five-inch thirty-eight main batteries, torpedoes, and loaded with AA."

Fite came to life. "Fire-control radar?"

Dale shook her head and Fite appeared visibly relieved. "Surface and air search, only, Captain." Her eyes moved restlessly around the room, finally coming to rest on Admiral Fujita. "I have an encryption, box — for NIS."

Fujita inclined his head toward Mark Allen who said, "Lieutenant Ross is in charge of ciphers — computers. See him after the meeting, Ms. McIntyre."

McIntyre looked around. "Lieutenant Ross?"

Mark Allen smiled and said, "He's sitting next to you."

"Oh," she said, turning to Ross and smiling lavishly. Brent returned the smile and mumbled a greeting.

Mark Allen said to Fujita, "May I introduce the staff, Admiral?"

Grimacing, the old admiral nodded slowly. Mark Allen stood and quickly introduced the officers and gave a brief description of each man's duties. The woman's green eyes moved with the introductions and the old Japanese officers stared back almost foolishly, like schoolboys looking for approval. Fujita was obviously disconcerted and drummed the table impatiently. A woman had invaded his realm. To him this could only mean trouble, and he could see it on the faces of his men. Brent Ross had seen the admiral's hostility to women over two years ago when the Israeli intelligence agent, Sarah Aranson, had come aboard. Fujita drove her off the ship.

"We need submarines. We do not have the capacity to reconnoiter the Marianas and Tomonuto Atoll by air," Fujita said.

The CIA agent pulled a single sheet from her valise and sighed. "As you know," she said, staring at the document, "the US Navy does not have enough subs to maintain its own surveillance stations. However, with the shortage, several WW II museum boats have been refitted and one, the *Blackfin,* is on loan to the CIA. However, we had plans for her off the Crimean Peninsula."

"Can we have her?" Fujita asked, eyes gleaming like a hungry schoolboy eyeing a candy bar. "Ms. McIntyre," he conceded again. Brent almost laughed. The old man would do anything to gain a new weapon.

"I can request it," she said.

"And add my signature," Mark Allen said with youthful eagerness. "I'll make a request through my own channels. Where is she?"

"New York." Her eyes ran down another document. "She is only partially manned. She has an exec, two other officers, and only thirty men."

"The *Blackfin* is of the Gato class. I made two patrols on the *Grouper* in '42 as the exec. Send me," Mark Allen said, staring at Admiral Fujita.

The woman's voice was casual. "Can you command her, Admiral Allen?"

Mark Allen swallowed hard. "I didn't expect the command. Lord, I'm rusty, of course. And how can you offer me the command when we don't have her?"

"Of course you don't have her." She tapped the desk thoughtfully. "She isn't due to be operational in the Black Sea for another year when two Dallas class boats are due for overhaul. But with your request, I think you'll get her, and we would need a captain. That's what's holding us up now, the shortage of experienced diesel-boat skippers."

"You said she has an exec," Allen said.

"Lieutenant Reginald Williams," she said, glancing at her notes. "An experienced sub man, but only in nuclear boats."

Fujita broke in impatiently. "Put in your requests. This could be academic if we are refused. I will contact the Imperial Palace and see what pressures can be put on the Pentagon from there." And then emphatically, "I want that sub." He nodded at Dale. "You may be seated, Ms. McIntyre," he said.

The woman seated herself, and as she rocked to tuck under her skirt, she brushed against Brent Ross's arm. He could feel the hard muscle under the wool and found even the inadvertent touch exciting. His headache faded.

Fujita eyed his staff silently. He began to talk, emphasizing his words with the pointer's tip against the desk. "Remember to be alert not only when on watch on *Yonaga,* but when ashore. We have had problems with terrorists and Japanese Red Army swine. No man is to go ashore unarmed." He moved his eyes to the woman. "Where is your escort, Ms. McIntyre?"

She smiled, patted an armpit. "Here. My Baretta — nine-millimeter, seven-round automatic."

"You are alone?"

"Yes."

Fujita shook his head. "You do not have eyes in the back of your head. Our brave enemies like to attack from behind — especially unescorted women and children." He looked at Brent Ross. "See to it she is escorted home."

Brent nodded with forced solemnity. "Yes, sir." He saw both Mark Allen and Yoshi Matsuhara suppress smiles.

Fujita stood slowly and turned to a small paulownia

wood shrine attached to the wall under the emperor's picture. Built like a tiny, open cabin with a miniature log roof and framed with delicately carved lotus blossoms, it contained a number of icons set like markers in a graveyard; a talisman of the Eight Myriads of Deities, a Buddha from Three Thousand Worlds, a minute gold Buddha of exquisite workmanship from Minatogawa, a gold-and-platinum tiger representing the revered, *tora,* who wanders far, makes his kills but always returns home, and a number of good-luck charms from the shrines at Kochi and Yasakuni. Picking up a small, knobbed stick, the old sailor tapped a tiny gong hanging from the shrine three times — he considered odd numbers lucky, two and four signified death and were avoided.

Everyone stood and the Japanese and Brent clapped three times. Fujita reached far back into the past. "Oh, Bodhidharma," he said, naming the first patriarch of Zen who preached about enlightenment through intuition, "let each of us find enlightenment through intuition and meditation like the flash of a meteor's path. Let us transcend the illusion of ego and reality, live free in the world, free from the barrier of preconception, free from the known which is imagination, memory, and the past, and free from the unknown which is nothing but the future defiled by our memories." Running a finger over the lotus blossoms, he continued, "Free *Dai Nippon* from the slough of hedonism and irreverence for the emperor like the lotus which grows in mud but bursts out to blossom into a beautiful bloom." He raised a tiny hand and his voice swelled, "Let our nation find her glory again in the glow from the sacred *Mikado.*" He looked over his men slowly before continuing, this time calling on the most important Shinto god. "And Amaterasu-O-Mi-Kami, help us find a way to rid this world of terror, exorcise the devils—Kadafi, Khomeini, Arafat, Jumblatt, those of the Red Army, Nidal . . ."

He was interrupted by shouts of "Banzai!" and *"Tenno heiko banzai!"* ("Long live the emperor!")

He waved his men to silence. Finally, in a soft voice, he said, "You are dismissed."

Quietly, the staff rose and filed through the door. Brent led Dale McIntyre to a small conference room across the passageway.

Chapter IV

"When you come on board this ship you shed a couple of centuries," Dale said from a stiff-backed chair across the small table from Brent. The room was small, sparse, and designed for not more than four men. With two armed guards standing inside the door, the small space was filled to capacity. She waved at the guards. "My firing squad?"

Brent laughed. "The admiral's probably afraid you'll stowaway."

It was Dale's turn to laugh and Brent liked what he saw—even, polished white teeth and lines of good humor that came to life at the corners of her eyes and mouth. But they were deeper than he expected, indicated a few more years than he had first guessed.

"I'm Dale," she said.

"I'm Brent, Dale."

"I have a box for you," she said. He raised an eyebrow and held back a smile with effort. She reddened, obviously disquieted by the gaffe—or was it a Freudian slip. The green eyes averted to the deck and she reached down. "I mean, I have your encryption box." She placed a small package on the table and her aplomb returned quickly. "It's hard-wired and programmed to access your AN-UYK-Nineteen data processor. Your codes and ciphers will be safe for another million bytes."

Brent was all business. "The software?"

She shook her head. "Sorry, it's not ready. I'll give you a call when it comes in." She hunched forward. "I can't understand Fujita." She waved, "And the others."

"Like a time capsule," he offered.

"He's a living, breathing ghost of the past," she said.

"He also has the greatest military mind I have ever known, Dale."

"He's also the greatest bigot."

Brent felt anger stir. "He's a nineteenth-century man, Dale. From a different age."

"Eighteenth century and he'd better come of age."

He felt good humor slip away. "Japan needs him and we need him. Without Admiral Fujita, world terrorism would be running wild. Israel would have gone under three years ago, Japan would have been beaten into submission, the Middle East lost, America on the ropes, NATO destroyed . . ."

"I know. I know," she said impatiently. "I wasn't trying to antagonize you." She brushed a long golden strand of hair back from her eye. The gesture was graceful and completely feminine. The guards watched and Brent stared, fascinated. It had been a long time since Mayumi Hachiya. "But he was rude to me, Brent." Her voice became hard. "I don't allow insults. I felt like slapping him." She hunched forward. "He's not a god, Brent, and he didn't have to order me off the ship."

"What do you mean?"

"I mean I would never, under any circumstances, come on board this ship again, anyway."

"A woman does not belong on a warship."

134

"You're another Fujita."

"Can't you understand, Dale, thousands of men — lonely, forced to deny natural . . ."

"Why don't you say it — horny! Randy!"

"Of course. The presence of a woman could lead to — ah, disruption."

"I had no intention of *disrupting* Fujita and taking him to bed when I came on board this ship." A pixieish smile crept over her face. "Anyway, the thought is appalling." She touched his hand with a single finger while the guards watched wide-eyed. He pulled back despite the warmth of the touch and the deep tingling.

"I think I'd better escort you back to your office."

She laughed softly. "It's not necessary."

"Orders."

Her smile lost its humor. "Oh, yes. God himself has spoken. The eleventh commandment, 'Thou shalt not disobey Fujita's every whim'."

There was a sharp cracking sound as Brent slapped the desk with an open palm. "He's my superior officer. Of course I obey my orders."

Her lips curled down harshly. "You're the 'American Samurai,' aren't you?"

He shrugged. "That's what Kadafi and his killers call me."

"I've seen it in the press."

"The Japanese media are run by traitors."

The line of her lips became mocking and the polished emerald of the incongruous eyes penetrated his like lasers. "I hear you're good at chopping off heads."

Brent felt heat on his face and his voice was hard. "It's time to leave." He patted the encryption box. "I've got to deliver this," he said, rising.

Followed by Dale McIntyre and the two guards, Brent's temper cooled and he led the way aft to the ship's Combat Information Center (CIC). They walked through the chart house where two quartermasters were hand-correcting charts with pen and ink and then the radio room where both old tube sets and modern, transistorized receivers and transmitters sat side by side, bolted to the shelves. Ratings and officers turned and greeted Brent, offering congratulations on his victory and recovery. Brent smiled and returned the salutes with friendly, warm words, addressing each by his name. The woman's body did not go unnoticed as they passed.

Dale stiffened under the eyes and held her head high and smiled lightly in the mood of sparkle and pleasure all attractive women feel when hungry male eyes probe, penetrate, and disrobe. Like most women with alluring figures, she was not averse to standing in the limelight. Finally, they entered a compartment filled with banks of electronic equipment and plotting boards. The lights had been rheostated down to a dull rose glow to protect the night vision of the men on watch and to make the glowing scopes more easily read. The green glow of the scopes merging with the rose lights gave everyone a bilious cast, outlined veins and lips in blue and colored teeth purple as if one were viewing the cast of a cheap horror movie. Brent waved and pointed at the two guards who waited at the door.

The half-dozen men on watch came to their feet, shouting "Welcome back, Mr. Ross!" "How do you feel, Lieutenant?" "Shot down another one, Mr. Ross!" No one mentioned Takii.

"As you were. As you were," Brent said thickly. Shaking hands and greeting each man he felt the

136

strong force of comradeship permeating the room. He belonged here, was part of *Yonaga*. There were no doubts. At that moment, he felt he was in a room filled with brothers—the fraternity of war. Admiral Mark Allen was wrong.

Working his way toward the back of the compartment, Brent led Dale to a console where a tall, thin, scholarly young American with bifocals perched on his thin nose like an elongated drop of water stood grinning. Grasping Brent's hand, he offered congratulations on Brent's kill and his rapid recovery. Brent patted the young man's shoulder and introduced him to Dale.

"This is Electronics Technician Martin Reed," Brent said. "As you were," Brent said, gesturing at the console, which consisted of a keyboard beneath rows of dimly lighted switches and buttons, a green scope minus the customary sweeping beam of a radar scan, and more switches and buttons tilted down for easy access above the operator's head like the instrumentation in the cockpit of an airliner.

Reed settled back down into his padded chair and Brent handed him the encryption box. "Put it into operation at twenty-four hundred hours tomorrow night," Brent said.

"Aye, aye, sir."

Dale looked around the room in awe. "I thought the admiral was old-fashioned—believed in the old methods."

Both men laughed. Brent said, "Unless the 'old method' menaces his ship. Then he learns fast."

"Yes indeed," Martin agreed.

Dale waved at the console. "That's ESM, isn't it." She placed a hand on the countertop and leaned forward, other arm akimbo, hand planted on a sculpted hip perfectly outlined by the tight, hard finish of the wool skirt. A half-dozen heads turned for fleeting glances of the marvelous spectacle.

"Very good," Martin said. "ESM—Electronic Support Measures." He patted the machine pridefully. "This is the Raytheon SLQ Thirty-Two—the best. With its port and starboard antenna assemblies it gives us three-hundred-sixty-degree azimuth coverage in all bands and instantaneous frequency measuring—we call it IFM. It has its own digital processor. In its passive mode, this little baby intercepts electronic emissions, can identify them within thirty-two milliseconds by PRF—ah, sorry, Pulse Repetition Frequency, type of scan, scan period, and frequency by accessing its own eighty K threat library." He tapped the scope with a single finger. "And then we read out bearings and ranges here on its CRT."

"No emissions for an enemy to pick up."

"Yes. Absolutely undetectable Ms. McIntyre."

"It sounds an alarm when it has a contact?"

Martin nodded. "A buzzer in the operator's earphones and a gong everyone can hear."

"But it can go active," Dale observed.

"Very good, ma'am," Martin said, running a finger over four switches like the caress of a lover. "In the active mode, it becomes ECM—ah, sorry, Electronic Counter Measures, jams broadband signals, that is, on a wide frequency bracket, or spot-jamming on specific frequencies. In the old days, when we had to defend against missile attacks, that was a life or death function."

"Jamming the missiles' terminal guidance systems?"

"Correct, ma'am. But now, our search is concentrated on ship and aircraft radar homing in on us— and subs, too, of course. Can be just as deadly as missiles."

"But it's not on line with fire-control," Dale said.

The young technician smiled. "That's verboten Ms. McIntyre. *Glasnost,* you know." They all chuckled.

Brent stabbed a finger overhead. "All fire control is done up there, in the director with old-fashioned optical range finders."

"I see." The woman looked around the room, at the pulsing green radar scopes and their restless, sweeping beams, the men now staring at their sets instead of her body. "Why man this equipment in port. You're getting nothing but harbor clutter."

Brent spoke to the question. "Fujita's orders. Training, and we can spot small vessels that approach too close and our air search, L- and S-band, is effective." Dale nodded understanding.

Brent heard a guard cough loudly. "Time to leave, Ms. McIntyre," Brent said.

The woman said to Reed, "Thanks for the tour, Technician Reed."

The young man smiled up at Dale. "Come back soon, Ms. McIntyre."

Dale laughed, a dazzling display of genuine humor and flashing teeth as white as new snow. "Sorry. Fujita would have me hung from the yardarm and drawn and quartered."

A chuckle swept the room. Only then did Brent realize every man at every station had been listening to every word. He led Dale out of the room while the eyes followed.

Dale insisted on a detour to the pilot house before entering the elevator. With the guards following doggedly, they entered the compartment as wide as the bridge. The woodwork was oak, decks scrubbed

139

teak, and polished brass glistened everywhere like gold jewelry in Tiffany's window. Only two ratings were on watch. Both snapped to attention and then relaxed slightly at Brent's command of, "At ease — as you were."

In the front of the room under rows of armored brass portholes there was the usual huge wheel served with varnished line, the gyro repeater hooded in shining brass in front of it, a magnetic compass, speed across the bottom indicator, speed through the water indicator, four engine rev counters, and four engine-room telegraphs also polished with operating-room fervor. The rear of the bridge was the navigational area with its chart table, drafting machine and parallel rules, dividers, and pencils in their usual slots beneath the table. Above the table were dozens of volumes containing the infinite number of solutions to spherical triangle problems given the navigator by his elevations on stars, planets, or the sun, estimated position and Greenwich Civil Time. To one side was mounted a small radar repeater with an eyepiece in its coned hood, while to the other side the familiar wheel of a radio direction finder (RDF) projected down from the overhead. Banks of radios for ship-to-ship communications were bolted neatly onto shelves next to the radar repeater, and beneath the chart table rows of chart drawers were locked closed against the ship's roll.

"Beautiful. Beautiful," Dale said. "One could have surgery here."

"This is *Yonaga*," Brent said simply. He waved in an encompassing gesture. "Eight-inch armor. Don't forget, *Yonaga* is a member of the greatest class of battleships ever laid down. It would take a direct hit from a large-caliber shell to put this station out of action."

Dale gestured to the rear. "No LORAN? No modern aids to navigation?"

Brent shook his head. "Admiral Fujita insists on the old methods wherever possible. Commander Atsumi is probably the best navigator on earth."

The woman surprised Brent with her knowledge. "But in foul weather you can't get sights. We've got a boat in New York and I've done a lot of boating — long trips in the Caribbean and along the east coast. You would have to use DR exclusively."

Brent nodded. "Atsumi is uncanny at dead reckoning."

She smiled, a warm inviting look that almost brought Brent's hands up and made him ache to touch her. "He's had a lot of practice," he said, gripping the sides of his trousers. They turned toward the elevator.

Dock B-2 was the single largest facility at Yokosuka. Surrounded by warehouses and service buildings, the facility was used for replenishment and repair. It was fitted with the usual tracked cranes that leaned over the ships like tired old birds, raising and lowering pallets with bent beaks. *Yonaga* occupied most of the dock space with two of her Fletchers close astern. Scaffolding had been rigged up the carrier's side all the way to the signal bridge and yard workmen and ship's company were busy installing new navigation and signal lights, cargo lights, and replacing a half-dozen twenty-five-millimeter triple-mounts with new mounts. Gangs were everywhere, scraping and painting in man's endless war against the cancer of the sea, rust. And the sounds pounded home as they could never penetrate when one was inside a closed compartment in the ship; the rumble of the steel wheels of railroad transporters, whine and squeal of power cranes, truck engines in low gear straining under heavy loads, the machine-gun blasts of pneumatic tools, the electric hissing and popping of the huge automatic welders, the battlefield reports of the riveters' hammers.

Stepping off the gangway onto the dock, Brent was followed by Dale and two new guards, each carrying a 7.7 millimeter Arisaka slung over his shoulder. They were old hands who Brent had known for over two years. The leading rate was that of Azuma Kurosu, a Watertender First Class, who was lean and wiry and highly respected as one of the most capable members of the crew of Engine Room Three and the ship's champion at the violent sport of *kendo*. The man was a ferocious fighter and had fractured several skulls with his flashing stave while Brent had known him.

The second guard was Kenzo Nakayama, who was also a plank owner and the oldest seaman in the world. Although he was a capable armorer and knew his weapons better than most men knew their wives, he was a brawler and, despite his sixty-two years, his squat physique, barrel chest, and long arms that dangled at his sides simianlike gave the impression of a rolling, walking riot waiting for a chance to explode. His numerous fights had kept him broken down to his low rank. Both guards had the black hair and round, smooth faces of men decades younger. Brent knew Admiral Fujita had assigned the formidable pair because of their fierce reputations. Brent patted his armpit where his 6.5 millimeter Otsu—an automatic pistol that was so fast it was known as "the baby Nambu"—nestled in its leather holster.

As if ordered by a silent command, the group

stopped and turned and stared at *Yonaga* with the silence and awe you find gripping spectators staring at natural phenomena like the Grand Canyon or the great falls at Victoria. No man could ever become brazen or indifferent to the size of *Yonaga;* not Brent, not the old guards. Standing only a few feet from the ship and staring up, *Yonaga's* gracefully curved superstructure seemed to reach up into the low-hanging clouds like a steel Everest. The men scurrying on the giddying heights of the scaffolding were ants or other tiny insects, not humans at all. As the foursome stared, a small cloud detached itself from the overcast and crept over the vessel, concealing most of her forward director and upper works. Indeed, the leviathan did reach into the clouds.

"Incredible," Dale said. "As high as the sky and a mile long."

Brent chided her, "A fifth of a mile long, Dale."

"Is that all? My God," Dale breathed, "I still can't believe that's actually a ship—something built by men."

"There are new tankers that are longer."

"I've seen some in New York Harbor. Maybe they're longer, but they're not that massive." She groped for words. "Ah, that tall, intricate, ah—complex. This is a warship, an airdrome, a skyscraper, a city . . ."

"And Fujita . . ."

She looked at him with an eyebrow raised in surprise. "Why, yes . . . of course, it is Fujita."

With Watertender Kurosu leading and Seaman Kenzo following, they walked toward the gate house which was located between two huge warehouses. They passed concrete barriers staggered like old European "dragon's teeth" so that a vehicle could not pass. Spotted in sandbagged emplacements, a dozen

Nambus pointed their barrels at the ten-foot, barbed-wire, chain-link fence enclosing the entire area. Their gun captains exchanged salutes with Brent as they passed.

"You don't take any chances, do you, Brent?" Dale said, moving close to the American and brushing his sleeve with her arm. He felt a familiar excitement begin to race deep inside. He did not move away.

Brent waved at the gate house where a half-dozen seaman guards stood at the barrier with slung rifles while two other guards manned phones inside the small window-lined house. "Last year when the ship was in dry dock a couple of terrorists tried to ram a truckload of HE through our barriers and drop twelve tons of plastique into the dry dock. Could've knocked her off her blocks—been the end of everything."

"Obviously, they failed."

Brent's mind filled with thoughts of that day, the murderous Kathryn Suzuki—his incendiary lover for an unforgettable night—behind the wheel. The machine gun firing, the pistol bucking in his hand, the terrorist he shot from the fender, the smashed gate house, the riddled truck overturning, Kathryn looking up at him, blood welling from a wound in her lovely breast, pleading as he pulled the trigger of his Otsu, the small blue hole between her eyes, brains splattering the pavement, the spasmodic jerking as death rushed in. "Yes," Brent said simply. "They failed."

Passing the gate house and walking under the raised barrier, the chief petty officer in charge, Chief Teruhiko Yoshitomi, an original member of *Yonaga*'s crew and Yoshi Matsuhara's crew chief, snapped to attention along with his guards. Short and heavyset, he was a striking man with skin like tanned lemon, head crowned with a magnificent mane of white hair. He was the best mechanic on the ship and took great pride in his work. Every pilot wanted him, but Yoshi would not release him. "Good to see you well again, Mr. Ross. And congratulations on your kill. We do not get many from the B5N's third seat, and now you have two. Marvelous shooting, sir." The man's smile was broad and warm.

"Thank you, Chief Yoshitomi," Brent said, pausing. He waved toward a cluster of buildings that concealed the parking lot. "Any of our friends out there?"

"There must have been a hundred of them out there this morning, sir."

"Demonstrators?" Dale said. "I didn't see them when I parked. One or two bums, that's all."

"They were gone by ten hundred hours and the bums you saw were there to count and record traffic. Sometimes they even photograph everyone coming or leaving the ship."

Dale said to the old chief, "How did you know there were a hundred?"

"I could smell them, ma'am."

"Any now?" Brent asked.

Yoshitomi raised his nose and sniffed. "Twelve, sir."

"Japanese Red Army swine?"

"Probably, Mr. Ross," Yoshitomi said. "But they have their rights—constitutional rights." He shrugged helplessly.

"Democracy always protects the criminal," Brent said bitterly.

He exchanged salutes with the chief and turned toward the parking lot, Kurosu leading, Brent side by side with Dale and then the sauntering

145

Nakayama.

Chief Yoshitomi had been wrong in his prediction; there were eleven demonstrators. Walking in a ragged line and carrying signs, they paraded at the entrance to the parking lot. All were filthy, unkempt, shoulder-length hair disheveled, men unshaven. Five of the group were women; at least Brent thought they were women. It was hard to tell because all were dressed alike; trousers, sandals or tennis shoes, torn shirts hanging over their belts, and no hats. But at least some had beards and Brent assumed these to be men. Brent read a few of the signs: "Japanese Die For American Imperialists," "Blood For Oil," and the omnipresent "Yankee Go Home" paraded past. Drawing closer to the group, Brent patted his armpit and the guards unslung their Arisakas and held them at a casual high port like Kendo staves.

The demonstrators stopped, bunched together, blocking the entrance to the parking lot. Kurosu did not even pause and Brent pushed Dale back and quickly overtook Kurosu. He took the watertender by the arm and stopped him only feet from the line and a tall, angular Caucasian who appeared to be the leader. He was a strong-looking man with gray streaks in his tangled shoulder-length hair and snarled beard. His mustache and beard were fouled with forgotten specks of food and tobacco and his teeth were stained as if they had been dipped in lemon and tar. He reeked.

Brent had encountered the same situation six months earlier when leaving the ship with Yoshi Matsuhara. Challenged by the leader of the demonstrators, Eugene Neeb, an unlikely Communist from a wealthy family in Arcadia, California, he had fought his way through and broken Neeb's jaw in the melee. The fight had led to the ambush in Ueno

Park and the death of Yoshi's fiancée, Kimio Ursha-zawa. Brent killed Neeb. The memories were tortur-ous and painful. Was it happening again? It seemed like déjà vu. Why didn't the police clear these tramps and traitors away, Constitution or not? They were a travesty, a blot on civilization. And there wasn't a policeman in sight. He felt his muscles bunch and tighten, heart barging against his ribs, the familiar heat coiling deep, the crystal-bright sharpening of his senses. Atavistic rage was rising. He could kill—he wanted to kill.

"Yankee killer," the tall Caucasian shrieked in Brent's face, waving his sign menacingly to and fro in a short arc.

Gritting his teeth, the lieutenant choked back the fury and spoke in a surprisingly even, modulated timbre. "Move. I'll ask you once. Move."

The entire group stood immobile; only the signs moved in short arcs above their heads. They grunted and wheezed incoherently like a pack of Neander-thals. Then there were shouts of "Die, *Yonaga!*", "Nuke the Yankees!", "Yankee shit go home!" One hulking man waved his sign at Dale, screaming, "I'm going to shove this sign up your pussy, slut!"

Stunned by the sexual epithet, Brent felt the white heat break loose, the ravening beast of hatred and anger devouring the last vestige of reason, civiliza-tion. Snarling, he charged the leader who brought his sign down sharply, aiming at Brent's head. But before the blow could be driven home, Kurosu's Ari-saka flashed up in a blur and caught the man's hand, breaking both the handle of the sign and the demonstrator's wrist. The sign flew through the air and the man collapsed to his knees, clutching his wrist and screaming in pain.

The others rushed in, flailing out with signs and

fists. With Azuma Kurosu on one side and Kenzo Nakayama on the other and Dale close behind, Brent waded into the middle of the knot of terrorists who wailed and screamed like spirits in a purgatorial hell. The two guards made vicious weapons of their rifles, fighting them like two-handed staves, cracking jaws and, in particular, ears, with painfully disabling blows. Two men fell with broken jaws almost immediately while a third dark, squat man moved on Brent.

Broad-shouldered, he was a powerfully built man with dark, thick hair, head big-nosed and gaunt-boned with a heavy-bearded jaw. His complexion was dusky, and his birdlike eyes dilated and glittering with madness like those of an Arab in the grip of hashish. And, indeed, Brent knew he was right when the man bellowed in a spray of spittle, "I am Nazik abdul Habash. *Allah Akbar!*"

The power of the shout stopped everyone like a freeze frame in a Hollywood action drama. Then Nakayama moved toward the Arab. "No!" Brent said, grabbing the guard's arm. Brent smiled, an icy, frightening look, "he's my guest."

Dragging their two injured members back, the demonstrators formed a semicircle while Dale, Nakayama, and Kurosu stood behind Brent. There was the thumping sound of a dozen boots striking pavement and Brent saw Chief Teruhiko Yoshitomi and five guards rush up, form ranks with rifles clubbed. Now they outnumbered the enemy, could easily force their way through. But a strange compulsion, a cold force like a giant's hand, clutched at him, focusing his entire being on the sneering face before him.

"We will clear this rabble away for you, Mr. Ross," Chief Yoshitomi said.

"Why not massacre us, you cowardly swine," the

148

Arab wheedled in a voice that singed. "You are experts at killing helpless people."

"We've never bombed an airliner or shot up a school bus, 'peoples' hero,'" Brent taunted.

Yoshitomi waved his men forward. "No!" Brent commanded, gripping Yoshitomi's arm and still smarting from the sexual epithet hurled at Dale. "There is something to settle first." Brent was the senior officer present, had made the decision. The Japanese stepped back and leaned on their arms.

Habash's eyes flitted around like a reptile preparing to strike. He knew he was one-on-one with his hated enemy. Brent crouched and balled his fists, but left them at his sides. He was still weak from the effects of his wounds, but the flow of adrenaline had charged his muscles with new strength. Anyway, the old feeling to attack, to obliterate, was there—overwhelmed every restraint. He hated the beast before him and sized him up like a professional fighter. The Arab's arms were thick and ridged with the taut muscles of a man accustomed to hard labor or physical training. Lumpy with scar tissue, his balled fists were the size of pork loins. Brent guessed the man was an experienced brawler, perhaps even a professional assassin. Watching his enemy's feet, he saw the minute shift in weight.

The first blow came from the level of the knees and it came up so fast Brent barely had time to duck as it whistled past his cheek and scraped the skin from his temple. Instinctively, the American stepped to his left, dropped low, and brought his right up like a sledgehammer and caught the Arab on the right side of the chest, feeling the blow impact so hard his teeth clashed together and spittle flew from his mouth with a grunt. He felt ribs give, maybe break, and the man gasped and spray thick with

149

mucus whooshed from his lips. Cheers. Excited shouts.

But the man was a block of granite, muscled like a professional wrestler; he shifted his weight with the grace of a dancer, his left-handed swing bouncing off the point of Brent's shoulder and pounding off his temple.

Even though the blow glanced off Brent's head, in his weakened condition he felt as if someone had slammed an opaque door shut in his head and fired rockets across his retinas. He leaped back, shaking his head, clearing the darkness and the flashing lights. Grinning, Habash moved forward, lashing out like the brawler he was.

The swings were round and wide, almost as if the man was inviting Brent to move inside to take his easy shots. Dropping low, the American took the opening, coming up inside, accepting two powerful hits to the shoulders and the side of his head, clashing his teeth together and lacerating his tongue, the taste of his own blood thick and metallic. But he felt his counterpunch crash into the Arab's cheek in return. There was a sound like teeth biting into a green apple and Brent knew he had broken his enemy's cheekbone. But the huge arms were around him and Brent felt he was fighting a bear. Then he noticed the ridged scars on the man's forehead, partially hidden by the hairline. A warning flashed.

The Arab reared back like a poisonous reptile poised for the strike, and then the whipping motion of his head as the snake struck. The blow was aimed at Brent's nose and mouth and would have crushed the flimsy cartilage and sheared off his front teeth if it had landed. But the lieutenant had anticipated it and dropped, pushing with his hands with all of his power born of panic and rage, breaking the grip and

150

avoiding the murderous lunge. Off balance, Nazik abdul Habash was caught by Brent's two fists, fingers entwined to form a single lethal block like a tree stump that smashed into his stomach. Here Brent found the man's only soft spot and Habash doubled over gasping for air like a drowning man.

Leaping to the side, the American brought the locked fists down on the back of the man's skull, dropping him to the ground like a steer felled by the executioner's hammer. A deep-throated animalistic shout of triumph burst from Brent's lips and he was on his stricken enemy like a great white-smelling blood. But the man was not through, rolling and spitting, screaming into Brent's face, trying to bite his face, his throat. Brent lunged back, teeth bared. Rolling across the pavement, they scattered the blood-crazed spectators, clawing, punching, howling into each other's faces. They crashed into a pile of boxes and pallets, sending an avalanche of crates and trash into the excited crowd and over themsleves. Brent saw a sixteen-penny nail protruding from a board, smashed his enemy's shoulders down onto the rusty point. Habash screamed, tried to roll, but Brent smashed him down again and again, puncturing the man's back, spitting bloody saliva into the Arab's face.

Brent heard Dale's voice from far away. "Stop them! Stop them! For God's sake, stop them!"

Holding Habash down with a forearm across the throat, Brent brought his knee up into his enemy's crotch, twisted to free an arm, and smashed the man's nose. Teeth slashed at his temple and fingernails dug into his back. Two short, brutal punches broke off the Arabs teeth at the gumline and more blood sprayed onto his face. Now the Arab was on his back without the strength to roll and Brent pinned him with his own weight, elbowing up into a sitting position and then punching down with all the strength and power of his two hundred twenty pounds. The nose was flattened to the side over the left cheek which had caved in, both eyes bloodshot and deeply underscored with purple bruises that swelled them to slits. More punches broke the jaw and sent chips of enamel flying, ripped an ear so that it dangled.

"Stop! Stop!" Dale shouted, pulling on his shoulder.

Brent swung at the woman wildly, growling, hissing hate, possessed by a rampaging blood lust he had only felt twice before in his life. But it was back, the beast was loose, and there was no way to control it.

Strong hands were on his shoulders now, and he could hear Chief Yoshitomi. "Enough, Mr. Ross. It's finished, Mr. Ross."

"It's never finished."

It took four men to pull him off.

While two women tended to the writhing, moaning Nazik abdul Habash, Chief Yoshitomi and Dale McIntyre took Brent's arms and led the American through the sullen crowd which had been enlarged by a dozen more supporters who had raced around the corner of a nearby warehouse. Quickly, the outnumbered seaman guards fanned out and rifle-whipped the angry crowd back. Nevertheless, the demonstrators were not finished, a large Oriental slipping through the cordon and charging the American, knife glinting in his hand. "I'm going to cut off your dick, you murdering son-of-a-bitch," he yelled at Brent. "Then your whore won't like you anymore!"

Before anyone could react, Dale, her face contorted in a rictus of rage, leaped forward gracefully, spun like a world-class skater on the tip of one skate and brought a single foot up in a circular blur like a monkey's fist whirled around a seaman's head. Her skirts flew high, there was a glimpse of perfect hips, thighs, and tight, muscular buttocks and her toe caught the man in the throat. Hurled to the side by the rapierlike blow, he dropped instantly as if his legs had melted, knife flying, clutching his mouth and throat, gasping as though a noose had been tightened around his trachea. Immediately, he turned purple, veins in his forehead bulging black, eyes protruding from their sockets like cue balls, gagging, vomiting, strangling on his own gorge.

More blows from the guards, Azuma Kurosu and Kenzo Nakayama swinging their rifles with relish, and the crowd fell back. "American whore!" they screamed, shaking fists at Dale. "We will remember this, imperialist dogs!"

But Brent was numb, still in the grip of the killing frenzy and spitting blood. He was trembling as Yoshitomi and Dale led him to the woman's Honda Accord.

With Watertender Kurosu driving and Seaman Nakayama in the passenger's seat next to the driver, the foursome took the wide Tamagawa Dori to central Tokyo and the magnificent Imperial Hotel where Dale McIntyre had an apartment. "The office can wait until tomorrow," she had said simply as she gave the driver his directions.

She sat close to Brent, holding his hand gently because of his bruised knuckles and using a small linen handkerchief to dab at the blood that trickled out of the corner of his mouth. She had never seen such an explosion of temper. True, she was sure the disgusting sexual insult hurled at her had triggered the violence. Notwithstanding, the big Arab and Brent Ross had reverted back to the savagery of primeval creatures fighting over a carcass, attacking with fists, teeth, fingernails. And the intent had been obliteration. She was sure Brent would have killed the man with sadistic pleasure if the guards had not intervened.

The young American was one of the most attractive men she had ever met. Obviously brilliant, he was a blond giant who gave women pleasure to look at. Even under his dress blues, one could sense his body was cared for and honed rock-hard by exercise, and she could imagine the rack of his ribs under the fine skin, the knotted, rippling stomach muscles, the trim waist and tiny hips, the smooth power of the muscles of his arms and legs. Youth gave way to maturity in the thickening of his neck, the hair which crept up under his loosened collar. There was strength in his face, the broad, noble forehead, the straight Grecian nose, jaw like a fortress, the blue eyes that had sparked at the Arab like arcing electricity.

What a strange boy. What an enigma. At first sophisticated and urbane, but then the raging beast out of control. She wished she were younger. Much younger. She moved closer until her arm was against his, her thigh pressing.

He seemed not to notice. She felt piqued. The carrier had been exciting, knowing every man who looked at her, except that specter Fujita, would have traded his soul for a few minutes between her legs. Men had always responded to her. Had always made the first move. She ran her fingers over the back of his hand, felt the hair covering his wrist. A long-dormant heat stirred deep down and tingled with both delight and discomfort. She squirmed uneasily. *This really isn't the time or place,* she said to herself. The man had just fought for her life and his own — was bruised and hurt, still wrapped in the fury of the fight. She moved away, but his hand came to life. Gripped hers. She sagged back against him.

"You're feeling better?" she said as Kurosu whipped the Honda off the thoroughfare and entered the madhouse of downtown Tokyo traffic. Fortunately, the oil shortage had thinned traffic, but still, the streets were crowded and every car seemed to have a lunatic at the wheel, especially the cabs.

He worked his jaw. "Yes. I bit my tongue and my cheek and my jaw's sore." He moved his body against his seat belt. "Got me a couple good ones in the ribs, too. He was one tough mother . . . ah, I mean, ah — guy."

She laughed, pleased that he was back.

"I hope I didn't shock you," he said, looking straight ahead. "There's something in my family. An ungovernable, out-of-control something that comes on. My father was worse. They called him 'Trigger' because of it." He looked at her with wide, pleading eyes like the young boy he was, begging for understanding and approval.

"They really left you no options, did they, Brent?"

Obviously pleased by the answer and brightening, he shook his head. "You did all right yourself. You clobbered the slob. I never saw anything like it." He looked at her admiringly. "You're fast — quick. A hell of an athlete. Does the CIA teach all of you karate?"

She laughed. "No. I've lived in lower Manhattan for years." She smiled, her widest and warmest. "Call it on-the-job jungle-survival training."

He laughed and then became very serious. They won't forget."

She waved. "Those hoodlums—that tête-à-tête back there?"

"Yes. Don't kid yourself about those bums. That was backed, organized, and choreographed by the Japanese Red Army."

"You're sure."

He nodded grimly. "Fujita did you a service. You're better off staying clear of the ship. And be careful every place you go. They have long memories."

"I'm leaving in three more days."

"Where, Dale?"

"New York. I have a new assignment."

"Good. I'm glad."

But Dale McIntyre was not glad. She wanted this young man to want her to remain—be desperate to see her again, age difference be damned. But the immobile face was implacable, unreadable like a temple icon.

"This is it," Azuma Kurosu said, whipping the Honda to the curb in front of the hotel's brilliantly lighted entrance on the Hibiya Dori.

"You can't park here," Dale protested.

"We shall see," the watertender said, stepping from the car, Arisaka slung over his shoulder. Nakayama followed and took a station at the front fender while Azuma beckoned at the door.

"He's going to escort us up?"

"Right to your apartment door."

"Orders?"

"Of course, Dale, orders."

"You can't change them?"

Brent chuckled. "Not Admiral Fujita's." He glanced up at the soaring new thirty-one story Imperial Tower. Although the Imperial had opened its doors in 1890, it is one of the most modern in Tokyo with a nineteenth-floor pool, numerous restaurants, and a shopping arcade. Brent whistled. "Not shabby at all," he said.

"The CIA keeps several apartments here," Dale said. Quickly, she led Brent and the watertender through the busy lobby to a bank of elevators while dozens of curious eyes followed.

Already engaged in a heated argument with a hotel employee, Kenzo Nakayama remained with the car.

Brent was impressed with Dale McIntyre's apartment. On the thirtieth floor, it was richly furnished with deep carpets, a plump sofa, silk and velvet drapes, and floor-to-ceiling bay windows giving on a magnificent evening vista of greater Tokyo. Watertender Kurosu entered first with his rifle unslung and inspected the kitchen, living room, bedroom, including the huge walk-in closet, and bath. While Dale and Brent giggled, he even flushed the toilet with a broom handle to assure himself a bomb had not been rigged to the flushing handle. Then he stepped out into the hall and stood with ported arm and glowered back at astonished passersby.

Brent sat on the sofa while Dale dropped her jacket on a chair and sat close to him, her tight satin blouse accenting her large, rounded breasts. Carefully, she dabbed at his bruised face with a cloth dipped in a basin of soapy hot water. "A drink, Brent?" she asked, wiping the last of coagulated blood that had run down to the tip of his chin, and, leaning close, breast pressing against his bicep.

"Scotch?"

"Haig and Haig Pinch? Fifteen years old."

He smiled. "You just made a sale. A double, straight up, one ice cube, please."

She paused, "A twist of lemon?"

"In Scotch?"

"Why not? Adds a nice touch—a little finesse."

"Lemons are scarce in Japan."

She laughed. "I know. That's why it's a nice touch."

"Go for it. I feel reckless tonight, Dale."

Dale stood and walked to the kitchen. Although Brent was sore and fatigued to the marrow of his bones, he was entranced by the long stride, the sway of the undulating buttocks. He caught his breath. There was perfect balance there in the graceful sway of the hips from side to side; for each move a countermove like the harmony of counterpointed melodies in a Mozart symphony. *A work of art,* he said to himself. A mallet began to pound against his ribs and a tingling warmth spread low in his groin. He groaned as the door closed on the spectacle.

While Dale prepared the drinks, the young American stood and stared out of the huge bay window at the brightly lighted city. To the southwest, the Ginza—Tokyo's Fifth Avenue—with its huge department stores and elegant shops; to the west, the Imperial Palace with its vast gardens and its spectacular lighted fountain; to the south, the Azubu section with its block after block of jam-packed houses, to the east and north, Shinjuku with its forest of skyscrapers and blaring neon glaring obscenely, and, backdropping it all, the harbor with the myriad of lights of ships, gantries, cargo lights, and rows of amber sodium vapor lamps to penetrate fogs and mists. He heard a movement behind him and returned to the sofa.

Dale handed him his drink and he sighed gratefully as he sank back into the embrace of the cushions. She sat close, sipping her own Scotch and soda while he drank deeply. "That lemon gives it a nice accent," he said, holding the glass up and swirling the amber liquid around the solitary ice cube.

"We still have business," she said.

He raised an eyebrow.

She laughed. "Not that. I mean the software—can you pick it up here tomorrow night? We could have dinner here in the hotel—make it business and pleasure."

"How much pleasure?"

She laughed, a delightful, high musical sound. "You are feeling better, aren't you." She sipped her drink.

"Yes. Meeting you was like an IV of whole blood." He drank and began to enjoy the warm currents of well-being spreading through his tired body.

"You were just wounded, weren't you, Brent?"

Disgusted with himself, he waved his glass. "I didn't mean that—not that hero stuff."

"I know. It was a sweet thing for you to say, though."

He glanced at his watch and drained his glass. "I'd better leave. By now, Nakayama may be rioting with the Tokyo police."

"Take the Honda, Brent. It's better than a cab."

"You need it."

"Not really. I have one stop tomorrow at the office and it's actually easier to use the subway. You can return it tomorrow. Phone me—room three-oh-four-seven."

He rose slowly and hand in hand they walked to the door. He put his arms around her. "Brent," she said softly. "I'm old enough to be your mother."

He chuckled in her ear. "Were you careless in junior high school?"

She held his eyes with hers. "Really, Brent, I'm crowding middle age—only a couple years on the green side of the big four-oh . . ."

He stepped back, ran his eyes over her lean, curvaceous body with a look that saw everything. She blushed, but reveled in the sudden, hungry look that clouded the young man's face and widened his eyes. "You aren't exactly a matron," he said. "You wear those years the way Haig and Haig mellows with its fifteen."

She returned to his arms and held him close, thrilling at the press of his muscular chest, flat stomach, the hard muscles of his legs against her thighs. "Then the difference in age doesn't bother you?"

"No. You?"

She shook her head, held him closer.

His hands roamed her back restlessly, from her neck to her hips. "Then look out for my Oedipus complex," he said, chuckling.

She kissed him gently on the cheek and he left.

Chapter V

"One killed, two broken wrists, four broken jaws, and two fractured skulls," Police Captain Kamagasuo Kudo recited, standing in front of Admiral Fujita's desk.

Brent had been called into the admiral's office with Watertender First Class Azuma Kurosu and Seaman Kenzo Nakayama when the officer stormed aboard. Yoshi Matsuhara had requested to be present and he and the scribe, Commander Hakuseki Katsube, were the only other officers present. The only men seated were Katsube and Admiral Fujita. Flanking the desk, Brent and Yoshi stood at attention while Azuma Kurosu and Kenzo Nakayama stood rigidly just inside the door. Police Captain Kamagasuo Kudo dominated the center of the room in front of the admiral like a magistrate holding court.

"A dead man?" Brent said. "I didn't hit him that hard."

Kudo, a short, fat man of middle years, shifted his eyes to the American. "A blow to the trachea. It was crushed. He strangled." He eyed the big American from head to foot. "You are Brent Ross,

161

the American Samurai?"

Brent looked down on the police captain who had been crushed and creased by the weight of his work into a shape so singular he reminded the American of a giant old crab heaving across the sand of an aquarium. "Some members of the press call me that," Brent said with an amused glint in his eyes.

"You are a violent man, sir. A new corpse yesterday and two years ago you killed a man in an alley two kilometers from here and blinded another. Last year you shot a helpless woman in cold blood . . ."

"Helpless? In cold blood?" Fujita shouted, coming half out of his chair. The old legs gave out and he sank back and leaned over the oak, fists clenched. "She was a terrorist trying to blow us off our blocks in the dry dock. And those men in the alley attacked Brent Ross." He waved a hand in disgust. "Commander Matsuhara and our own seaman guards rescued Lieutenant Ross. He was wounded—could have bled to death. We never saw a single policeman that night—only the next day when it was safe and you were investigating. And yesterday there was no police presence and you knew there were demonstrations. This has been going on for years."

"We were not called, sir."

"I'm to wait for you?"

"Yes, Admiral. Obey the law. We will enforce it."

A red tinge forced its way through the parchment of Fujita's cheeks to lend an ominous blue hue to the old man's complexion. "You do not tell me to obey anything!" A tiny fist slammed down on the desk, "Where were you yesterday when that *gyangu* (gang of criminals) attacked my men and the woman they were escorting?" He turned to

162

Brent. "Did you ever see a policeman, Mr. Ross.

"No, sir."

"We are stretched thin, sir. There are riots in the Ginza, demonstrations outside the Imperial Palace . . ."

Fujita cut him off with a wave. "Do not tell me of your problems, Captain. I will come to an understanding with you." The old man's thin smile caught the policeman off guard. He expected a concession. Brent knew something else was brewing. "I will set up Nambus outside the parking lot and escort my supply trucks with my own armed guards. In that way, your overtaxed personnel can be freed to police the women's toilets in Ueno Park."

"Sir, that is grossly unfair. You can't send guards armed with machine guns and rifles into metropolitan Tokyo."

The lines of the admiral's face rearranged themselves into harsh patterns. "Watch me, Captain Kudo, and I warn you, do not try to stop me."

The policeman sighed with resignation, but there was no surrender in his voice. "I know what you are doing—I know you stand between world terrorism and Japan." He tapped a palm with a pudgy fist. "Without you we would have lost everything, been under Kadafi's heel." Fujita nodded and sank back for the first time. But, Admiral, *Yonaga* is not a sovereign state. We still have laws, a police force to enforce them, a Self Defense Force. You just cannot run rough shod over our laws, ignore our judicial system."

Fujita toyed with the single white hair hanging from his chin. "I am my own law, *Yonaga*'s judge and jury. I will choose the actions of my men and keep this in mind," he pressed down on the desk

163

with both hands, "no one attacks any member of my crew without digging his own grave first." His eyes bored into the captain. "You are a Japanese. How can you forget the value of honor, the sacredness of vengeance—the vengeance of the forty-seven ronin?" He patted the leather-bound copy of the *Hagakure* in its customary place on the desk and paraphrased one of his favorite passages: "Can you sleep on logs, eat dishonor, drink gall while your enemies dance around you like temple devils?"

The man shifted restlessly. There was pain in his voice, "That is unfair, Admiral. I cannot forget—I seek redress, sir. But the citizens of Tokyo pay me to uphold the law."

Fujita waved in irritation. "Uphold your law. But tell your men to give my men a wide berth. We do not savor the taste of gall and dishonor." He flattened both hands on the desk. "Keep in mind, we are samurai, follow Bushido and the instructions of the Mikado."

"He is near *hogyo*."

Brent was an expert in Japanese, but Kudo's use of *hogyo* was confusing. However, he quickly surmised from context and the demeanor of the speaker that *hogyo* was a honorific reserved for the emperor, a level of expression used exclusively for the Son of Heaven by the older Japanese who still observed old customs. Since the language of the ship was English, a tradition Fujita maintained from the turn of the century when the Navy had been patterned after the Royal Navy and English adopted from British advisers, Brent seldom heard Japanese spoken in flag country. However, when he did encounter the native tongue in other parts of the ship, he had learned and used the usual three distinct levels of politeness: talking down, or up, or

164

on a level of equality. There was no English equivalent for *hogyo,* and respect for the emperor had forced the policeman to lapse into his native tongue, using a fourth rare level, reserved for the emperor. Discreetly, Kudo had avoided the ordinary but polite word for death—*shikyo*—and actually said, *nearing demise.*

Fujita had no trouble with the honorific. "Impossible. He is a god. He is just moving on to another plane of existence. You must know that."

"Of course, Admiral. But he is still *hogyo.*"

"Crown Prince Akihito follows Bushido just like his father." The old admiral patted the *Hagakure.* "He will continue the tradition. Japan will remain free."

Kudo stirred restlessly and Brent knew the man had another troubling thought and would not leave until he was finished. He had guts. He moved his eyes back to Brent. "You are a follower of Kensei?"

It was a strange question to ask, and all eyes fell on the American. Brent knew the policeman felt he would be taken aback. His answer was prompt and brought surprise to Kudo's face, "You mean Miyamoto Musashi, who was known as the Kensei—the Sword Saint?"

"He lived four hundred years ago—our most famous samurai," Fujita said, tapping the desk impatiently. "What does Miyamoto Musashi have to do with Lieutenant Ross?"

Kudo's eyes never left Brent's. "Musashi gave birth to kendo." Everyone looked puzzled, but Brent began to see the drift, the subtle turn. Kudo continued, "Kendo that teaches . . ."

Fujita interrupted in midsentence, obviously on to the policeman's track, too. "Teaches a spiritual attitude for life, a code throughout one's existence on earth, respect for elders, hard work, training, living life to the fullest."

Kudo picked up the thread. "And it also teaches to strike with one's stave or rifle or whatever weapon is at hand quickly at several points. Top of the head, right torso, jaw, and, of course, the throat. I have already told you, there were two broken wrists, four broken jaws, two fractured skulls, and we found the dead man's throat crushed as if struck by an expert at kendo."

It was clear to Brent, Kenzo Nakayama, and Azuma Kurosu that Dale McIntyre's kick had killed the man. Without even glancing at each other, the three made a silent compact; no help to the police to indict the woman or anyone else—for that matter. The truth would remain locked within themselves. It was the right thing to do; the samurai thing to do. Honor was at stake. And Chief Yoshitomi and his men were equally immutable, and, perhaps, had not seen the blow that had been struck like a bolt of lightning, anyway. Any information about the woman's lethal attack would have to come from the demonstrators and obviously the policeman had not been able to discover the identity of the killer from them, either.

Watertender Azuma Kurosu stepped forward. "I am the ship's kendo champion," he said, staring at Kudo.

"You struck the fatal blow?"

"Perhaps."

"Perhaps? You do not know?"

Kurosu shrugged. "It was a melee . . ."

"I did it," Kenzo Nakayama said.

"You're both wrong," Brent said. "I distinctly remember hitting him with . . ."

While Fujita watched in amusement, the policeman waved in frustration. "Enough." He gestured at the watertender. "I will take this man in for questioning."

Fujita's face twitched. "You are a brave man, Captain Kudo, and you do have gall."

"I do my duty."

"Do your duty elsewhere, because Watertender Kurosu remains here."

"Sir! May I remind you, when both civilian and military law apply, civilian law takes precedence."

"No," Fujita said. "You may not remind me." He brought the knuckles of both fists together and Brent could see from the old man's expression that he was enjoying himself. "I told you I was judge and jury on *Yonaga*. I will administer punishment." He gestured at Kurosu. "Watertender Kurosu, I find you guilty of assault, and it is my decision to place you on report and restrict you from the ship's bilges for the remainder of the day."

The ridiculous statement was met with guffaws.

"This is ludicrous. I protest!" Kudo exploded, chin quivering.

"Protest all you like. I have made my decision."

Kudo whirled toward the door.

"I did not excuse you."

Kudo took two steps and was caught by Brent on one side and Yoshi Matsuhara on the other. Grabbing his arms and pinning them, the two officers lifted the fat policeman off the deck, turned him, and dragged him back to the admiral's desk. His face was purple and contorted with rage. "You cannot do this!"

"This is my ship—my command. You wait until I dismiss you, is that clear?" Kudo sputtered, incapable of speech.

"Do you understand me?" Fujita repeated.

"Yes. Yes," the captain hissed.

"Request permission to leave," Brent said softly into the man's ear that looked like a red cabbage.

The captain choked on the words, but said them: "Request permission to leave the ship."

"Sir!" Brent commanded.

"Sir!" Kudo repeated.

Fujita smirked with amusement. "Permission granted."

The policeman's departure was accompanied by chuckles and laughter.

Admiral Fujita dismissed everyone except Lieutenant Brent Ross and Commander Yoshi Matsuhara. The two officers remained standing. The admiral fingered the yellow paper of a signal, and in his usual protean fashion, put the policeman out of his mind and replaced him with a new thought. "I have some new information regarding the Arab presence in the Marianas." He stared up at Yoshi. "Our agents report two regiments of the enemy's best troops occupying both Saipan and Tinian. The Fifth Special Combat Battalion on Saipan and the Seventh Parachute Brigade occupying Tinian."

Both officers nodded. "Yes, sir. The units were reported at the last briefing, Admiral," Yoshi reminded him.

Brent saw a fleeting, bewildered look flee across the old face. The memory—the old man's suspect memory, his only concession to the years. But Fujita picked up the thread in casual tones. "These are fine troops—not just the usual cowardly Arabs."

This was new information. "Mercenaries, sir?" Brent asked.

"Yes. German, Russian, English, French . . ."

His face twisted with distaste in anticipation of what was to come, "American and Japanese."

"But no LRA's, sir," Yoshi said.

The admiral nodded agreement. "No aircraft have been seen operating. This has been confirmed by our observers on Aguijan."

"The Rosencrance staffel, sir?" Yoski asked.

"Puzzling," Fujita said. "No sign of them. Intelligence claims the staffel has been withdrawn."

"Sir . . ." Brent said. "With one carrier disabled, maybe they just don't have the air power and the logistical support to fight the Israeli Air Force, train carrier pilots, and maintain a strong fighter presence in the Marianas."

Fujita nodded. "True. Their losses have been heavy."

Yoshi said, "But new Messerschmitts are being built in East Germany and Daimler Benz is producing a new engine and there is no shortage of pilots when you can pay a million a year."

"I know—I know," the old admiral said. "But we have a respite, Yoshi. Intensify your training."

"Fuel, sir. Fuel?"

The admiral brightened. "Good news. The Department of National Parks has sent us new supplies and the needs of the Self Defense Force have been reduced since the carrier attack."

Yoshi smiled. "Good, sir. We can use every minute."

Brent said, "Admiral, the only way we can destroy the Arab units in the Marianas is with an amphibious force. We've got to land troops and kill them."

Fujita eyed the American. "Strange how your mind can parallel mine. Yes. Of course. That is the only way."

"But we have no amphibious force," Yoshi offered.

"True," Fujita said. He patted a dossier on his desk. "This is top secret," he said. "We are forming one. Three regiments of assault troops, a heavy weapons battalion, and a tank battalion. All volunteers and under my command."

"But we're a public park!"

"The landing force is being trained under the auspices of the Self Defense Force outside Narita."

"We don't have the ships, landing craft," Brent said. "You're talking about landing a full division."

"The Self Defense Force has three Miura class LST's and one Atsumi."

Brent interrupted. "I trained in amphibious warfare, sir. We need LCVP's (Landing Craft Vehicle And Personnel), LCU's (Utility Landing Craft), experienced officers. And four LST's can't carry a division. We need LSD's (Dock Landing Ships), transports."

"I know all this, Mr. Ross," the admiral said testily. He ran his hand over the dossier. "We are working on those problems. In fact, there are a number of old American vessels moored in the Hudson River that have been made available to us through the CIA. Admiral Mark Allen is working on the transfer at this moment. We will send a few officers there shortly."

"Good. Good," Brent and Yoshi choroused.

The admiral sat silently for a moment, fingering the *Hagakure,* and Brent knew the canny mind had moved somewhere else. "You still request permission to commit seppuku, Yoshi-san?" he asked in a suddenly soft voice.

"Yes, sir."

"Because of the woman—the woman you loved

170

who was killed by the terrorists in Ueno Park."

"Yes, Admiral. I was careless. I was remiss . . ."

"That's not true," Brent challenged. "I was as much to blame . . ."

"No!" Matsuhara said sharply. "I was her escort—her fiancé."

The admiral waved them to silence. "You are my air group commander, the best fighter pilot on earth, Yoshi-san." He sighed deeply. "We have lost so heavily—the spirits of hundreds of our finest samurai have journeyed to the Yasakuni Shrine." He fixed the air group commander with eyes like moist coals. "You know I still cannot honor your request. The emperor needs you, Japan needs you, and *Yonaga* needs you."

Matsuhara drew himself up very tall. "Yes, sir." He stabbed a finger upward. "I will seek it up there. It is right. That is the place for a fighter pilot. Much closer to the gods than down here."

Fujita's eyes followed the finger to the overhead. "Death is as light as a feather, Yoshi-san."

Yoshi finished the famous Meijian rescript, "Duty is as heavy as the mountain."

Fujita smiled. "And your shoulders are broad and strong. You have borne a heavy burden for *Yonaga*—as heavy as Fujisan."

"Thank you, sir." The pilot glanced at the brass clock hanging behind the admiral's desk. "May I be excused, sir. I have a new training command at Tokyo International."

The admiral nodded his assent and Yoshi Matsuhara turned to leave. The admiral's afterthought stopped him. "And Yoshi-san, I increased airport security to a full company of seaman guards with heavy machine guns and mortars."

Yoshi smiled for the first time. "Police Captain

Kudo should be delighted."

Brent and the admiral laughed while Yoshi left the room.

After the door closed, the narrow eyes moved to Brent's face and held him. He stared back. "You have a violent temper, Brent-san."

"I know, sir."

"It can work in your favor and it can kill—perhaps kill you." The old man drummed the desk. "You are very much like your father."

"His temper turned on himself."

"And it destroyed him, Brent-san."

"I know, Admiral."

"Yesterday, in the parking lot, you conducted yourself well—in the best traditions of Bushido."

Brent smiled. "When in doubt, choose battle. Attack first even if you face a thousand enemies."

The old face cracked with sudden good humor. "You have been studying the copy of the *Hagakure* I gave you, Brent-san."

"If a daimyo thinks of his samurai as his children, they will think of him as their parent, and their relationship will be in harmony."

The old man chuckled, a dry brittle sound, but, nevertheless, filled with good humor. "Very good, Brent-san. You have learned the most important passages."

Brent studied the incongruous smile on the usually stoic face. It gave the young American a queer twinge, almost of conscience, to see the evident pleasure the old man enjoyed just at the sight of him. He could not get used to the idea that he was admired—even regarded with deepest affection—by this talented seaman, this relic from the nineteenth century, brilliant strategist and tactician who had earned the dogged devotion of the entire crew and the admiration of half the world.

As Brent stared at the old man, the smile vanished and the eyes dropped. The chameleon returned and the voice was subdued, edged with pain as the old man moved on to another topic. "As I said before, Brent-san, you performed a fine service for your pilot, Lieutenant Yoshiro Takii." Brent waited silently, wondering about the sudden shift in conversation. In a moment he understood as the admiral reached under his desk and placed the magnificent Takii sword on his desk.

"Oh, no, sir," Brent said, raising his hands as if he were fending off an evil apparition.

"I must offer it to you, Brent-san. I am honor-bound. It is yours by right of *kaishaku*."

"I know, sir. But I have the Konoye sword by that right." There was agony in his voice, "One is enough. I don't want Yoshiro's. He was my friend. I—I . . ."

"You loved him."

"Yes."

"It is not unmanly for a samurai to love his friends, Brent-san." He raised the sword in an offertory gesture.

Brent shook his head again and took a step back as if he were menaced by a poisonous reptile. "No. Keep it, sir."

The old man dropped the sword. "All right, Brent-san. I have done my duty and I understand. I was compelled by honor to make the offer. You know that."

"Yes, sir."

The wrinkled brow added new creases, and the narrow eyes caught Brent's. "There is a chance I may give you independent duty far from this command."

173

"You can tell me no more?"

The old man shrugged his tiny shoulders. "Not at this moment. I must await a decision from Geneva. You would welcome it?"

"I am happy here, sir."

"It would further your career, Brent-san."

"You've been talking to Admiral Allen, sir."

The old man shook his head. "No, Brent-san. I know his sentiments. I know he has urged you to seek other duties."

Brent was not surprised at Fujita's knowledge. Nothing—absolutely nothing seemed to escape him. It was almost as if he had spies hidden in every compartment or had the gift of prescience which enabled him to open secret doors and rummage the minds of others like a burglar ransacking a room. Although his powers seemed mystical, Brent knew the admiral was a pragmatic man with a practical political sense, a sly awareness of other men's motives and how they might be levered to his own use, keeping a wary, testing eye on all those around him, conscious of their strengths and failings. "I am happy here, Admiral," Brent said. "But I am your subordinate and under your orders and I would happily accept any duty that would aid us in our war against world terrorism."

The old man nodded. "Well said like the fine officer you are. I dislike assigning men to tasks they find repugnant. Such assignments do not work in the best interests of morale or *Yonaga*. But if this new post materializes, it will fit your experience and talents precisely."

Brent shook his head and spoke with sincerity. "I am ready, sir, for any task. You know I will do my best."

The thin lips curled upward in pleasure. "Very

174

good, Lieutenant." He riffled through some papers. Put on his steel-rimmed glasses and squinted at a document. "Our software for the new encryption box?"

"I'm to pick it up this evening."

"At the Imperial Hotel."

Brent felt chagrined and his cheeks warmed. Of course Fujita knew, and he probably knew of the powerful attraction between Brent and Dale McIntyre.

"I will send four seaman guards with you, Brent-san."

"Not really necessary, sir. I'll be armed and I will only go to the hotel, pick up the software, and return to the ship." He waved a hand. "With a full company at the airport and an extended perimeter at this facility, I respectfully submit that we are overextended now."

"You will be gone for several hours." The old man was far ahead of Brent, seemed to be reading intimate pages of his mind. Brent shifted his weight uneasily. "Take one seaman guard. Post him on guard while you are—ah, transacting your business."

"Aye, aye, sir," Brent said, blushing furiously. "Am I dismissed?"

The old admiral motioned him out with a wave of his fingers and a knowing smile.

"I killed a man, didn't I, Brent?" Dale McIntyre said, seated on the couch next to him, drinking her Scotch and soda.

Followed by the doughty, irascible Watertender First Class Azuma Kurosu who had driven a *Yonaga* staff Mitsubishi, Brent had returned Dale's

Honda Accord to the rental agency in the basement garage of the Imperial and had then taken the elevator to the thirtieth floor with the rifle-toting watertender at his side. A dozen passengers had entered and left the car in its rise. All stared wide-eyed at the American and his bizarre companion. None dared utter a word.

When Dale opened the door, Brent had his breath taken away at the sight of her. Dressed in a tight green silk frock with snug black belt to accent her tiny waist, each nuance of each curve and undulation of her superb body was defined by the clinging cloth. Her hair was down, brushed into glistening folds all the way to her shoulders, back-lighted by the room and glowing like newly minted pieces of red gold and platinum. With the exception of a light touch of lipstick, she wore no cosmetics, her tanned skin glowing with ebullient health and tinged with the rose of excitement at the sight of him. But her expression had been solemn and there were traces of anguish under her eyes and at the corners of her mouth. There was trouble in the depths of the green eyes like a cloud shadow drifting across a green mountain lake. Brent sensed the tension and nervousness immediately. Her obvious disquiet made her even more desirable, brought to life an urge to circle her with his arms and console her, a powerful magnet that shocked a physical desire for her to life, and his body reacted free of his control, his heart pounding furiously, a clenched fist in his groin pushing hard. He swayed toward her.

But she had turned away and led him to the sofa where drinks waited on a large marble-top table. Now the moist green eyes were staring up at him in wide anguish and she repeated the indictment, "I

176

killed a man, didn't I? It's in all the papers. One man had a crushed trachea."

Brent drank his straight Scotch thoughtfully and circled the truth. "Who knows, Dale? It was a riot. Actually, two of my men claim they killed him."

"Oh!" Some of the tension drained from her face. "Your men?"

"Yes. Azuma Kurosu," he gestured at the door, "he's on guard just outside in the hall, and Kenzo Nakayama. They're both trained kendo fighters. In fact, Azuma is the ship's champion."

"I know Kendo can kill."

"That's what it's for."

"Just like karate, Brent. I wish I had never taken those damned lessons."

"You may have saved my life, or—ah, something more important."

She smiled fleetingly for the first time and then drank deeply. "And you, too. That filthy man and his foul threats with that sign." She shuddered and drank again, sighed some of the tension away as the Scotch began to spread. "That man had some very unsavory plans for me." She looked up. "Why are the threats always sexual?"

He sipped his drink thoughtfully. "Because, I guess, we all fear losing our sexual powers as much as our lives—maybe more. The threats alone strike a chord of fear. Worse than a dentist's drill on a nerve."

"Sex and violence go together."

"Of course, Dale. Men equate the two."

Her eyes widened. "Not all men?"

He shook his head. "Murderers—rapists. That's what they were doing to us—all of us—raping."

"Yes. Yes. It makes sense, Brent."

"You've heard those threats before, haven't you?"

"Yes. Back in New York. Bums. In alleys. And once I was mugged and the threats were the same and at the end of a knife. He threatened to put the knife—to do something that terrifies a woman more than anything else."

"I know."

She drained her glass. Recharged her drink and Brent's from a service on the table. "That's why I learned karate." Her gaze moved back to his eyes and held. "You're sure one of your men killed the demonstrator?"

Brent sipped the fiery liquid, filtering it between his teeth, enjoying the burnt wood flavor before swallowing it. "Even the police were convinced of that—wanted to arrest Azuma."

"But they didn't?"

Brent laughed, a lightness spreading upward and relaxing him. "There was a slight disagreement with Admiral Fujita."

She laughed, and a sparkle began to return to her eyes. "You know, Brent, I shouldn't worry about that dead vermin, should I?"

He shook his head. "Of course, not. I'm sure most of them were *Rengo Sekigun.*"

She raised an eyebrow in confusion.

"Japanese Red Army. Heartless killers of women and children."

She nodded understanding. "My department has a book on them."

"Oh? Well, so do we. In fact, we have a library. You met Bernstein, our Israeli liaison officer. He briefs us continuously on Middle East terrorist groups." He continued as if he were eyeing a report on the table before him, "Red Army cadres train in Libya, Syria, and Wadi Haddad's camp in Aden with the German Red Army, Baader-Meinhof,

PLO, PFLP, IRA, the Basques' ETA, Spanish GRAPO, and a dozen more I can't remember."

"Nice bunch of lads."

"Their Tokyo cell is known as one of the deadliest bands of killers on earth. Its leader, Hiromi Matsunaga, planned the LOD Airport massacre, Dale."

"Yes. I remember that, Brent. Three of them."

"Killed twenty-six innocent travelers with machine guns and grenades."

"I know." She filled his empty glass.

"Now do you feel better, Dale?"

"What do you mean?"

"I mean, would you feel depressed if you stepped on a cockroach?"

She smiled up at him and her eyes were warm. She moved closer and took his hand. "You're a sweet boy, Brent."

"*Boy!* You aren't singing another chorus of your 'September Song' again, Dale?"

She laughed, shedding her grim mood. "My 'toyboy'? Is that it?"

"You just want to ravish my pristine body. Right?"

She laughed again and ran a hand over his arm, her fingertips leaving small, burning trails on his bicep. "You do have a great physique, Brent."

"Sorry. I'm saving myself for my wedding night." Then with mock gravity, "There'll be blood on the sheets."

Her laugh was deep and free and he kissed it off her face, her mouth open, tongue hungry and wet, meeting his. He pressed her back into the cushions, feeling the maddening swell of her breasts against his chest. Burning deep in his groin, the heat built quickly, spreading like flame through oil, turning

179

his breath to gasps, and he trembled with the hunger for her. His hand found the rise of her breast, cupped it, toyed with the areola through the silk. She twisted, moaned, pulled hard on the back of his neck, darted her tongue over his lips, gums, dueled his.

Suddenly her hands were on his chest, pushing, and she twisted away. "No, Brent," she said breathlessly.

"Why? What's wrong?"

She shook her head. "I don't know. It just isn't right." She ran a hand through her hair and picked up her drink.

"Too fast? Too soon?"

She toyed with an ice cube with a single finger. "I'm not that sophomoric, but this *is* only the second time I've ever seen you." She drank. "But I guess some of that is there, yes." And then she gestured to the door, "And there's a man in the hall, just outside the door."

"That bothers you?"

"Yes."

He took a big swallow of Haig & Haig and suddenly saw a macabre kind of humor in the crazy set of circumstances that had thrown them together. "And you're not a child molester," he said slyly, changing the mood.

The sparkle returned. "You're uncanny." She rose slowly and pulled him to his feet with her. He put his arms around her and she snuggled close, speaking into his ear. "The hotel has a half-dozen fine restaurants. I'll give you the software and then we'll eat. This is a business meeting, you know."

"Why, of course. What ever gave you the idea I had anything else in mind?"

She was laughing as she disappeared into the

bedroom. When she reappeared, she was carrying a small package which Brent slid into an inside pocket of his tunic. She held his hands and looked up into his eyes, her eyes bright emeralds reflecting candlelight. "It's not that far from May to September, is it, Brent?"

"No. And autumn is the most beautiful season. The leaves are glorious and the sun and clouds put on spectacular shows."

She kissed him fiercely.

"That was spectacular," he said hoarsely.

Taking his hand, she led him to the door. Watertender Kurosu followed them into the elevator.

Dale felt a fulfilling sense of happiness as she led Brent to the first floor and the hotel's new French restaurant. In the crowded elevator she stood close to him, holding his big arm with both of her hands, basking in the envious stares of a half-dozen other women in the elevator. Men and women alike gawked curiously and somewhat fearfully at Watertender Kurosu, who stood at the back of the elevator and stared fiercely at every newcomer as he entered.

"I've never eaten there, but I hear it's great. Same cuisine as Maxine's and it's supposed to have the same decor," she said as she led Brent into a large, elaborate dining room with three magnificent crystal chandeliers, wall-to-ceiling velvet drapes and watered-silk wallpaper that matched the drapes.

"The cancan?" he asked.

She laughed. "No can-do," she punned.

The tuxedoed *maître d'hôtel,* a tall, thin, elderly Frenchman, who carried himself as erect as Napoleon on parade and commanded his waiters with the same authority, led the couple to a center table next to a small dance floor. "Madame, Monsieur Lieutenant," he said, gesturing.

To Dale's surprise, Brent rejected the table, insisting on a secluded booth in a corner that faced the room's only entrance. Designed as a corner unit, there were no chairs. Instead, a curved settee fit into the corner and there was room only for two diners to sit close together, side-by-side. Dale liked the arrangement as she slid in close to Brent. She might never see the young man again after tonight. She wanted the closeness. Felt a thrill in the touch of his hand on the thick leather seat.

A quick motion from the *maître d* and a small delicate waiter of about thirty hurried to the table. "Your waiter, Marcel Plubeau," the *maître d'hôtel* said. He left quickly, obviously irritated by Brent's insistence on changing tables. However, when he saw Kurosu approaching with his rifle casually slung across his shoulder, he stopped in midstride like a man walking into a glass door which was shut when he expected it to be open.

"This man is yours, monsieur?" the maître d'hôtel asked, aghast, turning to the American. Marcel Plubeau stood mutely, fingering his menus.

"Oui, monsieur," Brent said, mimicking the maître d'hôtel's grave demeanor.

"S'il vous plaît, monsieur, he cannot come into— ah, carrying that *carabine,* he . . ."

Brent smiled, ordered the watertender to take a post at the entrance. Azuma Kurosu snapped to attention, saluted, turned smartly, leather heels of his boots stomping the hardwood like three shots from his rifle and marched back to the door followed by a hundred disbelieving eyes in the now dead-silent room.

Brent explained to the maître d', "I am an officer from the carrier *Yonaga*. He has been assigned to me as a guard and is a well-disciplined seaman. I assure you he will not cause you any awkwardness or embarrassment."

Yonaga was a magic word and the Frenchman bowed and smiled weakly. However, Dale could see he was still in a state of shock and unconvinced. After all, a rifleman was standing at his door, *Yonaga* crewman notwithstanding, and glaring at his diners. Several had already left and more were rising. "Hotel security may be curious, *monsieur,*" he said, a slight tremor in his voice.

"Let them take their chances," Brent said. "Now bring me the menu."

Piqued, the maître d'hôtel wheeled on his heel and stalked off.

But hotel security was mysteriously absent and had been throughout the evening. Certainly, they had been forewarned by the row Seaman Kenzo Nakayama had had with a hotel employee on the sidewalk in front of the Imperial the previous day. Either they were hopelessly incompetent, scared, or had been contacted by someone in power and told to give the lieutenant and his guard wide latitude. Dale guessed either Fujita or a member of his staff had made discreet arrangements.

Nervously, Marcel Plubeau, immaculately dressed in a tuxedo and carrying a white linen napkin on his left arm, leaned over Dale. She smelled his cologne, strong and sweet like Chanel Number Five. *Strange, for a man,* she thought. She watched him over her menu as he leaned close over Brent, smiling into Brent's face while he handed the huge menu to the American. His long walnut-colored hair was carefully coiffed into a bob that fell to his left shoulder and was casually drawn back from the right cheek to display a large diamond earring in the pierced lobe of his right ear. His eyelashes were so long they curled, appearing soft and dark on his cheek. He smiled down at Brent, asking about champagnes, wines, and before-dinner drinks with a voice that was free of an accent and as soft and lyrical as a girl's. Dale found him utterly repulsive.

"I'm on Scotch and I'll stay with it," Brent said. He ordered his Haig & Haig and Dale stayed with her Scotch and soda.

While the waiter swayed to the bar, Brent enveloped Dale's hand in his. "I think that waiter has fallen in love with you, Brent," she said, pressing close, thrilling at the touch of his hard thigh against hers.

Brent raised an eyebrow in surprise, turned, and stared at the waiter who was standing at the bar. "Didn't notice, but he did smell beautiful."

Marcel minced back with the drinks and stood expectantly. "Ready, Dale?"

Dale shook her head and held up her drink. Brent dismissed the waiter with a curt, "I'll call you when we're ready." He turned to Dale with a puzzled look. "How could a beautiful woman like you not be ah — entangled?" He ran his eyes over her body and found her thigh with his hand and moved it up and down on the firm flesh. She reacted to the touch like a schoolgirl on her first date, squirmed, felt heat mount. She pushed it away. "No. Please, Brent," she pleaded, holding his hand. "Not here."

"Where?"

"I don't know," she said helplessly. "Please be a good boy."

"All right," he conceded. "But answer my question."

She sighed. "I've been married—I was married for ten years to Jonathan McIntyre."

"Divorced?"

"Yes."

"Children?"

"No."

"Why did you break up?"

"John never grew up. I think he felt he missed the sexual revolution when it chugged out of the station and spent our entire married life chasing the caboose. He was ten years older than I. When he was forty-two he bought a red Corvette and began to drive around with a green beret on his head and designer sunglasses on his nose, making all the singles' bars in tight Calvin Kleins."

"My God. He was chasing other women with you at home? He was insane." He tightened his grip on her hand.

"Thanks, Brent. You're sweet." She kissed his cheek and sipped her drink. She told him of her youth. Born on Long Island, she was the only child of a stockbroker and a New York socialite. Her earliest memories of her father were of a big, distant man who spent most of his days and nights in his office in Lower Manhattan.

She was educated in private schools and graduated from Bryn Mawr with a math major. Because she was away for most of her youth at school, her mother could spend her time with her bridge clubs and entertaining a succession of young lovers without interference. Immediately after graduation, it was obvious to Dale she was not wanted at home and she found a position with IBM as a computer programmer. When she married, she quit her job and moved into an apartment in Manhattan. At first she was happy, but then Jonathan cracked under his midlife crisis.

After her divorce, she took a job with the CIA as a computer expert. Quickly, she mastered the latest technology and was moved to codes and ciphers. She worked in Washington, Seattle, Hawaii, and New York and found the job exciting and interesting.

"You must have known other men."

"Of course, Brent."

"You never remarried?"

"No. That's not for me." Her tone was bitter. She drank. Eyed him over her drink. "And you, Brent. How did you ever wind up on *Yonaga?* Talk about crazy circumstances."

He smiled. Told her of his youth. The academy. The assignment to the carrier by NIS. "And that's about it," he concluded. "I'm on permanent liaison and will remain on board as long as Admiral Fujita wants me."

She drained her glass and smiled. "You may not remain there much longer."

Surprised at the statement, Brent tabled his drink with a thump. "Fujita said something like that just this afternoon. What is this all about?" He waved at Marcel in irritation and pointed at his empty glass.

"It's not top secret — you'll know tomorrow, anyway." She rattled the ice cubes. "You've got *Blackfin.*"

"So?" He shrugged his shoulders.

She looked up at him as Marcel quietly replaced their drinks and murmured apologies which they both ignored. "Admiral Mark Allen has command and . . ."

Brent finished her sentence, "And he has requested me."

"Yes. That's my information."

"And Fujita knew it." He drank deeply. "And he approved it or was still undecided. That's it."

"Well, he's not undecided anymore. It came through this afternoon. That was one condition the CIA laid on Fujita—we needed a qualified captain and staff."

"I know nothing about those old pig boats."

It was her turn to shrug. She turned her hands up in a hopeless gesture. "As Marcel would say, *'Cest la guerre.'* "

He shook his head and stared over his glass at the entrance where Azuma Kurosu stood with the Arisaka at his side. With the exception of one couple dining in the far corner, every table was deserted. "Maybe Allen will finally get his way," he said almost to himself.

"Brent, there is one thing." He moved his eyes to Dale. "There is an agreement. The subs, Zulus and Whiskeys that the Russians are supplying their allies and Gatos and Balaos we're giving the Japanese . . ."

"They must be all original? Right?"

"Right, Brent. But with the exception of communications. They can be fitted with modern communications gear. It just came over from Geneva an hour ago."

Brent slapped the table. "That's it. That's his lever." He took a stiff drink. But his mood changed quickly with a new thought. *"Blackfin's* moored in New York Harbor and you live in the city?"

"That's right."

"And you're returning tomorrow?"

She nodded. "Yes. I have duty in our New York

office."

"Can I see you?" He turned his hands up in an indecisive gesture, "If I'm assigned?"

"You'd better, Brent." She fumbled in her purse, removed a checkbook, and tore off a deposit slip and handed it to Brent. "Here's my address and phone number. I live in Lower Manhattan in a meat locker."

"A meat locker?"

Her laugh was as delightful as a mountain stream over pebbles. "It's not another word for bordello. I actually live in a ninety-year-old converted meat locker. It's very large and, I feel, charming."

"Like a loft?"

"Exactly."

His hand found her leg again. "We can be alone there, Dale?"

"Completely." He slid his hand up. She did not resist. Lost herself in the hot depths of his blue eyes.

"*Pardon, monsieur et madame.* The *cuisine* will close soon," Marcel said, materializing over the table.

"We'd better eat," Dale said.

Brent appeared disgruntled. "The orchestra. I want to dance."

"Not tonight, *monsieur.* Only on weekends."

Brent raised his menu and sipped his drink. "All right." He looked up at the waiter. "What do you suggest, Marcel?"

The Frenchman beamed with the pleasure of recognition and moved closer to Brent, holding his pad and pencil. "We have excellent *Escargots à la Bourguignon* this evening, *Monsieur* Lieutenant." He bunched his fingers, kissed them with full pursed lips, and cast them off to the sky.

"Snails? No thanks," Brent said.

A look of dismay shadowed Marcel's face, but he recovered quickly. "Perhaps, chicken."

"That's more like it." Brent looked at Dale. She nodded approval.

Marcel gazed over Brent's head with a dreamy look, gestured dramatically at the swinging kitchen door. "Our *cuisinier* prepares a superb *Supremes de Volaille Rossini*."

"That's boned chicken breasts with a *pâté*," Dale said.

"Oui, madame. Pâté de foi gras," he said, with the look of a man about to fall into bed with his lover. "Flavored with lean ham, parsley, beef stock Madeira." He stared at Brent and edged closer to the big American. "I would suggest *Soupe Albigeoise, Salade de Tomates . . ."* His face flushed, breath became short, and he cleared his throat with a tiny cough.

"Fine. Fine," Brent said. "I'll leave it to you."

The waiter pulled himself up. *Vin, monsieur,* a white *vin* with *poulet."*

"Your best white wine?" Brent asked.

"Pouilly-Fuissé, *monsieur, naturellement."*

"Naturally. Bring it," Brent said, impatiently waving at the swinging doors.

With a delighted look crossing his face, Marcel walked to the kitchen with quick, short steps.

"He sure knows his food—actually, loves it," Dale said.

Brent nodded solemnly. "He gets his kicks out of it. No doubt about that. I wanted to get rid of him before he had an orgasm."

Dale recoiled in mock horror. "Why, Brent, you're such a naughty boy."

189

Marcel returned quickly with the soup, and an assistant poured the wine. Brent raised his glass. "To the meat locker."

Dale touched her glass to his and drank. The salad was exquisite, and then the entree and more wine. They drank and ate and became intoxicated with each other and the liquor, all the while Marcel and his assistant hovered close, bringing more dishes, and the wineglasses were never allowed to become empty.

Toying with a half-empty glass, Dale found herself staring boldly at Brent's straight nose, strong jaw, thick, corded neck. His broad shoulders filled his coat, an expanse of fine blue wool that seemed yards wide. Touching his arm, she felt the bunched muscles like knots of iron. The closeness of the forged, hard body of Grecian perfection fanned a deep heat in her that spread through her body on the warm rays of alcohol, awakening a gnawing hunger that thrilled and tormented at the same time.

The waiter returned, but they refused dessert and sat quietly, looking at each other. Dale felt his hand again, moving up slowly, under her skirt.

"Please, Brent."

Showing the effects of liquor and his desire for her, his face glowed the color of sunset. "We're almost alone in here," he said. "Almost as alone as we've ever been." And he was right. Two more couples had entered while they ate but had taken tables across the room, seeking the dimly lighted privacy of corners, too. Marcel and his assistant had vanished into the kitchen and Dale wondered why they had been so slow in returning. Watertender Kurosu was barely visible, lounging in the shadows of the entrance.

Dale started and squirmed as Brent's hand touched the bare flesh above her hose, fingers hot and seeking. "No, Brent. Please." She grabbed his hand, but her muslces were weak and the hand insistent in its quest as old as mankind, stroking in a circular pattern ever upward, trailing hot paths on her firm flesh.

"I'm going to see that—what's under my hand—all of you, someday," he said huskily into her ear.

Rising from visceral depths, the heat flared like a struck match, her muscles melting as the hand found the elastic band of her panties, pulled it aside roughly and snaked under. She sagged back, heart pounding as if a mad drummer were under her breast and the rush of blood hummed in her ears, warmed her cheeks . . .

"Oh, Brent. No. This is torture." She was out of control and she knew it—felt she could pull this young man down onto the settee, appearances be damned, and have him here and now in front of God and everyone else. She heard a creaking and the slap, slap sound of the swinging doors and she looked up as steps approached. Brent turned his head and the fingers stopped just short of their goal.

A new waiter was approaching, a big, square man with a long stride. His right hand was under his napkin. Dale heard Brent's breath catch as if he had been punched in the solar plexus, and in a fleeting instant his hand grabbed her shoulder and he pushed her with one powerful motion into the corner while his other hand leaped to his left armpit. "Brent!" she managed to shout.

"Down!" he screamed, coming to his feet and turning the table over, glasses and silverware crashing to the floor and clattering across the deep car-

191

pet. The new waiter was across the dance floor and almost on them, pulling a long, vicious knife from its concealment under the linen napkin draped over his left arm. Dale felt fear like cold heavy oil spread through her guts. She tried to huddle within herself.

"Sabbah! *Allahu akbar*," the man cried, lunging for the American, who was unholstering his pistol. Dale knew Brent would never make it. Too much drinking. The distraction of her body. The sexual heat. It was all planned.

A huge man with wild eyes and black hair like long coils of loose springs, the killer had the face and savage leer of a hungry hyena. Young and powerful, he leaped over the table casually, like a hurdler, as Brent tore the Otsu from its holster. The knife was high. Glistening even in the dim light. "Infidel swine! Yankee dog. Sabbah! Sabbah!" Cold steel flashed downward.

Three shots, so fast they sounded like an automatic weapon, boomed in the room like artillery. The killer's wide-open mouth exploded with a gout of blood and shattered teeth as a bullet hit the base of the man's skull and ploughed out of his mouth. Another slug exited the man's head just between his eyes, hurling both eyeballs, splintered fragments of skull, gouts of yellow-gray brains and gore onto Dale who screamed in terror and revulsion. The big man's body twisted and collapsed at the top of his leap and instantly the powerful, vicious killing machine became just a dead, bleeding carcass with no direction or control, arms windmilling, legs water.

Dale tried to twist away, but the body crashed down on her, pinning her with over two hundred pounds of dead weight. The shattered head

192

thumped into hers, blood, splintered teeth, shreds of ripped tongue and gums and gore splattering her face and streaming down into her brassiere, soaking through the silk of her dress. A jugular had been severed and hot blood pulsed from a still-beating heart, spurting onto the side of her head, soaking her hair. She screamed wildly again and again.

She had known horror in her life, but never had she felt the atavistic explosion of distilled fear that drove her mindlessly to escape this frightful creature from her worst nightmare, pinning her down with his enormous weight. She pushed with her arms and legs, squirmed and turned to the side and thanked God through tears and sobs as the corpse slid in its own gore and rolled from her, tumbling to the floor with the muscle control of a rag doll.

Coming erect, she gagged, the smell of cordite and the acid taste of her own gorge scalding her mouth and throat. Just a few feet away, Watertender Kurosu was crouching on the dance floor, Arisaka leveled and smoking. No diners or waiters were visible. Pistol in his hand, Brent stood between the legs of the overturned table. "Sabbah. Sabbah assassin," he said. And then in panic, "Behind you, Kurosu!"

Two dark men brandishing stubby pistols burst through the entrance and charged. The leader was tall and lean like a terrier and the other was squat and round and gorilla-like. Flame leaped from their pistols. The Otsu barked, Kurosu staggered and whirled, and then the rifle boomed again—once, twice, but not as fast as before. Vibrating with crashing reverberations, the interior of the room sounded as if someone had lighted an entire package of firecrackers and then threw in a few cherry bombs at random. Blue smoke hung like a fog.

The tall leader stopped abruptly as if he had run into a stone wall and toppled backward onto the floor. The second man came on, pumping bullets into the watertender who dropped his Arisaka and slumped to the floor, clutching his stomach.

"No!" Brent screamed. Charging. Firing. A hail of bullets caught the assassin in the chest and neck. He threw his head back, screamed, vomiting blood, and tumbled loosely as if his bones had turned to jelly, pistol skidding across the hardwood of the dance floor.

Silence and then cries and shouts for mercy and help from diners who were hiding under their tables. A new commotion and a large man in a business suit ran through the entrance. He had a gun in his hand. Brent fired. The man dropped and rolled across the floor.

The voice of the *maître d'hôtel* came from a dark corner. "That was hotel security— You've killed hotel security!"

"I don't give a damn who he was! No one comes into this room with a gun!" In quick, precise movements, Brent ejected the clip from the Otsu and rammed a fresh one home into the base of the grip with the palm of his hand. There was a loud click as the spring-loaded locking pin snapped into place.

More noise at the entrance and Brent leveled his pistol as he worked his way past a dead assassin toward the watertender. "I'll kill any man who enters this room with a gun in his hand!" Brent shouted. The commotion stopped as Brent reached Kurosu's side.

A tense voice came from the foyer. "This is chief

of hotel security, Hiromitsu Ochiai. Put down your weapon. The police are on their way."

Brent was on his knees next to Azuma Kurosu. "No chance. If you want to stay alive, stay out of this room. I have a woman and a wounded man. Have a car at the entrance. No driver. We're leaving."

Brent leaned over the watertender, whispering. Azuma groaned back and suddenly went very limp. Dale thought she heard Brent whimper.

Slowly, Dale came to her feet, face smeared with thickening blood, hair matted, gore streaking her cheeks, her dress. She took several deep breaths, tried to shake the paralyzing horror from her mind, and felt her old steadiness begin to return. Wiping coagulated blood from her face with a napkin, she walked to Brent who was still leaning over Kurosu. The big lieutenant's shoulders were shaking. Dale stared down. Kurosu was relaxed and limp in the final embrace of death.

Hiromitsu Ochiai's tense voice from the foyer: "I will have a Mercedes sedan at the main entrance for you in three minutes."

Brent came to his feet slowly. "I need two men. They are to enter the room with their hands on top of their heads."

"Why should I do this? There are four dead men in that room."

"Five!"

"You may want them for hostages."

Brent looked around the room. Waved at the *maître d'* who was huddled with a waiter in a corner. "Over here! Over here!" Brent shouted, waving his pistol. Slowly the pair walked across the room.

Brent gestured at the watertender's body. "Pick him up."

"He's dead," the waiter said.

"He's going home," Brent said thickly. He leveled the Otsu. "Now pick him up."

Quickly the pair picked up Kurosu by the shoulders and legs and turned toward the entrance. "Hold it!" Brent said. He shouted at the foyer, "The entrance is to be cleared. No security, no police — no one at all. Understood?"

Ochiai's voice: "Understood."

Dale heard a flurry of subdued voices and the sounds of hurrying feet and Ochiai spoke again: "The foyer is cleared except for myself."

"The sidewalk?"

"No one. And the Mercedes just pulled up."

"Get rid of the driver and then take off."

"The police are on their way."

Brent waved the pistol irritably. "Hold them back or I'll take the *maître d'* and one of his waiters with me."

The voice was filled with frustration: "All right. All right. You can come now."

Holding Kurosu's feet, the waiter led with the *maître d'* gripping the dead watertender's shoulders. Brent followed and Dale came last. Hiromitsu Ochiai had been true to his word. The foyer and entrance were cleared and no one was on the sidewalk. A Mercedes SEL 560 was parked at the curb, keys in the ignition. Looking down the Hibiya Dori in both directions, Dale could see the revolving colored lights of police cars halting traffic at intersections. Brent ordered the men to put Azuma's body into the backseat and then stared down the Hibiya Dori, stopping on the revolving lights. "Both of you, get in there with him," he shouted.

"No! *S'il vous plaît, Monsieur Lieutenant.*"

"In. Now!" He waved the pistol.

Groaning, the *maître d' hôtel* and the waiter placed the corpse on the backseat. "In! In! One on each side." The Frenchmen groaned, moaned, and complied. Brent turned to Dale. "How do you feel?"

"Better."

"Can you drive?"

She was caught by his eyes, which glowed as if lamps were burning behind them. Steady and unblinking, the look was frightening—the blood lust of a predator; the same animalistic fever she had seen at dock B-2 in the terrible fight at the parking lot when he had blindly swung at her when she attempted to stop him. She tore her eyes away and managed a reasonably firm, "Yes. I can."

He waved her into the car.

Chapter VI

Only half of the glowing orb of the sun had crept over the horizon when a fatigued Brent Ross was summoned to Admiral Fujita's office for the second time. As usual, the scribe, Commander Hakuseki Katsube, was seated next to the admiral. In addition, Admiral Mark Allen, Yoshi Matsuhara, and Dale McIntyre were all standing in the crowded office. Surprisingly, Police Captain Kamagasu Kudo was present, this time subdued and standing off to one side unobtrusively instead of grabbing center stage in front of the admiral. The usual pair of seaman guards flanked the door and a communications rating manned the phones in the corner.

Brent felt drained—exhausted by the emotional roller coaster of the previous night, physical exertion, and the lack of sleep. He had been called into the admiral's office the first time on boarding and had given his description of the terrible events and was dismissed. Then Dale McIntyre had been called in as he left.

For the woman's protection and to keep her out

198

of the hands of the police, she had been given a cabin next to the admiral's. Frantically, she had showered and scrubbed the gore out of her hair and slipped on green fatigues which Fujita had ordered for her while her dress was sent to the ship's laundry. But nothing would ever wash the memories of the night from her mind.

Passing her as she entered the admiral's cabin, Brent would never forget the haunted look on her face. Puffed and underscored with blue pouches, the striking green eyes were wide and rimmed with tired lines, appearing as heavy and dead as stagnant swamp water—the look of one who had seen the Stygian Creek and grappled with the furies in the bowels of hell. She had brushed past Brent silently without even turning her head and had spent over an hour with the admiral while Brent answered an endless stream of questions from Mark Allen, Yoshi Matsuhara, and Colonel Irving Bernstein in Mark Allen's cabin.

Now, standing in front of the admiral, Brent's mind seemed fogged and out of balance, divorced from reality like a heavy drinker on the verge of stupefaction. Despite his strongest efforts, his thoughts wandered back to the bloody events like a film strip that insisted on repeating itself: the killer leaping over the table, knife glinting; the Arisaka roaring; the two assassins racing out of the foyer; the Otsu bucking; the roar of the weapons and acrid smell of gunpowder; Dale's screams; the security guard's insane charge; Kurosu's brave death that had temporarily left him a sobbing ruin; the ride back with a stunned Dale and the disintegrating waiter and *maître d' hôtel;* a half-dozen police cars following the Mercedes all the way to the parking lot; the seaman guards gently unloading Watertender Azuma Kurosu's body while the police parked at a discreet distance. Then, Chief Hospital Orderly Eiichi Horikoshi examining the corpse on the quarterdeck and dispatching it to the ship's crematorium in Fire Room Seven. And most galling, Horikoshi turning to Brent and saying sardonically, "Another one, Lieutenant. You are going to overwork the crew of the crematorium, yet, Mr. Ross."

Too filled with grief, soured rage, and self-recrimination to speak, Brent had turned on his heel and walked off silently. Then the self-doubts struck home. Had he been remiss? Had he been so possessed by the woman's sexuality he had become careless? Thrown away Kurosu's life for a quick, cheap feel of a woman's thighs? Disgust and self-loathing festered and turned his guts to acid.

Admiral Fujita's voice addressing the police captain jarred Brent back to the present, "Captain Kudo, we are all anxious to hear the results of your investigation of last night's incident." The admiral's demeanor was surprisingly cordial.

Kudo answered in a restrained voice. "It was a charnel house, Admiral. Six killed."

There was something wrong with the number. "Six?" Brent said through the fog.

"I do not have his name, Lieutenant, but a young waiter with long dark hair and an earring in his right ear had his throat cut in the kitchen," Kudo said.

Brent heard Dale's broken voice, "No. No."

Kudo continued, "The leader of the assassins was Ismael abu Hemeid. He was 'Sabbah.' We know very little about this group except that they are merciless killers and very professional."

Bernstein spoke and there was bitterness in his voice. "Kadafi's killer elite. *Sabbah*. Israelis know them well. The followers of 'the old man of the mountain,' Hasan ibn-al-Sabbah. Started his pride of assassins in Iran—Persia then—centuries ago. The cult has persisted till this day and now they are supported by the Libyans—given everything they want—food, liquor, women, or boys, if they prefer, training facilities. They still prefer the knife. Get high on hashish and will put cold steel into a great white, if ordered. And, of course, they find eternal paradise if killed while attacking."

Kudo nodded in gratitude, picked up his thought. "The other two were Muzammil Siddiqi and Ammar Abdulhamid. They were newly re-cruited by Hemeid for this job. They were just thugs from the dockyards of Tripoli . . ."

"A hotel security guard was killed?" the admiral said.

Kudo turned his lips under and squared his jaw. "Yes, Admiral. Security Guard Kiotaki Kawaguchi was hit by four bullets. He died instantly." He stared at Brent Ross while a heavy silence crept through the room like a thick, viscous fluid.

"I shot him," Brent said simply.

"He charged into the middle of a gun battle. Azuma Kurosu was dying," Dale said. She waved at Brent. "How could Brent know?" The finger stabbed at every man in the room. "All of you would have done the same." The men stared at her silently. She started to plead. "I would've shot him." The finger moved again, "You, you and you . . ." The voice trembled on the edge of hysteria.

Fujita's voice was uncharacteristically gentle. "Ms. McIntyre. I understand. Of course, the security guard was very foolish—stupid. He would have died at my hand, too."

Kudo said to Admiral Fujita, "He is dead, sir. That is all that matters."

Fujita's demeanor hardened. "You will not take Brent Ross anywhere for questioning."

"That is not why I requested to come on board, sir."

"Then why? What do you want here, if you do not want Mr. Ross?"

The police captain sighed. "It is dangerous for any of your men to go ashore."

Fujita's chuckle was dry with irony, tone mocking. "Indeed, Captain. Any other new information for me?"

Kudo squirmed uncomfortably and a red hue crept up from the multiple chins hanging over his tight white starched collar and flushed the bulging cheeks. "I am here to request that you restrict your men. Most of the Japanese people are with you, however, these terrorist attacks are impossible to stop."

"I know," Fujita answered. " 'Sabbah' tried to ram *Yonaga* with a ship loaded with explosives, dive a DC-3 into her. We had a petty officer murdered in a warehouse, an attempt to attack the ship with a truck bomb, two men killed in the gate house by that same truck . . ." He glanced at Brent Ross. "Two fights in the parking lot and a killing there." The eyes moved to Yoshi, "An ambush in Ueno Park that left a woman dead and two members of the crew went on leave and never returned. Their families never saw them." His hard gaze returned to the fat police captain. "And now, Watertender Azuma Kurosu, the man you would question over the death of a swine, is dead. We know about these cowardly terrorists—indeed, we do."

"I would suggest that you restrict your men, Admiral."

The admiral's black eyes wandered over the policeman like twin gun sights; the huge round head set on Kudo's neck like a pumpkin on a broomstick; the lemon-custard flesh of the jowls sagging down almost to the layered chins; the deep purple gash of the mouth; the spread legs braced in the stance of a pregnant woman in her third trimester, counterbalancing her enormous abdomen. The policeman had stepped over the line. Fujita's voice was cracking ice. "I will make those decisions, Captain Kudo."

"Why, of course, sir," Kudo said hastily. He waved his hands as if he were fending off an assailant. "Only a suggestion, sir."

Fujita nodded at the scribe, Katsube. "I have already canceled all liberty. Any personnel ashore on ship's business will be escorted by our own armed guards."

"You have the full cooperation of the police, Admiral. We are setting up roadblocks on all major thoroughfares entering the city and arresting anyone with a weapon."

The admiral's nod showed approval. "Long overdue, Captain."

"The Self Defense Force relieved some of our riot police in the downtown area. Now we have the personnel, Admiral."

The tiny admiral's fist struck the table. "No more good men will be thrown away. We lost one of our best last night."

The words whipped Brent's soul like a lash. He felt icy guilt avalanche like snow down a spring slope. Weak and fatigued, he felt as if he were sliding over the rim of consciousness. He tried to push it away, but his culpability seemed overwhelming. Cruelly, his mind's eye brought back every detail. His hand on the woman's leg, groping like a schoolboy trying to shed his virginity in the backseat of a car. Kurosu on the floor in front of him, bleeding, groaning. The watertender looking up and whispering through the blood welling up from his punctured lungs, "Sorry, Mr. Ross. I let you down," and then dying like a little boy dropping off to sleep. And other thoughts crowded in like maggots boiling up through rotten meat: the back of Konoye's neck, the sloppy decapitation; Takii's skinny neck, the feel of the great sword in its vicious arc, the thud and squirting blood. What had he become?

Brent took a step forward. "Admiral Fujita," he said loudly. All eyes turned to the young American. "I request permission to commit seppuku."

There were gasps. Fujita's eyes widened and he straightened. Brent heard Mark Allen's voice: "Insanity! He's over the edge! Get a psychiatrist."

204

Yoshi Matsuhara spoke: "You do not know what you are saying, Brent."

Bernstein grabbed the young man's arm: "You need rest, Brent. It's been an ordeal—a terrible strain."

Dale stepped close, panic in her eyes as the realization of Brent's words seeped in slowly. "That's suicide. You can't mean it?"

Kudo's eyes rolled and he said into Brent's ear, "No, young man. The police will not trouble you. We know it was self-defense."

Fujita waved them all to silence and his voice filled the room. "Why, Brent-san? Why this request?"

Brent held himself at stiff attention. "I am responsible."

"Not true, Brent," Dale shouted, grabbing his arm and pulling close.

Fujita ignored the woman. "Why are you responsible, Brent-san?"

Brent steeled himself. "I drank too much—was ah, involved with Ms. McIntyre when I should have been alert—left the protection of all of us to my man." He looked around, blue of his eyes deepened by moisture. "I was careless—surprised."

"Nonsense!" Mark Allen shouted. "Any of us can be surprised." He waved a fist in exasperation. "My God, you don't cut out your guts over that."

Fujita spread his fingers and waved his hand at Allen like a fan and then gestured for Dale to speak. Dale said, "Of course we were surprised. That killer burst out of the kitchen." She tugged on Brent's arm and stared up into his eyes imploringly. "But, Brent, you reacted so fast I didn't even know what was happening until that killer fell over me."

"Kurosu's dead," Brent said blankly. "My eyes, my whole concentration, were on you."

"Of course you were taken by the woman. But you killed two assassins and Ms. McIntyre was not even scratched," Yoshi said.

Brent stared at Yoshi and his eyes were hard. "You feel guilt over Kimio—blame yourself for her death and you have requested seppuku. Who are you to tell me?"

"I am a Japanese, Brent-san."

"You have said I am more Japanese than many."

"Do not take me literally. You are not Asian— not one of us—not expected to . . ."

Brent hurried on impatiently. "There are two forms of seppuku—one to deny guilt, the other to express it. I am guilty. Will you be my *kaishaku,* Yoshi-san?"

Mark Allen's voice: "This is crazy!"

"Enough! All of you!" Fujita's hand slapped the desk. "Why are my most valuable men so determined to kill themselves?" His eyes moved from Yoshi to Brent and back. "Our enemies will afford both of you ample opportunities to move on to a higher plane of existence." His gaze steadied on Brent and his hand found the *Hagakure* resting on the desk. "There is a time to live and a time to die. This is not your time to die, Brent-san. Your request is refused." The eyes moved to Mark Allen and then back to Yoshi Matsuhara and there was a challenge in the stare. "Commander," he said acidly. "Brent Ross has earned the position and respect of a samurai. Of all the men on this ship, you should know that better than anyone. You were born in America—came to this country as a young man just as Brent-san. Yet you consider yourself a samurai—live the life of Bushido. Asian or not, he has earned the Konoye sword honorably and fought alongside all of us bravely in the best tradition of Bushido." He slapped the desk. "I never want to hear such a remark from you again."

Yoshi's jaw worked and he managed a tight "Yes, sir." He returned to Brent Ross. "I meant no disrespect to you, Brent-san." He returned to the admiral. "It was my opinion and, Admiral, it still is."

"You are entitled to that," Fujita said. "But express it elsewhere." His eyes sought the overhead and he laced his fingers across his bony chest. He was somewhere else in the past. "According to the great sage Manu, 'Deeds proceed from the body, speech, the mind and produce either good or evil and the soul in conjunction with the body performs three kinds of deeds: good, indifferent, and evil'." The eyes descended to Brent Ross and the tone was soft and intimate. "No one can ever say your acts have been either indifferent or evil, Brent-san."

Brent took a deep breath and expelled it audibly. "Thank you, Admiral. But respectfully, sir, I alone am responsible for my acts and my conduct last night did not measure up to my standards and the standards of Bushido."

Mark Allen interrupted and his voice was anguished. "For Christ's sake, Brent. Come back to reality."

Fujita's expression hinted approval of the American admiral's words. He said to Mark Allen, "You need Lieutenant Ross in *Blackfin?*"

"Of course. You know I've requested his assignment."

Fujita spoke to Brent. "I am posting you to *Blackfin* as communications officer. You will be in New York the day after tomorrow. Prepare your gear, Lieutenant. Your orders will be cut immediately."

"Yes, sir." Brent wondered about the admiral's faith in him as a samurai. Was it weakening? Tainted with doubts? Did Fujita share Mark Allen's concern over his mental stability? Was he afraid terrorists would gun him down? Was he going mad? And why not? They had all been under crushing loads. Back-breaking pressures. The fighting had been incessant for years. And there were subtle philosophical and psychological dangers that could be more destructive than the enduring violence. How could he, an American to the core and a rational man, accept the Asian philosophy in which all things somehow are one, man part of the universal whole, flowing in the infinite river of life and at the same time believe in the natural law and world view of Christianity that had taught him from birth that man was created in the image of God and human nature the epitome of the universe. He had found himself trying to believe in both, but it required a splitting of the personality—a level of schizophrenia. Maybe Mark Allen was right.

Fujita's words to Dale McIntyre interrupted the wild Niagara in Brent's mind. "I understand you are to take a plane at Tokyo International at seventeen hundred hours this afternoon."

"Yes, Admiral."

The old sailor drummed the oak. "You will be escorted by my seaman guards." He turned to the scribe, Commander Hakuseki Katsube. "Orders to the executive office. Ms. McIntyre is to be driven to the airport in a staff car with two armed guards. One truck is to precede her vehicle and another is to follow. Each truck is to carry six seaman guards and a Nambu mounted on the cab and another over the tail gate. They are to stop for nothing—police, Self Defense Force. Nothing!" Katsube brushed furiously and nodded. He handed the document to the communications man who walked across the cabin from his station in the corner. Holding the ideograms, he returned to the phone and began to speak into it softly.

"Admiral, please," Dale said. "I must return to my hotel first."

The old man nodded to the communications man who looked up. "Amend the order," Fujita said.

Uneasily, Dale eyed the admiral and blurted, "May I speak alone to Lieutenant Ross, sir?"

"In a moment—across the passageway in the small conference room," the admiral said.

Kudo said to the admiral, "With your permission, I would like to interview the lady and the lieutenant." He waved a pad.

Fujita nodded his permission. The old man moved his eyes from face to face. There was fatigue on his face and the old eyes were tired. He spoke wearily. "This meeting is closed."

Everyone rose slowly.

Dale sat close to Brent and stared across the table at Police Captain Kudo who poised a pencil over a pad and spoke softly and with concern. "I do not wish to prolong your ordeal, but I need your statements."

"I understand," Brent said. Dale nodded her agreement. Quietly, Brent described the events of the night, sparing no detail, even his involvement with Dale. Dale followed with her own story. The quiver was gone from her voice and she felt her old confidence returning. Finally, satisfied, the fat policeman left.

Dale eyed Brent anxiously. He seemed strangely docile and subdued for one who had fought so ferociously in the parking lot; killed so quickly and ruthlessly at the hotel. The broad shoulders slumped and the deep blue eyes with all of their excitement and promise were now as cold and lifeless as cut glass. She was sure it was not just Azuma Kurosu's death that had devastated the young man. Certainly, she could not even imagine the pressures every man on *Yonaga* had felt. And Brent was so young. An American. The "American Samurai." But was it possible? An American and a samurai? The two clashed. Were diametrically opposed. She spoke softly into the young man's ear, "East is East, and West is West, and never the twain shall meet."

He turned to her, smiled for the first time, picked up the verse, " 'Till Earth and Sky stand presently at God's great Judgment Seat.' " He stared into her eyes. "You're trying to tell me something, Dale?"

"Maybe—Kipling tried a hundred years ago, Brent."

"You think I'm—ah, unbalanced?"

She pondered for a moment. "Suicide doesn't come from a perfectly healthy mind."

"You don't understand."

"The Japanese understood, but they aren't healthy. How can a follower of Bushido be healthy?"

He shrugged. "It's viewpoint, Dale. From their viewpoint seppuku is perfectly logical."

"When honor has been compromised. Right?"

"Yes. And western men do the same thing. You know that."

"But they're not honor-bound and ritualistic about it and they're considered sick—aberrations." She felt a deep turmoil. Anguish was in her voice. "You can't wear different faces at the same time. We're not made that way, Brent." She waved a hand. "The Japanese are different—they wallow in contradictions, thrive on it."

"I killed Azuma Kurosu. There's no contradiction there."

"Yes there is. I told you before. You reacted to the sound of the door—the hand under the napkin. You have the senses of a leopard." She pleaded, "I've never seen such speed. If you hadn't been fast, both of us would be dead, too. There was nothing you could do for him."

For the first time, she saw life flicker deep in the blue depths. "You really believe that?"

"You know I do."

He sighed. "You're a great girl, Dale." He leaned toward her as if he wanted to touch her, but then sat back. "It's all academic anyway. Fujita refused permission."

"Of course. He's intelligent, a pragmatist. He can't afford to throw you away and he knows it." She drummed the table. "Commander Matsuhara made the same request?"

"Yes. A gunfight. He lost his fiancée. Blames himself."

"Good Lord. I can't believe this, Brent." She looked at him, despair and frustration boiling deep. "Must you define your manhood with the calculus of death? Are you afraid to measure yourself against a woman? Is it safer to pull a trigger than to love a—ah, to love a woman?" And then she blurted it out, "To love me?"

He eyed her with a hint of awe in the blue depths. "You're an amazing woman, Dale. You use words like scalpels. I've never thought of it that way." He repeated, "The calculus of death," to himself slowly as if he were memorizing the phrase. A smile softened the stone of his jaw. "And love you?" He rubbed the stubble on his chin. "You're so bright, so beautiful. Oh, that would be so easy to do."

"Then do it."

His stare was enigmatic; warm yet still distant. "Someday," his wave was all encompassing, "when all of this is over."

She brightened with a new thought. "Your orders to *Blackfin* will be a good thing."

"I think Fujita—all of them agree with you."

"She's moored in the Hudson River—just a few

212

minutes from my place, Brent." He remained silent. "I'll see you?"

He moved his eyes to hers. The look was inscrutable, distant, like a meditating monk. "Yes. I'll see you again."

She was not convinced.

There was a knock and the door opened suddenly. It was the executive officer, Commander Mitake Arai. "Your escort is ready, Ms. McIntyre," he said, eyeing Brent Ross curiously and with concern.

"I'm ready," Dale said, coming to her feet.

Brent remained in the chair and stared as Dale turned toward the door. "Wait!" he shouted. He rose. "I'd like to walk you to the gangway."

"Delighted," she said, smiling warmly.

With Arai leading, they stepped into the passageway.

Two days later and seven hours before the chartered Constellation was to leave Tsuchiura with Brent, Admiral Mark Allen, and new crew members for *Blackfin,* Brent, Mark Allen, and Colonel Irving Bernstein were called to the admiral's office. Rest had restored Brent's energy and pulled him from the depths of his depression. His mind was crystal clear and the demons had vanished from his brain. But the wound of Kurosu's death was still raw and he awoke several times in cold sweats, his mind filled with visions of the watertender's death. It was not ended—would never end. And Dale was gone—in New York City now. He felt a void, an emptiness, a defeat.

213

There was a dispatch on the admiral's desk that Brent had just decoded that morning. The admiral was drumming it. "There is to be some kind of meeting under the auspices of the United Nations in New York City. The PLO and various Arab groups are to meet informally with American, British, and Israeli representatives. No Japanese have been invited."

The three officers nodded. All had been involved with the decoding of the signal and were familiar with its startling contents.

Brent said, "Admiral, the PLO is not a member of the United Nations."

Bernstein spoke to Brent. "True, Brent. But they maintain a representation in New York."

Mark Allen said, "The dispatch says nothing about the Libyans, Syrians, Jordanians, Egyptians, and the rest."

"True," Admiral Fujita agreed. "But something is afoot. I want representation—a report."

"That would be difficult, sir," Bernstein said.

"Yes, I know," Fujita said. "You know those people—ah, those vermin better than any other member of my staff, Colonel Bernstein. I am sending you."

Bernstein caught his breath. "But, sir. With Admiral Allen and Brent Ross both detached, who will do the decoding? Cryptographers Reed and Pierson are the best, but you need specially trained officers."

"I have requested replacements and they will be here at any moment." He tugged the single white hair hanging from his chin thoughtfully. "I have decided all of you will be my official representatives to this meeting—as innocuous as it may be—as useless. We must attempt to keep the restoring of *Blackfin* a secret."

"Respectfully, sir," Mark Allen said. "That is virtually impossible. *Blackfin* is moored in the Hudson River, clearly visible to hundreds of thousands of people. And we're taking thirty-one members of her crew with us. New York will be crawling with spies—every member of the Russian delegation to the UN is a KGB agent and the Arabs are no better. They'll spot us when we leave the plane at Kennedy."

"I know, Admiral Allen," Fujita said. "But we have no choice. You must make the effort."

"Officially, *Blackfin* has been contributed by the US Navy to Japan's National Parks Department as a museum, Admiral Fujita, correct?" Allen asked.

"Correct. A functioning, viable vessel, capable of sea-keeping on her own."

"And ostensibly Japan is to put her on exhibit as a relic of WW II—an enemy relic." Everyone stared at the American admiral silently. He showed his amazing encyclopedic mind. "A member of a force that destroyed over two hundred warships and nearly six million tons of merchant shipping?"

"Yes," Fujita said with a trace of bitterness.

Brent and Mark Allen exchanged a skeptical look. Bernstein spoke. "I didn't know about the UN. That's no good, Admiral Fujita. The Arabs will see through it immediately. It's flimsy, full of contradictions . . ."

Fujita tapped the oak with bony knuckles. "I agree, but we have no choice. The American Navy dictates that we pick her up in New York Harbor or not at all." He smiled slyly. "And remember, we Orientals are living contradictions—revel in them." He laughed humorlessly, thumped the desk with knuckles like withered roots. "You must try. You may cause some confusion and conceal our true intentions. Those are my orders."

There was a knock and the admiral gestured to the door and a seaman guard opened it. Two officers entered; one an American commander and the other wore the khakis of the Israeli Army.

"Your replacements," Admiral Fujita said.

"Carrino. Joseph Carrino," Mark Allen exclaimed, grabbing the American's hand. Carrino, a short, dark man with a definite Latin flavor to his visage, grabbed the American admiral's hand and shook it vigorously. Allen turned to Admiral Fujita. "You've got one of the best." He slapped Carrino's shoulder boisterously. "I taught him everything he knows."

Bernstein also had met an old acquaintance. "Marshall Katz," he said, shaking the Israeli's hand. *"Shalom."*

"Shalom," the Israeli, a thin, graying man of about sixty, answered. His cheeks were hollow, hair sparse, flesh hard and lined like an old saddle as if he had spent too many years in hot desert winds and had had every drop of moisture burned from his flesh. But his voice was strong, and when he shook hands all round, his grip was firm.

Admiral Fujita cleared his throat and everyone snapped to attention. "My orders," Carrino said, handing the admiral a long yellow envelope. Fujita accepted the envelope and then took Katz's orders. Quickly, the steel-rimmed glasses appeared and the documents were scanned. Admiral Fujita was obviously pleased. "Welcome aboard, gentlemen," he said.

"It's an honor to serve with you, Admiral," Carrino said.

"We are allies and all of Israel appreciates the sacrifices *Yonaga* has made to preserve our state and save the free world from terrorism," Katz said.

Fujita acknowledged the Israeli with a nod and slowly unfolded from his chair, his every move worn by a century of time. He spoke to the new officers. "You need to be briefed on our latest intelligence reports." He gestured at a chart on the bulkhead. "We have picked up signals from Aguijan and reports from native observers. There are reports of massacres on Saipan and Tinian." The men rumbled angrily. "And there is intense activity at the airfields. The Libyans are enlarging them and repair facilities are being built."

"They must be supplying them by submarine," Mark Allen said.

"Yes," Fujita said. "But there is still no aircraft activity." He stabbed low in the chart. "The enemy *Majestic* is in dry dock in Surabaya. Will not be ready for months." He moved the pointer to the western Carolines, "And the other carrier, the *Principe de Asturias,* two cruisers, and at least a dozen destroyers are here, in Tomonuto Atoll. Two depot ships, a tender and another oiler have been spotted." His eyes embraced the room. "We have time—time to train our pilots and sortie for our decisive battle. We need *Blackfin*. The Arabs will not expect a submarine." He stared at Mark Allen. "If we could pick off a carrier when they sortie

217

from Tomonuto to intercept us . . ."

"Great opportunity," Mark Allen agreed. "We should be ready."

The admiral spoke to Carrino and Katz. "You understand the situation?"

They chorused, "Yes, Admiral."

Carrino said, "Admiral, the Arab presence in the Marianas may pose the greatest threat of all, sir. All they need is some long-range aircraft."

"You are perceptive, Commander Carrino." He tugged on the whisker, surprised everyone. "An old Arab proverb warns: 'If the camel once gets his nose in the tent, his body will soon follow.' We are training a landing force. We will soon throw the beast out of the tent." The men chuckled. Brent had an impulse to shout, "Banzai," but controlled himself.

The old man's eyes moved over Brent, Mark Allen, and Irving Bernstein. "Show my new staff the communications gear and introduce them to the technicians and then you are dismissed to your new duties. And exercise caution in your new assignments. The streets of New York can be more dangerous than an Arab dive bomber."

The officers chuckled at the rare humor.

The admiral gestured at the paulownia wood shrine obeisantly. The officers snapped to attention and turned toward the shrine. Fujita and Brent Ross clapped twice. Fujita spoke. "May we follow the noble Eightfold Path of the Enlightened One, find the middle path between the pleasure of the senses and asceticism, and adhere to the Four Noble Truths. In this way we will be better men than our enemies and we will prevail, kill them all like the dogs they are." He clapped again and everyone knew he was not finished. "Our enemies are strong and are massing to destroy us like typhoons at the first parallel. But a strong tree bends with the storm, not breaking even under the weight of the heaviest snowfall. Our honorable *Tenno* (Heavenly Emperor)," he said reverently, resorting to the honorific for the gravely ill Hirohito, "gave us these words in 1946 in Japan's most desperate hour: 'Under the weight of winter snow, the pine tree's branches bend, but do not break.'" Turning slowly, his black eyes found every man and seemed to transfuse strength. "May the spirit of the Son of Heaven be with us in our quest—the quest for righteousness and honor." He was silent for a moment. "You are dismissed."

Yoshi Matsuhara was waiting in the passageway when Brent exited. He pulled the young American to his cabin, explaining, "I had to come back from the airfield to check on supplies—the new engines, and I wanted to see you before you left."

After he closed the door, Brent found a seat at the small table in the Spartan cabin and Yoshi sat across from him, pouring two drinks from a bottle of Johnnie Walker Black Label. "Just one," Brent said, raising the glass. "Today's a working day."

"To *Blackfin*," Yoshi said. They both drank.

"Your air groups?" Brent asked.

"Coming into shape. I have some fine pilots. But the torque of the new engine has made the Zero-sen a tricky aircraft. It forgives nothing." He sighed. "I lost a pilot yesterday. Ground looped into a petrol truck." He sipped his drink. "But I am expecting new engines today for the bombers. That's why I'm here."

"For the bombers?"

"Yes, Brent-san. Should make Kazuoshi Muira and Shusaku Endo happy." He pushed his glass back and forth in a short journey on the tabletop. Spoke to the table, "Maybe you were right about my request for seppuku."

Brent was not fooled. "You're trying to tell me I made a foolish decision, Yoshi-san. Aren't you?"

"Not foolish. No, it was a question of honor." The glass stopped and he tapped it on the table, causing the Scotch to slosh and peak. "But hasty, perhaps, made when you were upset — not yourself."

"And your decision? The same decision?"

"I think the same." The pilot drank. Fixed Brent's eyes with his, *"Yonaga* needs us, Brent-san. Seppuku must be put aside."

"Fujita has forbidden it. Is that why?"

"No. Put aside by us. Out of mind until this is all over. When we are calm and the emotions are placid again."

"If ever, Yoshi-san." Drinking, Brent stared high above Yoshi's head. He was far away, detached, "Do you think we — all of our power can influence history? What is happening on this planet?"

Yoshi chuckled. "You can ask some of the most amazing˚ things, my young friend."

Brent's voice was filled with impatience. "Answer me, Yoshi-san. Answer," he demanded.

The fighter pilot nodded, and his demeanor was earnest. "You mean the turn of the wheel of history—are the spokes gripped by the fates or turned by men?" He took a small drink and nursed the remainder of his Scotch before he answered his own question. "We are helpless, men do not make history, Brent-san, history makes us. We have no control over events. We flow with events like a man who has fallen into a flooded river."

"You've been reading Tolstoy, Yoshi-san."

Matsuhara laughed. "I'm glad he agrees with me."

"But men do make decisions—decisions that send us into battle," Brent noted.

"Of course, Brent-san. But they are in the river, too. As helpless in the current as we are." He drained his glass. "In a way, Kafka, in his madness, saw the world in correct perspective—a hostile, uncontrollable place, where we are all at the mercy of powerful, remote leaders who share the common madness—are as helpless as we are to control the wheel."

Brent was gripped with a sudden insight. "Then this is a terribly futile thing we do, Yoshi-san. We spend men and wealth like drunken gamblers throwing away chips for what? Sink the next carrier, take the next hill, the next trench, on and on without end. We achieve nothing at all."

"I disagree. We're stopping Kadafi."

"But the wheel turns and wars go on. We move on to the next battle and the next with no idea of where we are going and why. Killing, victories, give us the illusion we are going somewhere, but nothing changes and we just flounder deeper in the swamp." He drank. "And if it isn't Kadafi, it's Hitler, Attila the Hun, Genghis Khan, Idi Amin, the Ayatollah—take your pick."

"Just because we can't control the wheel does not mean there is not right and wrong. Every generation must face this. I did not mean to suggest our battles were futile. Of course I would prefer to be dedicated to some future life of wisdom and beauty—to add my iota to it instead of the sword. But that is not the way of mankind. We must fight and have fought since time began. What else is there for us to do?"

Brent pondered the strange circular logic for a moment. It seemed to make sense, but he knew it should not. "You amaze me, Yoshi-san."

"Why?"

"Your mind. Your power of reason. Your love of literature. The amount of reading you've done and such a wide scope."

"Thank you, Brent-san. But remember, my early schooling was in America and I had forty-two years in Sano-wan to catch up on my reading."

They both laughed. Then Brent felt suddenly troubled. "You won't seek death up there." He stabbed a finger upward.

The pilot shook his head. "No. I will fight with all my skill, but never deliberately seek death." He rattled his ice cubes. "And you?"

"The same. A trade. My life for your life."

Matsuhara looked away, asked self-consciously, "The woman?"

"What about her?"

"She is very attractive."

"One of the most desirable women I have ever met."

"You love her?"

222

Brent answered honestly, "I don't know. I've known her for a very short time."

"War compresses everything. You'll be in New York together—will you see her?"

"Perhaps."

Yoshi sighed, a deep mournful sound. "We all need our women, Brent-san."

Brent knew his friend's mind was with Kimio and the terrible loss he felt. He could say nothing. There were no more words left. He could only nod and clench his jaw.

They stood together as if by signal and shook hands firmly.

Chapter VII

With refueling stops at Midway Island and Los Angeles, the flight of the chartered Pan American Douglas DC-6 from Tsuchiura to New York's John F. Kennedy International Airport was a plodding twenty-five hour ordeal. With thirty-one volunteers for *Blackfin,* Brent Ross, Mark Allen, and Irving Bernstein and extra fuel tanks mounted in the rear of the fuselage, there were still twelve empty seats. However, to Brent, the vibrating old aircraft was still cramped and there was no way he could uncoil his six-foot-four-inch bulk comfortably, finding the trip harrowing and fatiguing. "Better in the third seat of a B5N," he grumbled to Mark Allen after a sudden downdraft dropped the old plane five hundred feet.

The old admiral grinned and gestured. "President Truman used one of these for his personal aircraft—the *Independence.* I flew in it once."

Brent looked around solemnly. "No wonder he had such a nasty temper." Mark Allen laughed.

While the four huge Pratt and Whitney engines

roared and the old transport vibrated its way over the ocean, Brent had hours to think, to reflect and ponder. No one condemned him for Watertender Kurosu's death except himself. He had tried to protect his man and he knew he had fought well— had killed two assassins that night. And poor Yoshi, so concerned. They had made a strange compact—to try not to die; almost laughable if you thought about it. But he felt better about Yoshi's chances, which as a fighter pilot were not very good anyway. And Admiral Mark Allen was in a jovial mood. He had finally torn Brent from *Yonaga* and Fujita's influence, which he felt was destructive. And old Admiral Fujita, he had been so anxious about Brent and the attempts he felt the Red Army would make on his life.

Fujita, the enigma, the *Fujisan* of strength, the ghost who defied time, the walking, living encyclopedia of history, the confidant of kings and statesmen who had known some of the most powerful and influential leaders of the twentieth century: Teddy Roosevelt, Woodrow Wilson, John J. Pershing, Lloyd George, Douglas Haig, Winston Churchill, Franklin Delano Roosevelt, Adolf Hitler and many, many more in every corner of the globe. Fujita the strategist and tactician, who with Isoroku Yamamoto had been the driving force in developing Japanese naval aviation and who had joined with Kameto Kuroshima and Minoru Genda to plan the attack on Pearl Harbor. And today, still the tenacious Fujita, the immovable boulder who blocked the flood of Arab terrorism.

The British had a whole history written around

225

Winston Churchill, who, with the temperament of a bulldog, had almost single-handedly rallied a nation on the verge of defeat to eventually triumph over Nazi Germany. Fujita was no less. Whipping together the few fighting forces of an impossibly divided Japan which refused to fight even when attacked, he had blunted and bloodied the Arab's strongest efforts. He handled *Yonaga* masterfully, as if the great carrier was an extension of himself, striking like a lurking predator only when the odds were in his favor and then withdrawing quickly like a phantom in the night, leaving his enemies cursing and bloody. Men did not follow him, they became shards of his will, not obeying it but possessed by it.

The eyes. Those strange black eyes that pierced as if they had a life of their own, exuding a mesmerizing power and command that dug into a man with preternatural force. From the first moment he met the old admiral, Brent knew he was special to him. True, the old man had known his father, Ted "Trigger" Ross, and admired him. But it was more than respect for his father. He knew Fujita had been impressed by his fighting skill, his respect for Bushido and gradual acceptance of it, his extraordinary vision and marksmanship—"Sharpest eyes on the ship," Fujita had said. There was a closeness, a condescension—if the admiral could ever feel that emotion—that was nearly paternal. Yoshi had noticed it, commented one day, "He had a son, once, vaporized at Hiroshima. Big boy, strong, intelligent, as much like you as a Japanese could be."

A surrogate son? In a way, perhaps. Did the old man feel he needed a change to preserve his mental stability? Certainly he had shown erratic warning signs, knew he had been on the verge of unhinging, possibly breaking down completely. Did Fujita actually feel *Blackfin* and New York City would be safer for him than duty in Japan? Sent him away to protect him? Hardly. *Yonaga* was as much a part of Fujita as his circulatory system; his heart, his lungs, his soul. The carrier and the emperor came first—came before everything; himself, family, crew, Brent Ross.

Life was a cheap, expendable commodity in war. Any commander who thought otherwise had no right to command. The bright, the witty, the talented were sacrificed in wholesale lots. No, indeed, a man did not search for safety when he fought a war. *Blackfin* would be no haven. There would be mortal danger in her mission and everyone knew it. Notwithstanding, Brent's ambience would be changed and he was convinced both Mark Allen and Admiral Fujita thought he needed it.

He shifted his weight in the knobby seat restlessly, staring down at the endless vista of the Pacific twenty-four-thousand feet below. Scattered blobs of low clouds drifted below like dollops of frosting dropped by a careless baker, casting shadows like flat, dark duplicates of themselves on the sea. In the distance, the puffs blended in a single mass becoming a gray-white line that stretched to the horizon like a luxurious carpet. High above at its zenith the white eye of the sun glared overpoweringly in a dazzling crystalline

227

void, reflecting from the sea in a silver sheen that ached his eyes, brushing the tops of the clouds with white like December frost. Such beauty. No wonder Yoshi and the other pilots loved their planes, the sky; even wanted to die there, "closer to the gods."

Suddenly, the beauty brought Dale back and she filled his mind. Actually, she had never left it. He had to see her again. In New York. He had her address and phone number. He felt anxious, and a familiar, warm excitement began to stir deep down. He squirmed uncomfortably. Could they love each other? It had been such a short courtship—if you could call it that. Yoshi had put it succinctly when he said, "War compresses everything."

Since the orbiting of the Chinese laser system, the incessant fighting had inflicted terrible casualties. With death so eager and greedy, he had felt the power of life at the other end of the balance grow. Courtship, convention, ritual, morals went by the board. He had known it with other women and they with him. Tradition was a luxury that belonged to the slow pace of peace—something he could not even remember. Since the "terrorist wars" began four years earlier, he had snatched at the flimsiest promise of life. Do men and women actually "love" during wartime? They desire, demand, and take from each other whatever they can get—conventions, morals, obligations be damned. Was that what he sought with Dale? Certainly, desire for her had been fanned by the prospects of death—the fatalism of every fighting man. But he told himself there was more to it than her body—

228

had to be. He chuckled, remembering the awed comment of the exhausted Israeli intelligence agent, Sarah Aranson, who two years earlier, after a marathon night of lovemaking said, "You're nothing but two hundred twenty pounds of super-heated sperm, you big oaf." Maybe that was all there was—would ever be. He sagged back, disturbed, confused and ill at ease, watching the Pacific crawl by below.

After they refueled at Los Angeles International, the flight became far more interesting. Crossing the continent, Brent never tired of looking down at the spectacular country stretching to the four horizons. It was a map—a relief with a bewildering amount of extra detail unfolding as if it were an endless parchment cranked over a drum. But the colors were subtle and there were shades never found on the printed sheet. The Rockies swept up and faded away like giant white-tipped breasts. Then the Midwest where towns and cities were laid out with rigorous precision in the geometric patterns and order so loved by the planners: highways showing gray and black, the glistening tops of occasional cars reflecting the sun; railways winding threads more difficult to see than the roads; lakes reflecting shimmering blue like chips of broken mirrors; rivers clear glossy ribbons meandering carelessly; woods dark patches of green merging into the dark browns of the ploughed fields surrounding them; farms with their sprinklers marked by green circles as if a giant had toyed with enormous compasses. And as they finally approached the east coast, ground mists blurred the horizon with occasional cloud shadows darkening patches of landscape while throwing others into high relief. Rarely could a man see this much of his country in a few hours, feel the size and beauty of it. It was impossible not to love it as he would a beautiful woman. It was his, and he was part of it. Maybe this was what patriotism was all about. Suddenly, a slowing in the rhythm of the engines interrupted his thoughts.

They began to let down and the No Smoking and Fasten Seat Belts signs flashed on. The same low clouds that had dogged them all the way across the continent were still there, but suddenly they broke away and Brent had a clear view of New York City and its boroughs. They were actually out over the Atlantic south of the city and making their turn to approach John F. Kennedy International Airport from the west. To the northwest he saw Staten Island, New Jersey, Newark; to the north, the Hudson River where *Blackfin* was moored and Manhattan with its forest of skyscrapers; to the northeast, the East River, Long Island Sound, the Bronx, Queens, and in the east, the green swath of Long Island stretching off into the Atlantic.

The sweeping turn took them low over Staten Island, the Narrows between Staten Island and Brooklyn, and then over row after row of tiny houses lined up like troops on parade, broken only by the green swaths of Greenwood Cemetery, Holy Cross Cemetery, Washington Cemetery, Trinity Cemetery, and Cypress Hills National Cemetery. Turning to Mark Allen, Brent waved out the window. "The only relief they get is in their cemeteries."

The old man smiled. "There's a lot of truth in what you say, Brent."

From his window seat, Brent saw the flaps drop, slowing the Douglas and giving it a nose-down attitude. Then there were loud thumps as the landing gear locked down and they were so low Brent could see people looking up. At a hundred twenty miles an hour they skimmed over the Belt Parkway, missing the top of a bus by only a few feet. "Christ, I could've transferred," Brent said. Mark Allen and Irving Bernstein laughed.

There was a new set of vibrations as the pilot pulled the throttles back to twenty-four inches of boost on all four engines and slipped the propellers into fully fine pitch. Then a thump and a screech as rubber tires wasted themselves on concrete and the plane shook and slowed, the pilot jamming his brake pedal.

"New York, we're here," Mark Allen said. "Brace yourself."

The ride to Manhattan and the docks was fast even in the rickety old chartered bus. The driver, a dark, sallow madman totally lacking in depth perception, charged down Linden Boulevard through the heart of Brooklyn en route to the Prospect Expressway and the Brooklyn Battery Tunnel. The route was explained on the bus's PA system by the driver in a mixture of ruptured Brooklynese and Puerto Rican. Luckily, the fuel shortage had lightened traffic, removing potential targets from the driver's path.

The view was depressing. Old rickety frame houses lined the expressway, interrupted here and there by ugly clusters of industrial buildings. Passing through Flatbush, many buildings were actually in decay, and north of Greenwood Cemetery some abandoned buildings took on the aspect of bombed-out ruins. Passing trains were scrawled obscenely with graffiti. "The logos of bums," he heard Mark Allen mutter.

"You'd think they could clean it up," Irving Bernstein said, obviously appalled by the spectacle.

"Corrupt administration—they just don't give a damn," Allen said.

Mark Allen said to Brent, "You know the men have a barracks on the dock next to *Blackfin?*"

Nodding, Brent glanced to the back where the thirty-one enlisted men sat quietly. They were a picked group, all veterans of the Self Defense Force and fluent in English, which would be the only language they would hear for the next six months—if they lived that long. Four older men had actually served in the Imperial Navy at the end of WW II as fifteen-year-old apprentice seamen. They had survived because the Imperial Navy had lacked the ships to send them to sea, which would have been certain death. One of these men, who was in charge of the draft, was Chief Torpedoman Masayori Fujiwara—a compact, solid man with arms and shoulders of timbers and boulders. After his brief service in WW II, he had spent a career in the Self Defense Force. Despite the objections of his wife and family, he had come out of retirement to serve Admiral Fujita. He was tough, reliable, and commanded men like a whip. In fact, he carried a short leather cane and was not adverse to laying it across the buttocks of crewmen who did not step lively enough to suit him. In extreme cases when the cane failed to illicit the desired enthusiasm, he did not hesitate to use his fists to expedite orders. He brought to mind the ancient naval adage, "Officers lead, petty officers drive." Drive, indeed. Brent was convinced Fujiwara could drive the devil back through the gates of hell.

The bus rumbled through the long, claustrophobic confines of the Brooklyn Battery Tunnel and then emerged into the brilliant sunlight of Lower Manhattan, turning north on Broadway. There were dozens of taxis and buses, but traffic was still thin, pedestrians crowding the sidewalks and staring long and curiously at the bus. Wide-eyed and silently, the sailors gazed back under Fujiwara's hard stare.

They left Wall Street to the right with its clutter of stolid-looking financial buildings, sidewalks crowded with men in Brooks Brothers suits, while to the left the Gothic spire of Trinity Church pointed a thin finger to the sky. It was a charming old building and Brent chuckled to himself, reflecting on its antique cemetery where each grave was now in land worth hundreds of thousands of dollars. There were "oohs" and "ahs" as they passed the hundred-and-ten story twin towers of the World Trade Center, soaring a quarter of a mile

233

into the sky.

Finally, the bus made a sharp turn at Fourteenth Street, rumbled to the Hudson River, and then turned north on West Street along the waterfront. When they reached Twenty-third Street, the driver wheeled into a hard left turn that sent a groan through the vehicle. Shouting unintelligibly and pointing, he pulled up to the gates of a nearly deserted parking lot just above the waterfront. A ten-foot chain-link fence crowned with barbed wire surrounded the area and the only opening was gated and barred with a striped barrier. Two marines in camouflaged fatigues and carrying M-16's at port arms stood in front of the barrier.

Mark Allen leaned out of the window, showed his orders, acknowledged the salutes of the sentries, and the barrier was raised. With a roar of loose connecting rods and belching clouds of black smoke, the driver turned the bus toward the front of a dilapidated barracks. Rows of warehouses and service buildings concealed the river and the usual bent backs of giant cranes loomed above the buildings like arthritic old men. Hysters and trucks passed, filling the air with their busy sounds and spewing smoke as if fuel was in long supply. All drivers wore the dungarees of US Navy personnel and they all stole glances at the bus and its occupants.

"Christ. Left over from the Civil War," Mark Allen muttered, staring at the barracks.

"The CIA screwed up on this one," Brent said.

"Wait till you see our hotel," Mark Allen announced ominously.

The bus jerked to a stop and the doors banged open with a hiss of compressed air. Carrying their own canvas barracks bags, the three officers disembarked and then a sharp command from Chief Torpedoman Masayori Fujiwara and the draft fell out, carrying sea bags and assorted gear. Every man had a camera slung over his shoulder. Quickly, two rows were formed and the ranks dressed, facing the chief torpedoman and the three officers standing in a row behind him. A shouted command and the men dressed right and then mustered, shouting their names and ratings. The bus roared off and a large group of US Navy enlisted men gathered in front of a service building and stared curiously. Brent had not seen a single civilian since they had entered the gates.

Fujiwara did a smart about-face and reported to Mark Allen, "All present and accounted for, sir."

"Very well."

Brent felt a pang of pride, *real pros,* ran through his mind.

Fujiwara, thoroughly briefed by Admiral Allen on the long flight, turned to the draft and, with a voice strident enough to fill Yankee Stadium, explained the assignment to their new barracks, restrictions from liberty for all hands and the necessity to be ready to board *Blackfin* at 0800 hours in the morning for their first duty. The sub was not ready to quarter her entire crew and the draft would be temporarily housed in the barracks. He turned to Admiral Allen and saluted smartly. "Anything else, Admiral Allen?"

The admiral eyed the ranks of rigid seamen.

235

"Yes, Chief." He spoke to the draft. "According to my orders, two petty officers will meet with the draft this afternoon and hold a briefing session in the barracks. They will provide you with identity tags and papers, and I understand they will bring a VCR, show pictures and try to answer all of your questions." His eyes roamed the ranks. "Time is of the essence and secrecy is essential—that's why you're restricted. Later, liberty may be permitted, but on a restricted basis. I served here before," he waved to the south, "at the old Brooklyn Navy Yard." He pointed to a small building next to the barracks. "That's your mess hall. After you stow your gear, you can report there for a meal. There will be no necessity for any man to leave this base." He eyed the cameras. "Not for any reason, and stow your cameras—pictures of *Blackfin* are prohibited." He nodded to the chief.

"Draft! Attention! Fall out!"

The men, led by Fujiwara, shouldered their sea bags and filed toward the barracks.

"All right, you two. It's time to meet our new home," Allen said. He gestured. "She's moored at Charlie Four—just behind that warehouse."

At that instant, a jeep careened around the warehouse and screeched to a stop in front of the officers. The driver, a black man wearing the paired gold bars of a senior lieutenant on his collar and the gold dolphin of the submarine service on his chest, leaped to the ground and snapped out a sharp salute. Not as tall as Brent, he was as broad, his musculature filling his shirt and clearly visible rippling in his sleeve when he saluted. His

236

waist was tiny and his tight belt made this point emphatically. The hair under his cap showed as freshly washed coal, skin black — so black, it appeared blue in the slanting rays of the afternoon sun. His forehead was deep and intelligent, cheeks strong and regal, the broad nose flattened and pugged like a street fighter, black eyes sparkling. Brent saw power, intelligence, and pride there, and an impression of hauteur which was not totally belied when the ominous visage broke into a toothy grin — a forced expression of friendliness devoid of warmth.

"Lieutenant Reginald Williams, executive officer of *Blackfin* and temporarily in command," the big Negro said in a basso profundo that would have shamed Pavarotti. Williams gripped Mark Allen's hand. "Heard a lot about you, Admiral. It will be a pleasure to serve under you."

"Thank you, Lieutenant. I relieve you," Mark Allen said. He handed the executive officer his orders.

Williams glanced at them and saluted. "I am relieved, sir."

Smiling, the admiral returned the salute and pocketed his orders. He quipped, "I'll be the first admiral to command a submarine in the history of naval warfare." Everyone chuckled.

"Colonel Irving Bernstein, Israeli Intelligence," Bernstein said. Williams took the colonel's hand and stared at him with a puzzled look.

Admiral Allen explained, "Colonel Bernstein is on a secret mission with us. He will remain with us for security and he has top security clearance."

Bernstein handed his orders to Williams, who examined them briefly and then snorted his approval. Turning to Brent, he extended his hand. Brent found the man's hand big, square, and strong. He was troubled. There was something familiar about the lieutenant.

"Brent Ross," Brent said. And then, "Haven't we met?"

"Almost," Williams said.

"Almost?"

"Yes, Mr. Ross. I was playing middle linebacker at USC when you made All American at the Academy." He eyed Brent from head to toe. There was genuine regret in his voice and a challenge in his eyes. "Too bad. We didn't schedule you. It could've been interesting."

Brent laughed. "Very interesting, Mr. Williams."

Fascinated by the exchange, Allen and Bernstein stared at the pair silently.

"You're big, even for a fullback," Williams noted.

"I played at two-forty."

"Everyone tried to take you low and with your height you could fall forward for five yards."

Brent laughed but felt uneasy.

"I would've taken you high—waist high—driven you back."

"It was tried."

"Not by me."

"They took them off—sometimes on stretchers."

Mark Allen interrupted with an amused grin on his face. "Sorry to interrupt Old Jocks Week, but there's a small matter of a war to fight."

Williams helped Bernstein and Allen with their bags and then the officers boarded the jeep and roared off toward the docks.

Brent first caught a glimpse of *Blackfin* as Williams wheeled the jeep around a warehouse and drove onto a mile-long pier. She was alone, not another vessel moored within a thousand yards of her. A single crane was busy and work parties were loading boxes and crates of canned food stuffs and piles of gear. Marine guards were everywhere. Admiral Allen signaled to Williams to stop near the bow. The officers alighted and then with the admiral leading, they walked the length of the ship.

"Built by the Electric Boat Company at Groton, Connecticut," Mark Allen said.

"Right, sir," Williams said, with surprise in his voice. "How did you know?"

"Electric Boat built theirs lower, sleeker than Manitowoc Shipbuilding or the navy yards at Portsmouth and Mare Island—the only other yards that built these boats."

"I'll be damned," Williams muttered.

Grinning, Brent and Bernstein eyed each other. Brent was accustomed to the admiral's incredible depth of knowledge. He studied the long, sleek hull.

There was an inherent deadliness about the low, streamlined shape of the cruiser. With her bridge set well forward of amidships because of her two huge engine rooms housing the four powerful diesel-electric engines, her deck gun, a stubby cannon, was mounted nearly amidships just abaft a

239

small deck extending from the bridge where two twenty-millimeter guns were bolted to the deck. The bridge was streamlined and rounded, reminiscent of the front of the classic Cord automobile of the thirties with glassed portholes in its forward section. A steel-framed periscope-support tower rose from the center of the bridge and her two periscopes stabbed upward like a pair of shorn saplings. A score of crewmen were visible on her decks and superstructure, most scraping rust and loose paint, leaving large patches of newly painted red lead behind.

"Lord. She's all original," Mark Allen said, awed.

"Part of the deal with Japan's Parks Department, Admiral," Williams smirked.

"You're an employee of the Parks Department?"

"Yes, Admiral. Resigned my commission and went to work for the CIA. Then I was hired by Japan's Department of Parks. That's how we all wound up here." The big black waved at the work parties and the white teeth flashed. "Great benefits. The pay's good and we get all the rice we can eat."

Chuckling, the quartet stopped at the foot of the gangway and Mark Allen said, "They used to call these subs Fleet Boats. They were designed with the speed and range to operate with the fleet. But, of course, that concept was rarely used and they made their reputations as commerce raiders." He turned to Williams. "Review her specs, Lieutenant. I'm a little rusty."

Obviously pleased by the request, Williams

turned and gestured at the boat. His mind and memory worked like a computer's and he spoke like a machine. "Length, three hundred twelve feet, beam, twenty-seven, displacement, one thousand five hundred twenty-six tons surfaced, two thousand twenty-four tons submerged." He stabbed a finger aft. "Her four old sixteen-cylinder Wintons were replaced by new engines, the Fairbanks-Morse Thirty-Eight-D, each with six-thousand horsepower and she can do twenty-four knots surfaced, nine knots submerged. Her batteries are new and fully charged." He pointed at the weapons. "One five-inch, twenty-five caliber, two-twenties, but we're adding two fifties on the 'cigarette deck,' " he indicated the small deck just abaft the bridge where the Orlikons were mounted. "And two more fifties and a twenty forward." The finger pointed to a small platform being welded to the front of the bridge. "She's of all-welded construction and her designed maximum operational depth is three hundred feet—not much when you consider the depths where our boomers operate."

"But she should be good for six hundred feet," Mark Allen added.

"She is," Williams assured him.

"Range?" Mark Allen queried.

"Nineteen thousand miles, Admiral."

Mark Allen scratched his chin. "Cruising at ten knots, on the surface?"

"Right, sir."

"You've increased her range, Mr. Williams."

"The Fairbanks-Morse engines are more efficient, sir."

241

"Have you taken her out?" Brent asked.

Williams shook his head. "We've run four dock trials, and the engines and power trains are perfect, but she's not ready for sea. Her hull's been checked by Electric Boat and it's as good as new. We've overhauled or replaced every valve and fitting, but we're still working on her main induction valve, installing our new communications gear and ECM and we only have half of a partially trained crew." He stared at Admiral Allen. "We need a lot of dry runs, Admiral."

"And we've got to build an efficient crew that's half Japanese and half American," Allen added.

Bernstein asked, "How many tubes?"

Williams eyed the Israeli. "Six forward and four aft."

"Fish?" Brent asked.

"Not aboard yet. We should get the new Mark Forty-Eight — we'll load them at night."

"No wires, no terminal guidance," Brent said.

"Right, Lieutenant," Williams acknowledged. "That's the agreement reached at Geneva."

Bernstein stared at the boat, obviously troubled. "How many of these boats were lost?"

There was a long silence. Finally, Admiral Allen said, "Fifty-two."

"Good Lord. All those men," Bernstein muttered to himself.

Brent stared at the boat silently. It was long, sleek, lethal, her every aspect was that of a killer. But the exchange had brought to mind a thought that has terrorized generations of men who have served in the silent, black depths. She could also

242

be a tomb—his steel mausoleum. Had been for thousands of others. The realization dropped in his stomach like a cold rock. New risks. Another way to die. Blasted by depth charges and bombs. A hideous shrieking end in collapsing compartments with air superheated by the compression of the depths—roasted lungs, drowning like rats in total darkness. He felt it again. Complete helplessness to control his own destiny. He was a pawn in the games played by other men in the Middle East, Geneva, in Tokyo, Washington—men who did not even know he existed and could care less.

With Admiral Mark Allen leading, the officers filed past a Marine guard who brought his M-16 to present arms and across the gangway to the sub's deck. Here a young ensign and a rating, each wearing duty belts and holstered forty-fives, snapped to attention and saluted. A log book and a telephone were on a table next to the enlisted man. Returning the salutes, the four men stepped onto the deck, which was actually a long steel platform built over the pressure hull, slotted and holed for the easy flow of water.

Williams gestured. "Ensign Frederick Hasse, our torpedo officer," he said. He said to Hasse, "Admiral Allen has taken command."

Brent heard the rating speak into a phone, his words echoed hollowly by the ship's PA system. "Captain's on board. Captain's on board."

A year out of the Academy, Hasse was a short, slender young man with dark-brown hair over bushy eyebrows and darting brown eyes that made it obvious the young man was finding it difficult to appear at ease. In fact, he stuttered a little as he grasped hands and exchanged greetings. And then answering Williams's query, "The chief engineer is in the engine room and Lieutenant Cadenbach is in the forward torpedo room."

"Have them meet me in the wardroom, immediately," Mark Allen said.

"Aye, aye, sir." Hasse turned to the rating. "Pass the word. Mr. Dunlap and Mr. Cadenbach to the wardroom." The rating picked up a phone and spoke hurriedly.

Admiral Allen gestured and Williams led, climbing up the side of the superstructure and stepping down into the bridge, a curved platform in the front of the superstructure protected by a steel windscreen. Brent saw a wheel, annunciators, a rudder angle indicator, and mounts for heavy binoculars. Williams gestured at an open hatch. "The only access to the pressure hull when under way." He slipped down through the round opening that was much like a manhole with a hinged cover. Brent noticed the cover was convex in shape to withstand pressure and it had a locking wheel in the center. The wheel had a crank for fast "dogging" and a short rope wrapped around a wooden handle hung from the outer rim of the cover. Speed. It was all built for speed.

They dropped into a cylindrical compartment about eight feet in diameter and about sixteen feet in length. It was jammed with a stunning array of equipment; gauges, meters, cranks, dials, scopes.

Brent was overwhelmed and depressed by the mass of unfamiliar gear. While in the Academy, he had had two orientation cruises on the *George K. Polk,* a nuclear powered SSBN of the Lafayette class that carried sixteen Trident missiles. Compared to *Blackfin,* the SSBN had been enormous and it had been completely computerized. He saw nothing that even remotely reminded him of a computer, all of the equipment surrounding him dating from the early forties. He felt a harsh wave of frustration and self-doubt rise, but remained silent.

Allen nodded and Williams gestured at two periscopes mounted in the middle of the room. "This is the command center of the boat and the captain makes his submerged attacks from her." He looked at Bernstein. "We're just above the pressure hull — in a sense, the conning tower is an extension of it. In fact, the control room is under our feet and the captain can shout commands down that hatch." He pointed to another open hatch. "He can con from there."

Allen looked around at the mass of equipment crammed into the tiny compartment. "Jesus Christ, she hasn't changed much." He stabbed a finger as he pivoted around. "Attack scope, speed indicator, depth gauge, water pressure gauge, engine-room controls, rev counter, telephone circuit board, sonar, radar, TDC, helm." His moist eyes revealed the emotion he felt. "It's all the same — it's all here, after all these years."

"We're getting new radar and sonar, sir," Williams said. "Even ECM."

"Approved at Geneva?" Allen asked.

"All wrapped up, sir," Williams said.

245

"Then the Russians must know about this ship—her true purpose," Bernstein said. "And if they know, Tass Pravda and Izvestia will broadcast it to the whole world. I can guarantee that."

Williams said to Bernstein, "Not really, Colonel. The US Navy is refitting six more of these boats—all museum boats. With all of our satellites destroyed and a shortage of AWACS, the Navy's desperate for reconnaissance and these old boats can do the job and they're a lot cheaper than 'nukes'—they're running a billion a copy. And it's been agreed that the old boats can be equipped with the latest sonar and radar. The Russians are doing the same with a half-dozen Whiskies and Zulus." Williams's white teeth glared against his black skin as he smiled. "We're kind of sneaking *Blackfin* through. 'Ivan' will never suspect."

Allen, in obvious high spirits, chuckled his approval. Brent was not convinced. Bernstein maintained a skeptical silence.

The four officers dropped through the hatch, down a ladder into the control room. Descending the ladder, Brent became conscious of a smell that he had barely detected in the conning tower, but now it became much stronger and seemed to permeate everything. He wrinkled his nose and sniffed the stuffy, humid atmosphere. Diesel oil and sweating human bodies. The universal smell of the diesel-electric submarine—and he knew it would become much, much worse with extended cruises, long dives, and the lack of water.

Stepping off the last rung, he found himself in a room, perhaps twice the size of the conning tower. With controls duplicating the controls in the conning tower, the control room was jammed with even more equipment and gauges, the overhead crisscrossed with pipes and valves. Four young ratings working on a variety of equipment came upright to attention.

"As you were—at ease," Admiral Allen said. The men returned to their work.

Brent was amazed by the amount of polished brass glowing from dials, gauges, switches, and levers. If the conning tower was the brain of the ship, the control room was the heart. He saw engine-room controls, fuel gauges, rows of voltmeters, ammeters, shaft-revolution indicators, rows of valves, cranks, levers. *Mind boggling,* he said to himself. This was a different world from the SSBN.

Bernstein was even more confused, staring at two large hand wheels mounted below rows of gauges and banks of lights. Mark Allen answered the quizzical stares. "That's the diving station. The diving officer stands about where you are, Colonel. The two large wheels control the bow and stern planes which are actually horizontal rudders. When we dive, the bow planes overcome the boat's positive buoyancy and her own momentum drives her under the surface." He grasped the wheel, which was wrapped with line and varnished. "When submerged, the operator watches the depth gauge and adjusts his planes to maintain depth."

"Like flying," Bernstein observed.

"Exactly," Mark Allen said. He moved his hand to the other wheel. "The stern planesman watches

247

the clinometer and it is his responsibility to keep the boat on an even keel."

"Power assisted?" Bernstein said.

"Of course," Allen said. "The latest power steering." Everyone chuckled at the admiral's quip.

He indicated the rows of gauges next to the diving station. "Those gauges indicate whether the various openings in the pressure hull are open or closed by burning red or green lights." He smiled. "We used to call it 'the Christmas tree.' "

"We still do, Admiral," Williams said. Allen pointed and the executive officer led the men forward, past more crewmen hard at work and the strangest toilet Brent had ever seen. In a tiny room, it was bolted to the deck against the curved side of the hull. It was surrounded by a maze of valves. Williams saw Bernstein's eyes widen and smiled. "Better not turn the wrong valve or the shit will not only hit the fan, but the overhead, the deck, and everything else within ten yards."

The men laughed.

"Why, there's a fire extinguisher in there," Bernstein said, pointing to a red cylinder with the usual funnel-shaped nozzle and Carbon Dioxide lettered in black on the tank. The extinguisher was mounted on the bulkhead next to the toilet.

Williams spoke gravely. "Yes, sir. Sometimes our cook prepares Mexican food and some of the men . . ."

He was interrupted by laughter. Bernstein was confused, looked around, face reddening, and finally joined the hilarity. Brent would never know if the Israeli caught the humor.

They stepped over the high coaming of a watertight door into a passageway lined with bulkheads of gleaming stainless steel. Curtained doors broke the sides. They were in officer country.

Bernstein said, "I've seen no batteries."

"You're walking on them, Colonel," Williams said. "The forward battery well is under the deck."

Mark Allen spoke. "If I remember, there were one hundred twenty-six cells in this compartment and another one hundred twenty-six in the aft compartment."

Williams nodded. "Good memory, Admiral. Six fore-and-aft rows of twenty-one cells."

"Must be a lot of weight there," Bernstein said.

"Right, Colonel. Each cell is twenty-one inches wide, fifteen inches long, and fifty-four inches high and weighs one thousand, six hundred fifty pounds."

Bernstein whistled. "There's a lot of boat to drive," Mark Allen said.

Williams stepped to a door and pulled a curtain aside and the four officers entered the wardroom. Not more than ten by twelve, the small room had a single table bolted to the center of the deck with two space-saving benches instead of chairs. A small refrigerator was built in under a stainless-steel drainboard and sink, and in the aft bulkhead, a closed pass-through led to the galley. Two cupboards with latched doors were above the sink and in a corner of the counter was a stack of a half-dozen copies of *Sports Illustrated*. A tiny desk was attached to the aft bulkhead. Overhead in the usual clutter of conduits, cables, and pipes was a speaker, two lights in big saucerlike fixtures, and an exhaust fan. In the center of the room, two officers were standing at attention.

The first, a senior lieutenant of average height who appeared to be about thirty years of age, stepped forward. Fair and streaked with platinum, his hair reminded Brent of dry sand in the morning sun, eyes blue-green and intelligent. "Chief Engineer Brooks Dunlap," the lieutenant said, shaking the admiral's hand.

Brent found Dunlap's hand big and rough, and he noticed grease on the sleeve of the engineer's tan shirt. When Dunlap smiled, deep lines fell off from the corners of his eyes and mouth, dark as if grease had been ground into his flesh and indicating more years than Brent had first guessed. He smelled of diesel oil and solvents and his fingernails were black. Brent felt sudden confidence—an insight that told him he was in the presence of a master mechanic, a man who knew his engines and probably loved them as well.

The second officer was a tall rail of a young junior lieutenant in his early twenties. His most prominent feature was a sharp, chiseled nose that appeared even larger in a narrow face with sunken cheeks and pointed chin. His eyes were brown, bright, and alert. Brent smiled to himself as he reached for the young man's hand—he looked just like a youthful John Carradine. Although his hand felt like a bag full of rocks, the grip was firm and his smile friendly. "Lieutenant Charlie Cadenbach," he said in a high, thin voice. "Navigator and assistant attack officer." He shook hands all around.

Admiral Mark Allen gestured and the officers seated themselves. Allen eyed the new officers. "How much experience do you"—he moved his eyes to Williams, "do all of you have with these old fleet boats?"

Williams spoke for the trio. "We all were in the recommissioning crew of *Fifer* at Mare Island."

"She's a Gato?"

"Yes, Admiral. We were involved in every aspect, Admiral. Engineering, ordnance . . ."

"Sea trials?"

"Yes, Admiral. We shook her down and every one of the enlisted men on board *Blackfin* was in that crew."

"Very good," Mark Allen said, obviously relieved.

Brooks Dunlap spoke to Admiral Allen. "It'll be an honor to serve with you, Admiral. I've heard a lot about you—*Yonaga*—the battles you've fought for all of us."

Allen acknowledged the statement with a gracious nod. Dunlap turned to Brent Ross. "Heard a lot about you, too, Mr. Ross. The American Samurai."

"Also, the All American," Williams said with narrowed eyes.

Brent thought he detected an edge of sarcasm. "I've flattened a lot of linebackers in my time—left my cleat marks right up their butts," he said, staring across the table directly into the Negro's black eyes. Williams straightened as if someone had jabbed him in the small of the back with a sharp stick.

251

Allen's voice brought a halt to the exchange. "How many enlisted men do you have assigned?" he asked.

Williams moved his eyes from Brent slowly. "Thirty-two, sir."

"We have thirty-one men in our draft, all experienced submariners, too, but not in these boats. We need ten—fifteen more men and there are only five of us." He rapped the table with his knuckles. "I need four more officers."

"We have ten more enlisted volunteers coming aboard tomorrow and I expect three new officers."

"Only three?"

"Sorry, sir. That's all."

"It'll have to do. Are they experienced submariners?"

"I don't know, Admiral. The CIA just informed me about the numbers. That's it."

Mark Allen glanced at the chief engineer. "What is the condition of the engineering department?"

"We've had four dock trials, Admiral, and the engines are four-oh." He made a circle with his thumb and forefinger and held it up for all to see. "We're on shore power, but our auxiliary engines are operational. I have a fine crew, but not enough men to maintain three steaming sections."

"Yes. Yes," Mark Allen said impatiently. "We brought twelve machinists for you." He turned back to Williams. "I would like to take her on her first sea trial within a week."

The black thumbed his chin. "The boat should be ready, sir. It's the crew."

"Will Electric Boat help us?"

"They've been great, sir. Four of their engineers are staying in a hotel nearby and are on call. Two of them are old retired men who actually worked on the design of these subs. Real pros."

"Good. Good," Allen said, rubbing his hands together. "What about ordnance?"

Williams nodded to Charlie Cadenbach. "Our ammunition and torpedoes are stored in a shed at the end of the pier, Admiral," Cadenbach said. "There is no ordnance on board except small arms."

"Very well." Mark Allen glanced at the pass-through. "I saw dry stores being loaded."

"The galley's operating, sir." Suddenly anguished, Williams shot a glance to the rear. "I'm sorry, gentlemen. Would you like something? Coffee? A sandwich?" He waved at one of the cabinets, "A highball?"

Allen's eyes flashed. "Liquor?"

"Why, yes," Williams said, reading the hard look on the admiral's face with his own anxiety.

"Throw it overboard. Now!" Mark Allen bellowed.

"Pablo!" Williams shouted. "Pablo Fortuno!" The swinging doors to the galley flew open and a short, dark man with the flat, wide nostrils and thick, full lips so common to the people of the South Pacific Islands entered. With jet-black hair that appeared as if it had been rinsed in India ink, the short, stocky man's skin was pockmarked and his stomach bulged under his whites like so many naval cooks Brent had known. There was an anxious look on the man's face and he was wringing

253

his hands like a housewife caught with her lover. Obviously he had been listening behind the closed doors.

Williams said to the cook, "Empty the liquor locker and throw the booze overboard."

Allen said to the cook, "Every bottle. I'll court-martial you myself if you cheat."

"Aye, aye, sir," Fortuno said, opening the locker. In a moment there was a clink and clatter as the cook gathered a half-dozen bottles. Brent noticed one was Johnnie Walker Black Label. He winced. The cook dropped the bottles in a bag and fled.

"There will be no drinking on board this ship. My standing orders. Under way or in port." Allen moved his eyes from face to face in short jerky movements. "Understood?"

"Aye, aye, sir," the men chorused. Brent was awed. He was seeing a new side to Admiral Mark Allen.

Mark Allen's fingers began a tattoo on the table and the anger vanished as quickly as it had appeared. "We have another problem. The day after tomorrow, Thursday, Lieutenant Brent Ross, Colonel Irving Bernstein, and I must be at the UN at ten hundred hours to meet with certain groups from the Middle East." The fingers stopped and the hand became a club. He turned to Williams. "You're the exec. Draw me up a schedule of orientation procedures for the new hands. We will start at zero eight hundred hours tomorrow. We'll run them through their diving and surface stations here at the dock until they can perform in their sleep." He struck the table for emphasis. "Maybe we can start shaking her down in a week."

"Aye, aye, sir," Williams said, relieved at the admiral's change in demeanor.

"Anything else?" Allen asked. There was a short silence broken only by the sounds of the overhead fan.

Bernstein gestured at a display of Japanese flags on the bulkhead behind Brooks Dunlap. "What's that about?"

The men turned. Brooks said, "That's *Blackfin's* score in WW II." He stabbed a finger. "The merchant flags represent thirty-eight merchantmen sunk and the ensigns represent five warships."

"There's a cartoon dolphin firing a torpedo from a crossbow in the upper corner," Bernstein noted.

Williams smiled. "It was a Disney generation, Colonel. That's the ship's logo."

Bernstein was not satisfied. "The locomotive, trucks, stars, a crane . . ." He pointed. "That other flag and the pennant?"

Williams said, "The stars represent eight patrols, the blue-red-yellow pennant is the Presidential Unit Citation, flags with white centers represent ships damaged but not sunk, the locomotive, trucks, and crane were destroyed when she penetrated Minami Daito Harbor and shot up the town."

"Good Lord," the Israeli said. "Shot up a town." He moved his finger to a new aiming point. "That flag. It looks French."

"Right, Colonel," Williams said. "It is. She knocked off a Vichy French 'can' off Indochina."

"You weren't at war with them."

Dunlap and Cadenbach laughed. *"Blackfin* was,"

255

the engineer said.

The Americans chuckled and looked at each other while the Israeli sat stolidly.

"Quite a historical vessel," Bernstein said.

Williams nodded agreement, spoke to the Israeli. "She was commissioned in November of '41 — just in time for the kickoff. Her eight patrols were all made in Japanese home waters. Over a hundred fifty thousand tons of enemy shipping sunk. She got her Presidential Unit Citation for her raid on Minami Daito. She was decommissioned in '47 and placed in the Reserve Fleet, New London Group." He smiled. "But the old girl came to life again late in '51 during the Korean War and landed reconnaissance personnel behind North Korean lines. In '54 she was designated 'out of commission in reserve.' Then in 1960 she was towed from Mare Island to Seattle where she became a Naval Reserve training vessel. She was stricken from the lists . . ."

" 'Stricken from the lists?' " Bernstein interrupted.

Williams nodded. "Yes. That's 'Navy' for 'too old,' ready for the scrap yard — razor blades and hairpins."

"But obviously, she wasn't scrapped."

"Some old submariners stepped in — raised money, and with the help of the Navy League bought her, had her towed to New York Harbor and made a memorial of her."

Bernstein tugged on the point of his beard. "Quite a career — quite a fighter."

"Our ship has had a distinguished career, gentle-

256

men," Allen said suddenly. "Will we live up to it?"

There were shouts of, "Hear! Hear!"

Good Lord, he's another Fujita, Brent said to himself.

"There's one other thing, Admiral," Williams said. "All of your cabins have been ripped apart — new wiring, pumps. It'll be a couple of days before you can use them." He gestured at Dunlap and Cadenbach, "We're bunking in the chiefs' quarters."

"Accommodations have been arranged for us in a hotel nearby," Mark Allen said. "The Oakmont Suites."

Dunlap, Cadenbach, and Williams exchanged a strange look. "I beg your pardon, sir," Dunlap said cautiously. "But that's not exactly the Waldorf."

"I know, but it's nearby."

"Yes, Admiral."

"That's all that counts," Mark Allen said.

The officers shrugged.

Mark Allen tugged on his ear thoughtfully, turned to Williams. "Mr. Williams," he said. "As CO, I should stay aboard. Please exchange billets with me — if you don't mind staying at the Oakmont Suites."

"But, sir, the chiefs' quarters are very uncomfortable . . ."

"Mr. Williams," Allen interrupted sharply. "If you don't mind."

"I'll get my gear together," Williams conceded.

"Very well," Mark Allen said. "That's settled." He gestured to the door. "Come, gentlemen, I want a tour." His eyes moved from Williams to

Dunlap to Cadenbach. "From periscopes to bilges, from tubes to tubes."

"Aye, aye, sir," the officers chorused. They came to their feet.

With Reginald Williams leading, the group moved toward the bow to the forward torpedo room. Set in vertical banks of three, the solid brass doors of all six tubes were open. Twenty-one inches in diameter, they were huge, moldings glistening with polished brass, nestled in a jungle of valves, endless piping, springs, levers, and switches. Three torpedomen who had had their heads inside the twenty-one-inch openings polishing the stainless steel, came to attention. "As you were," Mark Allen said. Self-consciously, the men returned to work.

The admiral pointed to brass rollers and loading trays beneath bunks secured to the ship's sides. "The fish are stored there under those bunks and are actually reloaded by hand with lines, pulleys, and rammers," he said.

Bernstein eyed the tubes. "How do they fire them," he asked.

Mark Allen nodded to his executive officer. Williams took his cue. "They're fired electrically from the conning tower." He pointed to a panel mounted on the bulkhead between the two banks of tubes. The panel had six glass windows and six switches below the windows. That's a firing panel. It's similar to one in the conning tower. If the firing circuit fails, the chief torpedoman can hand-fire the fish by turning those valves and pulling those levers." He gestured to two banks of valves

258

and levers.

Mark Allen nodded. "Rigged a little different from *Grouper*," he said.

"There will be differences, sir. She was wired with new firing circuits in '51. As you know, no two boats are exactly the same," Williams said.

"True. True," Mark Allen acknowledged. He turned to Brooks Dunlap. "Let's see your country, Chief Engineer."

"Aye, aye, sir," Dunlap said, turning to the stern. As the officers left, the three torpedomen sighed with relief.

Following the engineer's lead, the group moved aft through watertight doors, back through the control room, and into the maneuvering room. Crewmen were working everywhere, adjusting and testing equipment. To a man, they came to attention as the admiral passed. Mark Allen smiled, nodded, and repeated, "As you were. At ease."

Stopping in the middle of the maneuvering room, Williams waved at a panel at least eight feet long cluttered with volt meters, ammeters, indicators, levers. "Control stand," he said. He pointed at a pair of annunciators. "Remote controls for engine shutdown, and that," he pointed at the meters, "is an auxiliary switchboard." They passed another head and a small lathe crowded in a corner against a bulkhead.

Another watertight door and they passed the radio room and galley. The galley was no larger than a closet and a single cook labored there making sandwiches and coffee. The compactness of the small cylinder came home again to Brent Ross. In

259

the crews' quarters, the chain-suspended bunks were pulled against the sides and secured away from the center line of the ship. Entering the forward engine room through the usual watertight door, Brent found a narrow passageway between two giant Fairbanks-Morse engines. The floor plates were of corrugated steel. Four machinist mates were hard at work on one of the sixteen-cylinder engines, tools scattered on the plates. Quickly, they came to attention and stepped aside. Allen acknowledged them and they returned to work after the party squeezed past.

"A SSBN is an auditorium compared to this," Brent muttered. The officers chuckled.

Brooks Dunlap gestured aft. "Each of these engines is connected to a generator, and both port and starboard are identical engine generator sets." He pointed forward. "Over there under the grating is one of our auxiliary diesels geared to another generator which is almost under our feet." He stomped the grating with his foot. "You can't see them, but under the port engine we have two vapor compressor distillers for making fresh water." He smiled at Brent. "But this is no SSBN. If we're lucky, one bath per week per man—unless, of course, you're lucky enough to be on the bridge in a rain squall."

"What's back there?" Bernstein asked, pointing to the stern.

"The aft engine room and the stern tubes," Dunlap said. He began to walk aft.

"Belay that," Mark Allen said. He glanced at his watch. "Colonel Bernstein, Lieutenant Brent Ross, and Mr. Williams, it's time to check into your hotel." He stared at Williams. "I would like to confer with you, Mr. Williams, before you go ashore."

"Aye, aye, sir," the big black said.

With the admiral leading, the officers turned and walked toward the wardroom.

While Brent and Colonel Bernstein waited for Reginald Williams on the dock, Brent spotted a pair of pay phones near the main gate. Quickly, he made his way to the phones while Bernstein wisely remained at a discreet distance. Brent dialed Dale's number and she answered immediately.

"Oh, Brent, it's so good to hear your voice."

"Yours, too." He explained his assignment and the location of the sub, forgetting that Dale already knew the particulars, had arranged the details of the transfer.

"I know. I know," she said. "I've been waiting for your call. When will I see you?"

"We're all restricted."

"Oh, Lord."

"I'm staying at the Oakmont Suites."

"That fleabag?"

"Your CIA arranged it."

"I had nothing to do with that. I know the hotel's near Pier Sixty-eight."

"I haven't seen it yet."

"Practically on the corner of Twenty-third and West, Brent. That's off the base. That doesn't sound restricted. Why can't I see you there?"

With the thought of seeing Dale alone, Brent felt the fire begin to mount deep in his groin. He closed his eyes and shook his head. "Sorry, Dale. I don't have that right—the others are restricted to the ship or the base. It would be dishonorable."

"But I'm CIA!"

"I know, Dale."

"When will I see you?" There was anguish in her tone.

Misery twisted his voice. "I don't know." He thought for a moment. "Duty tomorrow and I have a meeting at the UN Thursday."

"Thursday? Damn, I'll be in DC. Why the UN?"

"A representative of the PLO wants to meet with Fujita's representatives."

"They're a bunch of murdering bums. What about other Arab groups?"

"Unknown, Dale." He tapped the coin box in frustration. "Friday night—I'll try to get liberty Friday night."

"Oh, yes, yes. You can come to my place. I'll cook for you. Just the two of us."

Again he felt the heat rise, twisted uncomfortably. "The meat locker?"

She laughed. "Yes, that's right. You have the address. It's not far from Pier Sixty-eight." The timbre of her voice dropped to a deep, ominous tone. "There's a rumor your friend Kenneth Rosencrance is in town."

Brent felt his heart leap and the veins in his neck began to pound. "Rosencrance?" Dale McIntyre seemed to know everything.

"Yes, recruiting more killers, and he's representing Kadafi in some diplomatic mission to meet with some Iraqi and Iranian diplomats."

"Keep me informed — I have something to settle with him."

"I know. And, Brent, have you heard the latest about the Ayatollah Khomeini?" Silence. "Scuttlebutt has it he's calling off the war against Iraq. Iran and Iraq will throw in with Kadafi in the *jihad* against Israel and *Yonaga*."

"Jesus Christ, a hundred million fanatical Muslims."

"That's why I think Rosencrance is here — to meet with the Iraqis and Iranians at the UN."

"That doesn't make sense."

"Yes it does — if you're an Arab. Neither group will enter the other's capital. At the UN — or Geneva, for that matter — neither nation loses face. And all the machinery's here — at the UN."

"But I mean Rosencrance is a fighter pilot — a killer. That's all he is. He's no diplomat."

"You underestimate him, Brent. He's adopted the Muslim faith and has become Kadafi's favorite. He's in charge of all fighters, and rumor has it Moammar trusts him more than his own generals."

He punched the coin box so hard the bell rang. "Brent! You still there?"

"Yes. Yes. I just want to see you, Dale."

"Friday night, Brent."

"All right. If I can't make it, I'll phone you."

"Make it, damn it."

"All right, Dale. I'll make it." He could see Wil-

263

liams and Bernstein approaching. "Got to leave."

"I miss you, Brent. I think of you all the time."

"You're never out of my thoughts, Dale."

"Friday."

"Friday, if I have to jump ship—wars, the UN be damned."

Reluctantly, they both hung up.

The Oakmont Suites appeared to have been built at the turn of the century and then forgotten— never visited by a painter, carpenter, carpet man, or—as Brent discovered later—a plumber. Seventeen stories high, it was built of unreinforced brick which had settled so that the exterior lines of decaying grout appeared slightly wavy like strata in earthquake country.

"Jesus," Brent said, entering the dilapidated lobby. "We've entered a time warp. I wonder if George Washington slept here?"

Williams snorted. "Valley Forge was probably luxurious compared to this."

They passed a half-dozen collapsing leather sofas, two of which held bums who were sound asleep. One sleeper had a shopping cart filled with trash tied to his wrist with a rope. Bernstein was appalled. "You don't see this in Israel," he said.

"Richest country in the world, we keep telling ourselves, and you find thousands of them—all over New York," Williams said, edging up to the counter. He pointed at one sleeping tramp who was black. "Completely integrated," he added sarcastically.

The three men looked for the night clerk. Brent finally found him almost concealed behind an antique switchboard reading a battered *Hustler* magazine and sipping a glass of wine. A cheap bottle of Burgundy was on the desk in front of him. Williams slapped the counter and the man looked up. Smiling defensively, he rose and walked to the counter. He was very old, bald and thin in the way peculiar to men who derive most of their sustenance from the sugar in wine—white flesh lined like crumpled paper, rheumy bloodshot eyes, stooped posture. "Ah, gentlemen," he said in a hoarse, wine-addled voice with a surprisingly cultured timbre. "You wish to be our guests?"

"Right. Three rooms," Williams said. "They've been reserved under 'Mark Allen.' "

The clerk fingered a register, the skin of his arms clinging to his bones like dead flesh ready to slough off. "Ah, yes. Two rooms were reserved by the Profile Boat Works."

"Three rooms," Williams insisted.

The man looked up. There was fear on his face. "Sorry, sir," he wheedled. "A suite with two doubles and a single next to it and we have no vacancies." His voice began to tremble. "I'm sorry. I'm very, very sorry."

Williams looked at Brent. "You and I bunk together and Colonel Bernstein can take the single. He has the rank. Okay?"

Bernstein and Brent nodded, picked up the small bags both carried, and followed Williams to the elevator which looked exactly like a giant bird cage built for a six-foot canary.

265

"No vacancies," Bernstein snorted.

"No doubt the place is overrun by the jet set," Brent added.

"Just another Hilton," Williams said, pulling the steel mesh door of the elevator aside. They entered the car silently.

The room was large, with two floor-to-ceiling windows, two battered beds, and a mahogany nightstand supporting a lamp with a huge ornate shade like millinery Lillian Russell would have worn on a spring morning. The light switches were round and required a circular twist to operate. Thrown into the middle of the room on the wide planks of the hardwood floor was a threadbare rug. The bathroom was large, containing a sink with two leaky faucets and a huge Victorian tub resting on four cast-iron feet. A masterpiece of nineteenth-century engineering, the toilet's tank was at the ceiling with a long chain hanging down from the flushing handle. When the chain was pulled, the flood of water shook the entire room. Brent soon discovered the bathroom door was warped and would not close. In fact, everything seemed bent, warped, twisted, and out of plumb. Right angles were scarce.

"There's no place like home," Williams said, throwing his small bag on one of the beds.

"Seen better," Brent said.

"Are you hungry?" Williams asked.

"Negative. Ate on the plane—or maybe I should say I was poisoned."

Williams nodded. "I ate on the ship just before you came on board." He reached into his bag and pulled out a half-dozen sandwiches. "Pablo fixed these for us—better than trying to eat anything in this neighborhood. Anyway, in a sense, the admiral has restricted us."

His conversation with Dale came back to Brent with a sharp impact. "I know."

Williams smiled slyly. "I brought something to break the monotony." He pulled a bottle of Haig & Haig from his bag. Brent raised an eyebrow. Williams explained. "The admiral ordered Pablo to throw all of the booze in the wardroom overboard—right?"

Brent smiled. "That was my interpretation."

"Well, this was in my locker."

Laughing, the two officers moved to the window where there was a table with a pitcher and two glasses. Pouring two stiff drinks, the executive officer said, "We should invite Colonel Bernstein."

Brent was seeing a friendly side to the man he had never suspected existed. He shook his head. "He said he was exhausted—was going to hit the sack."

Williams raised his glass. "*Blackfin*. And call me Reggie."

"Okay, Reggie." Brent raised his glass and drank with the executive officer. Brent spoke thoughtfully. "I know nothing about Fleet Boats—*Blackfin*."

"You're an expert in communications."

Brent nodded. "That's what they tell me."

The big black took a drink. "You've been in on

Glasnost—the latest dope on negotiations, Brent, correct?"

Brent shrugged. "Only what came over on *Yonaga*. Why?"

Williams drained his glass. Refilled both glasses. "What do you know about the Russian RBU six-thousand depth charge launcher?"

Brent drank. Nodded. "Yes. I know about it. A six-barrel mortar that can fire six three-hundred-millimeter charges six thousand meters ahead of the attacking vessel."

"Right. A real bitch—automatic reloading, and each charge weighs four hundred pounds. Will we be up against it?"

"It's out, Reggie. All mortar systems are out along with the homing Five-Three-Three torpedo."

Williams sighed, drank, and toyed with his glass. *"Blackfin* would have no chance against the Five-Three-Three—passive and active homing, the wire. . ." He tapped his glass on the table and then emptied it.

Brent began to wonder about the man's capacity, but matched the exec's pace and emptied his own glass. Immediately, Williams refilled the glasses. "Sonar and old-fashioned six-hundred-pound charges with hydrostatic fuses—that came out of Geneva—and that's all, Reggie."

"That's enough. One charge within fourteen feet and we're kaput." He turned his palms up in a gesture of helplessness. Brent felt tiny frozen insects run up and down his spine and took a big gulp of Scotch. Reginald continued, "Do you think the Russians will honor the agreement, Brent?"

"They've shown a definite weakness in the honor department," Brent said. "But, yes, they're very reluctant to give anyone their latest technology. It goes back to the Six Day War when the Egyptians surrendered hundreds of tanks and whole batteries of the Russian's latest SAM missiles and fire control systems intact to the Israelis. Most of the electronics gear was shipped to the Pentagon. The Russians never got over that."

Again the glasses were refilled, and Brent felt the room move. He shook his head and drank some more. He felt warm and relaxed for the first time in a week. And Reggie was suddenly a fine old friend, his early animosity wiped clean by the Haig & Haig. He drank again, although he knew he had had too much. The room began to turn. Suddenly, Brent pushed himself to his feet, emptied his glass, and said, "I'd better hit the sack." He moved unsteadily to one of the beds and collapsed on his back.

Williams continued to drink and talk, but his enunciation began to suffer. "You're gonna havta run a couple quick openers against me."

"Any time, Reggie."

The executive officer studied his Scotch. Took a drink. "We'll get up a game o' flag."

"That's not contact."

"It'll be for you an' me."

"You're on, Reggie. We'll get some of the crew. A bottle of Haig and Haig says you never hold me to no gain."

Williams grunted his approval, threw his head back, gulped his drink and rolled his glass, clattering across the table, breaking on the floor. Weaving slightly, he made his way to his bed, collapsed on his back with a sigh. "How do ya feel about roomin' with a nigger?"

Brent laughed at the cruel question. "What took you so long, man?"

"You think I'm a stereotype?"

"With a question like that you are."

"Then what am I to you?"

"My executive officer who is a little arrogant and I don't particularly like him."

Williams snickered. "Cool man. And I think you're conceited and overrated."

Mellowed by the scotch and on the verge of sleep from fatigue and jet lag, Brent thought the remark funny. He laughed so hard he shook the bed.

"You think I'm funny."

"A riot. But I'm liable to take you up on that when I sober up."

"Would you like to hear about a real riot — South-Central Los Angeles where I was born?"

"I've heard it before. But if it'll help unwind your psyche, tell me."

Reginald ignored the retort, began to tell his story while Brent smiled and drifted off into a quasi dreamworld where his companion's voice droned on, interrupting like an early bird's song intruding on a dreamer.

"I was born in south-central Los Angeles — Watts. A rotten hole."

Brent stirred from the dream. "Yeah, I've been there."

"Been there—you're a brave man."

"I wanted to see the Watts Towers—Simon Rodia's art—so I went. No one bothered me."

"You're big."

"Size helps."

Williams moved on, talking to the cracks in the ceiling. "My mother was LaTanya Williams—single . . . I didn't know my father."

Brent felt a compulsion to speak, but his muscles were jelly and even the lumpy mattress seemed comfortable and enfolding like Dale's soft hand. The thoughts were there, but his mouth would not form the words. He listened quietly as Williams spoke.

In a hard, uneven voice, Reginald told of the housing project, his two older brothers, Clarence and Rodney. The tiny apartment, welfare, the blaring television set, the lack of food, patched clothing. Clarence and Rodney growing to early manhood and leaving school to run with street gangs. Large amounts of money mysteriously appearing in the hands of his brothers. His mother's fears. Then, when Reggie was twelve, Clarence nearly cut in half by a Mac-10. "A drug deal, they said. A drug deal went sour."

Drugs. That was all he heard about. Even the kids in elementary and junior high school talked of snow, crack, and pot, and many were using. Rodney dealing in the streets—arrested when he was sixteen for selling a "controlled substance" and sent away. LaTanya, heartbroken and horrified. Doting on Reginald who had reached six feet by the time he was thirteen years old. A brilliant student. A gifted athlete.

The release of Rodney at the age of seventeen and his conviction of murder by the time he was eighteen. "A payback for Clarence," he told a devastated LaTanya.

Reggie became his mother's life. Avoiding gangs, gang members, drugs, cigarettes, and liquor. Playing first string linebacker as a sophomore. Straight-A grades. Earning All City honors as a junior, Player of the Year as a senior. Then the recruiters, the choice of USC because of its reputation and the nearness to his mother.

The sea. Reggie loved the sea. And he never saw it until he was thirteen. And the Pacific was only twelve miles away. Where did he find this love for the sea? Watching old Errol Flynn movies on television? Did he fall in love with Olivia De Haviland? Maybe. The sea—wide, free, uncluttered, and in beautiful Technicolor. A spacious place where a boy from the slums could fill his lungs with clean air and live like a human being.

There was a door. A way in. The NROTC. He joined it. Got his commission six months after his degree in Electrical Engineering. Then the Navy, a decent wage, and the house he bought for his mother in the Baldwin Hills section of West Los Angeles.

Brent stirred from his stupor. Something Reginald said did not make sense—no sense at all. He thought for a moment, worked his jaw. Finally the words came. "You wanted the sea, freedom, room to live, breathe fresh air . . ." He was convulsed by fits of laughter that cramped his stom-

272

ach muscles. "And you—you chose sub duty? *Blackfin?*" More laughter. The irony was overwhelming. He finally controlled himself. "Christ—can't you smell it? Diesel oil, sweat, and when we're submerged, you'll smell the heads—the crap."

"You think I'm funny!"

"Better than Rodney Dangerfield."

"Whitey can't understand."

"That's a cop-out."

"You think I haven't taken shit—felt heat because of my color?"

"No. When you're six feet tall and weigh two twenty, people are friendly."

"I'm six one and weigh two thirty."

"Then they're friendlier. So don't give me that bullshit. You've done all right with your life."

Williams rolled to his side and faced Brent angrily. "Someday, we'll settle this in detail—my terms, my way."

"Anytime. Any place." Brent knew the big black was toying with the idea of coming after him. A sudden alertness pushed some of the effect of the alcohol aside and his muscles bunched, his heartbeat picked up. But Williams rolled back and put his hands behind his head. Brent relaxed again.

They both lay sullenly and stared at the ceiling. Sleep was long in coming.

Chapter VIII

The next day added to Brent's confusion. With sixty-three men and five officers on board *Blackfin,* new equipment being installed, stores coming aboard, new guns for the superstructure, the ship's wiring ripped out amidships, there was little room to walk, to stop and discuss problems. With almost equal numbers of Japanese and American crewmen, each Japanese was assigned an American "buddy" to introduce him to the ship. It did not work. With four Electric Boat engineers trying to install and explain new wiring in the control room, people fell over one another and a fight broke out at the diving station. Finally, in exasperation and frustration, Mark Allen divided the crew into port and starboard sections and sent one section to the barracks for classroom instruction under Ensign Fred Hasse and two chiefs. The effect was immediate and refreshing and there was room enough for a man to walk again and function.

A surprisingly docile and completely professional Lieutenant Reginald Williams led Brent to the radio room. The big black had been taciturn and distant when they first rose and said nothing over breakfast, which they took in a corner of the small mess hall reserved for officers. By the time he boarded *Blackfin,* he had shrugged back into his cloak of authority and had resumed the role of the consummate officer.

Entering the combination radio room and cryptocenter, they found two enlisted men hunched over some new equipment. They came to attention. "This is Lieutenant Ross," the executive officer said. "He's your new communications officer." He waved. "Show him the new gear, Simpson."

The PA system blared, "Mr. Williams to the bridge."

Williams waved and rushed to the ladder.

"Cryptologic Technician First Class Don Simpson," the first petty officer said, a fair-haired young man with a deep, intelligent brow and strong jaw. He gestured to his companion, a squat, dark, barrel-chested youngster with arms so long his huge hands hung almost to his knees as if he were carrying two beef roasts. His wide forehead was narrow, showing as a tan line between his shock of bushy black hair and heavy eyebrows that moved with his moods with a life of their own like huge black caterpillars. His eyes were deep-set and in dark, bony hollows. A black slash of hair protruded over the collar of his skivvy shirt. Simpson spoke. "This is Crog—ah, I mean Radioman Second Tony Romero."

" 'Crog?' " Brent said.

Romero smiled. " 'Crog', for 'Cro-Magnon.' " He

gave Simpson a playful shove. "Got the name in boot camp, Mr. Ross." He shrugged. "If it gets too bad, I kick ass."

Eyeing the squat, powerful build, Brent had no doubts about the man's ability to do just that.

Crog continued, "But you can call me 'Crog', sir." A big smile cracked the wide face. "I've gotten used to it, and we'll be in the conning tower together as part of the attack team, Mr. Ross. We're short sonarmen so I have the sonar which is back to back with your TDC."

Brent's confusion was read by the man instantly. "The Torpedo Data Computer. It's on the new Watch Quarter and Station Bill."

"Very well, Crog," Brent said, embarrassed by his ignorance. He gestured at the new equipment.

Obviously pleased with the opportunity to show his knowledge, Crog glanced at Simpson and said, "No ELF—extremely low frequency equipment, Mr. Ross."

"Then we're deaf and dumb submerged?"

"Not completely, sir. We do have a dozen BRT-Ones, transmitting buoys."

Brent had heard of the transmitting buoy, but had never seen one. Containing a cassette recorder and radio transmitter, the buoy was released by the submarine with a preset delay before transmitting, giving the sub time to escape the area before the transmission began. "Delay?"

"Fifteen to sixty minutes, Mr. Ross."

Brent ran his eyes over the equipment. "Surface equipment."

"I'm afraid so, sir," Romero said. "Got to have

276

our 'whip' above the surface to transmit or receive." He patted a receiver fondly. "Great stuff. The ICS-Two."

"Oh, yes," Brent said. "The Integrated Communications System, Model Two. *Yonaga* has the Model Eleven."

The radioman nodded knowingly. "You had a much more elaborate and powerful system, sir." Simpson watched intelligently and silently, absorbing the exchange. Crog continued, "This compact little gem is ideal for a sub. It's capable of all types of ship-to-ship, ship-to-air and ship-to-shore communications."

"VLF, MF, and HF bands?"

"Yes, sir. VHF and UHF, too. And when we had satellites, it could monitor *Satcom* circuits, too . . . "

Brent scratched his head. "Frequency range?"

Crog smiled. "Ten kilohertz to thirty megahertz. And, sir, it can handle voice, data, teletype, and morse signals."

"Christ, I'm impressed," Brent said. "Damn near as versatile as the ICS-Eleven."

The squat radioman nodded. "Not as powerful. Power output varies with range requirements—up to five hundred watts."

Brent was pleased, not only with the equipment but with Radioman Second Class Romero as well. Every officer depended on his key enlisted personnel and, obviously, he had found a polished professional in Tony "Crog" Romero.

Brent turned to the cryptographer. "You know we'll be 'packet switching,' Simpson." Brent said, testing.

"I know, sir. And we have the gear," Simpson said, smiling confidently.

Crog looked at Simpson and then Brent in confusion. Obviously pleased with his chance to impress his new officer and Crog, Simpson explained to the radioman, "Packet switching is a new system used for top secret transmissions. A message is broken down into thousands of fragments—packets. Each packet contains a coded address of the addressee and the transmitting computer automatically routes the packets over any free route in the communications network." He indicated a computer wired to one of the receivers, "A TBC Twenty-Two and the encryption box is there, below the computer and the hot printer." He pointed to a printer on a shelf below the encryption box. "We're set up to reassemble and decode both Navy and CIA transmissions."

Crog nodded. "Yes, I see." He scratched his narrow forehead. "But only if we have the codes."

Brent smiled. "That's right, Romero." He patted the printer. "And Crog, you'll be doing double duty—both of you will. We're short-handed. Simpson is our only Cryptologic technician. So learn each other's duties."

The men nodded. "We know, sir," they chorused.

There was the sound of feet on the ladder and three strange officers passed the radio room. Immediately, Brent heard the PA system blare, "Mr. Williams, Mr. Ross, Mr. Cadenbach, Mr. Dunlap to the wardroom."

Brent said, "As you were," turned, and walked

an obstacle course of sweating crewmen and scattered tools to the wardroom.

When he entered, he saw three new officers standing before Admiral Mark Allen. Within seconds, Charlie Cadenbach, Brooks Dunlap, and Reginald Williams crowded in behind Brent Ross. Mark Allen introduced the officers in the usual descending order of seniority. The new officers were young, two ensigns and a lieutenant junior grade.

"This is Lieutenant Bernard Pittman," the admiral said, gesturing to a tall, thin man of about thirty, with shifty blue eyes and a disconcerting look of latent panic on his face. And then in quick succession the admiral introduced Ensign Robert Owen, a heavyset youngster with a friendly smile and Ensign Herbert Battle, a short, wiry-looking young man with bright eager, brown eyes that flitted restlessly over everyone and everything. After hands were shaken all around, the admiral gestured and the officers seated themselves at the table. Mess Manager Pablo Fortuno entered and served coffee and placed a plate of cookies in the center of the table.

The admiral asked each man about his qualifications. All had served on SSN's or SSBN's, but none on the old diesel-electric boats. Then a quick review of *Blackfin*'s status of readiness and her mission. Brent saw Bernard Pittman's eyes widen in alarm. Brent began to feel uneasy about the man.

"Sir . . ." Ensign Battle said. "You mentioned sea trials in a week—I know nothing about these boats—absolutely nothing, sir." The other two officers nodded concurrence.

"I know," Mark Allen said. "Four of us have served on diesel-electric boats and the rest of you," his eyes embraced the entire room, "will learn very fast or the first time we submerge will be our last." He gestured to Reginald Williams. "Mr. Williams will take you on a quick orientation tour and you will be billeted at a nearby hotel, the Oakmont Suites, until the wardroom is put back together—in about four days."

He went over the officers' responsibilities: Lieutenant Reginald Williams, executive officer and assistant attack officer; Lieutenant Frederick Hasse, who was absent, torpedo officer; Lieutenant Brent Ross, communications, radar, and the TDC; Lieutenant Brooks Dunlap, engineering; Lieutenant Charlie Cadenbach, navigator; Lieutenant Bernard Pittman, sonar; Ensign Robert Owen, supply; and Ensign Herbert Battle, diving officer."

He studied each officer. "Any questions?"

Bernard Pittman waved a hand. "You have designated me sonar officer." He clattered his cup on the table nervously. "The equipment I've seen on this boat is ancient. I've had experience with the SQS-Twenty-Six sonar, sir, on *John Adams*. It had five hundred seventy-six transducer elements bow mounted, and I've had some work with the BQQ-Five on the *Los Angeles* with a similar array. Both these systems display predicted transmission paths in ambient conditions, take into account salinity, temperature, propagation distortions, and a dozen other factors. These are the best active sonars in the world, sir." He waved helplessly. "But I know very little about these antiques."

Mark Allen drummed the table. "I'm familiar with the new equipment and I don't need a lecture." Pittman winced and reddened. Brent had trouble concealing a smile. Mark Allen pressed on, showing his knowledge. "I know you are accustomed to integrated combat systems—active sonar, passive flank array sonar, passive towed arrays, and combat control systems that can give fire-control solutions." He tapped his chin with a closed fist and stared at Pittman. "We were promised new sonar. However, I have discovered we can overhaul, install new transducers and solid state circuits and that's it."

"That's it? Then we'll operate with old WWII equipment?" Pittman waved. "The units I saw in the conning tower and control room?"

"Remember, Mr. Pittman, although you have worked with highly exotic, glamorous units with colorful displays, high-powered computers and rows of pretty, flashing lights; basically sonar hasn't changed since the 'Asdic' of 1917. It's still the same. All an active sonar can do is 'ping,' bounce a signal off a target and locate and range by measuring return-signal Doppler shift. That's all they do!" Mark Allen struck the table for emphasis. "That's all any of them can do on the *John Adams, Los Angeles* or the *Blackfin*".

Pittman's sigh was heavy with resignation. "Then I'll be working with basic, WWII equipment. No integrated systems."

"Yes. You will work with WWII units—the

Mark Four, both active and passive. No computer enhancement or solutions."

"Passive? The old hydrophones, sir?"

"Yes."

"They haven't changed since 1916."

"I don't make the rules, Mr. Pittman," Mark Allen said with finality.

Herbert Battle asked, "Sir, since we can't make our own automatic comparison checks and have no threat libraries, can we access NATO's Ocean Surveillance Information System, their sound libraries, seabed listening posts, their automatic computer comparison checks." He tapped the table. "They could locate and identify subs that could be hunting us."

Allen sighed. "Good thinking, Mr. Battle. The SOSUS (Sound Surveillance System) hydrophones strung across the western and northern Pacific will pick up a shark's hiccup—and it'll pick us up as well. But it's been agreed at Geneva, these systems, as well as NATO, are out." There was a groan. "Sorry, gentlemen, I repeat, we'll get no information from the Navy's seabed detectors or towed arrays. I want to make it perfectly clear that help from either the Navy's SOSUS system, Acoustics Research Center or the Anti-Submarine Warfare Center is prohibited." The men looked at each other. "But the Libyans will receive no help from the Warsaw Pact and Soviet detectors, either. We're on our own and so are they."

"Do you believe in this *Glasnost*, sir?" Robert Owen asked bluntly.

"Do we have a choice, gentlemen?"

"Ours is to do or die," Pittman said.

"That's what they pay you for," Brent Ross said suddenly.

Silence while Brent and Bernard Pittman glared at each other.

Mark Allen broke the silence. "After your tour, the new officers and Mr. Ross report back here." He gestured to a stack of manuals. "I want to go over your assignments, and the best thing to do is study your manuals and become acquainted with your stations and your men as soon as possible. And, incidentally, as crowded as things are, we're ten men short and, apparently, we'll get no new men — we'll steam short-handed." He slapped the table. "Learn the whole boat — every function. All of you will be standing OD (Officer of the Deck) and JOD (Junior Officer of the Deck) watches."

The new men looked at each other, their feelings of uncertainty so strong, it was a palpable force that put an edge on the entire room. Mark Allen sensed it. "I know, at this moment, you must be experiencing total confusion. Don't condemn yourselves. It's natural. But you're picked men, will learn fast. The one big difference you'll find between this boat and a modern nuclear sub is the lack of computers, and consequently, the lack of visual displays at the diving station, sonar, TDC, engine room, the control boards. But *Blackfin* is still a sub, has all the characteristics and problems of any other sub. She's slow, can't dive very deep, but she's still a descendant of the old *Holland,* just like those 'nukes' you served on. And we can play dead — lie absolutely silent on the bottom while those nukes can never shut down their pressure cookers—boil and bubble like volcanoes. Why, they're the noisiest things at sea." The gray-green eyes moved around the table. The old man looked very tired. "I expect no miracles. But I do expect hard work and a willingness to accept new challenges—and one other quality." His eyes narrowed and the words came as if he were chopping them off with a hatchet. "Resoluteness in the face of the enemy—in the face of danger." The men nodded. "And remember, we have a long journey ahead of us before we even reach our patrol area. By then, I promise you, you will know *Blackfin* better than you know your wives—or," he glanced at Brent, "your girlfriends." There was a tension relieving chuckle. "You are dismissed."

Brent spent the next two hours in the radio room with Don Simpson, Tony Romero, and two middle-aged Japanese radiomen assigned to Brent's department. The Japanese were Petty Officer Goroku Kumano and Petty Officer Shiro Matsuoka. Kumano, a stubby man with thinning black hair, had spent eight years in the Merchant Marine and ten in the Self Defense Force. Matsuoka, a tough, leathery fisherman's son from Kyushu, had spent his adult life at sea, including seventeen years in the Self Defense Force. Both men were bright, resourceful and learned quickly, digesting the manuals as if English was their first language instead of their second. They had traded their green fatigues for the blue working uniforms worn by the Americans: blue working cap, blue chambray shirt, black socks, dungaree trousers. Now every member of the crew wore identical uniforms, both dress and working. "They're members of the same crew and by God, they'll all look alike if I have to stamp *Blackfin* across their butts," Reginald Williams had announced that morning.

Brent soon discovered all four men were thoroughly versed in Morse code, international semaphore signals with hand-held flags and could recognize flag and pennant hoists. These qualities were absolutely essential because his crew was required to stand signal watches when surfaced in addition to lookout duties. He needed more men, but he knew he might receive two "strikers" and no more. But strikers were seamen aspiring to ratings, would know very little, and would have to be taught by himself and his men. He was just leaving the radio room to visit the conning tower and study the TDC, when the PA called him to the wardroom.

The rest of the afternoon was spent studying communications manuals with Pittman, Owen, and Battle. Brent spent most of his time reading old pamphlets on the TDC—Torpedo Data Computer. All bore the date, 1942. "Computers," he snorted to himself. "Back then?"

Late in the afternoon when everyone was fatigued and Brent had trouble focusing his eyes, Admiral Allen entered. He sagged into a chair. He looked haggard and very old. He ordered Pittman, Owen, and Battle to inspect the engine room where Chief Engineer Brooks Dunlap was awaiting them. As they left, he turned to Brent. "Our new radar and ESM will be installed tomorrow. It's your department. We're getting the SPS-Ten, D-band surface and air search radar."

"Christ, the 'Ten' is a thirty-year-old tube set."

"Westinghouse has upgraded it. Tubes are out, no one can replace them anymore. Our unit is solid state with a new CRT (cathode ray tube)."

"ESM?"

Mark Allen smiled slowly. "We'll do a little better with electronic support measures than we did with sonar. We're getting a WLR-Eight."

Brent Ross beamed. "That's great stuff, Sir."

"Modified."

"Oh," Brent managed suspiciously.

Mark Allen chuckled. "We just don't have the room for the entire system."

"The computers? It has two and it isn't worth a damn without them, sir."

"We'll get one. The Sylvania PSP-Three-Hundred."

"Good. Good. Then we'll have automatic signal acquisition, analysis and processing, anyway."

"Right, Brent. And measurement of signal direction of arrival, analysis of frequency, modulation and pulse width, Brent."

"But no threat library or priority searches and threat warning."

"Those functions are out, Brent." He ran his fingertips over the white stubble on his chin. "We won't have room in the conning tower for it so I'm having it installed in the control room next to the diving station. Anyway, we'll only use it just before surfacing and when surfaced."

"Yes, sir."

A troubled look darkened the old face. "We have a problem, Brent."

Brent looked up expectantly. Mark Allen continued. "I can't go with you to the UN tomorrow." He waved his arms helplessly. "Look at this mess. There's a million and one things to do and no time. I can serve Admiral Fujita better by remaining here. You and Bernstein attend and I'm sending the exec as my representative."

"I think it's a nothing meeting, sir."

"But we've been ordered."

"Of course, Admiral."

Mark Allen drummed his fingers on the table as if he were playing an instrument. "There's a chance—a very remote chance that we can make the first move toward an understanding."

"With the PLO? They're bush players in this league. The big players are Kadafi, Hafez Assad, Saddam Hussein, Walid Jumblatt . . . "

"I know. I know, Brent. But Arafat has a lot of influence in all Arab circles."

"Khomeini's jumping in."

"How did you know that, Brent?"

Brent explained his conversation with Dale McIntyre.

Mark Allen nodded dejectedly. "Doesn't look good." He moved his eyes to Brent. Suddenly a sly smile twisted his lips and he said casually, "Oh, by the way, you're starboard section and the officers of the starboard section have liberty Friday night. I hope you can use it."

Brent blushed like a schoolboy. "I might think of something to do, sir."

The ride to UN Headquarters was short, almost directly across town to the East River and the foot of Forty-second Street. However, with the fuel shortage, cabs were hard to find. And one passenger had been added at the last moment; Chief Torpedoman Masayori Fujiwara was sent along by Admiral Allen. "An adviser and a bodyguard. You don't want any of those Arabs to get behind you," the admiral had warned.

Brent welcomed the tough chief. His Otsu was back on the sub and he felt naked without it. No one could carry a pistol past the UN's metal detectors anyway. Three cabs passed before Fujiwara finally stepped boldly out onto West Avenue and forced one to stop. The driver cursed, shouting he had another fare to pick up. Fujiwara slapped the windshield with his leather cane and grabbed the man by the collar. Instantly, the driver decided he was available. Quickly, Brent Ross, Reginald Williams, and Colonel Irving Bernstein tumbled into the rear of the cab. Fujiwara sat next to the driver. With the sailors all dressed in their service dress blues, Bernstein's desert fatigues looked strangely out of place. But the Israeli had said over and over, "I'll not dress for anything but combat until my country is at peace."

Even in a world of magnificent towers, the thirty-nine story vertical glass box of the UN's Secretariat Building presented a dramatic profile, rising from a cluster of satellite buildings. With white marble end walls and side walls of green glass set in an aluminum grid, the tower and the entire complex was set in a beautifully landscaped site.

Exiting the cab on First Avenue, the group approached the seven nickel-bronze entrance doors of the General Assembly Building, passing pools and statuary. Williams read an inscription on the pedestal of a bronze statue. " 'Let us beat our swords into plowshares.' "

Bernstein snorted scornfully, "Yeah, we'll plow Kadafi under." The men snickered.

At the door a guard examined their identification and consulted a register, politely informing them that their meeting was to be held in Conference Room Two. The Arab delegation had already arrived and was waiting for them with a British arbitrator. He pointed to a hallway opening off the left side of the lobby. Quickly, they walked past an information desk, past a bronze of Poseidon, and under a replica of the first *Sputnik*. Finally, they found Conference Room Two.

They entered through two solid oak doors and found a long room with a polished table. Six men were in the room, seated at the table. All were dressed in smart business suits with the exception of one who wore a magnificent silk burnoose. Open embassy cases were on the table. Three were smoking and the room stank of Egyptian tobacco.

A tall, slender man of middle years rose from his position at the head of the table. Speaking through a warm, toothy smile, he had the most dulcet voice this side of the Royal Shakespeare Company. "I'm Neville Hathaway, aide to the British ambassador. The secretary-general asked me to look in on this show. He's awfully keen to help out, and all that."

Looking at the Englishman, Brent chuckled. With thinning gray hair slicked straight back, a pencil-thin mustache, a large Adam's apple, high forehead, large aristocratic nose, gaunt physique and perfectly tailored tweeds, the man was so completely British he could have leaped from the pages of *Punch*. He even had a gold-rimmed pince-nez perched precariously on his nose.

Brent's eyes were caught by the man seated next to Hathaway. It was the renegade American killer, Kenneth Rosencrance. About thirty years old, Rosencrance was a big, pasty-white man with a huge leonine head and a full shock of white-blond hair, colorless lips, and the sunken cheeks of a cadaver. His blue-gray eyes were fixed on Brent with the intensity of laser beams, the look satisfied as if he were seated in his fighter, waiting for Brent Ross and, at last, bringing him into his sights. Not one man of the Arab delegation rose.

"Delighted to see you again, Lieutenant Ross," the flyer said sarcastically.

"Oh, you know each other," Hathaway said. "Good show."

Staring at the flyer, Brent felt an old anger begin to resurge, deep down. He knew Rosencrance quite well—too well. He remembered the fistfight in *Yonaga*'s sick bay over a year ago when he had almost killed Rosencrance. The American's vow to kill Brent. There was nothing redeeming about Rosencrance; he was a killer without principles who killed for money and the perverted thrill he derived from killing. Brent suspected the man would still kill even if he were not paid the million a year in salary and fifty-thousand-dollar bonuses for each victory. It was rumored he had painted seventeen Japanese flags on the fuselage of his ME 109.

"Yes, Mr. Hathaway," Brent said casually. "We're old friends." He stared at Rosencrance, "It's been a long time, Captain," Brent said. "We do have some unfinished business."

The colorless lips turned down. "Yes we do, ol' buddy. I assure you I haven't forgotten."

"I'd be delighted to do it again—any place, any time."

"I'll see to the arrangements," Rosencrance said curtly.

Hathaway gestured at the empty chairs. "Please be seated, gentlemen, and we'll get to it straightaway."

Bernstein nodded and the four men sat. Hathaway introduced the first three men of the Arab delegation, all thin, dark, Semitic in appearance: Iman Younis, splendid in his burnoose, was the personal representative of Yassir Arafat and the PLO; Jai Ahmed a Syrian who represented Hafez Assad, the Popular Front for the Liberation of Palestine—General Command, Abu Nidal, Nabih Berri of the Shi'ite Amal militia and another half-dozen terrorist factions based in Lebanon; Ali Sabagh, an Iranian representing the Ayatollah Khomeini.

Bernstein and Brent exchanged a startled look and then stared at the Iranian.

291

Rosencrance interrupted Hathaway and introduced the last man of his delegation, a big white-haired man in his late fifties with the thick lips of a sensualist and the beady black eyes of a cobra. "This is Captain Wolfgang 'Zebra' Vatz, one of my best pilots. He's snuffed ten Nips." Fujiwara came erect angrily. Brent placed a hand on his arm. Vatz nodded at the chief and the thick red lips curled cruelly into a sneer.

Brent had never met the German, but knew him by reputation. A great pilot, it was said he had flown the ME 262 jet for the Luftwaffe as Adolph Galland's wingman when Vatz was only sixteen years of age. Now one of Kadafi's highest paid killers, he flew often as Rosencrance's wingman in a flamboyantly painted, white-striped ME 109. Thus the sobriquet, "Zebra." He was a merciless killer and had gained infamy by riddling two parachuting Japanese pilots and was suspected of the machine-gunning of four sailors in a life raft.

Despite Brent's efforts, Fujiwara struggled to his feet and Brent pulled him back with a scraping of chairs on hardwood. Hathaway's eyes widened and he almost dropped his pince-nez. He spoke to Fujiwara and Rosencrance like a scolding schoolmaster, "I say, chaps. We're here to solve problems." Brent felt Fujiwara relax, but the torpedoman's breath was short, and anger flushed his face. Hathaway nodded at Colonel Bernstein, who he recognized as the senior officer. "Please introduce your men and then we'll get cracking."

Colonel Bernstein rose and introduced his delegation. Their opposite numbers were sullen, glaring at each man with undisguised hostility. There were no handshakes. Brent had a deep sense of foreboding and unease. Was this really an attempt at some type of reconciliation, or a trap?

Hathaway tapped his pince-nez on the table. "As all of you know, this meeting is being held in the friendly offices of the UN in an attempt to come to some kind of understanding—" He waved his hand. "Find a common ground on which we can agree and put an end to the bloody fighting between you that has been going on for over four years without profit for anyone."

Rosencrance raised a hand; Hathaway nodded. The American said, "We asked for this meeting because we have been instructed to do precisely that—attempt to end the fighting."

The Englishman beamed. "Bully. That's ripping."

Brent was surprised, Rosencrance had actually sounded sincere.

Rosencrance glanced at some notes and continued. "A few conditions must be met—first, *Yonaga* must never enter the Mediterranean again, the monitor *Mikasa* must be withdrawn, the Israelis must withdraw from the West Bank and the Sinai." Brent heard Bernstein gasp. Rosencrance droned on. "Admiral Fujita must apologize for the destruction of the DC-3 over Tokyo Bay that was the incident that started hostilities . . . "

Brent interrupted. "That happened over four years ago."

"That's right. Innocent people were murdered."

"What was the guilt of the twelve hundred Japanese you garroted on *Mayeda Maru* in Tripoli

Harbor?"

"Justifiable retaliation."

Hathaway tapped his pince-nez on the table in alarm. "I say, gentlemen. Things are getting a bit out of hand. Daresay, let's . . ."

Everyone ignored him. Ali Sabagh leaped to his feet as Hathaway watched openmouthed. The Iranian spoke in a high-squeaky tones like an out-of-tune violin. "I have been instructed to inform you by the Ayatollah himself, if you do not cease hostilities against the forces of the free Muslims of the world, we will unite behind Allah in an unstoppable *jihad* with Colonel Kadafi's forces that will obliterate all evil from the face of this planet." He stabbed a finger at Bernstein. "And we will start with the Jews."

"Hear! Hear!" Vatz screamed. "We will finish it!" He gestured at the six blue-tattooed numbers on the Israeli's arm. "You are one of them."

Bernstein jumped to his feet. "Auschwitz, class of '45, you son-of-a-bitch. I got away!" Brent grabbed the back of Bernstein's shirt.

Hathaway came to his feet. "Dear me, gentlemen," he cried. "Please calm yourselves. This will be a hard slog, but not impossible . . ."

Brent pulled Bernstein back, pleading, "One minute, Colonel." Then shouted the Arabs to silence, "Will you pull out of the Marianas? Indonesia? Reduce the price of oil? Permit free trade in the Middle East and Mediterranean? Free access to the Persian Gulf for all nations?"

"Quite," Hathaway said to the Arabs. "That's cricket, don't you think, chaps?" The Englishman

294

was speaking to the walls.

Rosencrance laughed raucously, sneered at Brent. "Jesus Christ, man. Do you want a free ticket to Disneyland, too?"

Hathaway held up his hands in futility, glaring at Rosencrance. "Blast it, man. You're a boorish cad, sir. You're making a muck of the whole lot."

"Well, daresay, bully for you, old sod," Rosencrance taunted, mimicking the Englishman through his chuckles.

Williams said to Brent, "This is bullshit, man. They want everything and will give nothing."

Rosencrance glared at Brent. Gestured at *Yonaga*'s delegation. "What the fuck is this, ol' buddy. You show up with a Kike, slant, nigger, and you're nothing but a half-Jap yourself."

Williams bolted from his chair followed by Fujiwara. Williams shouted, "You son-of-a-bitch!"

"Shut up, nigger!" Rosencrance shouted. "This is none of your fuckin' business. Go back to the apes."

Williams lunged. Brent grabbed him. Rosencrance was on his feet. Then everyone in the room left his chair and started cursing and screaming at the same time.

Hathaway shouted and pleaded. "Please, gentlemen. The object of this meeting is peace!"

Rosencrance pointed at Reginald Williams, shouting, "Then get that spade out of here!"

Williams began to break loose. Fujiwara grabbed his other arm. "No, Reggie," Brent pleaded. "I promised Admiral Fujita 'no violence.' "

295

"I don't even know him," Williams screamed. With that he broke away and charged Rosencrance.

Hathaway pounded a button on the table before him.

Rosencrance squatted low, met Reginald's charge with a quick kick to the midriff while Vatz attacked the American from behind.

"Oh, the hell with it," Brent said, wading in, catching Vatz with a right to the side of the head that sent the German staggering. Younis, Sabagh, and Ahmed jumped in, trying to hit Williams and Brent from behind. But Bernstein and Fujiwara leaped over the table, knocking over chairs and smashing a small side table, knocking off and breaking a pitcher and a dozen glasses.

Brandishing his leather cane, Fujiwara shouted, "Banzai! Banzai!" Brent heard hard slapping sounds and screams of pain as the chief lashed out with the vicious weapon. More shouts of, "Banzai!"

Brent took up the cry. "Banzai!"

Rosencrance and Williams were exchanging blows; surprisingly the American renegade was holding his own. He was no coward.

A small body hit Brent from behind, staggering him. Then Vatz whirled, bringing up a fist that caught Brent on the side of the head. There was a shock that traveled down his spine and neon lights flashed on and off. There was a salty taste in his mouth. He whirled, hitting the German with a three punch combination that broke his nose, sent teeth flying, and ripped Brent's knuckles. Vatz

296

dropped as if executed.

Williams was down, apparently unconscious, hit on the head from behind by the burnoosed Arab with a broken chair, and punched from the front by Rosencrance. Rosencrance had the broken pitcher in his hand, raised over Reggie's face. "I'm gonna improve your looks, you jig son-of-a-bitch!" he bellowed.

"No!" Brent screamed, lunging. He caught the arm, twisted the wrist back.

Crying in pain, Rosencrance dropped the pitcher and whirled, bringing up his right and catching Brent in the ribs. Brent felt a sharp pain as if stabbed in the chest with a hot knife, and the breath exploded from his lips. Quickly, he recovered, weaving, catching the American with two quick left jabs and then a right uppercut to the jaw that landed with so much force he felt the shock all the way to the shoulder, knuckles cracking and his skin ripping free. Eyes glazed, Rosencrance reeled back on rubbery legs.

"Banzai! Banzai!" both Brent and Fujiwara shouted.

Suddenly, there were shouts from the door and the room filled with security personnel wielding clubs. Within seconds the combatants were separated, staggering back, bloody, gasping, spitting threats and oaths.

A security man shouted, "All of you out or I'll have you arrested. Now! Out!"

Hathaway picked at the pieces of his pince-nez scattered across the table. He spoke to himself. "I've had a jugful of this lot."

Sullenly, the men filed from the room. Brent helped Reginald Williams from the floor and led him through the door. He could hear Rosencrance hissing, "This isn't finished. Not yet. I'll get you. Both of you — pricks." And then with his eyes sparking with the distilled essence of hatred, he said to Brent, "I'm going to 'Banzai' your ass, ol' buddy. You're nothing but a fuckin' white Jap."

Brent spoke calmly. "I'll kill you if I have to do it in Libya."

Glaring, Rosencrance spat, "I'll get you a visa, ol' buddy."

"Tally ho, gentlemen. Tally ho," Hathaway said. "Boff the bloody buggers. That's the only way." He was laughing as the last man left.

Brent heard Reginald Williams mutter as he helped the executive officer through the lobby surrounded by security men, "I was half wrong."

"Half wrong?"

"Yeah. You're not overrated."

Admiral Mark Allen was grim when he received the reports from the four-man delegation. "They weren't interested in settling a thing, Admiral," Williams said from his chair in the wardroom.

"Rosencrance deliberately wrecked the meeting, sir," Brent added.

"They're up to something — they're holding meetings, cementing their bloody *jihad,* Admiral," Bernstein said.

Brent said to Mark Allen, "There was something strange about the whole thing, as if it were choreographed to break up." He scratched his temple pensively with a single finger. "There was no Iraqi representative there."

"What about Jordanian and Egyptian?"

"No, Admiral, but they're already committed to the *jihad*."

"True, Brent."

Brent stared at the far bulkhead. "It was almost as if Rosencrance was trying to impress the Iranian representative."

"That's right, Brent," Reginald said. "He was trying to show him what savages we are—goaded us."

"Baited us," Bernstein added.

Brent continued, "And he sure as hell hooked the guy." He turned to Mark Allen. "Kadafi's got Iran in his hip pocket."

"I agree," Bernstein said. The Israeli drummed the table. "I've got to report to the Israeli consulate. They want a full report, Admiral."

"And then a new assignment, Colonel?" Mark Allen asked.

"I'll probably return to *Yonaga* and relieve Marshall Katz. At least, Admiral Fujita has made the request."

"What Fujita wants, Fujita gets," Mark Allen said. A modest chuckle broke through the depressed atmosphere of the room. The admiral continued, "We've got to press our preparations. Now it is even more obvious that we are up against the most formidable alliance on this planet." He focused the gray-green eyes on his executive officer. "Mr. Williams, did anyone even mention this sub?"

"No, sir. But I was unconscious part of the time." Everyone laughed.

"Not a word, sir," Brent said.

"Good. Good," Mark Allen said.

Brent brought up a troubling thought. "Admiral, we'll have to use the Panama Canal?"

Mark Allen nodded. "We don't have the time to double Cape Horn."

Brent shook his head. "They'll be watching, sir. They'll know when we sortie from here, transit the canal, and enter the Pacific."

"I know. We'll hope they buy the museum-boat story and if not," he slapped the table, "I don't give a damn. We'll sink them anyway."

The men slapped each other on the back. Stifling an urge to shout, "Banzai," Brent smiled inwardly. The old admiral had learned something about dramatics from Admiral Fujita.

Mark Allen continued, "Tomorrow we'll run through our first drills—special sea detail, fire and collision, diving stations, attack submerged and battle surface, if time." He sagged back. "And in case you've forgotten, there will be liberty for the starboard section tomorrow night—officers only. The port section on Sunday and the men next week." There were murmurs of approval. "Gentlemen, you are dismissed."

The officers filed through the door.

"One-sixty Caddington," Brent told the cabbie, as he settled back into the cushions.

"That's Tribeca, Lieutenant," the cabbie said,

jamming the cab into drive and firing away from the curb like a fighter from a catapult.

"I thought it was Greenwich Village," Brent said.

The cabbie shook his head. "Not any more—they call it Tribeca for 'triangle below Canal Street.' It's just south of Little Italy."

Brent shrugged and gritted his teeth as the driver shot south on the Westside Highway. It seemed like only seconds before he screeched off the expressway at the Canal Street exit and then south and into a neighborhood of very old brick buildings. "Christ, these are antiques," Brent said.

The cabbie laughed as he whipped around a bus without reducing speed and turned the corner of Varick Street—an avenue lined with hulking, dark old buildings like rows of glowering old men. "Some of these buildings are almost two hundred years old." The driver waved. "Used to be the center of the town's meat and produce markets." He gestured at an eight story with windows only on the top floor. "That one's still in use. The offices are on the top floor. You can tell, when they cut 'em up into lofts, they cut windows into all the floors."

"But these others have been converted into apartments." Brent waved at some buildings with rows of windows.

"Yes, sir," the cabbie said. "Lofts—big places. They go for a million or more." He roared into a turn at too high a speed, slid sideways with a screech of agonized tires, turned into his slide, and straightened out with a violent fishtail.

Brent forced down a harsh acid taste that left his stomach and tried to force its way through his teeth. "Jesus, man. I'm not in any hurry. I want to use every one of my three score and ten."

"Sorry, Lieutenant. But I'm really not driving fast. There are too many cops around."

"They couldn't catch you—they couldn't even see you. Like trying to net an artillery shell."

The cabbie laughed and slowed the cab. Brent looked at the old buildings, most of which still had their loading docks and heavy refrigerator doors and commented, "A million or more, you said."

The cabbie laughed. "This is no low rent area, Lieutenant." He jerked the cab violently to the curb in front of a dark, glowering six-story brick building, jammed his brake pedal to the floor, and left at least twenty feet of screeching rubber on the pavement. "One-sixty Caddington, sir," he said calmly.

Brent bolted from the cab thanking God, Amaterasu, and any other deity and kami that came to mind.

Dale heard the screech of tires like the scream of a mugged woman. Looking down from the sixth floor, she could see the big, young American leap eagerly from the cab. *He can't wait to see me,* she said to herself.

Walking quickly to a large mirror in the living room, she turned up a floor lamp next to it. Staring intently, she fluffed her long golden hair up with quick motions, ran her eyes over her tight blue satin pants and white blouse. She moved closer to the mirror. Even in the unforgiving light, there were no lines in her neck, sags in her face or breasts. But, still, evidence of the years was there for her to see—for anyone to see. Tiny clusters of lines tracking downward from the corners of her eyes. She palmed her cheeks, pushed upward but the lines did not vanish, only changed direction, curling to the sides. Like all beautiful women, age held particular horror for Dale McIntyre. She turned down the lamp to its dimmest setting and the lines were not as pronounced. She nodded grudging approval.

Stepping back, she ran her hands down over her breasts, to her waist and over her hips. Solid. Just like when she was eighteen. She was much more pleased with her body than her face. Her hips, buttocks, even her thighs, showed through the satin and flowed provocatively when she moved. And her breasts, peaked and firm, crowded the blouse. She liked the way the points of her nipples showed through. To get the effect, she had chosen a flimsy lace brassiere. Tracing the hands back up, she rubbed her flat abdomen and felt the smooth satin under her hands. "Oversexed bitch," she said. "An old woman lusting after a young man." She glanced at the door to the bedroom. A king-size bed was visible. She shook her head. "I'll keep him out of there. There's got to be more to it than that."

When the young man had phoned that morning, he had seemed eager, happy, and anxious to see her—a far cry from the suicidal wreck she remembered after the terrible gun battle in the Imperial Hotel. She knew then Brent needed a change and apparently the duty in New York—the *Blackfin*, new acquaintances, different responsibilities, and, above all, freedom from the destructive clash of cultures, were precisely the needed prescription. And there had been too much death on *Yonaga;* too many of his friends had died. She had seen the bond that had grown between Brent and his shipmates—the terrible, haunted look when he spoke of Watertender Kurosu. And it was in his eyes when he looked at Admiral Fujita or spoke to his best friend, the pilot Yoshi Matsuhara, and a dozen others. What was this brotherhood that welded men in war? Certainly, women had their cliques, close friends, bridge clubs. But they didn't die for each other. She was convinced a piece of Brent Ross had died with the watertender—perhaps, part of him went with each dead friend. She felt chilled. Grabbed her elbows and rubbed at the chill.

She heard a heavy door slam, and then the elevator motor hummed. Her impulse was to rush to the door; she had been on edge and anxious since his phone call that morning. But she held back. *Mustn't seem too anxious,* she told herself.

The bell rang. Rang and rang again. She made him wait despite the impulse to run to the door. Finally, she opened it and he was there—big, broad, magnificent, smiling, and confident in his blue uniform. And he was very youthful. She could only stand there mutely for a long moment,

304

staring at him, feeling an ineffable joy flow through her entire being. Then she led him in, closed the door, and kissed him on the lips, long, hard, and wet with hunger. He held her for a long moment, running his hands over her back, tracing the ridge of her spine like a string of polished beads, following it down to her tight buttocks. Pulling her hips hard against him, he kissed her neck, her ear. "I've missed you, Brent," she whispered with a tremulous voice.

"Oh, Lord, I've missed you, Dale."

With an effort, she broke the embrace and led him into the living room which was actually a large corner of the loft walled off from the rest of the apartment by floor-to-ceiling oak panels. She pulled him down on a plump, rich sofa done in purple velvet. There was a bottle of Johnnie Walker Black Label on a small marble-top table in front of them. "The usual?" she asked.

"Yes."

She poured Brent straight Scotch and herself a Scotch and soda. He sipped his drink and waved his glass at the huge beams overhead, the floor-to-ceiling windows that were at least twelve feet high, the thick, scarred oak planking of the floor, the luxurious furnishings. "I've never seen a place like this," he said. "It's built like a fortress." He pointed at the ceiling, "Those must be twenty-by-twenty beams."

She drank. "The building's over a hundred years old — used to be a meat refrigerator." She waved. "The offices were in here."

"It's huge."

"Three thousand square feet, Brent."

While she spoke, he ran his fingers through the silk of her hair, held glistening strands between his thumb and forefinger, examining it like precious gems. It was so fine and silky it formed a silk sheet, lustrous as watered satin and flowing down to her shoulders. When she moved her head, it flickered with flashing diamonds and highlights. "Golden," he said, awed. "Jason should've met you—he wouldn't have had to fight a dragon for the golden fleece."

She tabled her drink. Pulled him down and kissed him, long, hard, and deep. The big arms were around her, pulling her so close she could feel the muscles in his arms and chest tense and bunch. A familiar deep heat and the wild pounding of her heart warned her. She pushed him away. "You are your old self," she said slyly.

He laughed. She pulled him to his feet. "Come along, Brent. I have a meal that would have pleased Jason and the rest of the gods."

He tried to pull her back down, but she slipped away. He pointed at the sofa, "I liked the hors d'oeuvres right here."

She laughed. "Come along. You're a growing boy and you need your nourishment."

He ignored her, pulled her close, ran his hands over her breasts, waist, hips, and she felt her resolve melting like ice left in the summer sun. She broke away and actually pulled him into the dining room.

The meal was superb. New York steak broiled just right, stuffed baked potato, asparagus with hollandaise sauce, a dessert of chocolate mousse. Brent ate like a famished man. Dale was pleased. A man with that appetite had to be well.

After dinner they sat close together on the sofa, sipping Benedictine and brandy. He told her of *Blackfin,* the riot at the UN, Rosencrance, the Arabs, the Englishman. "It's no use," he said. "They're arrogant—can only be persuaded by force."

"So. What's new?" she asked bitterly.

"What do you mean?"

"Hasn't it always been that way?"

He rubbed his chin. "It's an old argument," he acknowledged. He drank. "Mine is the oldest profession."

"That might surprise a few thousand women up on Broadway." Toying with her pony, she said thoughtfully, "The rumble at CIA headquarters is that the Arabs know what you're up to with *Blackfin.* Be careful."

"We haven't fooled anyone?"

She shook her head, emptied her pony. "I don't think so."

He drank the last of his liqueur and slid his hand up her leg and rubbed her thigh. She made no attempt to stop him. "Why do we spend our time talking about politics?" he asked.

"Maybe it's because those people halfway around this earth dictate how we shall live—or die." She shuddered.

"You feel that way, too?" he said.

"Helpless? Yes. Sometimes."

"Oh, the hell with it," he said with finality. He

pulled her close and kissed her open mouth, tongue darting and finding hers, twisting together, kneading, pressing wildly. The heat shot skyward and she could feel her heartbeat in her whole being; against her chest, her neck, and deep down where the heat was building to a maddening frenzy. The hand resumed its journey up her leg. He kissed her nose, cheek, eyes, and whispered in her ear as he ran his hand over her abdomen and down where she felt the maddening rush of blood.

"Why did you wear these damned pants?" He groped for a button and then the zipper.

"Please, Brent."

He pushed her back and suddenly he was on top of her, his weight pushing her down into the cushions. His mouth was clamped over hers, and she twisted and moaned. Without conscious thought, her legs parted and he was between them, trembling hands caressing her breasts, her waist, her hips. She felt a pulling and the blouse was ripped from her body, then the brassiere, and he was kissing her breasts, running his tongue over the areolas and nipples pulling hard on her buttocks and stabbing his arousal against her.

She twisted. Moaned. Kissed the side of his head, his hair, his cheek, clutched at his back, ran her hands through his hair, trembling, an aching, hot void deep within screaming to be filled. "No. No, Brent."

"You're out of your mind."

"I mean, not here." She pushed him aside, tugged on his hand until he rose. She led him to the bedroom.

The next morning, Brent was exhausted. He had never known such frantic lovemaking. When they first entered the bedroom, she had stripped long before Brent had been able to disrobe. Despite the terrible urgency, he paused to look at her as she sank back onto the bed. He stared wide-eyed, her body a work of art — the beauty of Degas and the delicacy of Mozart. "Hurry, Brent. Please. Hurry."

He tore off his remaining garments and slid over her, feeling himself trapped in the crucifix of her legs and arms, the hot depths.

She had no intention of releasing him. Even long after midnight when they were both spent and he slid to the side of the bed and reached for his clothes which were scattered over most of the room like discarded rags, she pulled him back. "No, darling. I want you all night and in the morning for breakfast."

"It's hard to get a cab. I'll be late."

"I'll drive you."

Her hand groped low, seeking him out and massaging gently, erasing all objections. Moaning, he pushed her back and lowered his body on hers. She threw her head back, laughed, chortled like a delighted child on Christmas morning and trapped him with her legs again.

Now it was time to leave and Brent stood before a full-length mirror, shrugging into his coat. Dale was already dressed and he could smell fresh coffee. Her voice came from the kitchen, "Breakfast, dear."

"You can drive me?" he asked, walking to the kitchen.

"No problem." She walked into the circle of his arms as if they had been made for her. He kissed her. "I'll see you again?" she asked.

"Try to keep me away."

She laughed, the delightful, trilling sound of a brook over pebbles.

Chapter IX

The next week found order established in the madhouse. Admiral Allen did not see his first sea trials in four days, but all of the new equipment was installed, including a modest threat library for the ESM which was casually slipped down the torpedo hatch while Navy inspectors conveniently looked the other way. Port and starboard liberty was held for all hands. Carefully instructed and released to liberty in groups of four, two Americans with two Japanese "buddies," the crew was discreet and disciplined. There was no drunkenness; no incidents.

Brent spent his liberties with Dale. They never left her apartment. It became their personal sanctum, a place where the world was sealed out, a place where they lived supremely for each other. Brent found every moment of their lovemaking unique. Dale approached their unions with artistry, like the movements of a Schubert symphony—each lyrical motif of their lovemaking building on itself, ranging, varying, yet moving always to another theme which in turn built on itself until the blending of the lush melodies climaxed in crashing completion and Brent finally rolled to his side in exhausted euphoria.

But Dale was troubled. Brent could see it in her eyes, hear it in her voice. One morning just before dawn, lying side-by-side after a night of frantic lovemaking, she awoke from a nightmare, crying.

He held her tightly as she sobbed against his cheek. "What is it, darling? What is it?" he pleaded.

It was a moment before she could talk. "It's us—what is there for us?"

"What do you mean?"

"I mean, what is there for us in this world ruled by a bunch of homicidal maniacs?"

Although roused from a deep sleep, and surprised by the question, Brent answered thoughtfully after a silent moment. "If we knuckle down to them we deserve to be destroyed."

"In a few days they'll take you from me—tear us apart."

"I know, Dale."

She lay silent again, staring at the ceiling. "Maybe it's for the best."

He rolled toward her, shocked. "Why do you say that?"

She ran a finger over his cheek, down a cord of his neck, found the hair on his chest and the bare tracks of long-healed knife wounds. Softly and with great sadness she said, "Brent, when you're my age, I'll be fifty-two years old."

"Is that important?"

312

"Of course."

"Why?"

"You want some kind of long-term commitment from me — don't you, Brent?"

"There is no long term in this world, Dale."

"You mean there are moments and that's it?"

"Yes. The Japanese would say life is a succession of moments, so live each one to the fullest. Nothing else is worth recording."

Sighing, she drew his head down and kissed him. "The Japanese are wise, Brent. Maybe we should leave it all outside. I'm sorry."

As the sun, reddened and diffused by the morning mists, crept into the room, she inclined her pelvis toward him and her hand groped low, gently caressing. He seized one of her buttocks in each hand and pulled her to him. Breathing in choking gasps, she rolled to her back, spreading her knees and pulling him between them. They made love for the last time.

The four Fairbanks-Morse engines rumbled and vibrated *Blackfin*'s steel hull, spewing acrid exhaust into the dark mists of the morning air. Standing on the bridge with Admiral Mark Allen and the helmsman, a competent, experienced second-class quartermaster named Harold Sturgis, Brent felt an amalgam of excitement and anxiety as Admiral Allen prepared to take the sub to sea for her first sea trial. The engines were warmed up and primed, batteries fully charged, the Special Sea Detail posted. All lines to the dock had been "singled up" and seamen were standing by the four cleats, ready to cast off. The sailing list with the names and addresses and next of kin of every man on board had been taken ashore by the four engineers from Electric Boat who had left an hour before.

Binoculars hanging at their waists and leaning on their safety rails, two lookouts were standing high on their platform attached to the periscope shears. A sixth man, Captain David Jordan, stood next to Admiral Allen. Jordan, a round, heavyset man in his late fifties with a bald pate and cherubic cheeks, had retired from the Navy after twenty-seven years in submarines. Iconoclastic and with a salty, earthy tongue, his vocabulary was more fitting for the mess hall than the wardroom. It was said, when angry, his store of expletives could leave a chief boatswain's mate standing in wonder and envy. In fact, his outspokenness had barred him from flag rank. However, everyone respected his knowledge of submarines, regarding him as one of the premier submarine men in the country. The route that found him assigned to *Blackfin* had been circuitous. An employee of the CIA, he was ostensibly a consultant for the Profile Boat Works. A dummy CIA company, Profile had a contract with Japan's Department of Public Parks and had subcontracted David Jordan to the department for an indefinite period of time ". . . to advise and train."

Jordan turned to Mark Allen. "There's a fairly heavy current in the river at this hour, Admiral — because of the ebb tide. You'll have to back into it."

"I can see it making around the buoys and pilings," Mark Allen said.

The old admiral gave his commands with confidence and a youthful zest Brent had never seen. "Take in the brow!"

A chief boatswain's mate shouted a command and a pair of sailors on the dock pulled the gangway ashore.

Mark Allen turned to Brent and stabbed a finger downward. Brent leaned over the open hatch to the conning tower and shouted, "Stand by to answer bells!"

Mark Allen shouted to the deck crew, "Take in two and three!" The middle lines were lifted from their cleats and tossed to seamen waiting on the submarine's deck. Hurriedly, the lines were coiled in their stowage bins under the deck.

"Take in four!" Allen shouted, leaving only the number one line from the bow still cleated to the dock. Berthed on the downstream side of the dock, the current tended to push the boat away from the berth. Admiral Allen read the set perfectly. As the stern began to swing with the flow, he shouted, "Slack one!" And then to Quartermaster Sturgis, "All back one-third." Sturgis pulled the annunciators back with a ringing of bells and the rumble of the diesels picked up. The slack in number-one line began to lessen. Allen turned back to the men at the bow. "Take in one!" The line was cast off and hauled aboard. "Left standard rudder!" he shouted at the helmsman.

"Left standard rudder, sir," Sturgis said, glancing

at the rudder angle indicator.

As the boat gathered sternway, Jordan warned, "Watch the set here, Admiral."

The old captain had hardly uttered his warning when the stern began to swing downstream. "Starboard back full, port ahead two-thirds," Allen shouted, anxiously leaning over the windscreen and staring over the stern.

There was a clanging of bells and shouts from below. Immediately, the boat began to tremble and shake as the engines strained against each other, twisting *Blackfin* so that she seemed to be trying to turn on her own length. Slowly and with white water boiling up from the screws, the stern stopped its slide to starboard and gradually resumed its turn to port.

Allen grunted with satisfaction. "All stop." The shaking stopped. "All back one-third." Smartly, *Blackfin* cleared the end of the pier and backed toward the center of the river.

Suddenly, Brent saw something black and shadowy emerging from a bank of low mist hanging in the middle of the river. "Tug and tow bearing one-six-five, range one thousand," he said to Mark Allen. His sighting was followed by shouts from the starboard lookout.

Allen threw a quick glance toward the sighting. "Very well."

Jordan said to Mark Allen, "The 'honey barge,' Admiral—enough shit there to feed Kadafi for a year."

"I see him. We're well clear." Allen shouted at the chief boatswain's mate, standing on the forecastle. "Secure the Special Sea Detail." Immediately, the chief and his crew vanished down the forward hatch and dogged it.

Looking around anxiously, Jordan said, "There's more traffic in this stream than whores on Broadway, Admiral."

"I know, Captain."

With the sub clear of the dock, but with a misty channel ahead, Mark Allen shouted, "All stop." The vibrations faded and the vessel slowed, idling exhaust firing into the air and burbling in the water as the boat rocked gently. "All ahead one-third. Right standard rudder." The admiral glanced at the gyro repeater, "Steady up on one-nine-zero." He shouted at the lookouts. "Keep a weather eye out. There's a lot of traffic and visibility's poor." And then down the hatch. "I want to know why radar didn't report that tug and tow off our starboard quarter!"

There was an embarrassed babble. "We have her, sir."

"Bully for you. You're just a little late."

The voice from the conning tower; "We have a lot of clutter, sir."

"Very well, but keep alert. We have terrible visibility up here."

"Steady on one-nine-zero, speed eight," the helmsman said.

"Very well."

David Jordan spoke, circling an arm. "There are cities on every quarter." He stabbed a finger toward the sea. "Ellis Island, Governors Island, Liberty Island, Statue of Liberty. A lot of garbage for radar scopes."

"I know, Captain." The admiral shouted into the bridge speaker, "Navigator, you should be cutting us in."

Cadenbach's tinny voice came back. "I've started my DR track, sir." Radar's giving me good readings. Do you wish a course for the narrows?"

"Negative. We'll pilot from here." Turning to Brent, Allen gestured at the parting mists. "That's Ellis Island and that's Governors Island. Give me a course between them."

Brent bent over the gyro repeater, squinted through the gun sight of the bearing ring. "One-eight-five, sir."

"Very well. Come left to one-eight-five." Brent shouted the changes into the speaker to Cadenbach.

"Steady on one-eight-five, sir."

"Very well."

A voice from the conning tower; "Radar reports a vessel underway bearing zero-three-zero, range two-thousand."

A lookout shouted, "Tanker, bearing zero-three-zero, range two-thousand."

"Is her bearing steady?"

"Negative, Admiral."

Brent picked up the big ship in his glasses. "I have her, sir. We'll pass well clear."

Allen punched the windscreen. "Damn this fog. What a way to start on your first run, with a new crew, too."

Almost as if his words had been heard by the gods, the mists parted abruptly, brilliant shafts of the morning sun breaking through. Allen's sigh was audible.

Within minutes, *Blackfin* steamed into the middle of the Upper Bay. A small change in course and she pointed her bows into the center of the Narrows. Lower New York Bay was ahead and then the open Atlantic — *Blackfin*'s natural habitat, a place where she had room to dive, maneuver, and hunt — and, perhaps, die.

Passing through the Narrows, Brent could see morning traffic — mostly buses — on Brooklyn's Belt Parkway to his left and the docks and buildings of Staten Island to his right. Then the magnificent span of the Verrazano Bridge swept overhead and he felt the first surges of the open sea take *Blackfin* by the bow. The boat rose heavily to each swell, sluicing water over her deck eagerly as if she sensed her freedom and charged for it impatiently.

Leaving Coney Island's Norton Point to port and Hoffman and Swinburne Islands to starboard, *Blackfin* charged into the open Atlantic at last. Here the sea is capricious, can have many moods and faces. This day it seemed to smile at Brent. Staring off into the infinite acres of the vast wasteland, he saw swells moving down from the northeast — rows of slow, oily combers advancing relentlessly to pass in smooth weighty majesty beneath the ship's hull. Heavy and with very little freeboard, the sub rolled and pitched sluggishly as she rode with the seas, deck awash like a great basking whale, climbing lazily up the gentle slopes and dropping ponderously into the valleys.

In the eastern sky, the sun crept higher in the

319

pristine blue sky, glaring off the last traces of fog, painting a few persistent patches with soft pinks and misty rose. But the sky was not clear all around. To the north off the invisible Hamptons a long row of thunderheads soared to thirty-thousand feet and rolled like great gray curtains swirled by the wind. Beneath them, line squalls dumped rain into the sea uselessly like slabs of slate. But every other quadrant was free of threat, showing only an occasional train of high cirrus scudding like frightened sheep before the wind. Turning his head and drinking it all in, Brent felt a joy build and grow, a swelling happiness he had not known for months.

Uninterrupted by land mass, the swells grew larger, the wave patterns building up into successive ranges of small green cliffs.

"All ahead standard," Mark Allen said.

At sixteen knots, the low, heavy vessel on the very edge of negative buoyancy no longer rode with the seas. Instead, she challenged them, burying her nose in the swells, throwing spray and blue-green water high into the sky, the seas rolling over the foredeck, sweeping her from stem to stern and splashing angrily against the bridge. Brent grasped the windscreen and sank deeper into his foul-weather jacket, feeling the spume hit his face like tiny steel darts, filling his lungs with the pure air, reveling in a joy only known by men who challenge the sea.

Captain Jordan said to Mark Allen, "I suggest you 'blow her out,' Admiral. The old girl could be constipated."

Mark Allen shouted down the hatch, "Radar, give me a report — S-Band."

"Two targets bearing zero-nine-seven and zero eight five. Range eighteen and twenty miles. Another at two-one-zero, range forty," the voice came back. "Do you want A-Band (air search), too, sir?"

"Negative, radar." Allen pushed the bridge speaker button, "Sonar, begin a beam to beam search." Immediately, the rhythmic "pinging" of the underwater search began. The admiral said to the captain, "Might as well give them all some practice." Jordan grunted his approval.

Mark Allen turned to Quartermaster Sturgis. "All ahead flank."

The helmsman pushed the annunciators full forward. The rhythm of the four big engines picked up, exhausts firing from *Blackfin*'s quarters in big blue clouds and explosions of spray that flashed rainbows in the sun. Now the war with the swells was even more violent, the bow thundering into the seas, parting them like a club instead of a blade, the sub's empty ballast tanks reverberating with low, booming sounds like great temple drums. Astern, the wake boiled white, leaving a spreading scar to the horizon. Banners of water shot high into the sky and rained down onto the bridge, soaking everyone. Gripping the windscreen, Brent bent his knees and rode the sub like a man roped to the back of a wild horse. His knees began to ache and his thigh muscles tired quickly from the unaccustomed strain. The fun was gone.

Allen keyed the speaker button. "Control room.

Pitometer reading."

A voice came back, "The pitometer log reads twenty-five knots, sir."

"Very well." Mark Allen spoke into the speaker. "Chief engineer report."

A voice came back. "Dunlap here, sir. All engines and power trains operating normally, sir."

"Very well. Control, Mr. Williams report."

There was a pause before Williams's voice returned. "All stations secure and functioning normally, Admiral."

"Very well. All ahead one-third." The wild ride slowed and everyone sighed with relief.

Captain Jordan said, "I suggest you conduct your drills, Admiral."

"Very well," Mark Allen said. He turned to Brent. "We'll exercise at fire control and emergency drills — as many as possible."

"Diving stations, sir?"

The old man nodded. "Yes. But we won't flood our tanks. A dry run."

"Good idea," Jordan said.

For four hours, the crew ran through drills. Over and over the same drills were called. Mark Allen and David Jordan left the bridge to Brent, and when Brent was called to stations, other officers relieved him. Meticulously, Mark Allen and David Jordan inspected every station in every drill, both men taking notes in little black books. Finally, with the sun low on the horizon and the crew near exhaustion, Mark Allen resumed command on the bridge and turned the boat for home.

322

"I'm sorry, darling. I can't see you tonight."

Brent gripped the phone tighter. "But why, Dale? Why?"

"I just got the call. I've got to catch the first flight to Washington."

"When will you be back?"

"I don't know. I don't know." Her voice began to break.

"Your home office is New York?"

"Yes, Brent."

"You'll be back."

"But I don't know when."

He kicked the side of the booth. "I'll be gone soon."

"I know."

"Write me, or send me messages through channels."

"I will. And Brent—you mean a lot to me. You're everything. Take care of yourself."

"You're never out of my thoughts, Dale."

"Please be careful."

"I'm always careful, Dale."

"And Brent, I love you."

Holding the phone tight against his ear, he ground his teeth together.

"Brent. Brent. You didn't want to hear that, did you? We've avoided that word."

"Of course I wanted to hear it." He sighed. "I love you, Dale."

"Oh, darling, you've made me so happy."

"When I see you again, I'll make you happier."

"That's a promise?"

"It's a promise, Dale."

"I've got to leave—got to leave."

After he left the booth, he thrust his hands into the pockets of his foul-weather jacket and walked slowly back to the ship.

Two days later, *Blackfin* made her first dive. With David Jordan on the bridge with Mark Allen, Brent Ross, and Quartermaster Sturgis, *Blackfin* steamed out into Lower New York Bay past the hundred-fathom line. It was a perfect day: sky clear, sea calm, with only a small swell running and a light force two breeze from the northeast. Everyone was tense.

Mark Allen said to David Jordan, "We'll take this slow." The old captain nodded. Allen pointed at Brent and turned to the speaker, "All stations, rig for dive." Brent shouted the command down the hatch into the conning tower.

Immediately, enlisted men in each compartment went through their check-off lists, closing vents, valves, and completing the dozens of other tasks required before a sub can submerge. Mark Allen leaned over the speaker anxiously. "All stations report."

Jordan and Allen had carefully choreographed this first dive. In fact, each compartment would be inspected by off duty officers before actually opening the ballast tanks regardless of how many green lights were shown by the "Christmas tree."

Ensign Hasse's voice squeaked in the speaker.

"Forward torpedo room rigged for dive." Then Williams's voice came through from the control room followed by Lieutenant Cadenbach, Lieutenant Dunlap, all reporting, "Rigged for dive."

Mark Allen leaned over the speaker. "Rig out the bow planes!" Housed flat against the sides of the bow like huge leaves, the bow planes began to rotate and turn out until perpendicular to the hull and slanted slightly forward, their leading edges digging into the water.

"Lookouts below." The two lookouts tumbled anxiously from their perches on the periscope shears and vanished down the hatch.

Mark Allen looked all around. The bow had already been forced below the surface by the planes. "Let's pull the plug—clear the bridge!"

Brent was down the hatch and into the conning tower first, followed by David Jordan. Both men stood next to the TDC. Within a minute the phones, helm, radar, sonar, and plotting table were manned: Quartermaster Harold Sturgis taking his place at the helm and engine-room controls; Sonarman Crog Romero the sonar; Yeoman Randolph "Randy" Davidson at the phones and fastening his headset; Petty Officer Tadashi Takiguichi the radar. Reginald Williams came up the hatch from the control room and took his position next to the periscopes and Lieutenant Charlie Cadenbach hunched over his tiny table next to Sturgis.

Mark Allen, the official OD, came last. Dropping through the hatch, he shouted, "Dive! Dive! Dive!" and hit the dive alarm with the heel of his hand. The horn blared through the boat like an

325

old auto horn. "Oogah! Oogah!" Holding the wire hatch lanyard in his hand and bowing his back, the admiral jerked the hatch cover home with a clang of metal on metal. A few swift whirls of the steel wheel in the center of the hatch dogged it watertight. Then, he dropped down into the conning tower. Immediately, operators at the diving station threw levers and popping sounds were heard as the vents of the main ballast clanged open.

"Green board!" a man shouted.

"Green air!" another man shouted. "Pressure in the boat." Brent felt pressure on his eardrums as air was pumped into the boat to test for leaks.

"Very well," Mark Allen said. He shouted down the hatch into the control room. "Secure the air and take her down to sixty-four feet." He turned to Jordan. "This will give me two and a half feet of periscope."

"Sixty-four feet," the diving officer, Ensign Herbert Battle repeated. Leaning over his two planesmen, he gave his instruction in a calm voice.

Allen turned to Cadenbach who was hunched over his table, staring at a chart and fingering parallel rules. "Navigator, depth under keel."

"One hundred ten fathoms, sir."

Brent could hear the venting of air as water rushed into the main ballast tanks, the hum of electric motors as the batteries took over. The boat inclined downward. Slapping and gurgling, the sea crept up the bridge and conning tower, green water covering the tiny glass eye-ports. Then an awesome quietness as the boat completely submerged and

Brent felt the pressure begin to build against his eardrums again. Despite the whirling fans of the ventilating system, the heat began, and very quickly the conning tower became uncomfortable with the warmth and smell of closely packed bodies. Everyone had a strange rosy flush in the reddish glow of the battle lamps.

"Passing fifty feet, sir," Herbert Battle shouted up the hatch.

"Blow negative and level off," Mark Allen said. "All ahead standard."

"Passing sixty, blowing negative, and leveling, sir."

"Very well. Up 'scope." Williams pushed the pickle-control button hanging from the overhead and there was a sharp metallic pop of an electrical relay snapping shut. With a creaking of sheaves, the periscope began to rise from its well.

"Level on sixty-four feet, sir."

"Very well." Allen stooped over, caught the handles of the periscope as they came out of the well, extended them like a cross as the base of the periscope came clear of the deck, pressed his eyes against the rubber-lined eyepiece, rising smoothly with the tube to a standing position as it locked into place. He spun it around slowly, chuckling. He nodded to Jordan. "Nothing." He stepped away.

Jordan draped his arms over the handles casually and stared into the lens like the old professional he was. He flicked the magnification control from one and one-half to six, turned the scope, stared hard at something off the starboard quarter, and gestured to Mark Allen. "Not quite, Admiral. Hulled down on the horizon — we have company."

Mark Allen took the periscope. "The 'honey barge.' "

"Have you ever sunk a load of shit, Admiral?" Jordan asked casually.

"What?"

"A practice attack. Why not? She can't be doing more than five knots." He waved an arm in an encompassing gesture. "A perfect setup. Clear weather, calm sea. You have a good crew. Go for it. Put a fish up her ass."

Mark Allen smacked his lips and hit the General Alarm button with the heel of his hand. Instantly, the musical bong, bong of the alarm sounded throughout the boat. By the time Brent had reached up to the Torpedo Data Computer and threw the On switch, the attack periscope was already up and Mark Allen was staring into it.

Reginald Williams, the assistant attack officer, moved opposite Mark Allen, staring at the bearing and range scales on the shaft of the periscope. He had hung an instrument called an Is-Was around his neck. Used for matching target bearing with target course, it was made of celluloid and looked much like an old circular slide rule. An ancient instrument, it dated back to the old S-boats.

David Jordan took a place next to the helmsman and the engine-room controls, watching every move, listening to every command. Obeying a gesture from the admiral, Charlie Cadenbach dropped down the ladder into the control room and continued tracking the ship's course in "Plot." The congestion was eased slightly.

Brent looked around the tiny compartment at the intent faces. These few men were the attack team who delivered *Blackfin*'s lethal cargo from this crowded eight-by-sixteen-foot compartment. In one way or another, every other man in the crew had no other function except to support the few isolated in the steel tank of the conning tower; to obey every command, every whim, and live or die by the decisions of that single old man staring through the periscope.

"Conning tower manned and ready," Williams said.

"Very well."

"Forward torpedo room manned and ready, engine rooms One and Two manned and ready, forward battery room manned and ready" came in as the talker reported from the phone board.

Brent stared at the TDC as its motors came up to speed with low-pitched whines. A primitive kind of computer, he had learned to appreciate its complexities and ability to solve problems with multiple variables and provide a real time schematic diagram of the relative positions of the submarine and her target. It even computed the gyro angles required to direct the torpedoes to their target and transmitted them to the torpedo rooms electrically.

About four feet tall, the top panel was black with twelve circular dials highlighted with white etched letters and calibrations. Each was labeled: Target Speed, Target Length, Target, Own Ship, Relative Target Bearing, Own Course, Time, and a Distance to Track indicator which had a grid face.

Brent had spent long hours at the machine with other members of the attack team back at Charlie Four making dry runs. He had learned to set the machine's dials by turning the eight small cranks beneath them, feeding in target length, speed, range, bearing, and course while at the same time entering *Blackfin*'s speed and course. Then the wait for the red solution light that could spell a horrible death for an unsuspecting crew.

"Ship is at battle stations," Davidson reported.

"Very well," the admiral said as he stared through the periscope. "Down 'scope!" Stepping back, he pulled a microphone down from the overhead. "Now hear this," he said. "We're going to make a practice attack on a barge being towed out of the harbor. All commands will be obeyed just as if this is the real thing. However, we won't flood tubes and obviously we won't fire fish—we don't have any, anyway." He looked around the room. "All right, stand by. Right standard rudder. Steady up on two-six-zero." The helm was put over.

"Steady on two-six-zero," Sturgis said.

"Very well. Up 'scope!" Staring into the lens, he said to Williams, "Stand by, XO, first bearing." He stared rigidly into the eyepiece. "Bearing! Mark!"

Standing on the opposite side of the periscope from Mark Allen, Reggie watched the spot where the vertical cross hair on its barrel matched the azimuth circle etched on the overhead around it. "Zero-eight-zero," he read.

Brent entered the information into the TDC.

330

"She has a short antenna mast," Mark Allen said. "Make its height twenty-five feet. Total height from waterline to masthead about forty-five feet." His hand moved to a small wheel on the side of the periscope. At first he turned it rapidly, but slowed, matching the split images in the range finder. He stopped. "Range! Mark!"

"Eight-five-five-zero," Williams said, reading a range opposite the twenty-five-foot masthead height markers on a dial at the bottom of the instrument.

Brent turned his cranks.

"Down 'scope," Allen said stepping back. He said to Reginald and Brent, "Angle on the bow is tough — it's flat and wide. Make it port thirty." Williams adjusted the Is-Was.

Brent turned a dial and the TDC hummed. The target was thirty degrees away from coming directly at *Blackfin*. "Initial range eighty-five hundred," Brent said. "Speed five." Williams glanced at his instrument and nodded concurrence.

Mark Allen turned to Brent. "What's the distance to the track?"

The admiral was asking him for the distance from the submarine to the target's projected track. Brent looked at the grid, made a quick reading of coordinates. The problem was really quite simple, something taught in freshman geometry. A thirty-sixty-ninety triangle. "Four-two-seven-five, sir."

"Our speed through water?"

Quartermaster Sturgis glanced at the log, "Four knots, sir."

"All ahead full." And down the hatch, "Control,

sixty-five feet." There was clink of annunciators and the hum of the electric motors grew. Allen spoke to Williams. "We'll make this observation fast. Stand by. Up 'scope!" Williams pushed the button of the pickle.

Mark Allen leaned over, caught the handles as they came out of the well, and began his observation half doubled over, trying for minimum exposure of the periscope head. "Bearing, mark! Range, mark! Down 'scope."

"Bearing zero-six-zero, range six-five-zero-zero."

Allen turned to Brent who was cranking the new data into the TDC. "Angle on the bow, sixty."

Brent glanced at his grid. "Distance to track three-five-two-five."

"Very well. Our speed through water."

"Nine knots, sir," Sturgis said.

Allen said to Takiguchi, "How long was the periscope above water?"

The sonar man glanced at a stopwatch. "Nine seconds, sir."

"Good." Allen tapped the shaft of the periscope. "All ahead standard. Flood tubes one, two, three, and four." Almost a minute ticked off.

"Tubes one, two, three, and four flooded, sir."

All was quiet for several minutes. Finally, Mark Allen barked, "Open outer doors." He turned to the periscope. "This will be a shooting observation. Up 'scope!" The periscope slithered out of its lair. "Bearing mark! Range mark!"

"Bearing zero-seven-zero, range two-five-zero-zero, sir."

"Angle on the bow, zero-eight-five." Allen

332

stepped back, "Down 'scope!"

Brent cranked his dials furiously and shouted, "Set!" indicating the bearing from the periscope had been set into the TDC.

Mark Allen spoke to Davidson. "Torpedo firing order normal. Depth eighteen feet, speed medium." Davidson spoke into his headset.

A red "F" glowed on the angle solver dial of the TDC. "I have a solution light," Brent said. "You can fire anytime, sir."

"Very well. Simulate firing one! Shoot!"

Williams pulled a phone from the bulkhead and reached up to the firing panel, a long metal box with ten windows, four of which showed red lights. Beneath the windows were a row of switches, and beneath the switches the firing key, a plunger fitted with a round brass plate curved to fit a man's hand. Williams simulated throwing a switch and pushing the key. "Fire One," he said into the phone.

"One fired electrically" came from the talker.

Williams waited a few seconds and repeated the process. "Fire Two . . . Fire Three . . . Fire Four," and the same procedure was repeated.

Jordan smiled and said, "All fish running hot, straight, and normal." The men smiled at each other. Then Jordan shouted, "Boom! Boom! Boom! Boom!" Everyone looked at him. "Congratulations, men," he said with an impish smile. "You can paint a turd on your conning tower."

Laughter swept the compartment. Allen leaned over the open hatch. "Mr. Cadenbach. Give me a course back to the Narrows."

"I would suggest three-five-zero" came back.

"Right standard rudder, steady up on three-five-zero."

Turning his helm and staring at his rudder-angle indicator, the quartermaster repeated the command. "Steady on three-five-zero," he said.

"Very well. All ahead one-third. Prepare to surface." The command rang through the boat.

He turned to Crog. "Sonar, give me a reading on the tug and tow."

Hands on earphones, Crog leaned forward and studied his scope. "Bearing three-zero-zero, range twelve hundred yards, sir."

"Up 'scope." The periscope slid up and Mark Allen rotated around in a complete circle and stopped, staring off the port bow. He grunted with satisfaction. "Very good, sonar. Down 'scope." He shouted down the hatch, "Surface! Surface! Surface!"

The Klaxon blared through the boat and Battle's shout could be heard. "Blow negative to the mark! Six degrees up!"

Hissing under high-pressure, air jolted into the main ballast tanks, blowing out water. *Blackfin* shuddered and then inclined upward.

Mark Allen called down into the control room, "Maneuvering room, stand by to light off four main engines. I want sixteen knots." He turned to Brent and gestured at the hatch. "Stand by, Mr. Ross."

Brent climbed three steps up the bridge ladder and stood just under the hatch, gripping the handle of the hand wheel. He could hear water splashing and gurgling, draining off the bridge. Ensign Battle's shout came up, "Five-oh-feet, four-oh-feet, three-oh-feet . . ."

"Crack the hatch!"

Brent whirled the wheel and air began to blow out the slightly open hatch. He heard Battle's voice. "Pressure, three-eighths-inch," indicating a slightly higher pressure inside the boat than outside.

"Two-five-feet and holding steady" came from Battle again.

"Open the hatch! Section Two to steaming stations."

Brent completed undogging the hatch and unsnapped the safety latch. Counterbalanced by a large, coiled-steel spring, the heavy bronze hatch cover flung itself open with a huge rush of air, banging the side of the bridge and locking open with a thud. Brent, followed by Allen, Jordan, two lookouts and a helmsman, Seaman First Class Jay Overstreet, scampered onto the bridge, which was streaming water out of its scuppers. Quickly, four pairs of binoculars scanned the horizons and Overstreet took the wheel.

"Steer three-five-zero," Mark Allen said.

"Three-five-zero, sir. Ship is steady on three-five-zero, Admiral."

Allen scanned the horizon ahead, then shouted down the hatch, "Open the main induction valve!" He turned to Overstreet. "All ahead two-thirds!" With a thump, the main induction valve located just abaft the bridge and under the cigarette deck, opened. Immediately, there was a roar as the main engines sprang to life and *Blackfin* surged ahead with her new power. Allen shouted into the speaker, "Start the high pressure blow!"

There was a clang in the bowels of the ship followed by a high-pitched screech like the cry of an animal caught in the jaws of a steel trap as the turbo blow began forcing high pressure air into the main ballast tanks, expelling water and kicking up spray from the vents along the sides of the boat. Slowly, the submarine began to shrug herself higher out of the seas.

The tug and tow were passing only a thousand yards off the port beam. Jordan waved. "Some mighty surprised sailors over there."

Brent and the admiral chuckled. Tadashi Takiguchi's voice came up through the hatch. "Radar shows two vessels a thousand yards off the port beam, others bearing two-zero-zero, range fourteen miles, one-three-five, range twenty-three miles and three bearing three-five-five, clearing the Narrows at thirty-one miles, thirty-three, and thirty-four."

"Radar. Give me a bearing on the center of the channel."

"Three-five-five, Admiral."

"Very well." To the helmsman, "Come left to three-five-five."

Jordan waved a hand the length of the boat. "She's running fully surfaced, Admiral."

Allen nodded. Turned to the speaker, "Secure the high pressure blow." Mercifully, the screaming animal died.

Lieutenant Brooks Dunlap's voice came through the speaker. "Permission to charge batteries, sir."

"Permission granted." The pulse of the main engines slowed with the new load as switches were thrown and amperes began to flow from the four eleven hundred kilowatt Elliot generators and into the batteries. Mark Allen turned to Brent. He was obviously in an expansive mood. "This is your watch?"

"Correct, sir. This is my section."

"Well take her in, Lieutenant. Course three-five-five, speed twelve. I'll lay below to my cabin. Call me when you make a landfall."

"Aye, aye, sir."

Mark Allen and David Jordan disappeared down the hatch.

Chapter X

The next week was hectic. Each morning *Blackfin* stood out to sea or steamed into Long Island Sound to conduct drills. Beginning with the second day, a Navy destroyer accompanied *Blackfin*, serving as both target and attacker. Hours were spent in deep water, running silent and rigged for depth charge. On two occasions, the admiral took the submarine to the bottom where she settled into the mud while the crew stood at their stations silently, listening to the screws of the destroyer thrashing across the surface hundreds of feet above their heads. Dummy charges were dropped and on one occasion, two actually bounced off the bridge.

"Well, lads," David Jordan grinned. "You just earned the Navy Cross or the emperor's personal citation — posthumous, of course." No one laughed.

The efficiency of the crew grew, the attack team becoming a well-oiled unit. However, Mark Allen was often confused by the destroyer's zigzag and on several occasions pounded the periscope with frustration. Brent Ross, Reginald Williams, Ensign Freddie Hasse, Lieutenant Charles Cadenbach, and

Lieutenant Bernard Pittman took turns at the attack periscope. With the instincts of the hunter, Brent took to the periscope like a natural, outperforming all of the other officers. Immediately, he showed a talent for picking the base course out of the destroyer's zigzag.

Hasse and Pittman were extremely slow attack officers. While the pair fumbled their approaches, Brent found his long, dry periods standing before the TDC dull and irritating. His wandering mind inevitably found its way back to Dale. He could see her, feel her, smell her. The silk of her hair slipped through his fingers, her body pressed against his. He would shake his head, concentrate on the face of the TDC. He memorized every word, every number of the face plate:

US Navy Bu. of Ord.
Mk.3 Mod. 5
Contract WXSD-13913 Serial No. 240
Volt ll5DC 115 AC
Insp. E.K.W. Ord. Dwg. No. 291807
Date 1944
Arma Corp.
Brooklyn N.Y.

One afternoon he found himself debating with himself over Inspector E.K.W. Had the inspector been an old man? A fat, middle-aged woman? No. Probably a young, beautiful girl whose lover was at sea. That was it. She had been doing her bit building this killing machine. He laughed aloud and the other men looked at him. His face flushed.

On the fourth day ammunition and twenty-four

Mark 48 torpedoes were loaded. Because of restrictions imposed by the Soviets and Americans meeting at Geneva, all torpedo guidance systems were prohibited. Mark 6 contact fuses were installed and new circuits wired so that the torpedoes' gyros could be controlled from the TDC. One with a dummy warhead was fired from one of the boat's new Mark 68 tubes and the weapon functioned perfectly, tracking straight, true, and maintaining its depth. Driven by a gas-piston engine and designed to overtake and hit new Soviet high-speed attack submarines, the torpedo had a range of thirty miles and a speed of fifty-five knots. "Incredible," Mark Allen said. "Makes the old Mark 14 look like erratic junk."

On the fifth day, the submarine's hull and upper works were sprayed with a new RAM (radar absorbent material), Deflecton Four. Thick like a rubberized paint, Deflecton Four had been developed by the Air Force in its research for the defunct stealth bomber. "It's a radar repellent," Mark Allen said that afternoon in the wardroom. "And it's been modified by the Navy to distort sonar returns—better than the sonar absorbers they've been using on the latest SSBN's."

"Respectfully, sir, that can't work. I helped develop some of the latest materials and none of them were very efficient," Williams said politely.

Mark Allen nodded. "True, XO. They've had problems. However, it does confuse radar signals and diffuse them. With our low silhouette, it just might make us almost undetectable."

"Almost," Brent and Williams chorused.

Each evening Brent phoned Dale. However, there

was no answer. Had he lost her? Was she gone forever? She had told him she loved him. And he had said the same. Had he meant it? He did not know simply because he did not know what this elusive "love" was all about and he had told her as much. Certainly, he had grown attached to her. Certainly, he was unhappy when he could not see her. Maybe, on the stern of one of Kadafi's destroyers, there was a six-hundred-pound depth charge that would solve these problems forever. He shuddered.

On the sixth day, Cryptologist Donald Simpson called Brent to the radio room. He held a printout in his hand and was studying it with a confused look. "Doesn't make sense, Mr. Ross," he said. "Sixty-two groups and they don't fit any of our programs. Came out of the encryption box this way. Must be a code we aren't hard-wired for, sir."

Brent examined the message. The first group was five "C's" and the remaining groups were numbers, except the Greenwich Civil Time of transmission which was typed across the top. Brent felt a surge of excitement. The new top secret CISRA code, developed by Israeli Intelligence and the CIA and reserved for transmissions pertaining to *Yonaga* and the forces under the control of Admiral Fujita. The basis of the code was unique, a computer-generated system that expressed the alphabet as an eight-figure sub-routine which in turn was based on random combinations and permutations of a ten-figure master. Thus far, Arab and Russian monitors had found it impossible to break. But with the brute force of main frames located in Moscow, Damascus, and Tripoli, it was only a matter of time and everyone knew this. However, the master was changed randomly and the whole process began again. "C Code," Brent said simply. "This is my baby."

He took the printout to his cabin and pulled a small but powerful NEC lap-top computer from a drawer and placed it on his desk. Quickly, he typed in the eight-figure digital control code governed by the moon phase and Greenwich Civil Time of reception plus three. The NEC digested the information in a millisecond and flashed, *READY TO DE-CODE*.

As Brent typed in the numbers, the message unfolded letter by letter across the screen:

```
TOP SECRET
091736Z— —27649
ARAB NAV OPS— —BLACKFIN OPS
FM. COMYONAGA— —TO. COMBLACKFIN
INFO— —COMCIAXX COMISINTXX COMPAC

REPAIRS ARAB CARRIER SURABAYA COMPLETED
APPROX FOUR WEEKS XX DESTINATION TOMONUTO
ATOLL XX ENEMY FORCES TOMONUTO— —ONE
CARRIER TWO CRUISERS TWELVE DESTROYERS
TWO OILERS THREE REPLENISHMENT VESSELSXX

BLACKFIN PROCEED TO TOMONUTO ATOLL
IMMEDIATELYXX ENGAGE AND DESTROYXX
```

Brent leaned back and chuckled. "Is that all?" he said aloud. "That's Fujita." Fragmented memories of one of the old admiral's favorite passages from the *Hagakure* replaced the grin with a hard set to the jaw: "Meditation on inevitable death should be performed daily . . . One should meditate upon being ripped apart by arrows, spears, and swords, being carried away by surging waves, being thrown into a great fire, committing seppuku . . . and every day without fail one should consider himself as dead. This is the way of the samurai."

Grimly, he ran the message out through his printer, tore off the sheet, and walked to Admiral Allen's cabin.

An hour later, all eight officers were crowded into the wardroom, seated before coffee mugs kept full by the ubiquitous mess manager, Pablo Fortuno. Every man was seated except Admiral Allen, who stood in front of a chart mounted on the bulkhead. "Gentlemen," he began. "It's time we started to earn our pay." He read the CISRA message. A rumble filled the room and the men hunched forward eagerly.

Picking up a pointer, he stabbed the chart in the western Pacific. "Tomonuto Atoll—in the western Carolines. The enemy force will be assembled in approximately five weeks. Two carriers, two cruisers, and a dozen 'cans.' Heavy odds even for *Yonaga*. I intend to reduce those odds." There were shouts of "Hear! Hear!"

Allen moved the pointer to the Marianas. "As all of you know, the enemy is establishing air bases here on Saipan and Tinian. These bases pose a mortal threat to *Yonaga* and all of Japan, for that matter. If those dominoes fall, the terrorists will run wild and the US is next in line. All of you know this, or you wouldn't be here." He slapped the table with the pointer. "If we can just pick off one of those carriers, *Yonaga* might be able to handle the rest of it."

"Might, sir?" Hasse said.

"Yes. To clean out all of the vermin, we must mount an amphibious assault on Saipan and Tinian. An amphibious force is now being trained."

"We took those islands in WW II, sir," Ensign Battle noted.

"I know," Allen said, smiling. "I was there." He turned back to the chart. "Lieutenant Cadenbach and I have calculated our run." The tip of the pointer slid down the chart. "Seventy-eight hundred miles total. Our first run will be south from New York to this point off the Antilles. Then southwest through the Mono Passage between the Dominican Republic and Puerto Rico and into the Caribbean."

"Speed of advance, sir," Lieutenant Bernard Pittman asked.

"SOA twenty-one-knots." Pittman whistled. Allen waved at the engineering officer, Lieutenant Brooks Dunlap. "No strain on engineering?"

"That's right, sir. No problem for our new Fairbanks-Morse engines," Lieutenant Brooks Dunlap said.

Allen returned to the chart. "Southwest across the Caribbean to Panama and then west to Pearl Harbor where we'll top off our tanks and take on stores." He turned to the table and tapped the pointer on the floor. "Then our run of twenty-eight hundred miles to our patrol area off Tomonuto Atoll."

"ETA (Estimated time of arrival), sir?"

"Twenty days from today."

"How many entrances does the atoll have, sir?" Ensign Robert Owen asked.

"Two. But only one can handle vessels of deep

344

draft." Allen waved to Charlie Cadenbach. Quickly the navigator tacked a chart of Tomonuto Atoll next to the chart of the Pacific. Allen gestured with his pointer. "According to our sailing directions it's enormous, eighteen miles long and about six and a half miles wide at its widest." He circled the atoll with the pointer, "Almost a perfect ellipse—it's circled with a coral reef. A few of the larger reefs appear like long, narrow islands. In fact, some have enough soil to support thick stands of coconut trees. From a distance the trees appear like a fringe on the horizon. Ideal anchorage." He sighed. "The Marshalls, Gilberts, and Carolines have dozens of these atolls—the best natural anchorages in the world. Any one of them could accommodate every ship on earth with plenty of room to spare. I anchored in several when serving with Admiral Nimitz in Task Force Fifty-Eight."

Allen moved the pointer to a break in the reef. "We'll station ourselves here—off the entrance. We'll patrol submerged during the day and surface at night to recharge our batteries. If we keep our speed submerged at three knots and keep our use of our main engines at a minimum, we have enough fuel to patrol for maybe five months—here off the entrance. In fact, we could run out of food before we run out of fuel." He thumped the chart. "The Arabs are inefficient, but I would expect a 'can' to be either running a 'ping line' off the entrance, here, or to be anchored in the entrance with sonar on passive—or two can's manning both stations."

"We could still run out of fuel before they sortie, Admiral," Battle said. "They could remain at anchor for six months, sir."

"*Yonaga* will take care of that problem."

"Sir?"

Allen nodded at the young diving officer. "As soon as we're on station, we will send a signal. *Yonaga* will sortie and run south. The Arabs will have to stand out or be caught by her air groups in the anchorage." He pushed the long white hair back from his forehead. "That will be our chance." He slapped the table with the pointer so hard, it sounded like a pistol shot. "We'll fish one—maybe both of them."

More shouts of "Hear! Hear!"

Pittman interrupted the shouts. "Sir. The worst case scenario—if *Yonaga* doesn't rendezvous or if she's sunk." He waved a hand at the chart, "As Ensign Battle said, we could run low on fuel and it must be two thousand miles from Tomonuto to Japan."

"True," Mark Allen said. "However, the CIA has anchored a tanker here, at Kossol Passage at the northern end of the Palau archipelago. It's camouflaged and anchored close ashore." He struck the chart. "That's only three hundred eighty miles from our patrol. We can refuel and replenish there."

"The Palauan government has agreed to this?"

"Let's say they're looking the other way." There were chuckles. "Gentlemen, prepare the boat for sea. I intend to get underway within an hour. You are dismissed."

Talking excitedly, the officers filed out of the room. Pablo Fortuno dashed from the galley and hurried into the mess hall. Waving his arms in excitement, he began talking to a dozen men.

346

At twenty-one knots and steaming directly south on course one-eight-zero, the bridge of *Blackfin* was swept by spray and sometimes solid sheets of water. Despite the near-suicidal nature of their mission, the rough ride as the boat slammed into the swells at twenty knots like an enraged bull, Brent enjoyed being at sea again. He chuckled to himself and clung to the windscreen railing as the sea with its many moods capriciously punished the sub again and again with sledgehammer blows from attacking swells.

Crossing the thirtieth parallel, more power had to be called on to counteract the set of the Gulf Stream which flowed with a three-knot speed. The sky darkened, and for days on end the sun showed with the dim glow of a failing lamp. Repeatedly, Brent heard the navigator, Lieutenant Charlie Cadenbach, curse when he was unable to make precise sights at dawn and dusk. Geneva refused to allow the installation of a modern inertial navigation system (SINS).

The topside steaming watch consisted of four lookouts—one assigned to each of the four sectors around the ship—a helmsman and the Officer of the Deck. All six men on bridge watch wore binoculars over their foul-weather clothes. There was a chance an Arab Whiskey or Zulu might be lying in wait for them. Zigzagging was out of the question, and knowing the best defense against a lurking submarine was speed, *Blackfin* was forced to rely on her powerful engines and the alert eyes of her bridge watch. All men were carefully instructed to keep a close watch for low-lying dark hulls, periscopes, or mysterious streaks in the water. At night the running lights were not burned, the only light on the bridge coming from a tiny red light in the gyro repeater and the dim reddish glow coming out of the open hatch to the conning tower. As a further precaution, all watertight doors were latched shut, ready for instant dogging. Any ship picked up by radar was given a wide berth.

When they entered the Horse Latitudes, the wind began to shift without warning, sometimes whipping sheets of spray from the waves like white cotton from a burst mattress, flinging spume into Brent's face, and other times following the boat and not felt at all. Nearing the Antilles and turning southwest, the sky filled with a solid mass of scudding cirrus and cumulonimbus, taking on ominous black-gray hues, the sea glittering like molten lead. They were nearing a storm.

Stirred up by a hurricane just south of the equator, the wave patterns built up into a series of marching mountain ranges. The submarine took them like a battering ram, bursting through each with a burst of water like an exploding torpedo. Solid water tumbled and streaked her length, sweeping over her as if she were submerging, pouring over the bridge and leaking into the conning tower through the hatch that was latched but not dogged. After each mountain came a valley and the boat sheered off into the cavern ahead of her. Sometimes the screws broke clear and the vibrations shook every plate, every rivet. Then she slid forward like a skier on a down slope and finally bottomed in the valley between crests, where the wind was blocked and an eerie silence made the looming cliff ahead appear even more menacing. Then she threw her head up, attacking her new adversary and repeating the cycle again.

Mercifully, as they approached the Mono Passage between Santo Domingo and Puerto Rico, the storm gradually lessened and finally charged off to the south and west, leaving the skies an aching blue void, the seas calm. Entering the passage and hugging the coast of Santo Domingo, Admiral Mark Allen waved and said, "Hispaniola, the Pearl of the Antilles." His mood as bright and cheerful as the weather. "Loads of history here." He stabbed a finger ahead to the Caribbean. "The Spanish gold galleons, Drake, Morgan, Kidd, Captain Blood—they all sailed here."

"And now *Blackfin,* sir."

The admiral laughed. "Right, Brent. And now *Blackfin.*"

It took almost two days to cross the broad expanse of the Caribbean. Brent was impressed with the beauty of the area. It was warm, calm and peaceful after the Atlantic. But it was treacherous, capable of producing in very short time the most violent storms and hurricanes. However, throughout their transit, the sea was on its best behavior.

It was a brilliant morning when they made their landfall on Cristobal, the port on the Caribbean side of the Panama Canal. Passing through the breakwater into Limon Bay, the signal tower on the beach began flashing a challenge. Crog was summoned to the bridge and quickly the radioman flashed a "K."

"Proceed to the entrance to the canal, sir," Crog said, flashing the shore station a "Roger." "You will

349

make transit immediately. Pilot en route. Stand by."

At that moment a lookout shouted, "Boat approaching at a high speed, bearing three-two-five, range one thousand."

"Very well. All stop," Mark Allen said. "Deck crew stand by to receive small boat. Port side to."

In a moment the small speed boat came alongside and the pilot, a small, dark man of about thirty with obvious Latin antecedents, climbed up onto the bridge. He introduced himself. "Pedro Garcia," he said, his black mustache lifting with his grin. He took a single sighting through the bearing ring and said to Admiral Allen, "I suggest you come to one-seven-zero, speed slow."

"Very well." Mark Allen nodded to Brent who was officially the OD. Brent gave the commands and *Blackfin* headed for the canal.

As they approached Gatun Locks, Garcia waved and spoke proudly. "Over seventy years old, but still one of the marvels of the world. Took a half-million men ten years to build it."

"*Blackfin* will make the transit alone," Garcia said as they entered the huge one-thousand by one-hundred-ten-foot chamber. The gates closed and the moss-covered lock flooded, lifting the boat. "Three lifts," Garcia said. "We'll leave this lock eighty-two feet above sea level.

The gates at the far end opened and *Blackfin* entered Gatun Lake. Roaring, the engines pushed her south and then east, weaving between islands and narrow cuts in the hills. It was very hot and the humidity was oppressive. Brent was kept busy, responding to requests for frequent course changes. "Twenty-three changes in course in a fifty-mile run,

Lieutenant," Garcia said, sighting through the bearing ring.

Finally they entered Miraflores Lock and were lowered to the level of the Pacific Ocean. Then the short run to Balboa Harbor and Garcia was taken off by a pilot boat. *"Vaya con Dios,"* he said, climbing down into the boat. Brent and Mark Allen waved.

Mark Allen turned to Brent. "Steam one-eight-zero, all ahead standard until you clear that headland to starboard and those islands." He stabbed a finger. "I'll be in plot with Cadenbach. I'll call up a course change when we're well clear. Then we'll set our course for Pearl."

Brent repeated the order and Mark Allen went below.

Steaming on a northwesterly course for the Hawaiian Islands, the sea was calm, skies cluttered with clusters of clouds. Line squalls were seen and occasionally the bridge crew was drenched by a sudden downpour, the submarine charging through the small but intense rainstorms. Only two freighters were sighted on the long run.

Ten days after leaving Panama and three hundred eighty miles from the Hawaiian Islands, they were sighted by the Martin PBM flying boat. Dropping low, the graceful, gull-winged patrol bomber circled *Blackfin*. Although Brent instructed Cryptologic Technician Simpson and Petty Officer Goroku Kumano to guard FM-Ten and Bridge to Bridge circuits, nothing came over the airways. Instead, after four complete circuits of the submarine, a hand-held Aldis lamp flashed a single-letter challenge from the cockpit. Instantly, Crog responded with the correct return. The big Martin disappeared to the west. Mark Allen snickered, "They're learning to be careful."

Just two hours later Electronics Warfare Technician Matthew Dante, a bright young petty officer from Villa Park, California, called Brent from the radio room to the ESM console in the control room. "I've been getting a lot of UHF and VHF garbage—even a clear channel AM station in Los Angeles with the call letters KFI, but something big is trying to bust through all of it." Slipping an earphone from one ear, he pointed to his tactical warning board where a red light suddenly began to glow steadily between two flickering lights.

"There it is!" Dante tapped his keyboard, studied some meters and the display on his screen. "We've got him. A big mother, fifty-five hundred megahertz. Signature characteristics of a naval vessel. Bearing zero-zero-five, range one-seven-five. Closing at thirty-two knots. There's a lot of interference, but listen to him, Mr. Ross." He threw a switch and static followed by a fuzzy beep came through a bulkhead mounted speaker.

"I hear him. Is he ranging us?"

"No, but a good operator would've picked us up, sir. We're at his extreme range and the beep would be a steady tone if he had us. You know we can pick him up before he gets a return off of us." He clapped his hands over his earphones. "At this range the curvature of the earth is causing most of his search to go right over us. We're getting the downside of his beam, though. His antenna must be about eight-feet wide, over a hundred feet above the waterline, and his beam width is five degrees—

could be an old Hull class destroyer, but, actually, he should be getting a return off of us — weak, maybe, but we should be on his 'scope. Maybe he's asleep or a total screw-up." He tapped the tube. "Or that RAM, Deflecton Four, works." He fingered a few keys, turned a knob and a green light glowed. "He's not in our threat library."

"IFF (Identification Friend or Foe)?"

"Nothing yet. Shall I inform the Admiral?"

"I'll do it and stay on it, Dante." Brent picked up the phone and called the admiral.

"Must be a picket called by the PBM. They've been a little more careful ever since December 7, 1941," Mark Allen said from the bridge. "Report to the bridge, Brent. We need your good eyes up here." Brent turned to the ladder.

With a combined closing speed of over fifty knots, the vessels were within thirty miles of each other after an hour and a half of steaming. Still, the stranger's radar did not fix *Blackfin*. Allen was jubilant.

Brent was staring through his binoculars when the strange ship heaved over the horizon; radar cluttered mast first, then the upper works of what was obviously a destroyer and then the knifelike bow.

Dante's voice came through the speaker: "He has us on his radar, Admiral."

"Very well." Mark Allen turned to Brent. "He should. After all, his lookouts can see us." Both men laughed.

Suddenly, the sounds of a shrill bell ringing came up through the hatch and every man on the bridge turned his head. Radarman Dante's alarmed voice shrieked through. "Bridge, he's switched to eight-thousand megahertz—that's fire control, Admiral!"

"Stand by to dive. Battle stations submerged!" Mark Allen roared. Immediately, the horn boomed through the submarine and scores of hard leather shoes pounded on steel decks and floor plates, the crew rushing to diving stations.

Dante's frantic voice came through the speaker. "He's secured his fire control, Admiral. And I have his IFF. Friendly, sir."

Mark Allen shouted down the hatch, "Secure from diving stations, secure the diving horn. Section three return to steaming stations." A light began to blink. Allen turned to the signalman. "Answer his challenge."

Crog turned the light on the stranger and signals were exchanged. The ship identified herself as the USS *Somers*. *Blackfin* reduced speed.

"Hull class," Brent said to Mark Allen.

"That's right, Mr. Ross," Mark Allen said, staring through his binoculars. "He must've mistaken us for a Zulu or Whiskey. We all look alike from a distance." He was obviously relieved but Brent noticed his face was unusually pale and the veins stood out on his forehead and temples like blue lines.

The light tapped out a signal from the *Somers's* signal bridge. "I am your escort. Follow in my wake." The ship slowed and began to make a wide turn.

Brent heard Mark Allen clear his throat with a loud "Harrumph!" The old man turned to Crog. "Signalman, request name and rank of commanding officer of *Somers*."

There was an exchange of flashes and Crog said, "Commander Bruce Doheny commanding, sir."

354

Mark Allen chuckled. "Send a signal—Admiral Mark Allen commanding *Blackfin*. Follow in my wake." Everyone on the bridge laughed as Crog worked the shutters. *Somers* fell in astern of *Blackfin*.

A few hours later radar traced most of east coasts of Oahu and Molokai and the peaks of both islands were visible on the horizon. Numerous steamers and fishing boats were sighted and ESM reported numerous J-band and S-band radars. Entering the Kaiwi Channel between Oahu and Molokai with *Somers* five hundred yards astern, the sea was a mirror and the sky brilliant. Off-duty crewmen crowded the deck as *Blackfin* steamed past the forest of skyscrapers at Waikiki and Honolulu and turned north toward the entrance of Pearl Harbor. The inevitable light began flashing from the Aloha Tower and Crog flashed his "K."

Mark Allen spoke, "Request permission to stand in, Crog."

The radioman worked the handle of the light and the shutters clacked. "Permission granted, sir. Proceed to the sub base, berth at Sugar Twelve."

"Very well." Allen gestured to Brent.

Brent squatted and peered through the sights of the bearing ring, "Three-five-five splits the channel, Admiral."

"Take her in, Mr. Ross."

Brent gave the orders and *Blackfin* entered the narrow channel to Pearl Harbor. Ahead, he could see the soaring beauty of Oahu climbing in green hilly escarpments to the cloud-shrouded heights of the Koolau Mountains. Hawaiian flora has special intense greenness all its own and the sprawl of concrete towers in Honolulu and Waikiki seemed particularly obscene when viewed against this glorious backdrop. "Progress," Brent muttered to himself.

Slowly, *Blackfin* stood in, passing naval housing to port, Bishop's Point to starboard, then the marine barracks, the shipyard, and the slow turn to the right past Ford Island to the north and the lonely white buoys of "Battleship Row." Lettered in black, the rows of grisly white bollards were grave markers: Oklahoma, Nevada, Tennessee, West Virginia, California, Vestal, Arizona, Maryland. Slowly they passed the white, sagging, low bridge of the Arizona Memorial and the crew stared silently.

Somers dropped off and headed for her berth at the shipyard and Allen ordered another right turn and *Blackfin* made for her berth at the submarine base. Within a few minutes, she was firmly secured to the dock at *Sugar Twelve*.

Mark Allen was visibly upset. At first, Brent thought the memorials to the old dead and wounded battleships had depressed him. But it was not that at all. Mark Allen waved. "Look at all those ships. Destroyers, frigates, tenders—they don't have the fuel to keep them at sea."

Brent nodded. "And they're converting them, sir." He pointed to a nest of destroyers. "ASROC launchers are gone and so are their surface to air Tartar missiles." He pointed at several silolike structures, "They're installing the Phalanx, twenty-millimeter AA Gatlings."

Mark Allen nodded. "Twenties and forties in multiple mounts, automatic seventy-six-millimeter and five-inch dual purpose guns, too." He punched the screen. "And they don't have the fuel to keep them at sea."

"All lines secure," came up from the chief boatswain's mate. "Brow secured, sir." A group of officers waiting on the dock began streaming across the gangway.

Allen knuckled the screen and climbed down to the main deck.

Fuel tanks topped off and, with stores jamming every space, even the heads, *Blackfin* stood out the next morning. Steaming on a westerly course, the submarine left Johnson Island to the south and then Wake to the north, so close radar emanations were picked up by the ESM. Ships were infrequent and, when detected, avoided. They crossed the International date line and then the Marshall and Gilbert Islands were left to the south and the long run parallel to the Caroline Islands began. Here they found inter-island traffic cluttering their scope with many small steamers plying the trade routes between islands and atolls. All were carefully avoided.

Conditions on board *Blackfin* were much better than Brent had first anticipated. The crew had settled down into a routine almost immediately after leaving New York. There were no problems in the racial mix of American and Japanese. Two cooks and a baker prepared three good meals daily, designed to satisfy both Western and Eastern palates. The freezer was filled with steaks, roasts, hamburger, and fish. Up by 0300, the baker prepared rolls, bread, cakes and cookies. The pantry was open to all hands. Every man, regardless of the hour, had the right to open the refrigerator and help himself to rice, tofu sushi, tempura, bacon, eggs, or cold cuts for sandwiches. As usual on warships, a "Joe Pot" was kept hot with fresh coffee twenty-four hours a day, and tea was available for anyone who wanted it.

Brent was pleasantly surprised by the amount of fresh water available. In fact, the new evaporators provided enough water for at least two showers a week for all hands. The washing machine was in almost constant use. Off-duty enlisted men liked to congregate in the crew's mess, after battery room, the torpedo rooms or control room. The Americans taught the Japanese poker and the Japanese showed the Americans their game of Go—an intricate game played with black and white stones on a board checkered with nineteen horizontal lines and nineteen vertical lines. With a large store of video cassettes on board, movies were shown in the forward battery room and in the wardroom every day.

On the day *Blackfin* crossed longitude one fifty-five east, Brent had the morning watch when Mark Allen climbed up on the bridge and wearily raised his binoculars. "Down there, Brent. Only a hundred miles south of us."

"What is it, sir?"

The admiral appeared sick and old. Sighing, he leaned against the windscreen, "Truk. It was Japan's Gibraltar of the Pacific. Their biggest base—headquarters for their combined fleet. It was supposed to cancel out Pearl Harbor."

Brent chuckled. "According to my history courses, Task Force Fifty-Eight canceled it."

"We hit the place in February of '44. But we never took it."

"Let it wither on the vine, Admiral?"

The old man nodded. "Used it for bombing practice." He stabbed a finger astern. "Did the same thing back there in the Marshalls. Bypassed Wotje, Jaluit, Mille, and used their garrisons for bombing and gunnery practice." He pointed southeast. "Ponape, too."

"Good planning, sir."

"Tarawa wasn't." Mark Allen threw a thumb astern. "It's back there in the Gilberts." His voice became bitter as hard memories returned. "We didn't need it, I was against it and said as much. But the 'braid,' in their infinite wisdom, knew better." He ran a fist over the rail. "Bloody foul up, didn't even figure the tides right—lost a thousand fine boys—hundreds of them shot down in the water before they even reached the beach. It's beastly hot down there, almost on the equator. You could smell the rotting meat a mile at sea." The fist punched the steel windscreen. "Should've bypassed it—we never used it. It was all for nothing."

Silently, the old admiral drummed his fingers on the windscreen. Brent could see he was upset—these waters, the old ghosts.

The reminiscences continued. "Remember I mentioned a tanker would be stationed in the Palaus?"

"Yes, sir."

"We invaded it, you know, and that was another useless slaughter. I was against it and so was Douglas MacArthur." He ran a palm over his forehead, brushing his hair back. "We only took two worthless islands out of hundreds, Peleliu and Angaur at the southern tip of the archipelago—two-thousand more boys thrown away. We never used it,

359

either. All those gold-star mothers never knew their sons died for nothing."

Brent found nothing to say, remained quiet like a mourner seated beside next-of-kin at a wake.

The approach on Tomonuto Atoll was made cautiously. Because the entrance was on the southwest coast, *Blackfin* steamed around the northern coast of the atoll. Just out of radar range, Mark Allen, Reginald Williams, and Brent Ross gathered in plot with the navigator, Charlie Cadenbach. Mark Allen ran a finger north of the atoll. "We'll maintain this course—two-seven-zero, on the ninth parallel and make a radar search of Tomonuto."

Cadenbach dropped his parallel rules. "Sir, that's only seventy-miles north of the atoll. They'll pick us up on their ESM's."

"Of course. But we need a reading on their precise anchorage. We can't plan on doing it visually. They're probably anchored about here." He struck the chart in the middle of the atoll. "Not too close to the entrance. They wouldn't want to give a sub a chance at a lucky long shot through the entrance." He slid his finger to the west. "The Philippines, Yap, the Palaus. Dozens of small steamers ply these waters—we've been picking up their radars ever since we entered the Marshalls." He traced a straight line west. "We'll follow this steamer route past the atoll until we're out of radar range." He looked up. "They'll take us for another inter-island steamer." He turned back to the chart. "And then we'll turn off not only our radar but all electronic equipment except the ESM, which doesn't transmit a signal." He looped his finger back southeast. "And then we'll double back and make a fast run in on the entrance and begin our patrol."

"Sir," Williams said. "What about Libyan aerial reconnaissance?"

The old man shook his head. "No chance. There are no airstrips at Tomonuto, and those heavy ME One-Oh-Nines and JU Eighty-Sevens need at least twenty-six knots of wind over the deck to take off."

The officers eyed each other. All of them had doubts, but no one had a better plan.

At a hundred eighty miles, ESM detected three surface search radars emanating from the atoll. "Big stuff," Matthew Dante reported with Mark Allen, Brent Ross, and a half-dozen officers and crewmen crowded behind him. "Two are searching E and F bands. My threat library indicates the Majestic class carrier and the Spanish *Principe de Asturias*. The third is a S-band search probably coming from a Gearing class picket destroyer."

"Damn," Mark Allen said. "I wanted a crack at that Majestic when she stood in. She's early—a week early. Must've missed her by hours."

Eighty miles directly north of Tomonuto, radar traced the entire atoll in detail. Eighteen ships were anchored almost in the middle of the atoll, precisely where Mark Allen had indicated they would be. A single blip was stationary at the entrance.

Continuing its westerly heading, *Blackfin* steamed slowly out of radar range. Then all electronics equipment, except ESM, was secured, course altered to the southeast and speed increased to twenty-two knots. When radar emanations were detected at a hundred fifty miles from the atoll, the submarine submerged.

Nineteen hours later, *Blackfin* approached the entrance, cloaked in the darkness of midnight. Detecting no active sonar, Allen brought the submarine to the surface eight miles from the channel. Immediately, the diesels began charging the depleted battery. Brent heard a lookout pray to Deflecton Four.

Standing together on the bridge, Brent and Mark Allen stared into their binoculars and spoke in hushed tones as if enemy ears were nearby and could overhear. Allen said, "They're confident or stupid. One 'can' in the entrance. No way to run a war." He turned to Brent. "Send the signal to *Yonaga* reporting we're on station." He rubbed his chin. "How long will it take to transmit the signal?"

"A millisecond, sir—if we get an immediate acknowledgment."

"Good. The shorter the better. But wait until we submerge at dawn—they could pick it up with their RDF's (radio direction finders)."

Just before dawn the boat submerged to sixty-four feet and began patroling ten thousand yards off the entrance. With the electric motors turning over only fast enough to maintain depth and steerageway and on "silent running," the destroyer anchored just inside the entrance was unaware of the deadly menace waiting in ambush. From the conning tower, the OOD periodically raised the periscope and took a quick look around. The destroyer never moved. Finally, Mark Allen called Brent into his cabin and ordered him to send the message.

"Use TACAMO (Take Charge and Move Out)." he said.

TACAMO sent a compressed computerized code with a signal strength of only 200 watts. The transmission depended upon the reception of the signal

362

by a U.S. Navy DC-6 orbiting over the western Pacific, trailing a four-mile-long antenna. Upon receiving the signal, the DC-6 was to relay it to *Yonaga*.

Brent moved to the radio room and stood behind Cryptologic Technician Simpson. "Ready to transmit, sir," Simpson said. "Anytime we can get the antenna up."

Brent moved to the foot of the ladder to the conning tower and looked up at Reginald Williams, who was officer of the deck and stood next to the Number Two, or night periscope. The attack periscope tapered to a small 1.4-inch exit lens, making it hard to spot, but allowing only a limited amount of light to penetrate the forty-foot length of the tube. With a much larger aperture and lens, the night periscope compensated for the lower visibility at night, transmitting much more light and sharper images. However, it could be spotted much more easily.

Brent said to the executive officer, "Radio room's ready, Mr. Williams."

"Very well. Up 'scope." Williams rotated the periscope through three hundred sixty degrees. "Down 'scope." He turned to the quartermaster of the watch. "Raise the antenna on my mark." Brent pumped a fist. Williams shouted, "Mark!"

An electric motor whirred and the whip antenna shot up to the surface. A green light glowed on the panel in front of Simpson. The quartermaster yelled, "Locked!"

"Transmit!" Brent shouted.

Simpson punched a key and immediately shouted, "Complete, sir."

"Transmission completed," Brent informed Williams.

"Down antenna!" Williams ordered.

Simpson clamped his hands over his earphones, turned to Brent and smiled. "Acknowledged, sir. First crack."

"Four-oh," Brent said. He brought a phone to his ear and reported to Admiral Allen.

Four nights later a half hour before dawn, Crog, who was standing the sonar watch, reported, "Cavitations, many screws of different sizes. A large force moving toward the entrance. Range eleven to twelve thousand yards. Making more noise than a virgin on her wedding night."

Admiral Allen and Brent Ross hurried to the control room. The old man gasped and wheezed and his face was unusually pale. In fact, Brent had to help him through the last watertight door opening on the control room. Here the red battle lamps gave his face a ghostly red pallor, veins black under the thin skin.

Hoarsely, Allen ordered the ESM antenna raised for a quick reading. Technician Matthew Dante called out, "They've fired up another dozen radars, Admiral. My threat library indicates emanations from cruisers *London* and *Llandaff* and at least ten Gearing class destroyers."

"Tracking party to the conning tower," Mark Allen shouted. He looked at Brent, pointed to the ladder. Brent understood. Usually the captain of the boat was the first man up the ladder. Allen needed help. Brent bounded up the ladder and reached down and almost pulled the admiral up into the conning tower. While the admiral steadied himself by leaning on the night periscope, the assistant attack officer, Lieutenant Reginald Williams, the helmsman, Quartermaster Harold Sturgis, Sonar Operator Radioman Tony "Crog" Romero, Talker Yeoman Randolph "Randy" Davidson, and Radarman Tadashi Takiguchi all scrambled up the ladder and took their stations.

"Manned and ready, manned and ready," echoed through the small chamber.

"General quarters? Torpedo attack submerged, Admiral?" Williams asked, dropping the cord of the "Is-Was" around his neck.

Negative. Negative." The old man rubbed his forehead. Began to speak. Tightened his jaw and gritted his teeth. Every man stared at him. He sighed. Took a deep breath as if preparing to leap into icy water and rasped, "Stand by to surface." He looked around at the surprised faces.

Williams said, "Admiral, respectfully, we're only seven thousand yards from that 'can' in the entrance. Even with Deflecton Four they may get a return. Aw, hell, Admiral, they should see us."

"Don't tell me my business, XO," Allen snapped. He glared at the startled faces surrounding him. Patting the Number Two periscope he said, "I'll use the night 'scope for this observation." Grasping the pickle, Williams took his position behind the periscope.

To Brent there was no rationale behind the admiral's decision to surface. Everyone knew they should remain submerged and take up a firing position on either side of the channel and wait for the enemy to exit. It would be an easy firing problem — a golden opportunity dreamed of by all submariners. The old admiral appeared sick, out of sorts and highly agitated. "Sir . . ." Brent said. "We're in an ideal attack position. May I suggest . . . "

"No! You may not . . . " The old man staggered. Williams steadied him. Allen pulled away, holding the tube of the periscope like a drunk clinging to a lamppost. He glared at Brent. "Why in hell are all of my subordinates trying to tell me how to run this war?" He punched the tube. "Damn it! Just follow my fuckin' orders!"

Everyone was shocked. Obscenities were out of character for the admiral and the decision was wrong.

"Up 'scope!" The tube slid upward, Allen grasped the handles, snapped them down and took a quick look around. "Down 'scope! All clear." He leaned over the hatch to the control room. "Surface! Surface! Surface!"

Davidson punched a button and the Klaxon hooted. The diving officer, Ensign Battle, shouted, "Blow negative to the mark! Ten degrees up!"

With high pressure air driving the water out of her main ballast tanks and her planes up sharply, *Blackfin* clawed for the surface. Allen pulled the microphone down from the overhead. "Torpedo attack surface." He turned to the executive officer. "Mr. Williams take the TDC. Mr. Ross on the bridge with me. Secure radar. Section Two to steaming stations." He looked at Brent and stabbed a finger upward. "Stand by to crack the hatch."

"Sir, this is crazy," Williams dared, face twisted by anger. "I protest your orders."

366

"Protest all you goddamned well please. Just follow my fuckin' orders. You're on report."

"He's right, sir," Brent said.

"What is this—mutiny? Another *Caine*? All you shit-assed punks trying to tell me my business? Up the ladder, Lieutenant, before I have you relieved." Brent hesitated. "On the double!"

Reluctantly, Brent climbed up the ladder. The old man was sick—out of his mind. A man that old should not be in command. There was only one Fujita. Now it was too late—maybe, too late for all of them. In a moment Brent could hear water gurgling and splashing off the upper works, and he gripped the hand wheel. "Passing three-oh-feet!" Battle reported.

"Crack the hatch!"

"Pressure one-half inch!" he heard from the diving station. Brent whirled the wheel, took a soaking as he threw back the bronze cover, scampering out onto the deck followed by Admiral Allen, who he pulled through the hatch. The old man's arms felt bony, like a skeleton's. In just seconds, the lookouts were above Brent's head on their perch and Mark Allen was at his side, gasping for air. Clumsily, the admiral locked his binoculars into the TBT (Target Bearing Transmitter), a waterproof instrument that automatically transmitted target bearings to the TDC in the conning tower. Brent swung his glasses to the destroyer. Bow on, it was big and black in the entrance. He glanced to the east. A weak rosy hue hinted at the coming dawn.

The main induction valve slammed open and the engines roared to life. Deep in the bowels of the ship, the turbo blow began its banshee screech and

Blackfin began to rise higher in the water. Brent felt his stomach contort as if he were about to become sick. Unless the destroyer's lookouts and sonarman were blind, deaf mutes, they must have been spotted.

"All ahead one-third, steer two-nine-zero," Mark Allen said. It was his last command. Suddenly, he came bolt upright as if his spine had been replaced by a steel beam. Rocking back and forth and clutching his temples frantically as if he were trying to suppress an explosion, he shrieked—an agonizing cry that pierced Brent's ears over the howl of the turbo blow, the roar of four diesel engines, and the hiss of air and water venting from the main ballast tanks. Brent whirled from the enemy destroyer just as the admiral vomited a yellow projectilelike stream that hit the windscreen and splattered onto Brent's jacket and face. Twisting violently, the tortured old man fell away from Brent, bounced from the steel screen, and collapsed onto the deck as if felled by a blow from a mace. He screamed once more and then was as still as death.

"Hospital corpsman!" Brent shouted frantically down the hatch. "Hospital corpsman to the bridge on the double!"

Within seconds, Reginald Williams and a Japanese medical orderly named Chisato Yasuda were bending over the admiral. "Con the ship, Brent," Williams shouted.

"I think he has had a stroke or a heart attack, Mr. Williams," Yasuda said. "I feel no pulse."

"You're in command, Reggie," Brent said.

Before Williams could answer, the night was split by an enormous flash as the two bow-mounted five-inch guns of the Gearing fired. Then the boom of the guns followed by the sound of ripping canvas as the shells tore overhead.

Williams shouted a stream of commands: "Lookouts below, clear the bridge, stand by to dive. Yasuda, lower the admiral. Take him to his cabin." He gestured to a lookout. "Help the corpsman." Yasuda and the lookout lowered the inert form down into conning tower where Crog and Harold Sturgis grabbed him and in turn lowered the limp body into the control room. More flashes and two towers of water shot up next to the sub, soaking the men on the bridge.

As the bow planes locked out with a thump, Brent and the lookouts tumbled down the ladder.

"Dive! Dive! Dive! Emergency!" Williams shouted, dropping through the hatch last and hitting the alarm button. As he dogged the hatch, the boat inclined sharply downward, water splashing over the bridge and trickling through the hatch until he dogged it with hard clockwise whirls of the wheel. Brent felt a rush of air as Herbert Battle opened the negative-tank flood valve, taking in nearly eight-tons of water forward of amidships, tilting the bow down even more. Almost simultaneously, two blasts shook the boat, a pair of shells exploding side by side not more than twenty feet off the starboard bow.

"Watch your angle, Mr. Battle!" Williams yelled. "We don't want our stern out of the water. They'll shoot our ass off."

"Ten degrees and holding, sir," Battle said from the diving station.

"Very well."

Brent took his post in front of the TDC and Williams balanced himself by leaning on the periscope. He answered the reports from the control room — "Flooding negative," "Green board," "Green air," "Pressure in the boat" — with "Very well," and "Secure the air."

As more shells exploded alongside, he shouted down the hatch, "Plot! Depth under keel?"

Lieutenant Cadenbach's voice came back. "One-eight-zero, sir."

"Bottom?"

"Coral and sand."

"Shit!" Williams said. "Take her down to one-five-zero feet, left full rudder, all ahead flank."

Brent heard the pitch of the four electric motors whine higher, and the boat surged forward as an electrician at the Maneuvering Control Stand opened the main motor rheostats full to the stops, pouring every volt in the battery into the propellers.

"Passing fifty feet," Battle said from his diving station. Everyone breathed easier — they were safe from the destroyer's shells.

"Very well. Navigator, give me a course for the hundred fathom line."

Cadenbach's voice came back from the control room almost immediately, as if he had anticipated the question. "Suggest course one-nine-zero."

"Steady on one-nine-zero," Williams said to Sturgis.

"Passing two-three-five," the helmsman said.

Yeoman Davidson spoke: "Medical orderly Yasuda reports the admiral is dead."

There was stunned silence. Brent could not believe the report, and neither could Williams.

"You're sure?" Williams said.

Davidson spoke into his mouthpiece. "Yasuda believes the admiral had a stroke and then suffered cardiac arrest."

Brent punched the TDC in grief, anger and disbelief. There was no time for mourning. It must come later. They must preserve the boat and their own lives.

Crog spoke. "The can's started her engines, Mr. Williams." He hunched forward, hands on earphones, staring at the scope of the old Mark IV sonar, which was calibrated from zero to only five thousand yards, "I hear a clanking, sir. She's slipping her anchor chain and she's pinging." He clutched his earphones. "A powerful signal—I've never heard sonar this strong."

Williams turned to the hatch, "Mr. Cadenbach. Range to deep water and what is the bottom?"

"Range six and one half miles to the hundred-fathom curve, bottom's sand and it drops off fast, sir, into the West Caroline Basin. Three hundred fathoms at seven miles."

"Steady on one-nine-zero," Sturgis said.

"Very well. Let me know when we pass one hundred-feet, Quartermaster," Williams said. Sturgis glanced at the clutter of instruments on the bulkhead in front of him. Besides a helm, rudder angle indicator and engine room controls, the second class quartermaster monitored a compass repeater, pitometer repeater, compartment pressure gauge, and depth indicator repeater calibrated to a maximum of six hundred feet.

"The can's underway, sir," Crog said. "Speed ten and increasing, range nine thousand." He looked up. "She's directly astern and it's hard to read her because of the cavitations of our own screws, and I've lost the other ships. But her big sonar's bustin' through everything."

"Our speed through water?"

"We're making nine knots, sir," Sturgis said, glancing at the pitometer. He shifted his eyes to the depth gauge. "Passing one hundred feet, Mr. Williams."

"Very well." Williams leaned over the hatch. "Navigator! Dawn?"

Cadenbach's voice came back. "Zero-five-forty—five minutes ago."

"Damn!"

Another element had entered the situation. The carriers were underway, and with dawn came the threat of aerial attack. The men exchanged uneasy looks.

"She's picking up speed," Crog said. "Range seven thousand." Everyone could hear the destroyer's echo ranging apparatus hunting them. "Ping! Ping!" Fast, harsh, continuous, and implacable.

"Is he ranging us?"

"Not yet, Mr. Williams."

"Passing one-two-zero feet," Sturgis said.

Brent felt the down-angle soften as Ensign Battle instructed his planesmen to begin leveling. Battle's voice came up through the hatch. "Passing one-three-zero, leveling at one-five-zero, sir."

"Very well. Rig for silent running. Rig for depth charge," Williams said to the talker, Randy Davidson. Randy spoke into his headset.

Brent heard the whine of the motors drop as

372

Blackfin rheostated down to minimum speed — only speed enough to maintain depth and steerageway. Throughout the ship, watertight hatches were dogged down, sea valves and hull fittings tightly shut, fans turned off, and the ventilation system secured. Immediately, the heat shot upward and the smell of sweat and fear permeated the boat. Usually dogged for "rig for depth charge," Williams ordered the hatch between the conning tower and the control room to remain open.

Crog had his sound-head cranked full astern. "He's coming on fast, sir."

Brent felt a familiar cold spring begin to flex in his viscera, sour gorge rising. Men were coming for him. Men he did not know, eager to inflict a horrible death on him.

Cadenbach's voice: "Depth under keel, two-three-zero.

"Take her down to two-zero-zero."

Brent could hear Battle's calm voice instructing his planesmen and the boat inclined down sharply to at least fifteen degrees.

With the submarine dropping deeper into the safety of the depths, Brent felt the pressure on his stomach lessen. The deep is a submarine's natural habitat. The deeper the safer, the thick cushion of ocean overhead her shelter. In the depths there is no motion, no sound except what is put there by man in his search for other men to kill. Light is soft or nonexistent, currents gentle, the abundant life snapping, popping, hissing in low key and in harmony with the primordial quietness and solitude of the depths. The destroyer was about to rip all of this to shreds.

"He has us," Crog said quietly. Everyone could hear the destroyer's echo-ranging bouncing off the hull, the "thump, thump, thump," of his screws.

"Right full rudder, all ahead emergency," Williams shouted. "We'll make him overshoot us."

Brent knew the executive officer's thinking was good—if it worked. No doubt, the destroyer's attack team had plotted *Blackfin*'s course and had projected their own to intersect it. Williams hoped to cut his track and force the enemy to drop his depth charges long and into empty ocean.

The sharp, churning sounds of the screws and pings grew in intensity and seemed to quicken, reverberating in the thick atmosphere of the boat, now overhead but slightly astern. Everyone stared at the overhead, anxious eyes following the sounds. Slowly, the thumps and pings "Dopplered" down.

"He's passed us," Crog said.

There were three clicks followed by two more. "Shit," Williams said. "Hydrostatic detonators." Crog turned down his gain control. Brent could see his hand shaking.

Five tremendous blasts jarred the boat and she shook like a bone in the teeth of a wild dog. The great jarring explosions compressed the hull, booming through the boat like the inside of a drum struck by a giant. Dust rose and pieces of cork packing rained on Brent's head. He gripped the TDC.

"Passing two-seven-zero," Sturgis shouted.

"Left full rudder. Come back to one-nine-zero. All ahead flank."

Crog cranked his sound head around. "He's steaming two-zero-zero and turning to his right."

Williams yelled down the hatch. "Bottom?"

"Sixty fathoms and sand."

"Take her down flat to the bottom."

The sounds of the motors lessened and the boat began a gentle descent to the bottom.

"She's turning, Mr. Williams. The can's coming around," Crog said.

"The other ships?"

The soundman cranked his soundhead around. "Big screws at slow speed like the carriers and cruisers are laying to. Two sets of high speed screws exiting the anchorage."

"Keeping the heavy ships in until they deal with us," Brent said.

"And sending two more cans."

"Passing two-five-zero feet," Sturgis said.

Minutes that seemed an eternity passed before the boat finally dropped gently onto the bottom at three hundred seventy feet and the motors were secured. The boat lay on the bottom as silent as a tomb. Brent could feel pressure on his eardrums and the ship's hull creaked, popped and groaned. Sweat streamed down his face, his chest, soaked his collar, the back of his shirt. With seventy-one men breathing oxygen and exhaling carbon dioxide, the atmosphere was heavy and stifling. The bulkheads seemed to be crowding him and he yearned for the ventilating system. Glancing at the pressure gauge, he felt a chill despite the heat—there was one hundred sixty-four pounds of water pressure on every square inch of hull. And pings seemed to be coming from every direction. But they were too deep—something was amiss.

Williams said, "They'll be making their runs.

Hang on."

"Maybe their charts are off, too," Brent said.

"What do you mean?"

"According to Cadenbach, we are still far short of deep water. Yet we're almost down to four hundred feet. Either we're in an uncharted canyon or the charts are off."

Williams shouted down the hatch, "Navigator. According to your DR track, what is the depth here?"

"Two-nine-zero feet, sir."

"I'll be damned," Williams said. "Damn near a hundred feet off."

"A can's making a run, sir," Crog said.

"Turn on your speaker."

Crog threw a switch and immediately the enemy's noises were amplified, the compartment resounding with propeller beats, pings — even the hissing of steam, the whine of reduction gears and turbines, and the furious slashing sound of his prow and hull ripping water. The pings were hammering off *Blackfin*'s hull like solid shot, increasing in intensity and coming more rapidly. Now more screws could be heard.

Crog said, "They're lining up — all three of 'em. Like the Easter parade." And then bitterly, "Their pings shouldn't be this strong — not at this depth. That's new equipment. They've been cheating."

"They're Arabs — what in hell do you expect?" Williams said harshly.

Suddenly the sounds of the leading destroyer dropped in pitch, seemed to come from every bearing like a halo of death. "He's directly overhead."

"Turn off the speaker."

Even with the speaker off, the noise still penetrated the hull. The thrashing of screws, pings, and then the depths were ripped by a catastrophic roar. And another. And another. A shower of six-hundred-pound charges. *Blackfin* jerked and twisted, her hull creaking and groaning.

Holding on to the TDC, Brent's mind whirled through the terror. *Fourteen feet,* he thought. One charge within fourteen feet and *Blackfin*'s pressure hull would collapse like a crushed egg before the mass of the Pacific absorbed the blast. They needed another two hundred feet of water and it was not there to be had.

More screws, another murderous shower, and the boat shuddered, the lights blinking off and on. "Here comes the third one," Crog said.

Thumps, pings, screws clubbing the water. Then Brent heard a half-dozen clicks very close to the hull. This would be close. A convulsive, prolonged roar. The boat reverberated like a huge tuning fork, the interior a great sounding cavern. It convulsed, bounced off the bottom and back down again in a cloud of mud. The lights went out. There were cries of terror.

"Emergency lights!" Williams shouted, the hard authority in his voice restoring order. The faint emergency lights flickered on. He stabbed a finger overhead. "They're exploding over us. We're deeper than they expected." He rubbed his chin. "Where are they?"

"In a column, sir. Bearing zero-eight-zero, lead ship at a range of one thousand yards and turning back," Crog said.

Williams whirled to Davidson. "Tell Lieutenant

377

Dunlap to stand by to release five-hundred-gallons of oil and call the forward torpedo room. Tell Ensign Hasse to flood tubes One and Two and to open the outer doors." He turned to Brent. "Set both fish for gyro angle zero, depth one hundred."

Brent was confused. "They'll hit nothing—just sink to the bottom and probably self-destruct, if deep enough."

"I know." Brent set his dials and Williams moved to the firing panel.

"TDC set," Brent reported.

"Tubes One and Two flooded," Davidson said.

Two windows glowed red. Williams pushed the firing key and the boat shuddered. "One fired electrically," Davidson reported. The second plunger was pushed and Davidson made his report.

Crog looked up. "They're making another run, sir." Everyone could hear the sounds coming from the starboard side.

Williams continued. "Tell Ensign Hasse to stuff broken planking, life jackets, anything that will float, into tube Number One and fire at my command."

"The Number Two tube, sir?"

Williams gritted his teeth, eyed Brent with a sidelong look. "Call Yasuda. Tell him to pump oxygen into the admiral's lungs, into his intestines . . . "

"No!" Brent shouted, stepping toward Williams. Every head turned.

"Back to your station, Mr. Ross. I'm in command!"

"That's unconscionable! Savage."

"Do you wish to be relieved?"

Brent gritted his teeth. This was the second time

378

he had been asked that question in an hour. He looked up as the sounds of the destroyers grew. "No, I'll remain."

Williams turned back to the talker. "Tell Yasuda to load the admiral's body into tube Number Two."

Several minutes passed and then the deadly shower resumed. Williams had been right; the depth charges seemed to be set just a trifle shallow. But as long as the destroyers remained, there was no chance the submarine could attack the carriers and eventually, a deep-set charge could crush the boat. Her pressure hull was taking a terrible pounding. Again the lights went out but were restored quickly.

Just as the third destroyer turned away, Davidson reported, "Tubes One and Two ready, sir. Outer doors open."

"Tell Lieutenant Dunlap to release the oil." The executive officer stepped to the firing panel and fired both torpedoes. Brent shuddered with the boat. Williams said to Davidson, "Call the forward torpedo room. Tell Ensign Hasse to load and fire three more loads of debris out of tubes One and Two manually, without my command and on the double."

"At least two destroyers, a cruiser, and one carrier standing out," Crog shouted.

"Damn!" Williams said, repeatedly slapping the periscope tube. "The other carrier?"

Crog shook his head. "A lot of noise, but I don't hear her screws."

"Good. Good."

Several more minutes passed. The boat jarred as Hasse fired the tubes, and the heat in the boat grew. Finally, Crog said, "Funny, Mr. Williams. The cans that were attacking us are headed south—maybe two, three thousand-yards and they're laying to."

Williams shouted down the hatch, "Mr. Cadenbach, what's the current?"

"We're in the Equatorial Countercurrent. The set is about two knots south."

Williams rubbed his hands. "Good. Good. They've found the oil and—and the debris."

"The trash," Brent said bitterly.

"We'll settle this later, Mr. Ross."

"We have several things to settle, Mr. Williams." Brent knew Williams had made the correct decision—a decision the admiral himself would have made. The preservation of the boat was paramount, took precedence over everything. Yet he wanted to pound Williams with his fists, break his jaw, punish him. When the admiral died, he felt as if he had lost his father. In a strange tragic way, he had felt the loss of a father twice.

"They're taking off, sir," Crog said. "Five cans, a carrier, and a cruiser on a northwesterly heading."

"The other carrier?"

"Still in the anchorage with at least five cans and a cruiser, Sir."

Williams clapped his hands together. "Good! Good! We'll nail that other bastard." He said to Davidson, "Damage control—I want a report."

Yeoman Davidson made the request and everyone waited silently. Finally he reported: "Lieutenant Pittman reports two sea valves ruptured, at least four cells have cracked tops, the bilge pump under the aft battery room has been knocked off its foundation, and one air compressor has a cracked hous-

380

ing."

"Very well." Although the damage was serious, it was not disabling. The main engines, drive shafts, and bearings were intact, propellers not bent. The cells could be repaired by drawing a hot soldering iron across the cracks, melting the mastic, and re-sealing the cracks. The bilge pump was out, but its vents could be cross-connected to the pump under the forward battery room. The air compressor could still be used and, in an emergency, jury-rigged to the other compressor which was undamaged. *Black-fin* was still a viable fighting machine.

Williams pulled down the microphone. "We've given the cans the slip. They think we're dead and we'll show them this is a gross exaggeration." There was a cheer. "Apparently the enemy has split his force into two battle groups. One has stood out and is headed northwest. I'm sure the rest of them will follow. They're probably setting a trap for *Yonaga*—put her on the vice from two directions. Well, we'll set one of our own. When the carrier sorties, those cans will come out full bore and ping-ing. We don't want to be spotted again in shallow water so we'll move to the northwest astern of the force that just stood out. I expect the second force to follow and probably split off to the east after clearing the northern end of the atoll. We'll see to it she doesn't get that far." More cheers. He turned to Crog. "Take a full sweep around."

Crog cranked the sonar handle. "All I get is the departing battle group. The other ships must've an-chored—they haven't stood out, sir—that's for sure."

"Anchored? I'll be damned." He turned to David-

381

son. "Secure from silent running and secure from 'rig for depth charge.' All ahead one-third. Control, bring her up to sixty-two feet — flat. Quartermaster, come right to two-nine-zero."

Brent heard the hum of electric motors and then the boat rocked gently and began to rise. Sturgis put the helm over. The fans came on and the ventilation system began to blow air throughout the boat. Everyone sighed with relief.

Battle's voice came up through the hatch from the diving station, "Request more speed, sir. She isn't responding to the planes."

"Very well. All ahead two-thirds."

"Steady on two-nine-zero," Sturgis said.

Brent knew Reginald was gambling. The force could exit and turn east, or, for that matter, steam south or not exit at all. *Blackfin* would have no chance. However, the odds were that the enemy would sortie and northwest would be their course. The executive officer, who was actually the captain now, had made the best decision.

At five knots, *Blackfin* inclined upward gently. Passing the hundred-foot mark, the angle of inclination decreased still more, Battle obeying the command to "Bring her up flat." Within three more minutes the boat was at sixty-eight feet with zero inclination. Gradually, it eased up to sixty-two feet. "Sixty-two feet!" came up through the hatch.

"Very well." Williams turned to Davidson. "Lieutenant Pittman to the conning tower immediately. Replace him with Chief Fujiwara." Seconds later, Pittman, who was in charge of damage control when at general quarters, puffed up the ladder. "You're on the TDC, Mr. Pittman," Williams said to the tall, thin lieutenant.

"I'm relieved?" Brent asked incredulously. Every man in the compartment stared at Brent.

"Yes. You're attack officer," Williams said.

Brent was stunned. "Attack officer? But you're officially the captain."

"I know. That's my decision. None of us have had much experience, but you had the best record during shakedown. I'll be your assistant whenever that carrier sorties." He punched the periscope. "Right now, I want that carrier more than anything else on earth, and you're going to get her for us, Mr. Ross." He slapped the Number Two periscope. "Up 'scope!"

Unable to believe what he had heard, Brent punched the pickle and the tube slid up. Bending low, Williams caught the handles and rose with the rubber cushion off the eyepiece pressed to his eyes. Quickly he swung around. He chuckled. "Some smoke to the northwest and the atoll is on the horizon off our starboard side." He shouted down the hatch. "Mr. Cadenbach, we're off the southwest coast of Tomonuto. I'll get you two tangents on the atoll. You'll have to cut us in with those two sights. That's all I can do. There are no prominent points of land — just palm trees and we can't surface."

"Aye, aye, sir. My DR track has us ten thousand yards off the southwest coast."

"Stand by, Mr. Ross," Williams said, peering into the periscope. "Bearing mark!"

"Zero-nine-five," Brent said, reading the azimuth. Davidson shouted the bearing down the hatch.

"Bearing mark!"

"Zero-three-two." Again, Davidson relayed the

bearing. "Down 'scope!"

In a few seconds, Cadenbach's voice came up the hatch. "Good fix, sir. We're ten thousand one hundred yards off the southwest coast."

"Very well. We'll hold her here and hope they come to us." He turned to Brent. "Mr. Ross, send a message to *Yonaga*. Use CISRA and TACOMA— one enemy carrier, five destroyers, and one cruiser stood out at Tomonuto sixteen-thirty hours. Course two-nine-zero, SOA about twenty knots."

Brent made his way down to his cabin, encoded the message, and handed it to Cryptologist Simpson. The message was sent in the usual millisecond burst.

It was a long wait. The ship secured from general quarters but the tracking party remained in the conning tower. For over three hours the submarine cruised off the the western coast of the atoll waiting for her quarry, every man praying Lieutenant Reginald Williams had made a correct guess.

At eighteen hundred hours, with the sun dying in a welter of bloody scarlets on the western horizon, the enemy sortied. Crog was the first to detect them. "Sonar contact!" he shouted. "Exiting the atoll. Destroyers! And they're pinging—ten thousand yards, bearing three-one-zero."

"General quarters!" Williams shouted. And then to Brent, "Mr. Ross, take the con. Course one-one-zero, speed three." He dropped the Is-Was around his neck and took the assistant attack officer's station behind the periscopes.

"Aye aye, sir. I have the con." Brent turned to the hatch. "Depth?"

"Sixty feet," Battle answered.

"Control. Bring her up two feet — easy," Brent said. He patted the night periscope. "Up 'scope!"

Williams punched the pickle. Bending low, Brent rose with the periscope and snapped the handles down as the instrument locked into place. At sixty-two feet, the periscope head would be well clear of the sea.

Battle's voice. "Sixty-two feet, sir."

"Very well." Brent trained the periscope to the port bow, snapped to maximum magnification and then back. In the gloom far to the southeast, he could see dark shapes moving. He said to the radarman, Petty Officer Takiguchi, "ESM?"

Takiguchi squinted at his display on the WLR-8, tapped out a command on his computer's keyboard, and studied the greenish display rippling like a waterfall across the tube. "Five Gearings, a Llandaff class cruiser and the Majestic class carrier — all in our threat library, sir. All vessels searching S and J bands, Mr. Ross."

"Hot damn! The Majestic," Williams exulted. "We want that son-of-a-bitch, Brent."

"I'll do my damnedest." Brent shouted down the hatch. "Mr. Cadenbach, depth under keel?"

"Two hundred fathoms, sir, and it drops off to three thousand fathoms a mile to the west — the West Caroline Basin."

Brent was pleased. They had plenty of water beneath them — a place of shelter, of safety where the depth charges would have a hard time finding them. Depending on Deflecton Four and luck, he kept the periscope up. The shapes grew. "I think you guessed right, Reggie," he said. "It looks like the carrier and cruiser are in column with the carrier leading.

There's a can on the point and two cans on both sides. But they're spread thin—covering both heavy ships." He hunched close to the tube. "Damn! They're swinging far to the west." He turned to Williams. "We'll have no chance if they maintain this course."

"They must swing north—they've got to. That's where *Yonaga* is," Williams said as if he were trying to convince himself.

Brent returned to the eyepiece. The ships were hulled down and fast disappearing over the horizon. "You must be right. We'll assume they'll come to a northerly course. Anyway, we have no choice." He turned to Sturgis. "Right standard rudder, steady up on two-nine-zero, all ahead full." He said to Williams, "We'll surface as soon as we're on our new course, cut a cord across the arc of their swing north at flank speed."

"A straight line—the shortest distance, Mr. Ross."

Brent nodded. "And hope we guessed right. Anyway, as I said, we have no choice."

Within five minutes, the boat had swung to her reciprocal course and surfaced. Brent and Reginald Williams took the bridge with the four lookouts and the official OOD, Ensign Frederick Hasse. Seaman Jay Overstreet manned the helm and annunciators.

Williams had resumed command. Before coming to the bridge, he had dropped down into Plot and studied the charts with Cadenbach. Staring into his binoculars, he said, "If I'm right, we should intercept them very close to the intersection of the one hundred fortieth meridian and tenth parallel—about eighty miles." He punched the windscreen. "Damn!

I'd give my right ball for a radar search."

"They'd pick us up for sure."

"I know, Mr. Ross." He looked up at the lookouts. "Keep a sharp eye! Radar's secured. You've got to spot them." He waved and pointed although none of the lookouts could see his finger in the darkness. "They should be out there — off the port bow!"

For over three hours the boat charged and slashed through the sea at twenty-four knots. The sky was almost clear, the moon full, visibility good. With a southerly set to the swell, the bow rammed its way through the seas in a regular rhythmic pattern, sending spray and sheets of water as high as the periscope shears. Brent, Hasse, Overstreet, and Reginald were protected by the windscreen, the lookouts by nothing but a rail. Within minutes, the lookouts were drenched.

Hasse tapped Brent's shoulder and pointed astern. The tropical sea churned by the whirling screws was flashing and glowing with phosphorescence as if fires were being ignited in the turbulence. "The Japanese would say sea *kamis* were following us," Brent said.

"With torches," Hasse added.

They were shocked by a lookout's shout, "Object bearing two-one-zero, range eight — ten miles."

All glasses swung to the port quarter. Brent focused on the black upper works of a destroyer, clearly delineated by the moonlit sky behind it. It looked unearthly, two dimensional like a painted matte in a cheap Hollywood movie. "You were right, Mr. Williams," Brent said. "Must be the point can, but we're farther ahead of them than I expected."

"They must be doing twenty knots. I figured twenty-four." Reginald let his binoculars dangle at his waist. "Take the con, Brent. You're the attack officer." He turned to the ensign. "Remain here, Mr. Hasse. We need your eyes."

Brent leaned over the hatch. "Station the tracking party," he shouted. "Torpedo surface!"

"They have good radar," Williams said.

"I know. We'll track from ahead and then submerge."

"A couple of cans may steam right over us."

"Pray to Deflecton Four and bored sonarmen," Brent said. He pointed to the north. "Force four wind, maybe twelve knots. Good chop to hide our 'scope." He locked his binoculars into the TBT.

With the courses of the battle group and the submarine converging, the carrier came into view within fifteen minutes. Brent studied the big, hulking black shape through his glasses and his stomach dropped out of his body. The enemy had changed course again to the west. The range was at least eight miles and opening and *Blackfin* would have no chance unless he could cut across to the west and set up on the enemy's track. "Left to two-eight-zero," he shouted. "All ahead flank!" He yelled into the speaker, "Engineering, give me every turn you can get out of those engines!"

The boat swung to the left and he felt the rhythm of the engines pick up in the steel deck under his feet. A voice came through the speaker. "Twenty-six-knots, sir. That's all she has."

"The shaft bearings?"

"Cool and smooth, Mr. Ross."

Pittman's voice come up through the hatch from his station at the TDC. "Shall we track, sir? I'm getting readings from your TBT."

"Not yet. Let them ride." He stared at the shapes on the horizon. They were larger again. "Seven, eight miles," he said to himself.

"They've changed course, Mr. Ross. They're closing fast," one of the lookouts shouted.

"Very well." Brent leaned over the hatch. "ESM?"

Takiguchi's voice came back. "Sevens and D-band searches."

"Are they ranging?"

"Negative, sir. They're sweeping right over us."

Brent sighed with relief. But he knew they would be sighted soon — even the phosphorescent wake could give them away. "Lookouts below! Clear the bridge!" The lookouts and everyone except Brent scrambled down the hatch. After a last look around, he dropped down the hatch and hit the diving alarm with the palm of his hand. As the alarm honked through the boat, he dogged the hatch and then dropped to the hatch over the control room. "Torpedo attack submerged, take her down to sixty-two feet."

Turning to the attack periscope, he said to Sturgis, "Quartermaster, left to two seven-five, all ahead one-third." He could hear the soft whine of the electric drive in the soothing quietness of the increasing depth, feel the pressure begin to build against his eardrums, shouts of crewmen reporting their stations "manned and ready." He acknowledged "Green air," "Green board," and "Pressure in the boat."

Battle's voice: "Level on sixty-two-feet, sir."

Sturgis's voice: "Steady on two-seven-five, sir."

Brent patted the attack periscope. "Up 'scope." The tube rose and Brent came up with the eyepiece. A quick look told him the lead enemy destroyer would pass well to the west, but the two starboard escorts would pass very close. He said to Crog without moving his eyes from the lens, "Sonar, turn on the speaker." The only man seated, Crog reached over the Mark IV and threw a switch. Immediately, the pings came through—strong, forceful, and penetrating. However, no one was ranging them yet.

Brent swung the periscope head to the carrier. Still over four miles away, she appeared as a big black hulk slashing through the moonlight. He was well ahead of her with an angle on the bow of no more than ten degrees starboard. An attack from ahead at a sharp angle would be a difficult firing problem because the target length was shortened by the angle. Ideally, the best torpedo track angle was one that intersected the target at ninety degrees. With a little luck he might get his right angle. "There's a can leading, then the carrier, and then the cruiser. Four more cans are off the beams of the carrier and cruiser," Brent said. He spoke to Reginald Williams. "Check me on the Majestic—length, seven hundred feet, height of mast, one hundred fifty, she draws twenty-five feet, maximum speed twenty-four."

Williams glanced at a chart taped to a bulkhead behind Davidson. "Correct."

"Stand by for first observation. Bearing mark!"

Reginald read the azimuth. "Two-seven-eight."

Brent grasped the wheel of the range finder, turned it until the two halves of the split image

390

merged into a coherent whole. "Range mark!"

"Six-three-zero-zero."

"Angle on the bow, starboard twenty. Course zero-one-zero." He snapped the periscope handles up to signal the observation was completed. Williams punched the pickle. Stepping back from the tube, Brent said to Sturgis, "Right to two-eight-zero."

Brent heard Bernard Pittman muttering to himself as he cranked the information into the TDC. Fidgeting nervously, perspiration covered his forehead and he swallowed hard, his pointed Adam's apple working up and down as if it were a meal that had stuck in his throat. Pittman said, "Initial range six-two-five-zero, speed nineteen, distance to the track three-nine-five-zero."

The pings grew louder and Brent was sure they would be spotted, but the leading Gearing continued on its plodding track and began to pass their bows. But the destroyer off the carrier's starboard side posed the mortal danger. When they fired their torpedoes — and Brent hoped to fire after the lead Gearing passed — the lead destroyer would be forced to make a complete reversal in course before attacking. By that time, he hoped to have a cushion of at least four hundred feet of ocean above him. But, of course, there was still the other destroyer, off the cruiser's starboard side. He put it out of his mind.

Brent glanced at his watch. Two minutes had passed. He said to Randy Davidson, "Flood tubes One through Six. Up 'scope." Quickly, he focused. "Bearing mark!"

"Two-eight-zero."

"Range mark!"

"Five-one-three-five."

"Angle on the bow, zero-three-zero."

Williams keyed his Is-Was, Pittman worked his cranks furiously. Pittman said, "Range five-one-three-zero, speed nineteen, course zero-one-zero, distance to track two-five-seven-zero."

Crog spoke. "The lead can is crossing our bows from port to starboard, there's another can bearing three-zero-five, range on my rim at five thousand yards."

Brent had no choice, he ignored the destroyer. "Turn off the speaker. Open outer doors tubes One through Six. This will be a shooting observation. Up 'scope."

"Bearing mark!

"Three-three-three."

"Range mark!"

"Three-five-zero-zero."

"Angle on the bow sixty-five. Down 'scope."

They could hear the pinging of a destroyer and even the thump thump of her screws penetrated *Blackfin*'s hull. "I have a solution light!" Pittman shouted as if he were staring at a miracle.

"When will the distance to the track be under two thousand yards?"

There was a long silence. "Damn it, man, answer! The whole western hemisphere is waiting."

Pittman sputtered and then managed, "In thirty-five-seconds, Mr. Ross."

"Set depth twenty feet, speed fast, one-hundred-fifty-percent spread." Pittman looked confused. Brent shouted angrily, "The first astern, four into the hull, and the last to pass ahead. Seven second intervals. Crank it in!"

Pittman gulped, looked up in confused helplessness. Williams pushed him aside and turned the cranks. "Set!" he said. "Gyro angle last fish right twenty-three degrees."

"Very well." With a spread of one-hundred-fifty-percent, Brent hoped to compensate for any errors—hoped for at least three hits which should be fatal.

Williams moved to the firing panel where six windows glowed red while Pittman looked like a man who would have liked to have vanished into thin air.

Brent took a deep breath. The survival of *Yonaga,* Fujita, Matsuhara, and all of the others who were so dear to him depended on what happened in the next three minutes. He shouted down the hatch, "Watch your trim, Mr. Battle. We're going to fire six fish in the next forty-two-seconds and be ready to take her down fast." He turned to Williams. "Up 'scope!"

A quick look. The set up looked perfect, but the destroyer off their port side was bearing down. "No change!" He snapped the handles up and the tube slid down. He looked up. "Shoot!"

Williams threw a switch and pushed the firing key. There was the sound of compressed-air blasting followed by a thump and the boat lurched. "One fired electrically," Davidson reported, starting a stopwatch. Five more times the order was given until all forward tubes were empty.

"Torpedo run?"

Pittman stared at the TDC, spoke in a tremulous voice. "One-nine-seven-zero, sir."

A quick calculation. About a minute and ten seconds before the first impact. Brent shouted a barrage of orders: "Take her down fast to four hundred feet. Right full rudder, steady up on one-zero-zero, all ahead flank, rig for depth charge!"

Battle yanked the handle of the tank vent and Brent felt the rush of air as the negative flood valve opened wide, tons of water pouring into the forward ballast tanks. *Blackfin* angled sharply downward.

"Passing one hundred, sir."

"Time to target, first fish?" Brent asked.

Sturgis glanced at his stop watch, "Seventeen seconds, sir."

"Turn on the speaker." Crog threw the switch. The pings of the destroyers came in loud and clear, the escort off their port bow drowning out the others. Even the thrashing of her screws was audible and distinct. And there was a high pitched whine like a flock of mosquitoes. The torpedoes. They could hear their torpedoes.

Suddenly there was a tremendous roar as the first warhead exploded against the side of the carrier, eight hundred pounds of torpex ripping frames and tearing strakes of plates like paper, hurling a column of water and debris two hundred feet into the air. The shock wave shook the boat. Then another and another and the men cheered.

"We've hit the son-of-a-bitch," Williams shrieked. He waved a fist at the overhead. "You just fumbled on the one-yard line, you dicks." Everyone chuckled.

"Can's changing course, sir. She's making a run." The laughter stopped.

"Very well," Williams said. He turned to Brent. "Great job. At least three hits. I have the con. Take

over the TDC. Mr. Pittman, return to your duties."
Pittman dropped down the hatch like a frightened
gopher going to ground.

"Passing one-fifty," Sturgis said.

Through the pings of the advancing destroyer
they could hear the shriek of tortured metal followed by crashing bangs, hissing, rushing sounds of
water. "Ship breaking up sounds," Crog announced.
More happy yells.

The noise of the churning screws, the powerful
pings bouncing off the hull grew in strength and
became more rapid, silencing the boisterous spirits.
Soon the whole boat echoed with the sounds and
the Doppler began to drop. "Here they come."

There was a flurry of clicks, and the depths were
ripped by a barrage of charges. Four exploded
under the boat's stern and at least two above her
bow. Leaping and twisting like a harpooned whale,
Blackfin's bow was hammered down into a steep
dive of over thirty degrees. Writhing, groaning, the
boat plunged down into the depths, more charges
exploding above her. Those men not clinging to
supports were hurled from their feet. There were
cries of fear and pain. Crog was knocked from his
seat and Takiguchi fell across him. Brent held onto
an overhead pipe. Then the lights went out and the
vibrations began.

"Blow negative! Emergency lights!" Nothing happened. Either the commands were not heard, the
crewmen injured, or equipment damaged. The lights
remained out and the descent continued.

The vibrations increased, *Blackfin* shaking and
trembling like the victim of an epileptic seizure and
a fearful rhythmic, clattering sound of metal

pounding metal filled the boat. One thousand five hundred twenty six tons of steel with her ballast tanks brimming with nine hundred tons of water, the boat was a pitch-black steel coffin plunging steeply into depths that would crush her like paper.

Brent could feel the pressure building in his eardrums and the specter of collapsing compartments and compressed air heating to hundreds of degrees, searing his lungs, and drowning him in his own blood before the onrushing water reached him, filled him with horror.

The dim red lights flickered on. "Damage report! Damage report!" Williams shouted. Davidson yelled into his mouthpiece, but there was no answer.

While Brent helped Takiguchi and Crog from the deck, the vibrations stopped suddenly and the whine of electric motors faded.

"Passing two hundred fifty," Sturgis said calmly.

Williams shouted down the hatch, "Mr. Battle, our trim, for Christ's sake, our trim."

"I'm blowing negative, sir, and the planes are full up."

Brent felt the angle begin to flatten, but he knew the boat's downward momentum would be hard to stop before fatal depths were reached. Apparently, Battle had started to blow negative on his own initiative before hearing Williams's command in the bedlam. The young man's resourcefulness might save their lives.

Davidson said, "Damage report. Port shaft and screw bent. Chief Fukumoto shut down the port motors. Seals intact. Two saltwater valves were ruptured, but they're being repaired. Auxiliary engine Number One has been knocked off its foundation.

Two machinist's mates are unconscious and a third has a broken arm."

"The battery?"

"No report, sir."

"Very well. Silent running."

The inclination of the boat became less severe. "Passing four-hundred."

More blasts, however, they were far overhead and wide. Gradually, with the pumps forcing air into the ballast tanks and water out, *Blackfin*'s plunge slowed and the angle of descent approached zero. But their sanctuary could still become their grave.

"Passing five-hundred."

Brent glanced at the pressure gauge. The white needle was passing two hundred twenty pounds — two hundred twenty pounds of pressure on every square inch of hull and increasing. He felt a cold electric prickle race up his spine to his neck.

The heat had become unbearable, air stagnant and foul, and the smell of sweat and unwashed bodies was overpowering. Brent's hair was matted and his soaked shirt clung to him as if glued. And someone in the control room had obviously lost sphincter control, the smell drifting up through the hatch.

"Tell that man to clean himself up," Williams shouted. There was an embarrassed babble.

"Five seventy-five and holding," Battle announced calmly as the boat flattened to zero inclination.

"Can you hold her here?"

"Yes, sir. No problem."

Brent heard Williams mutter, "I'm going to promote that man."

There were sighs of relief and the men looked at

each other like condemned men reprieved at the last minute. They had survived because two men, Ensign Battle and Chief Fukumoto, had acted quickly on their own volition. Now they should be safe in their sanctuary. The lights came on.

"Starboard ahead two-thirds. Come right to one-eight-zero. And Crog, turn on the speaker." Over the fading sounds of the destroyers' screws, they could hear the death throes of the dying carrier. The gurgling of rushing water, hiss of escaping air, the bang and crash of collapsing bulkheads, and Brent thought he heard high-pitched shrieks. Men screaming. Was it possible he could hear the death shouts of men dying hideously in flooding compartments—a fate he had expected for himself? He tried to shut it out, put his mind elsewhere. But it was impossible. The boat was very quiet and the men kept their eyes fixed on their equipment.

"She's on her way down," Williams said. "In six thousand feet of water."

The destroyers made two more halfhearted runs and then disappeared to the north. The breaking up sounds of the carrier finally stopped. Lieutenant Brooks Dunlap reported the port shaft bent, a shaft main bearing burned out and the propeller damaged. Shaft, bearing and propeller were unrepairable at sea. One machinist's mate had a broken arm and another a concussion. The boat was capable of six knots submerged on the starboard motors only; perhaps, eighteen on the surface. Williams brought them to a northerly heading.

Finally, sixteen hours after submerging, *Blackfin* surfaced cautiously into the afternoon sunlight, complete sweeps by both periscope and ESM made before blowing negative. When Brent cracked the hatch, the blast of fresh air jolted him like a split of cold champagne. Then, standing at Reginald's side, he stared at a flat sea covered with the "dust" of disaster: casks, lumber, empty aircraft fuel tanks, the wing of a JU 87 close aboard, bottles, barrels, stretching to the horizon astern and to the west. Williams muttered, "We've cut the odds." He pointed. "Men."

Brent focused his glasses — a life raft jammed with survivors, some even clinged to the sides. "Will you pick them up?"

"No way." Williams gestured to the southeast, "Let 'em paddle back to Tomonuto. Good exercise and it's a nice day." The lookouts and Overstreet snickered.

Williams said to Brent, "Send a message — one carrier sunk, second enemy battle group departed Tomonuto on a northerly heading, one cruiser and five destroyers. SOA unknown. *Blackfin* damaged. Proceeding Tokyo Bay."

"TACAMO?"

"Yes."

"CISRA?"

"Not necessary. The whole damned world knows we're here. Used standard encryption — Baker Three. It'll take less time."

Brent spoke into the speaker and gave his instructions to Cryptologist Simpson. Within a minute, Simpson reported the transmission made and receipted for.

Williams shifted uneasily. "I intend to hold a brief memorial service for Admiral Allen in the mess hall whenever conditions permit. I expect all off-duty personnel to attend." He bit his lip and then continued self-consciously, "But I'll leave your attendance up to you—make your own decision."

Brent stared ahead silently. He was still angry at the admiral's fate. Dropping his glasses to his waist, he said, "The samurai would say, 'The sword must be taken from its sheath to have life.' " He gripped the rail with both hands. "I'm trying to think of him that way—unsheathed even in death—a useful end." He clutched his glasses, brought them up. "I'll be there."

Williams nodded and smiled. Slowly, he made a sweeping gesture at the littered ocean, "We've cut the odds, Brent."

Brent spoke without interrupting his search, "Yes. Now Fujita will go after them. One carrier, two cruisers, and ten cans against *Yonaga*. The odds are even."

Williams laughed.